THE GRAIL OF HEARTS is a breathtaking novel of magic and wonder in the grand tradition of Marion Zimmer Bradley's *The Mists of Avalon*. A most exceptional fable combining the best of the Grail and Arthurian mythos, THE GRAIL OF HEARTS is the spellbinding saga of Parsifal and the Grail, of The Fisher King . . . and the Wandering Jew—told for the first time from a *woman's* point of view— an unforgettable tale by one of the brightest voices in the fantasy field today.

PRAISE FOR
THE GRAIL OF HEARTS

"THE GRAIL OF HEARTS is a hauntingly beautiful dream born of myth and the writer's art."

—Joan D. Vinge

"The rich brocade of THE GRAIL OF HEARTS is breathtaking, shot through with the red of Roman wine, the gold of oriental jewels, the white of samite robes, and the dark brown of earth and wood and old blood. I could not put it down."

—Jane Yolen

"Something very different in fantasy: a subtle interweaving of medieval myth, the heartbreak and tragedy of the Wandering Jew, and the shining legendry of the Grail, with the sound of Wagnerian opera hovering in the background . . . Moving, visually evocative and intriguing, and simply very, very good."

—Diane Duane

ADDITIONAL PRAISE
FOR THE GRAIL OF HEARTS

"Provocative, intense and original. Shwartz skillfully explores the crux perilous of Judaeo-Christian religious history and Arthurian myth. The redemptive saga of Kundry, the eternal fallen woman in thrall to time, illuminates modern notions as women, faith, and fate."
—Carole Nelson Douglas

"THE GRAIL OF HEARTS is a wondrous and magical retelling of the legend of the Holy Grail. It builds many bridges, across religious lines and between the past and the present."
—Father Andrew Greeley

"Shwartz's best book . . . an outstanding addition to the growing body of historically informed fantasy. Highly recommended."
—Booklist

"Lyrical, passionate, and thrilling at the same time, THE GRAIL OF HEARTS is a book in the tradition of the finest grand opera, with both style and substance."
—Esther Friesner

"With THE GRAIL OF HEARTS, Susan Shwartz spreads her nets very wide and takes on a theme of great complexity and grand scale. She brings it off. She brings it off very well, with careful scholarship and prose that sometimes sings. The scope is broad, the philosophy is intimate, and there is something to reward the reader on every page. I congratulate the author for a stunning achievement."
—Morgan Llywelyn

Tor books by Susan Shwartz

THE GRAIL OF HEARTS

SUSAN SHWARTZ

TOR
fantasy

A TOM DOHERTY ASSOCIATES BOOK
NEW YORK

THE GRAIL OF HEARTS

Copyright © 1992 by Susan Shwartz

Cover art by Dennis Nolan

A Tor Book
Published by Tom Doherty Associates, Inc.
175 Fifth Avenue
New York, N.Y. 10010

Tor ® is a registered trademark of Tom Doherty Associates, Inc.

ISBN: 0-812-55409-4
Library of Congress Catalog Card Number: 91-35972

First edition: February 1992
First mass market printing: February 1993

Printed in the United States of America

0 9 8 7 6 5 4 3 2 1

*To all the people who build bridges
instead of walls.*

I owe thanks to almost all of my friends and acquaintances for trespassing on their patience during the writing of *The Grail of Hearts*. Special thanks go to Richard Curtis, Thomas Doherty, and Claire Eddy, and to Jane Yolen, Esther Friesner, Judith Tarr, Evangeline Morphos, Marj Krueger, Sandra Miesel, Kit and Howard Kerr, Harry and Laura Turtledove, Ben-Zion Rapaport, and Parke Godwin.

"When thou dost ask me blessing, I'll kneel down,
And ask for thee forgiveness. So we'll live,
And pray, and sing, and tell old tales, and laugh
At gilded butterflies, and hear poor rogues
Talk of court news; and we'll talk with them too,
Who loses and who wins, who's in, who's out,
And take upon's the mystery of things
As if we were God's spies . . ."

William Shakespeare, *King Lear*,
Act V, scene iii, lines 10–17

1

THE Fisher King's small boat rocked gently on Lake Brumbane at the heart of Broceliande. The evening breeze brought on the blue hour. The water became opaque like the matrix of a black opal, set in the golds and greens of lime and beech trees. A dragonfly richly gemmed as a reliquary skimmed it, then flew off buzzing toward the depths of Broceliande. The leaves panted in the haze and brooding heat.

Amfortas might serve the Grail, but he could not command the fish. He glanced down at the barren waters. Today had been one of the very few free days he ever allowed himself, and it had turned out a disappointment. A last shaft of sunset stained the lake bronze. The water shifted and glimmered. Amfortas had seen mosaics with that sheen in the apses of the great churches in Byzantium. A face from off those apses, distorted by ripples from the boat's passage, stared back at him: dark, melancholy eyes and brows that frowned from years in the desert sun. By now, he had lost most of his desert weathering; even the creases at his eyes from squinting against sun and sand had eased, though they puddled with sweat.

Despite the heat, he still wore light mail (folly to wear mail in the water; worse folly to go without so near his great enemy) and a white silk surcoat emblazoned with the dove of his house and Order wrought in fine silks and bullion. He still wore his dark hair cropped for comfort under the helm he never needed now. He could have been a warrior at peace, little of such peace though he felt, or a priest garbed for war.

Priest and king? he asked his sea-change reflection wryly.

I am not Melchizedek, nor was meant to be . . . by anyone but
his father. Titurel had unloaded an old man's burdens on
him, unwanted, unexpected, then demanded that he thank
God for the command that had made him trade the auster-
ity of desert wars and the gallantry of Europe for the silent
hallows of Montsalvasche. They were buried here in Broceliande: Titurel in his living tomb, Amfortas on a throne.

And Bron, his brother, buried beneath the altar he
should have served. *Would God I had died for thee.* Amfortas
scowled at the blinding glint of sun on water.

Some of the youngest squires whispered that this forest
held magic. Amfortas could believe it. *All that power*, he
thought at the trees beyond his lake's shore, *yet you cannot
provide me even one decent fish*. He had better fortune as a
fisher of souls.

Wonders did happen in Broceliande: it was truly said
that travelers brave, foolish, or saintly enough to enter it
emerged changed—wherever they emerged. The wood
seemed to draw power up from its roots, which, in turn,
seemed to stretch like a net across the known world, snar-
ing souls.

Unmarked save to the young, the holy, or the mad,
Broceliande's paths snatched up travelers like chips in a
millrace and tossed them onto unexpected shores: Camelot
of the Kings, or the sacred shores from which Solomon's
ship translated those few marked out by holiness to Sarras,
or the more worldly lands in which a man with courage and
good weapons might find wealth and adventure.

Parts of it were wild, dangerous; other parts of it, like the
circle of land and forest around Montsalvasche, were holy
ground, warded—yet no less dangerous either to remain
upon or to pass outside.

Times had been that Amfortas had been a knight to ride
down such roads, a knight like Gahmuret the Angevin or
Uther Pendragon before he was crowned and ceased to
wander. Times had been when the map of the known world
was as familiar to him as his armor or the acclaim of noble
ladies. He had fought at Zazamanc, Sibilja, and Satalye. He
had helped to liberate al-Andalus, charging at the sides of
the knights of Calatrava and Evora.

He had been offered crowns, but refused even the vanity of a crest to his helm. He had been offered command of armies, but had ridden away with one or two squires, God's errant.

Blessed beyond any man's deserts, he had even knelt, dazed by wonder, at the Holy Sepulchre; he had wept at Golgotha. The names fluttered in the heat, bright as the fireflies that flickered now in the mossy depths of Broceliande, and as swift to fade.

Soon the bells would toll, and Amfortas's day on the water—the indulgence that the old knights referred to half reproachfully as his hunting day—would be over. He would return to his ordeal of sanctity. Holiness had dragged him back by the chain mail to this castle, which had been his father Titurel's, and his father's before him, and so on for all those many generations back to the first Bron, for whom his brother had been named, and to that Bron's father, Joseph of Arimathea. Thus was the law: when the king who ruled Montsalvasche, earthly home of the Grail, grew too weak to wield it, his son was summoned from whatever life he had made for himself.

It had been an easy enough law to obey once: not now.

At least once each day, Amfortas, king by default, must march before the knights of the company—many of whom had known him since he bestrode his first pony—and hold aloft the Grail. Air and light and sounds shifted; the world itself trembled and transformed around him. Only that daily, painful miracle sustained Titurel in life and maintained many of the elder men such as Gurnemanz, who had been his father's squire before becoming his, in health. They were strong yet, those terrible old men, to inflict their service upon him and compel him to serve them in return. Should he deny their need, deny them a sight of the Grail, it would not be long before they weakened, gummed their bread, and spoke in the cracked high voices of those turned once again to childhood. No, he could not condemn men he admired to such a fate—nor deny his father continued life, though life itself had become a burden.

Amfortas shuddered, thinking of the weight of the Grail. Each day, he must thrust it aloft; each day, it felt as if he struggled against a whole ponderous world clasped between his hands, fighting to crush him into base clay. Hot and piercing, the Grail's fire exploded along his sinews until he thought he and Chalice alike must glow from within with a light from beyond the circles of the moon. No man should have to bear such a burden; yet it was his, and that of his line, since the Last Supper.

A tiny muscle twitched along Amfortas's jaw. It was not all hell (blasphemous as even a breath of that suggestion was), this stewardship of the Grail. Always there came the moment when fire consumed his mind, and he was not son, or king, or Amfortas, but merely a being in joy. But that moment passed too quickly—and the return to the world was anguish as sharp as the burning. Amfortas never set the Chalice down to cover it without expecting to see his palms charred or marked with bleeding wounds. That a man could be burnt, unconsumed, seemed to him no less a miracle than the healing and the food the Grail provided.

Lake Brumbane rippled, and Amfortas bent to his line. Just one more cast, perhaps, before evensong. He had never had time to fish before he became master of Montsalvasche. In the days of his knighthood, he would have scorned it as tame sport, unworthy of an instant's leisure. *And yet*, his father had lectured him, *Our Lord was a fisher of souls*. So now he fished, and he cherished the brief freedom it gave him.

It was a poor exchange for the adventures now denied him—the splendor of banner and trumpets in which lances splintered; the just battle against enemies of law and God, outside a great city with its rulers watching and praising him. Amfortas gazed at the lake as if his old life were embedded in mosaic on its surface. Always after his labors had come the pleasures he had earned. He would lay aside his armor for light silks, rich with bullion and tassels. Then he would walk, arm in arm with his fellows, through narrow, white-walled cities where sunlight struck like a blow, pooling and gleaming in the thin red wine they drank from dented cups. The local men dodged them where they went. The brine and musk of the harbor rose as they listened to the songs of dark-haired women whose teeth shone like the sun and whose tempers were as hot as the summer itself.

Those had been the good years. Then music had not been hymns, chants, and bells—ah, there rang the bells of Montsalvasche! The lake trembled as the bells pealed, summoning men to prayer and Amfortas to his ordeal.

Amfortas had been an active man, and now he was forced to contemplation. God knows, he did not deny the virtue of Montsalvasche nor the sanctity of its purpose or his father's jealously guarded right to command his obedience. It was no sin to regret the life he had laid aside. All he had left of it was his arms—and even they had been augmented. With a fishing rod, Amfortas thought wryly, and the Spear. Even here in this tiny boat, in a peaceful lake warded by the conjoined powers of Broceliande and Montsalvasche, Amfortas carried his old sword to protect the Spear he bore, infinitely older and more precious.

It looked little different from the *pilum* that had helped Rome's legionaries to rule the world. But that was before one realized that it was precisely as old as those legionaries and that it was no trick of the wandering light that made its tip glow, no caprice of rain or dew that made it seem at times to drip with dark moisture. For this was the sacred Lance that had pierced Christ's side at the Crucifixion as a legionary sought to prove him dead.

Spear and Grail were paired for all eternity; when a blind man pierced Christ's side, blood and water had gushed into the cup set by the base of the cross, mingling with the vinegar it had held—sour mercy to a dying man, held to his lips by a sponge on the end of that very Lance. Some blood had run down the Lance, dripped into the blind man's face, and restored his sight. Joseph of Arimathea, founder of Amfortas's line, had taken up the cup even as he gave orders for Christ's body to be placed in his own tomb. When the body disappeared and Rome-in-Judaea pressed too closely, he had taken care to preserve it and his family. As a trader in tin and murex and all the riches of the world, he knew the world. He and his son Bron established a refuge here in Broceliande, and Bron ruled it after Joseph was gathered to his fathers.

But the Spear had disappeared, to be found centuries later by knights attempting to regain the Holy Land their sins had cost them. Instead, battered by the green banners of holy war, they lost their lives as well as the Lance; and Titurel, latest knight of Joseph's line, came too late to relieve them. Among the bodies, he found the Lance and added its care to the burdens of his line.

In all of Amfortas's days of errantry, he had performed no such deed to show him worthy of the burden he now bore. *Lord, I am not worthy,* he thought. *Give me this day my daily plea. Let this cup be lifted from me.* He shuddered at the echoes of memory that evoked. Gurnemanz would call that blasphemy.

He must serve. Now there was no one else.

Again, the peal of bells, with their rumbling undercurrents. Even as he floated in this cockleshell of a boat, savoring his last moments of freedom, the squires were preparing inexorably for evening service. His father was waiting for sustenance. Amfortas had hoped for a fish caught with his own hands to tempt the old man; but what was a fish when weighed against the nourishment provided by the Grail?

For all the fish that Lake Brumbane gave him, it might as well be the Dead Sea. Life here was all Dead Sea fruit, turning to ashes in eager hands and mouths—and the damnable thing was that only Amfortas knew it! Titurel, in his adventuring, had slain his thousands and begotten his sons. And what was the nothing at all that Amfortas might be granted? Grail knights were supposed to be celibate, except for the master of Montsalvasche. Bron had been content. But isolated as they were here in Broceliande, where would Amfortas find a queen to carry on the line, to inflict his burden upon yet another man?

Perhaps it was better that his line not go on, triply exiled as it was from the world. Once, by fiat of its founder. Twice by holiness. Thrice by Broceliande, wherever in the world it lay; after this long at Montsalvasche, Amfortas was not at all certain that the forest was *in* the world at all.

Of late, few pilgrims had come to Montsalvasche. That too was yet another sign of Amfortas's unworthiness. He had always welcomed pilgrims, not so much for what he could give them, but for the news they brought.

And now, he mused, *do I even know what year it is or how the kings I served fare in the Holy Lands?*

The world's time did not matter in Montsalvasche. It could be here, in the woods, but not *of* them. Broceliande stretched over the mountains between the fabulous Iberian realms where Christian and Moor battled to rule lands whose names sounded as if they were sounded by tabor or nakar and accompanied by a swirl of banners—Aragon, Castile, Asturias, León—and the land of the Frankish paladins.

In a sense, all woods were Broceliande, and all roads led through it. From Montsalvasche to Camelot; to Carbonek; to the Middle Sea; and, too close for easy thought, the mountain castle of Klingsor the wizard. Klingsor had vowed long ago to steal the Grail and whatever other relics he might and use them for his own heathen rites. That was, Amfortas had always thought, the one vow he might keep.

The king clenched his teeth. *Hate the sin, but love the sinner.* It was a charity he had never managed: Klingsor was not just his faith's enemy, but his own.

Montsalvasche was barred against Klingsor. It was built on sanctified ground. In addition to that warding, Klingsor would be stopped by men like those who served at Montsalvasche—out of the world—and those at Camelot as long as they held true. They were the paladins in these fallen times, they and whatever men existed beyond where Broceliande drifted in the circles of the world.

Sweet Lord, how far have we drifted since my youth? Time was . . . time was . . . sun and moon rose here, devoid of sequence, as he sometimes thought. Only the discipline of the bells imposed any order on the hours and days.

Lord, I am not worthy, Amfortas pleaded; but there was no one else and no mercy.

Again, the bells, commanding him to duty. Broceliande whispered and rustled, and torches moved in its blackening depths. Travelers must be passing by. Hope blazed up in the king, who quenched it ruthlessly. These days, it was the rare traveler Broceliande permitted to reach Montsalvasche; this group too would be deflected with no more—if the wood granted them that much grace—than a confused vision of a white stag caracoling by a lake, a crown upon its antlers.

But light approached from a more familiar direction. In a moment, one of the torchbearers would come close enough for Amfortas to see the dove blazoned on his cloak, the flare of firelight on the hilt of the long sword he carried: Gurnemanz, come to retrieve his tardy lord, with never a word of reproach but many an eloquent glance. Amfortas knew he was not the man his father was, or the man his brother might have been; his chance to be his own man had been cut short.

He should never have been here, where, daily, he was devoured by holiness and the eyes of the knights, ravenous for ecstasy, as he held aloft the Grail.

Abruptly, the flickering torchlight maddened him. There had been fires in the deserts of his youth, bonfires to rival the sunset once in a mad quest he had made when newly knighted to seek Mount Sinai. Al-Marrekh, he of the Spear, shone red; and red light gleamed off the Lance and from the torches. Higher in the sky, pitiless Saturn watched as Gurnemanz hurried to reclaim the Grail king for his nightly excruciation.

This fat land, these old men—how did they presume to think that they could ward the Grail? Let Sarras reclaim it and keep it, there in the ascetic desert—not this leafy prison where they held him and tormented him with holiness, when he sought only to be free.

The torches on the other side of Lake Brumbane flickered and beckoned. So did Gurnemanz. "My lord!" His voice, only faintly chiding, rang across the lake.

A long spill of firelight slashed across the lake. There had been a woman dancing in the firelight once, Medusa and Lilith combined, black serpents of hair twisting about her brown bare throat and over her mouth and lustrous teeth. That night, they had drunk bitter red wine and laughed at the laughing, flushed faces mirrored in the dented brass cup they shared (among the other pleasures they had shared), before they tumbled onto shabby linen sheets, mouths and bodies hotly joined for the night. Not a lady to bring to

Montsalvasche, no; but a fine and dangerous companion, like wrestling with a cheetah, tamed for the hunt.

The next morning, pounding below him on the taverna's door and the shouting of his name in the narrow street brought Amfortas out of deep, satisfying sleep. He drew himself away from the clinging hair and twining fingers of his bedmate, who muttered sleepy reproach. *Damn*, could they not let him escape for even one night?

His shirt flapping about him, the rest of his garments in one hand, he stalked outside, hot words on his lips.

They cooled as he looked at Gurnemanz. He had withered overnight. His eyes were red, his garments rent. Grim-faced, he would not speak to Amfortas until they had put the taverna well behind them. Then he pushed him into the shadow of a crumbling wall the way, years ago, he had cuffed a rebellious page into obedience.

"Word came at dawn," his father's squire said. "Your brother's dead. Klingsor offered truce."

"A fool to trust him . . ." Amfortas burst out.

"Your brother was a saint!" Gurnemanz stared the younger man down. "When the King heard how Klingsor ambushed him . . ."

"My father too?" Amfortas whispered. The sun of Outremer hammered against his senses. Not even the wall steadied him as Broceliande reached out and snared him. His eyes blurred and in the moment between the pain and unconsciousness, vision struck . . . *The old man, plunging from his throne to clasp the rusty, cloak-wrapped bundle that had been his heir. "Bron, my son, my son. Would God I had died for thee!" And toppling so the knights thought he had. When they raised Titurel, the King's face had blurred, like wax marred by a clumsy thumb, and he could not move.*

"Not dead, man!" Gurnemanz's hands pressed against his shoulders, bearing Amfortas up, blotting out the memory of other, softer hands late last night. "But not fit to serve. The order's come. You must go back. Today."

Amfortas jerked free of the older man's hands and sank to his knees. Retching, he brought up the wine and sins and joys of the night before. Then he wept for the death of his brother, whom he had, after all, loved, and the wreck of his father and his king. Gurnemanz stood by, his shadow falling upon Amfortas's shoulders as he trembled. He offered no more and no other comfort: not to a king he surely must disdain.

Without a word, the older man handed him a leather water bottle and gestured: *Cleanse yourself*. The water pouring down his face looked like tears; tears of rage at the trap he was caught in, his hatred of it, and of himself.

When he was empty, Gurnemanz bowed deeply and followed him to the camp.

As squire—or as guard that I do not flee? I would not have fled . . . would I?

The fury of that day rushed back upon him now. What? Not one night free, never, if he should live—which God avert—as long as Titurel? Amfortas seized the oars. Just one jolt of his shoulders would drive the boat toward the farther shore and brief escape from the sacred wards of Montsalvasche.

The lake's surface trembled, waiting, with the perturbations of the bells. In their cloaks, each as heavy in this heat as a bishop's cope poured from lead, the knights were assembling to walk through Montsalvasche, past the keep and into the chapel, a great dome of space cut within living rock that resounded with the throbbing of the bells, the echoes of chant, and the presence of the Grail. And his father, waiting for him. When he arrived, late, not even by a reproachful glance would they indicate how long and how painfully they had waited past the noon when it should have been displayed.

Well, just this once, just let them! A few negligent strokes of the oars shot the boat toward the far side of the lake.

"My lord!" Gurnemanz's fine voice, the terror of every squire on every drill field from here to Outremer, hailed him.

Amfortas drew breath to reply . . .

And the scream of a woman in mortal terror cut across the indigo sky.

2

IN Amfortas's forfeited life, bells had been a call to battle as welcome now as rebellion had been an instant ago. Arms and shoulders strained, thrusting the oars forward, and the tiny boat dashed into the shallows. He leapt for the shore, splashing his long surcoat as he raced toward the screams, sword and Lance welcome in his hands.

At last! Amfortas greeted the fight in torch-shot darkness with a sense of passionate relief, even welcome. Not even pausing to regret the kite-shaped shield he lacked or the mantle that might have shielded one arm, he found himself embattled, one man among four. The vaults of unaccustomed muscles—the arch of a foot, the stretch of thigh muscles as he held his ground or strained forward, the arm muscles for beating down an enemy's blade—ached, each familiar pain as sweet as desire.

Sweat, blood, and the mist off the lake were all one, sliding down swarthy faces; the torchlight spun, making teeth and eyes glisten in the treacherous shadows. Amfortas felt his own mouth stretch open into a square of effort, then into a grin. He was very happy. The ache of softened palm and fingers against hilt, the faint acid sting of a cut, the twist of a wrist muscle were all welcome as he fought.

He drove two men before him as he backed slyly deeper into the woods where a single torch burned steadily to show him his true enemy: a man in the metallic brocade *burud*, or surcoat, he remembered from Outremer and his battles at the *ribats*, the border posts. This man had locked his arms about a struggling woman and was trying to drag her deeper into the shadows of Broceliande, where centuries might

pass before anyone would know of his evil or find her
outraged bones.

The firelight flashed across her face. Amfortas gasped,
not just with the effort of the battle. She had the wild beauty
of desert and mountains, eyes and hair so black that they
made her face, tanned from the sun, seem fair; lips red and
bitter as pomegranates on the stem; and white past belief,
the rich curves of throat and bared breast as she tore at the
hands that ripped at her tattered gown.

A shift in the quivering of the air warned Amfortas that
he neared the perimeter of the land consecrated to Montsalvasche and warded by the Grail; three—no, two—more
strides and he would fight in Broceliande, vulnerable as any
traveler or this lady who now saw him and whose cheeks
flushed with hope and thankfulness.

He saw his opening and with a fierce joy pressed forward.
At the swing of a heavy sword at his head, he dodged rather
than risk the Spear in a parry that might have shattered the
ancient wood and brittle, darkened blade. He thrust it quivering into the ground and lunged forward, his long sword
an extension of his bloody will that left a man stretched
dead upon unsanctified ground. The impact still shocked
through his body as the man fell.

Amfortas laughed and turned toward his fellow. Idled for
years he may have been; but he *could* take them. He was
restored to life, to youth and knighthood. Once again, he
was an errant, an adventurer—not just God's paladin.
Humid air stung his throat like Greekish wine, while the
salt of his sweat stung his eyes.

Amfortas reached white heat. His blows fell as molten
metal pours from a crucible—almost in a trance of effort,
until the flames from the droplets scattered on the ground
burst into violent flame.

What it was to praise God, not for eternal peace, safe in
the cavern of Montsalvasche, but for making him His Warrior! He had forgotten that; he had forgotten much too
much. Amfortas dodged around trees, remembering a vicious fight with a robber in the narrow climbing streets of
Safed; a meeting in Alexandria by the ancient harbor of
Alexander with two mamluks. Then, as now, oaths and

warnings rose in five languages at once, a killer's argot familiar to his ears. Greek, Frankish, Arabic—languages he remembered; and some he did not. It was the tongue of the
ghazi, the border mercenary: some Saracen, some traitor,
and all his enemy.

Sword danced against sword in the torch-shot night
where branches and leaves took on the aspect of deep jun-
gle, and Amfortas laughed for joy.

The lady shouted. Hearing sound rather than sense, Amfortas dodged by instinct a blade that might have sheared
halfway through his shoulder. Angered, he thrust in return.
The man fell, clutching a leg that might, if he did not bleed
to death and were very, very lucky in his chirurgeon, let
him limp all the way to hell.

A third man turned and fled. Amfortas flicked a jeer of
a laugh at his back and turned to the man—that mighty
warrior—whose prowess barely served to drag the lady off
into the trees. The very roots and rocks seemed to aid her
as they caught in her garments and tugged her toward the
ground, keeping her where Amfortas might reach and rescue her. The man wrenched her around in front of him—a
paladin indeed, to use a half-bare lady as his shield.

His grip upon her naked arm must have twisted it sorely,
but she did not scream. Instead, she went limp. With an
oath, her abductor bent to adjust his balance. And in that
instant, she struck, biting the hand where its mailed half-
mitten did not protect it. He shouted and hurled her from
him as if shaking off a viper. She flung her arms out, as if to
clasp his legs and bring him down; but he kicked free and
strode forward to face Amfortas.

They were well matched. If Amfortas was the taller man
with the longer blade, this coward of an abductor had been
well trained, and his blade was of such a quality to make
Amfortas worry. Steel engaged, parried, and disengaged
with such force that his blade all but snapped. He knew
where in the world such blades came from. Steel of Damascus. From the glimmer of this one, it had spells in its forging
and spells, rather than holy relics, to guard its wielder.

So, did he fight a wizard's man—or, judging from arms
and silks, a wizard's mamluk? Only one wizard would dare

to pierce Broceliande with sin; and that was not Merlin. Wander in the wood at need he might, devil's son though rumor had him, he was a godly wight who served King Uther. It was not he.

Only one wizard would both dare invade the wood and own mamluks—his old neighbor and enemy Klingsor. Were Amfortas wise, he would take this man captive—assuming that he could. There must be some way that the knights could pierce the wizard's guard. Perhaps this man would know it.

As their blades crossed, Amfortas felt the strength drain from him. Already he had fought three and slain one, and he had not been in practice. Blades met again, a momentary cross that Amfortas begged for aid.

And aid came, though not as he expected it. Even as he allowed his enemy to beat him back one step . . . two . . . the lady rose from her huddle of rich rags and crept forward. The light of a guttering torch flashed on the dagger she held, which she had stolen from her ravisher as she fell. She forced herself into a stumbling run, her teeth bared, her dagger ready to strike.

She had aimed for a thigh, he saw. Perhaps she hoped to ensure that the man would try what he had on her on no other woman ever again. *What* a lady! Amfortas thought. He shouted with exultation, though, in the next moment, he had to gasp for breath.

Sparks flew as the blade sheared aside on the lamellar scales of the man's armor and slipped down, to score through his garments and slash his leg. He twisted aside and just barely avoided hamstringing. He thrust out, not quite strong enough for a kick, with the wounded leg, scattering black blood and sending the lady flying before he, too, fled faster than a limping man ought to be able to run.

Amfortas took one long stride in pursuit. Easy enough to cut him down or capture him now, thanks to the lady. My God, how her lord must treasure her, and not just for her beauty! Why had he never—? A groan halted him in midstride as the wretch disappeared into the dark forest.

There lay the lady, far too still. The mamluk's kick that had freed him had hurled her against a tree. Perhaps some bones were broken; please God, let them not be in her neck or back!

Amfortas's sweat cooled on him. He ached; he wanted no more than to fall where he stood and wait for his men to lead him tenderly away; yet he walked slowly over toward the fallen woman, laboriously knelt, and brushed the tangled hair from her face. His skin tingled as he raised her head to lie against his knee. Her black hair was soft, scented with ambergris and the salt of her tears.

Her face rolled upward: parted lips, a bruised cheek, and great vaults of fragile eyelids hemmed in by black brows and lashes. A beauty indeed to covet, had a man—or wizard—few scruples and less decency. Threads of what must once have been rich gold embroidery winked up and down with the lady's shallow breaths. Her bare throat was bruised, as if the man had ripped a necklace from her throat before tearing at her garments.

Amfortas glanced round, the instinctive search of a desert fighter for water. None closer than Lake Brumbane, he realized. Now, that was a good plan. Let him bear this lady up, and he would meet Gurnemanz and the guard that his old squire had doubtless assembled to reinforce their lord on his sudden eruption back into errantry. She could be brought to Montsalvasche and, in the sight of the Grail, healed of the wounds to body and spirit that she had suffered.

A good idea; a safe idea. "Look up, lady!" Amfortas whispered in Frankish. He tried several other tongues and several other messages of hope before, too gently to call the touch a slap, he touched her face, first one cheek, then the other, to wake her. She whimpered like a child, and her eyes fluttered open, filling with renewed fear that hurt him worse than any of the chance cuts he had taken that night.

"It was not I that hurt you, lady, brave lady," he murmured. "Not I, I beg you believe. See, it is over. Your attackers are dead, or wounded, one by your own hand, or fled."

He tried to show her the dove on his surcoat, but the blow that had almost taken his arm had slashed the fabric,

defacing the sigil. "See, I am Amfortas, son of Titurel,
Master of Montsalvasche; and truly I live to serve."

He swung her up into arms that protested a new burden,
but not for long. As much as his exhaustion, the scents of
her—fear and ambergris and sweet herbs on the tatters of
her gown—made him stagger forward; and she clutched at
his shoulders, her body pressing close, as he tried to steady
himself. It had been long since he had fought. It had been
long since he had done other things, too.

Her head shook back and forth where it rested against his
chest, and she half moaned, half whispered something he
bent his head to hear.

"No others . . . no other men."

"Lady, I promise you, your battle is over; and I shall
bring you to a place where brave men will protect and care
for you."

"*Not* let them see me, not like this!" she protested, her
cheeks turning crimson as she shook her head from side to
side and tried to hide her face. She burrowed against him.
Sweet Jesu, how long had it been? How long?

"Please, not like this," she begged. "My own place . . ."

Bemused by the weight and feel of her, Amfortas finally
began to understand. No matter what had happened (since
her skirts appeared intact, her chastity had not been
breached), the attempt to violate her had been made; and
she was ashamed. Ashamed without reason: no man of
Montsalvasche would blame a lady who had fought so val-
iantly to save herself. Nevertheless, out in the world, such
a lady might well face whispers and blame: how had she
come to such a pass? What could she have done or said to
invite attack?

Let Amfortas carry her to her pavilion where, no doubt,
women waited to tend their lady and ease her mind. There,
too, might even be the lady's chaplain: even a schismatic of
the Greeks might bring her soul's ease. Once he saw her
safe, Amfortas could return to his neglected duties, assuming even Gurnemanz would accuse him of neglect. After all,
he had protected innocence. *Am I not about my Father's
business?* he mused wryly.

But once again, the lady was murmuring.

"My lord, your arms . . ." Her voice was very sweet, huskier than a woman's wont, and, right now, surprised.

Amfortas flushed as he had not since he had won his spurs. Carefully, he set the lady down. "Don't be afraid," he warned. "They're right . . . ah!"

Where was the Spear? There! In the darkness, he had all but mistaken it for the bole of a tree. Torchlight picked out the fitful gleam of his sword, dangling from its cord about his wrist.

The blade was blood-smeared. It would have to be a distasteful sight for a gently nurtured woman, especially one who had survived a battle. He slipped it free of his wrist and bent to clean it, but her hand, strong despite its size, on his forestalled him. She drew the heavy blade closer and made as if to clean it upon the wine-dark shreds of silk she wore or even the long skeins of her hair.

"Let me serve," she whispered.

"Lady, I beg you, no! For mine own comfort, you need not do such things!" Amfortas was genuinely shocked.

Her eyes met his and filled with tears. "I owe you my life and more," she told him as he bent to clean and sheathe his blade, hastily lest the lady have other alarming notions of grateful service. Amfortas prayed her ordeal had not shattered her wits.

"Let me bear you to your women," he said. He lifted her as if there were no idea, ever, of permitting her to walk; she nestled confidingly against him. As if the weight of his mail did not lie between them, he felt the warmth of her.

"Can you tell me where your pavilion lies?" he asked. "Are torches placed? You must bring me through your guards."

Her head had fallen back, and he thought that, finally assured of safety, she might have swooned. Well, the sight of their lady in a strange knight's arms would probably make her guardians—not that Amfortas thought much of them— pause before they cut him down and he could explain.

Bearing the lady he had rescued, Amfortas strode deeper, ever deeper into Broceliande. The forest's shadows thickened and engulfed him, shutting out the shouts of his men come to seek him out.

3

AMFORTAS strode in haste through the twisted, darkening ways of Broceliande. Urgency was upon him to set the lady in his arms into the care of her attendants. She was trembling now with fear and shame; the women in her service would care for and reassure her before her very modesty made her sick. At such a time, the presence of any man could not help but cause her fear. As for her guards, he promised himself that he would have at least several words with them and perhaps with her lord, too, about how best to guard ladies whose courage did not accord with their strength or the ability of their knights to serve them. Or she might be a widow, long enough bereaved to have put off mourning clothes. He decided he would not think of why that thought made his heart beat faster.

Perhaps, he thought, it would be good to invite the entire household to stay at Montsalvasche for a time.

Good for whom? a voice jeered in his thoughts. *She is not your lady.*

She would not have been in such danger had she been my *lady,* he told the voice.

The lady—he had no time yet to ask her name—stirred in his arms, her hair brushing his chin. She wanted down, and he thought he understood why. He had rescued her from her attackers, but he too was a man—did she fear his touch? Just a moment ago, he had assumed that she could not but regard all men with revulsion. Now, the very idea cost him a pang before he dismissed his sorrow as unworthy.

"Lady, should you walk?" he asked.

As he walked, his hands had molded about what he held,

even while his body, unaccustomed to battle, had stiffened from his efforts. A cut at his temple stung from sweat and the dampness in the air. His eyes misted, and he shook his head, as if that would restore his mind to its usual clarity.

Around him flickered wisps of light, glimmering on beauties of tree or leaf that he and the woman in his arms might have been the first to see since Creation, when the morning stars sang together and all the sons of God shouted for joy. She sighed, and his palms grew warm from the warmth of her body.

"You are tired," she said, "and I must guide you from here."

He set her on her feet and told himself his reluctance came from his fear that she was still too unsteady to walk far. She was so brave, so courteous.

"You know where we are?" In the darkness, Amfortas was aware of her as a warmth, a voice, and a shadow; he himself would have thought they were lost. *Do you always take such care of the ladies you rescue, sir?* he demanded of himself. *Do you plan to wander till dawn comes and she loses what honor she has not lost already? And you presume to criticize her guards?* Again, he shook his head. His temples pounded. What a damnable time for the fevers that followed him from Outremer to recur.

"I see very well in the dark," she assured him, and took his hand to lead him through the darkness. Strictly he forbade himself to tremble from fever or from memories.

"There!" Her shoulder pressed against him and he felt, as well as heard, her laugh. Will-o'-the-wisps seemed to cluster about, casting a flickering, lunar light upon what might have been a palace, had it not been wrought of silk and poles. The lady traveled like a queen.

"Your men at arms?" He glanced about for armed men.

"Hidden." He rather thought that she must mean she had bowmen as well as swordsmen, stationed roundabout, chosen for keen sight like their lady's as well as skill and the discretion they would need if she often walked abroad alone. "Seeing me with you, they would not harm you."

She clapped her hands sharply together in the Eastern style. A panel of the tent billowed aside in a sudden splendor of firelight, and silk-clad ladies, some bearing torches, ran down what now looked like a clearly marked path toward them. Their veils and sleeves floated behind them like the wings of giant moths or like the petals of rare flowers that bloom only at night.

They greeted their mistress first with cries of dismay at her ragged state and bruises, then with consoling whispers. With soft yet quite inexorable hands, they forced Amfortas from her side and stood between them.

"The Lord Amfortas," she told them. "My preserver. See that he is cared for."

Dark eyes went wide and too bright in the torchlight. One woman, younger and smaller than the rest, pressed a corner of the saffron veil flung over her head against her eyes. Ladies of Outremer, Amfortas thought, and averted his eyes courteously. He thought he knew the type: daughters of knights who had chosen to forsake Europe for the Holy Land and the greater splendors of Saracen life there; who married there, often to ladies who had accepted baptism, and whose households, though Christian, blended East and West in a way that Amfortas had enjoyed greatly the few times he had guested in them. Daughters of such men would have the freedom of ladies in the West, yet feel most at ease removed from the gaze of strangers.

He saluted the ladies. Strangers in a strange land, they were; they might not kiss in courtesy, and, in courtesy, this were no time to ask. Sensing his restraint, they smiled approval and came forward, some to bear their lady away, some to wait on him.

Something else must be asked now, before he took another step.

"I should have asked before; I am at fault," he said. "But may I beg to know my lady's name? I would at least thank my hostess."

She laughed again, and he realized he had hoped to hear her laugh, warmth laced with faint—and so very gallant! he thought—mockery of the circumstances that had prevented him from asking.

"My name? You may call me Kundry."

That was no saint's name he knew, and no name of

Araby, either. Perhaps it was a name adopted to give her privacy while she journeyed. Noble ladies often did just that.

"My lady Kundry." Amfortas bowed deeply, faintly proud that he had managed not to flinch as the necessary courtesy strained ribs and muscles.

"Until we dine, my lord." She let her ladies bear her away.

Then a troop of them surrounded him, too, and swept him, bemused, into a place of aromatic lamplight and silken hangings.

As if they had known to expect a weary guest, a rich carpet was spread. Upon it gently steamed a large tub of chased silver. Amfortas's attendants gently pushed aside his hands, removing and bearing away the stained surcoat from which the insignia had been plucked, then easing him from his mail. Moving a little more quickly than sore muscles would have liked, but still too slowly for modesty, he climbed into the warm water on which red roses and fragrant oils floated, easing his hurts, soothing away the fever he thought he might have.

He revised still upward his opinion of the lady Kundry: only ladies of the highest nobility would have their guests tended by gently born maids. They brought him fruit juices and sherbet cooled in snow; just when he started to suspect that the lady might be Saracen and no Christian at all, they brought him wine. A bath sheet in their hands, they started to raise him from the water, to rub him with ointments to ease his body; their mirth, as he gestured them away, made him laugh too.

It had been many years since he had thus been tended, and that had been at the palace of a lord in Caesarea. But he was too eager to return to the presence of his hostess to savor it.

His request for his clothing brought gentle shrieks of mock outrage and an array of robes of honor held out for his choice: not a one of them was wrought of a fabric less costly than samite or taffeta, and they glittered with embroidery and gems like the robes of an emperor.

They displayed no white garments, and white was what

he had worn since he had returned to Montsalvasche. He waved away vanities of purple and scarlet, even the green, the achmardi that was as prized as purple in the East. Finally, concerned at the time he took, he chose an indigo shot with silver like a night sky through which a comet flies. The mantle that went with it was collared with white fur. He would have laid it aside, pleading the heat of summer. But a night breeze blew down from far-off mountains through opened panels in the great tent, and he tossed it about his shoulders, letting the heavy cords fall loosely. They applauded in delight, then held up a mirror, shimmering silver in the lamplight: a tall man, a lean man, eyes pale in a tanned face. Once again, he was a prince in Outremer, splendid, admired, and free. All thoughts of his father, his need, or the Grail itself had vanished.

Despite their vows that their lady was safe and *they*, at least, were not brigands, he belted on his sword, picked up the Spear, and stood forth fully armed.

The murmurs of the ladies were more potent than the wine as they led him through the hangings that curtained the bathing room from the center of the great tent. Then they withdrew, leaving not even a breath of laughter behind.

Lanterns of pierced bronze, wrought in cubes and spheres, hung from polished chains from the tent poles, casting jewels of light and shadows on brilliant carpets and hangings in the Persian style; chests of wood, inset with ebony, silver, and ivory; and braziers on which sweet sandalwood burned. In all corners of the tent and on the lids of the chests, tiny clusters of candles burnt. The pure smell of burning beeswax was familiar to Amfortas, reminding him—

"No one would think that you had just fought a battle, my lord," came the low voice of the lady Kundry.

"You could well be cause of a thousand such," Amfortas replied as he gazed with admiration at her.

Seated on a cushion before a low trestle table covered with a cloth was the lady Kundry. She wore a gown the color of the wine she poured for him into a golden goblet, and as closely fitted to her form as wine to goblet. Some women's magic—and a necklace as heavy with rubies as is a pomegranate with seeds—concealed the bruises on her throat. Her skin shone, as did her eyes as he approached, hesitated, and at her smile, seated himself at her side.

Dishes were on the table, and Kundry herself uncovered them. Here was heron; here, game; and here—"Lady, I labored all day to catch one fish, and now I see why I found none. They all swam to your lure!"

She laughed, delighted. Not content with serving him a portion of the delicately boned fish, she slipped from her cushions and knelt beside him to season it with tangy herbs before cutting it on his plate.

"I beseech you, lady, for my own comfort . . ." he protested, faltering. It was not fitting for a lady thus to serve a knight, especially a knight sworn to serve his fellows. When his words failed, he tried to raise her, to reseat her on her cushions or to give her his place. His hands faltered in the instant before he touched her. She shook her head at him, and the lamplight danced in the jewels at her brow.

"You are my guest."

"I am my lady's servant."

"Then"—she looked up as if he had said something witty and she were about to cap it—"you must obey me. Sit and eat!"

She would hear of nothing else; she would speak nothing about herself, but always turned the conversation, with an accomplished lady's skill, back to himself, his travels, his adventures. And he must make what deductions he could about her from her responses to him. He described the splendors of Byzantium, the heat of the bazaars in Alexandria, and the deserts of the Holy Land; her comments showed her familiar with all of them, and her tears as he spoke of pilgrims, kneeling at the Holy Sepulchre, lamenting on Golgotha, made him want to put out his hand and wipe them away. Had she lost her home or people she loved in all those wars?

"Well traveled for so young a lady," was all he dared to say.

She turned the compliment aside demurely. "Should I tell you I am older than I look?"

"She who is false shall ever win false praise. I praise you truly, so how can you be aught else but truth itself?"

She smiled at the courtly banter, at which she, no less than he, must have been schooled; but her eyes were thoughtful. Perhaps she still thought upon his tales of the Holy Land. He had not told her them to make her sorrowful.

Yet she was grave. He glanced down at her hand as she bent to fill his goblet. Rings she wore, but no marriage ring. Perhaps she *was* a widow. A lady of courage, a lady of virtue—else she would not have traveled and she would not have fought. The best thing he could do would be to bring her, this very night, to Montsalvasche where she could be guarded.

No: the best thing he could do would be to make her smile once more. Or try. Lord, it had been years since he had played such games. He took up his goblet, fingers brushing hers, and drank deep. "Perhaps it is I who am false. Perhaps *I* am actually Merlin himself . . ."

"I should have said Uther Pendragon, hastening to my aid," she told him. This time, her laughter rang out like a young girl's, and she poured him more wine. The ruby on her finger shone, and the dark wine quivered in pitcher and in cup.

Delighted with the success of his strategy, he drank to her.

He did not think it strange that no ladies sat with them or served them. The wine and the incense and the laughter mixed with the fever that had kindled in him until his head spun, and the slightest thing she said in that sweet, husky voice of hers rang out like unforgettable poetry. They both laughed a great deal. Amfortas remembered such laughter after other battles—a little too long, too shrill, as people who had been through too much convinced themselves that they were alive and happy to be so. He wanted to tell her how much about her he thought he knew, how much more he wanted to know; but always she had questions and forestalled him.

Though the candles burnt down, and the lamps dimmed,

he felt as if he sat in the noonday sun as she drew his life from him, story by story.

"So," she asked archly, "you fled your friends when you heard me cry for help?"

He peeled an orange and gave it to her. Covertly, as if studying a deer he stalked, he watched her lips part, then close upon the fruit.

"Lady, I am a great sinner. I would fly free of death if you cried for help."

"And do you repent?"

He should. Even now, it was not too late to rise and offer her his escort to Montsalvasche. Or, if she would not travel by night, it was high time for him to leave her camp, to spend the night in watchfulness and prayer.

Just one moment more to savor my old life . . .

She refilled his goblet yet again, and as she handed it to him, he captured her hand and kissed it. "Of serving you? Never!"

"I did not say you might do that," she told him, mock stern.

Mindful of the rules of the game of courts, he sighed and looked sorrowful. "I am betrayed. I was always taught that a man were wise to gain a lady's greeting and her kiss."

"And a ring?" She eyed him sidelong. "Shall you ask for that, too?"

"I would not so presume. Instead, I would repent, but—"

"You have already said you would *never* repent. But you know what is said," she chided him. " '*Come back, come back, even if you have broken your repentance a thousand times.*' "

"You have studied the Saracens, lady?" he marveled. The poet who wrote those lines was a mystic of no mean order—and no Christian faith.

"Aye, just as you have studied them yourself." She looked at him narrowly, and all her beauty flared up into a summer storm of anger. "And why should I not? Some Farsi and Arabic poetry has been written by ladies who are among the loveliest and most accomplished in the world."

"Lady Kundry, I meant no offense . . ." And how should

he presume? The ladies of Outremer were frequently quite learned; and that, too, was part of their dual heritage.

"Then, again, we are speaking of repentance," she went on with a pretty assumption of haughtiness that her dancing eyes contradicted. "I shall give you another lesson from the poetry that so shocked you. Repentance is"—she tapped her goblet against shining teeth—"'a door from the west until the day when the sun rises in the west.'"

"How rare. And how beautiful," Amfortas mused. Doctrinally, too, he thought it was true. Repentance, were it heartfelt, had to be eternal unless a man despaired. He did not think the poet had despaired, yet the poet was outside the Mercy. He shook his head. Surely He who had all miracles in His power would have mercy on such a poet.

Mercy . . . it was a thirst he saw every day in the faces of the men who watched him serve the Grail. A thirst . . . he watched the lady drink. Her eyes met his, and she flushed and glanced away.

As if nerving himself to tilt at a foe, he took another sip of wine. "But surely, lady, we might find poetry nearer to hand . . ."

She arched an eyebrow at him. "My lord can think of examples?"

The moment was upon him to give himself away, and he must not fail in courage here, as he had not in battle. Battle, he thought, would have been easier.

Even now, he might redeem the moment, might lead her to his home and woo her chastely—but how to do that in open sight of all those men? She could be won; she could be his. He knew that.

But must it be now?

Yes, heart and blood demanded. He was young again. He was free again, a man, and not a king circumscribed by what were almost priestly vows. And she was yielding. Even his blurring eyes could see that.

"Rise up," Amfortas said hoarsely, "my love, my fair one, and come away. For, lo, the winter is past, the rain is over and gone; the flowers appear on the earth; the time of the singing of birds is come, and the voice of the turtle is heard in our land."

Abruptly, he was far too hot. Sweat rose on his brow, and his hands shook. He rose, almost oversetting his goblet and the table, and strode to the darkest corner of the tent. He ached, almost as if he had taken a wound in his groin. Lifting a silken panel scented with attar of roses, he gazed out into the night. It had no answers for his questions: *shall I ask? Am I drunk? Have I been too bold already?* His longing was sweeter to him than the wine he had drunk.

No, Montsalvasche was too cold a place for such a wooing.

"There can be *no* repentance now for how I have behaved," he muttered, "for I would say yet more if I dared to dream you would hear it."

Kundry rose, her eyes enormous and so dark that her olive skin seemed pale by comparison. Her lips trembled, but she did not forbid Amfortas, so he went on.

"I would tell you, 'Behold, thou art fair, my love; behold, thou art fair.' And I have no right. Somewhere, you must have a lord—"

She shook her head, and hope filled him with a sudden, desperate fear. He should not have spoken—not yet, not at all, not ever.

"Lady, this is not right, this is too fast; you are not a . . . a . . ." He stammered, then blurted out the image that had tormented him all that long day. ". . . girl of tavern or harbor to be snatched up and enjoyed like a pomegranate or a cup of water in the heat of the moment." He drew himself up, trying finally for whatever dignity he could muster. He felt as naked as he had been in the bath, with all the ladies commenting on his scars. "I would court you by all the customs of my house and of yours."

There was no reason he should not. Except the coldness of the stones of Montsalvasche and the hunger in the eyes of the men who would watch him, watch her, weighing and judging. *How dare they?* Amfortas felt his eyes go blind with anger and desire. *Let he who is without sin . . .* This was sin, but sweet, so sweet, and he ached for it.

She swayed toward him, drawing a ring from her finger and handing it to him to kiss, then slip onto his little finger.

If he were not watching her lips so closely, he would have missed her words.

"Can you not simply think me easily won?"

He had his arms around her then, as he had longed to do since she had compelled him to set her down in the forest. He sighed with contentment. This time, her body rested compliant against his, and she pressed more closely against him as his hands roamed up and down her back and sides. She was beautiful, and she was yielding to him.

"Lady," he whispered. "My lady. Be my lady, and you will never know fear again. Only joy, I promise you."

His hands tightened as they caressed her, almost sculpting her form. Greatly daring, he slid his hand upon her left breast and felt her heartbeat fill his palm. His chin pressed against the crown of her head and he grew drunk on the scent of her hair.

"How can I see such need in you," she murmured against his throat, "and not ache to fill it?"

Her hands were deft on the ties of his mantle and his sword belt. As garment and belt tumbled to his feet, he lifted her chin and kissed her with longing, burying one hand in her dark hair to hold her mouth steady for him. She gasped, and her lips opened for him. Like a cup of water at midday, indeed. More than once, such a cup had saved lives. He was sure that this cup would save his.

Oh God, he was young again, free again, and he had won her!

Lifting her, plucking the gems from her hair, her fingers, her arms, and that shining throat of hers, he began to drain that cup. It would never run dry, he thought.

"Until the day break, and the shadows flee," she promised him and led him through the tent, a way he had not yet been, to a wide pallet, deeply cushioned and hung with layer upon layer of gauzy silk.

She held out her arms to him, like a lady waiting for her maids to disrobe her. His knees began to give way, but she caught his shoulders, protesting.

"You must not kneel."

"So beautiful . . . you deserve worship."

She pulled him upright with the same strength she had used to defend herself by the lake.

"That is not the worship that I want."

"What is?"

"You know; just a moment ago, you were perfect in all its rites."

Amfortas nodded and began to slip her gown from off her warm shoulders. "Until the day break, and the shadows flee away, I will get me to the mountain of myrrh, and to the hill of frankincense." He kissed her throat as he had longed to, and the deep valley between her scented breasts, and then he lost himself in wonder and desire and flame.

4

AS her bedmate's breathing slowed and steadied, Kundry tensed. Asleep at last, was he? It had taken hours to bring him to this point. Astonishing: she had grudged not a second of them. Cautiously, she raised herself on one elbow to study this knight . . . this Amfortas who called himself her servant. Relaxed in sleep, his face possessed the severity she had seen on monuments his people had left behind them in the Holy Land. They had left much, too much behind them, including battles and the remnants of their faith. Scars and youth had weathered down to austere symmetry; she could scarcely believe that a mouth that stern had stammered out poetry to her, that a body weathered like an old statue could belong to the same man who had loved her with the frenzy almost of a youth huddling and trembling in the shadows with his first girl.

His fever spent, Amfortas had held her as if she were fine glass, shot with rainbows by desert sunlight, and begged her to say he had not hurt her.

Injured me? If only he knew . . . And thank the God she feared to face that he did not. For all his scars, Amfortas was an innocent. Kundry knew the effect of every smile or twist of her body on the men who shared her bed. She had not known the effect of that question upon her, and had turned her face against his shoulder to hide the burning in her eyes. Tears? After all these years?

"Your honor is now mine, lady," he had said, raising his head from her breasts to look into her eyes. "I swear to you I will not betray your gift." He brushed her hair back from her brow, then off her shoulders and sides. His lips followed his hands. Used to feigning a pleasure she had never known with all her lovers in all her years, she had felt it in truth last night: his touch had drawn it from her. At the last, she had clung to him, whispered his name, and touched his face, astonished.

She had not thought, at her age, to find something new under the sun. It was a pity she might not stay to savor it.

And how long had it been since Kundry, the cankered rose of Sharon, had even thought of pity?

Preposterous. Better far to focus on the way he stroked her hair, the tenderness of his hands now that he feared he held her too hard. And another wonder: he had not gone immediately to sleep, but cradled her and whispered poetry in her ear for hours.

Men had whispered songs to her before, in Hebrew, Greek, and Latin, and only more recently in these successor tongues of Europe; but this time, this man had been different. Those men had paid for the privilege. This one . . . God have mercy upon her (only He never had and never would) . . . this one spoke of courting her, of bringing her as Lady to a castle where the very stones ought to conspire to dash her brains out, if she could be that lucky.

She was almost certain that was not the wine—or what she had put in it.

They had dueled with words, teased each other with verse about repentance before they turned to do what they must now repent. Only there was and never would be repentance for her, cursed as she was.

Kundry must have tensed, because the arm he had flung across her shoulders tightened. Protective even as he slept. She would have wept; but the few tears she had left would turn to gall. Instead, she lay absolutely still until he relaxed into deep sleep once more. Then, she slipped aside and reluctantly left her bed. Their bed.

Naked was vulnerable, though she had not felt so last night, standing before a man who had fought mamluks to protect her, but who sank to his knees at the sight of her bare body. She smiled at the sleeping man. Gleefully squandering a minor magic, she called smock and gown to her from the carpet where Amfortas had let them fall and slipped them on, making quick, deft work of the fastenings that the man she dare not call her lover had fumbled. Despite her resolve, she smiled, a secret reminiscent smile. She had lain with him as had been required of her. It was not the first time she had done such a thing. Likely, it was not the last time: she was practiced, hardened at her trade.

But this man had cherished her for her own sake; and that was something new.

Look not upon me, she murmured other words of that poem to herself, *because I am black, because the sun hath looked upon me; my mother's children were angry with me; they made me the keeper of the vineyards, but mine own vineyard have I not kept.*

So young, so new, he had called her, almost weeping on her breasts. *How can I ask you to mew yourself up with terrible old men and squires who dream only of swordplay and becoming saints?*

Put that way, it did sound quite fearsome, even were it possible. To her own horror, she wished that he had asked and that she were free to accept. Lady Kundry. Queen Kundry. Perfumed not with attar of roses, but with holiness.

But it could never be, not even as a dream. She was not what he thought, not young, but older by far than he and all his race.

Kundry bit her lip lest she start to laugh. She was afraid of laughter. It had been the cause of her ruin. But she had not been afraid to laugh with Amfortas, or at him—not as she had bantered, far too many years ago, with sleek tribunes newly come to Judaea from Rome or the Athens-trained sons of wealthy merchants.

Those had all been clients. This man—what? Could have made her happy. Foolishness, Kundry. If she had deserved happiness, she would have had it in Judaea. Would have had it and would never have met this Amfortas, for she would have been dead and dust before he and his "line" ever rampaged through her homeland—had her cursed laughter only not damned her to wander. The laughter she had shared with this man had been as warm as it must be short-lived.

Soon dawn would come, and she must give the signal,

whether she would or not. There were worse things than eternal loneliness, and she had been promised many of them if she did not obey. She hated her obedience.

She twisted up her hair with a red silk cord. Who was it who had dropped scarlet thread out her window and been saved from the fall of Jericho? Rahab—a harlot like and unlike herself. Where Rahab had let in messengers she trusted, Kundry must betray the man who trusted her. Who, in one night, had achieved what no man had done in all these weary centuries: he had touched a heart she had all but forgotten she owned.

She sighed and opened a secret flap of the great tent. From a slender pole, she hung a banner of the Tree Reversed—the sigil of Klingsor, her master.

Birds were singing outside. She was surprised that they sang as Klingsor's men crept into position. There were fewer than she remembered. Some had fled; some lay dead for wild beasts, unless Amfortas's men, foolishly kind, would provide the rite they called Christian burial. (She did not think that Klingsor would bother.) Last of all came Sir Ferris limping in, anger and pain twisting his face. She forced her face immobile. After all, how hard was it for a woman with her history to lie to a man, to any man? Just now, she had made herself a living lie to a man she prized; how much easier it was to lie to this . . . this mamluk who belonged to Klingsor as much as she herself.

Only she had had no choice. Klingsor's power over her was part of her curse long before she had lived out what would have been a life span for a normal woman. This Ferris, born a Frank, had sold himself to Klingsor for power, gold, and the promise, when Klingsor ruled the Grail, of a dukedom at least. A pity that Amfortas had not struck harder. Ferris was one whose death she would not regret at all.

"Were you planning to wait," he demanded, "till my wounds took fever? Where are his weapons?"

She hissed at him and pointed within. "His sword, too. You need not be afraid."

He glared at her, promising future vengeance; but she did not care.

"The Spear itself," she heard him mutter. "Dropped it where he dined . . . *here* we have it." His voice changed, became gloating.

"Klingsor . . . my lord Klingsor would scarcely begrudge me a sword as a trophy. But this . . . God's wounds, I can feel the power in this thing. No wonder my lord craves it. I wonder, though . . . shall he have it—or have I served long enough?"

Sir Ferris walked out, flourishing the Lance in mock salute at Kundry. He approached her closely, familiarly, and she recalled how Amfortas had recoiled, fearful of affronting her. It had been she who had gone to him.

"What ails you, woman?" Sir Ferris asked.

The man who lay asleep in her bed would slash the "sir" from this one's name and the sword and spurs from side and heels before he could spit, Kundry thought.

Ferris bent closer, tried to steal a kiss. Even as Kundry stepped back, she clawed at him with her nails.

"My lady Sphinx," he jeered. "As deadly, if not quite as old."

"Out with you. You have what you desire."

"Not all," he said. "Not all, my lady. You are no good to Klingsor, nor he to you. The time may come . . ."

She tossed her head. She could heat the renegade's armor so it burned into his flesh, she knew; but she would not waste a cantrip on the likes of him. Instead, she snapped out a verse she had once heard a woman of the Iberian shore hurl at a man who dogged her heels.

> "I am a lioness
> and will never allow my body
> to be anyone's resting place."

Ferris dared to sneer.

> "But if I did,
> I wouldn't yield to a dog—
> and O! the lions I've turned away!"

"A dog, am I?" he demanded. He had lived too long among the Moors not to feel that as a deadly insult—unlike the Europeans who sometimes treated favorite hounds better than their women. "A dog, you say? And who is this lion you did *not* turn away? Let us see this lion in your bed."

Kundry's hand dropped to her belt, but she had lost her knife by Lake Brumbane before Amfortas had come to rescue her. She had known of the plan to put her in danger; what she had not known was to what length Ferris and his cutthroats would go to make it look real, or the degree of lust and hatred that the mamluk felt for her.

"No!" she hissed.

"Oho, so you *liked* this one, did you? You liked him. Did he make you cry out and arch your back?" he mocked her. "What else did he make you do?" He sniffed, ostentatiously. "At least this one is clean."

How dare he talk about the man? Kundry wanted to draw a veil to shield him even from this wretch's gaze. Well, she would teach him. Raising her hands, Kundry muttered, summoning up old lessons, old magics, and old fire. After this many years in Klingsor's service, she had learned some magic. As Klingsor said, even a beggar at a miser's table will, sooner or later, pick up a crumb or two. Her master was the miser. She rather thought she had learned more than Klingsor knew. And she had kept it that way until now.

"None of your silly women's spells, lady. Klingsor protects his *faithful* servants. And the time when you could command me in anything is long gone. Soon, it shall be I who command—"

"At Judgment Day!" She thought she could bear Judgment just to see the doom meted out to such men as Ferris.

"Bridle that tongue, woman!" Ferris grabbed her, his right hand vise-tight upon her arm. He twisted it behind her back so she could neither strike nor kick at him without pain that brought her to her knees. It was such pain she could barely breathe, much less cast spells. He dragged her like a cat caught stealing fish to where Amfortas still lay.

"Let us see this paragon, this lion among men!" Ferris laughed. With the Lance that he had stolen in his left hand, he pricked away the covers from the sleeping man.

Kundry could not help but moan in shame and dread.

And Amfortas opened his eyes.

They went wide, aware, in that instant, of Kundry's pain and his danger. They held no fear, only rage that once again she—his lady, as he called her—had been outraged. Arms and legs tensed for battle. As the Spear thrust forward, he swung aside, heading—naked as the day his mother bore him—for the mamluk, who was determined to finish what he had left undone beside Lake Brumbane.

Ferris dragged Kundry before him as a shield and feinted at Amfortas, laughing as he struck.

"You jackal," Amfortas told him. "Apostate. Drop the lady."

"What is it to you? She let me in! Just as she let you!"

Amfortas's eyes flicked to her, the rage at her danger changing to shock and then, just as quickly, to shame, disillusionment, and sorrow.

Kundry wailed, courage and control gone. She had thought she could sink no lower. But now she knew differently: this rape of an innocent soul was the worst thing she had done . . . worse than what had started her on her accursed path.

She could have hurled herself down, pleading for forgiveness, but she had learned long ago there was no forgiveness for the likes of her.

Abruptly, though all the lanterns had long since guttered out, the light in the tent flickered as if a cloud passed high overhead. With it came a sudden wind; and thunder exploded.

"Do you appeal to me, sweet one?" A clear voice cut across the jeers and laments. A man stood at the entrance to the room, parting hangings already slashed by spear blows. He wore a long black surcoat with the Tree Reversed between broken pillars emblazoned upon it. He was sleek, too sleek, and a little too plump despite the restless eyes and hands. Despite his softness, men—or women—who took him for a fool deluded themselves to their own sorrow. His eyes betrayed him. Glancing about ceaselessly, they were powerful as basilisks, the instruments of a relentless, savage intellect. His mouth was too full, but he thinned his lips to hide the expression of one who never could be sated.

He was perfumed with civet, but Kundry thought she

could smell the Pit upon him: it had been long years since she had first read about Harpies who fouled and staled their food and spoiled the food of others. Klingsor was one such.

Amfortas drew his breath in a hiss of loathing. His naked body seemed to draw in upon itself. He bent to scoop up a sheet.

"To cover yourself? How chaste, this modesty of yours—and so misleading! Let us see what stirred our Kundry's heart!"

But Amfortas had laid aside shame as he had fear. Even as Klingsor laughed, the knight slashed out, using the length of fabric as a whip to break the mamluk's grip upon the Spear. Sir Ferris hissed as the silk snapped across his hand. Kundry smelled her perfume on the sheet, and other things; but her shame went beyond tears. How long had it been since she had felt so truly violated? Memories rose like the swell of sickness; madness threatened; and she forced her memories back as she had learned to do.

A welt rose upon Sir Ferris's hand, but he retained the Spear.

"And you, my Ferris. Not a word of greeting or of fealty?"

"My master!"

"Am I still your master? That was not what I heard you boast, moments ago. You need reminding. I take my own prizes, though. And I dispatch my enemies myself. Give me the Spear."

Fast as a cat striking, Kundry reached for it; and Ferris tossed her aside.

Amfortas's eyes followed her for just one instant. But in that moment, he had met her eyes, had known all; and his eyes had softened just a trifle. She would have to wander down the centuries now knowing that: she had betrayed him, and he had forgiven her.

"Easier prey than his brother, but still the perfect knight, isn't he, Ferris? In all things. You would know about knighthood, since you abandoned it, would you not? I tell you, I will have that Spear from you. Give it to me, or . . ." Klingsor raised a white hand for the Spear, but Ferris jerked it away.

"So we are going to play the fool, are we?" He sighed once, gestured, and Ferris dropped the Spear with an oath. Blood dripped from his fingers.

"See me later about your wounds, Ferris. I may be in a healing mood. I said, 'may be.' "

Klingsor picked up the Spear and started toward Amfortas.

The knight drew himself up and raised one hand.

"A warding sign?"

"The best I know." Amfortas sketched the sign of the cross in midair. "You cannot touch me. And by this sign, I command you—"

Klingsor burst into laughter that held a trace of rage.

"I believe you have to be in a state of grace for *that* particular spell to work. And you aren't precisely pure right now, are you, Amfortas? Not since Kundry set her spell on you. She is very pretty, very convincing, my Kundry. I would have been convinced myself by her sighs and moans."

Something flickered in Amfortas's eyes. It would have been sorrow if his face were not already grim enough for a battlefield.

Klingsor laughed. "Of course I watched. What is the point of being a wizard if you cannot please yourself as you wish? Of course"—he shook his head deprecatingly—"it has been a long time since such dalliance drew me."

"A long time since it could!" Kundry snapped.

Klingsor faced her, black eyes blazing in a face whose pallor began to change as his rage mounted. "I'll mark you for all time!" He flicked the Spear away from Amfortas, to lift the hair by Kundry's temple.

In that moment, Amfortas hurled himself between Klingsor and Kundry. Fear widened his eyes—fear for her.

"Run, my lady!" he shouted as he collided with the wizard.

Klingsor, astonished, took one step back. Then he blazed with fury, his eyes rolling back in his head as he muttered to himself, held up a hand, and ordered, in a voice that echoed like thunder, "Hold."

No longer shielded by wards or by his own sinlessness,

Amfortas toppled at Klingsor's feet, unable to lift as much as a hand to cover his genitals. The wizard stared him up and down insolently, the point of the Lance following his gaze and coming to rest, at last, where Amfortas least wished now to be touched.

"And shall I make you another like myself? You serve the Grail as priest, I believe. And I also believe—not that I put any faith in it—that it is written that 'he that is wounded in the stones, or has his privy member cut off, shall not enter into the Congregation of the Lord.' I am sure you understand me. Fitting, is it not? Kundry is *mine*, you see. With one blow, I avenge myself for the trespass on my property, make you unfit for your post, and rob you of one—no, two—of your treasures. Your house is cut off, unfit, as you believe, to wield the Grail.

"But I do not believe that nonsense. So, I shall take the Spear, and *I* shall wield it."

Klingsor moved the Spear forward, almost with a surgeon's precision, adjusted the blade a fraction. As his arm tensed to drive it home, Kundry summoned her power. No matter now that Klingsor would see her power as a challenge. She lashed out with it and the most frightful shriek she could conjure.

Her scream weakened the spell on her lover, who twisted his legs aside just as Klingsor thrust viciously with the Spear. It was almost enough. The Spear fleshed itself between Amfortas's hip and his groin.

The copper stink of blood fouled the air. Amfortas screamed, as Kundry shrieked again to deafen herself against his agony. She had heard such cries before . . . a man heart-thrust in battle, another pierced by an arrow in the eye . . . another, whose side was lanced and whose eyes and voice still tempted her toward the madness of laughter she feared most of all, after the curse that kept her alive and followed her in all her wanderings . . .

"In the name of God . . . go, bring aid!" She hardly recognized the voice that forced the words out as belonging to Amfortas. His eyes met hers, then rolled back in his head. "My lady, flee!"

Kundry hurled herself from the tent, running down the

forest track, running without care, in a perilous wood through which she had always traveled armed with knowledge. The sun shone, but it might as well have been black night. Thunder pealed out, and she knew what that meant: Klingsor, summoning aid from his keep.

She brought up for breath against a tree and hugged its rough bark, trying to summon her wits and whatever small power she had once had to shift time and paths—she only wished she could have wrenched time backward enough to undo her betrayal, yes, and even her memories of the splendid night before it.

Air and place shifted as she sought direction and Klingsor brought in his men. Now she heard thunder on a narrow track up ahead. When she ran toward it, she saw a troop of knights. Their white surcoats were pure of leaf or dust, and the doves blazoned on them shone like sunlight; but the horses they rode were lathered. From time to time, an outrider rose in his stirrups, as if searching for an ambush.

Kundry thrust herself into their path and cowered in the dust as the foremost horses reared, their iron-shod hooves almost striking her. She wished that they had, yet she had been sent to bring aid; and she must try.

The eldest knight leapt from his horse and tossed its reins to a squire. The horse's ears still were back, its eyes white, and it snaked its neck at her until he ran a hand down its flank.

"Now," snapped the knight, "you stop that. And you, too, lady. What is so wrong that you must risk being trampled and delay honest men on urgent business?"

Kundry gagged, choked out dry sobs, unable to find the tears that would free her voice. The old man grabbed her shoulders and shook her once, hard. That restored her somewhat, and she could point and gasp out Klingsor's name.

An awed mutter rose behind her. "This morning, the old king . . ."

". . . prophesied that a woman, and a great sinner . . ."

". . . should bring down Montsalvasche . . ."

". . . and only a man made wise through pity could redeem us."

"We thought it was delirium, since King Amfortas did not come home . . ."

"Is this the one?"

Blades rasped out, and Kundry found armed men's eyes upon her. She clung to the arm of the first knight who had questioned her, knowing that as long as he needed her to speak, she was safe.

"Enough gabbling, men! Now, woman, you say Klingsor's here? In Broceliande? Let's ride!"

"He's bringing in more men. Oh, hurry, hurry . . ."

"Lady, you must leave the path; you must let us ride . . ."

"In the name of mercy, go quickly, take me with you, I never meant—"

Abruptly, the knights' agitation, the mutters that her appearance had cost, and even her own guilt and grief became a hideous joke. She began to laugh, the ragged, gagging, hysterical laughter that had made her accursed. There had been thunder then, too, and darkness at noon, and no peace anywhere. Her laughter pealed up, high and shrill.

The younger knights recoiled. One or two of their elders made the sign of the cross.

"She is mad; unless I silence her, she will do a mischief to herself and hinder us," the eldest knight said. "Forgive me, lady."

His words were ruthless, but his tone was almost kind. And the fist that rocked her off her feet came as the coup to a mortally wounded man. The knights spurred their horses down the track, and the thunder from their hooves matched the thunder in her head. She was aware of a canopy of leaves and, far above them, blue sky, pulsing with light. Then sound, light, and laughter were extinguished at once.

5

AMFORTAS writhed around the agony in his thigh. His eyes rolled up, and he saw his enemy holding a Spear that dripped with his blood. He groaned. Klingsor had used the holy Spear that had struck him where he most offended! He had vowed to protect and venerate it. Instead, he had sinned, taken and trapped in the arms of a woman. So even the Spear had turned on him, punished him in the hands of his enemy, the man who had killed his brother and destroyed his father's life.

Redemption was not possible for such a crime.

In that moment, Klingsor might have struck again and killed him. Amfortas would even have thanked him for release from the agony and dread of death or mutilation. At least death would release him from a world of pain and shame. It was too simple a revenge, and his enemy knew it. Klingsor watched him as if contemplating a vision he had longed to see.

That too-smooth, sated face and its smile suddenly spun very far away. It was getting dark, though Amfortas knew dawn drew near. How cold he was! He shivered in spasms, as hot blood poured from between his legs. A little longer, and he would not need to worry about pain or penitence or betrayal—

He would thank God for such mercy.

But he would die with this sin upon him!

Desperate, he clawed a sheet free of the bed on which he had sinned and wadded it against the wound, then tied the ends around his thigh in as tight a knot as he could manage. That almost stopped the bleeding, though everything still felt far away. His ears roared, and he burned and shivered at once.

Thunder pealed out, and the steps of men in iron chausses neared. Was it Klingsor's men, come to look upon him in his shame, or the knights he had betrayed, come to save their unworthy lord? Either was equally unwelcome. Only he clung to a faint, small hope—that his men would find his body, that his father would forgive him and grant him at least the grace of burial. That hope grew, became a passion, and drove out his anguished vision of the face of the woman he had been so delighted to have won.

How could she have betrayed him? He would have sworn she had yielded him her heart as well as her body. He had sworn love and faith to her. The dark eyes, glazed with fear—fear for him?—and a desperate guilt, set his head spinning further. He ought to hate her; she was Klingsor's whore.

A fresh wave of pain made him shudder. He ought to look at his wound. He could not bear to. Klingsor had no use for whores except as catspaws: they would be well matched now, he and his enemy—save that Klingsor had defeated him.

Guilt and blood loss mazed him, driving him as far from Broceliande as Broceliande was from the world through which, in more innocent days, he had cut such a triumphant swath. Almost, he thought he could hear the horns and battle cries of his youth, but the light was fading and his life with it.

"My lord, my lord!"

The world returned and the intimate, devouring pain with it. Thanks be to God; Gurnemanz's familiar bellow, Gurnemanz's well-known sword strokes hammering above his head, Gurnemanz's shield atop him as he fought to rise. A mamluk screamed and tumbled to the floor, one more man's blood soaking the priceless carpets. For all his magic, Klingsor didn't heal him, didn't even try. His magic was strong only for destruction.

All around him knights fought the wizard's slaves, who formed a wall before their master. Klingsor himself did not deign to strike a blow. But then he was not a warrior, was he? No more than he could call himself a man. A wave of pain caught Amfortas in the belly; best not think of being unmanned. Origen had made himself a eunuch for God; Origen had been a heretic. Best that Amfortas not add *that* to his long tale of sins.

Amfortas bit his lip for a more manageable pain, and twisted the silk wrappings tight, still tighter, about his thigh. He fought to stand, but failed. At least, let him strike one blow! He crawled forward, hand outstretched for a dead man's sword, and clasped its hilt as if it were a rope and he a drowning man. Ah, he had the weight of it now, the knowledge of the steel.

"Klingsor!" he screamed hoarsely, appalled at how much of his reserves it took. His sight narrowed into a tunnel, with Klingsor's hateful smile at the end of it, and his ears roared.

Yet the wizard heard him. "My lord half-man?" he asked.

Amfortas had not enough blood left in him to flush for shame. Instead, he forced himself up and flung the sword at Klingsor, praying for victory with all his tainted soul. Let him strike just once at the wizard, avenge his brother's death, if not his own sin.

Klingsor laughed and flung wide one well-kept hand. The sword ripped through the tent; the lightning flashed; and when Amfortas's sight cleared, behold! He lay in a wilderness, on withered grass with dead men all about him. They were all unfamiliar, he realized, relieved almost to swooning.

The tunnel that was his sight wavered. Even its coin-small mouth was darkening . . . "Look up, my lord!" Gurnemanz was lifting his head, forcing wine between his lips. He let it trickle out down his neck and onto his bare chest. It was red as the wine he had drunk last night with . . . He shook his head.

Kundry. He must blot her name from his memory, or he would curse it and her; and unless he was even more wrong than usual, she had curse enough to bear. Ahhhh, Kundry, Kundry. Just last night, he would have sworn she loved him. But no, a previous curse, a previous lord had snatched her and her fragile faith away. He still had her ring. Best discard it. He tried to force it from his hand, but a wave of dizziness swept over him, and he had no strength to move.

"Shall I look for loyalty precisely where it vanishes, as fire in running water, dew in the sun?" he moaned. She had spoken of repentance before he kissed her. There had been guilt in her eyes as he woke to his betrayal. *God grant you grace, my lady. There is no grace for such as I.*

"What is that you're saying, my lord?" asked Gurnemanz. "Loyalty? Do you doubt it?"

"I am not your lord, cannot *be* your lord . . ."

"God save us, he's as mazed as old lord Titurel. Someone give me a cloak."

A soft weight of fabric dropped upon him, chest and belly, and he flinched at how close it fell to the wound near his groin—or, as he feared—in it. It was the splendor of indigo and fur that he had worn, a vanity to please a lady's eyes and his own pride, only last night, not the white mantle of his order that he had profaned. They would not let him have such a mantle now, he thought.

"Pfah! It stinks of civet!" Gurnemanz snapped. "Is that the best you can do? You, there, we need bandages."

"Leave me . . ."

"What, my lord? Leave you in the wilderness to bleed your life away, not that it's not half spilled already? Never fear. We will get you home. Look up!"

Obedient, Amfortas looked up and wished he hadn't. Tears poured down the old man's face, belying his cheerful words.

"Leave me . . . I cannot serve the Grail."

Gurnemanz's face twisted then, in anger and in grief. "You'll serve it, all right. You'll serve it because you're all we've got. Last night, when you did not return, your father swore you were in danger and mortal sin. He started to rave and froth at the mouth, and then he fainted. He's in worse case than ever I have seen him."

Amfortas shut his eyes and wished he could shut out Gurnemanz's words as well.

"Is he . . ."

That would be the last nail in his coffin, that while he had lain in a false witch's arms, his father had died. *At least I would not have to face his reproaches.* Now that was a truly despicable thought. He groaned with shame, then again, knowing Gurnemanz would interpret that as fear for his father's life.

"Not dead yet. He was raving, though. Something about how you could be redeemed only by a fool, made wise through pity."

"Nothing can redeem me."

Gurnemanz spat. "Save your breath, lord, if all you can talk is sin and foolery. Sounds like we've got *two* fools in the story, and I'm talking to—at—one of them. Save your strength, or what's left of it. We've got to get you back so he can be healed. In case you've forgotten, without sight of the Grail, and that speedily, he'll starve, that good old man. And he hasn't deserved it."

A low blow, Amfortas thought, but not as low as the one that had struck him down. And he deserved it.

"I cannot serve the Grail," Amfortas repeated. "Not now; not ever. That takes a whole man . . ." Klingsor's jeer of "half man" came back to him. Heretic and evil wizard he was, but there had been no error in his memory of the Law.

Gurnemanz thinned his lips. "Let's see." He pushed away Amfortas's hands and let out his breath in relief.

"Not a thing missing, except blood, and plenty of that. An inch over, though, and you'd be singing with the boys. An inch lower, and you'd be bled out by now. We've got to get you back and healed."

Relief—not a eunuch, not a half man!—made Amfortas faint. But he had to convince Gurnemanz. "Cannot! Knew that before . . . before this . . . shame my brother . . . my father . . . I am not fit . . ."

"That's all the old dispensation. We have a new law now, or hadn't you heard? For all the times you've knelt before the altar? So you let me preach it to you, *my lord*, and you learn it by heart. We are bringing you back to Montsalvasche to serve the Grail. Not to shame you, not to punish you, but because *we* need you. Now, maybe this is not your heart's desire. I know you never wished to rule in Montsalvasche. Knew it that time in Outremer. But Bron's dead and my king's as good as gone. So you're all we've got, and until this 'fool made wise by pity' turns up to take your place, you are damned well going to serve the damned Grail, if I have to drag you before the damned altar myself!"

Gurnemanz's voice broke and he turned away. Amfortas hid his face, too. All his life, Gurnemanz's service, Gurnemanz's unquestioned devotion, had supported him. And now, to have the old man despise him!

"Is that understood?" The very question Gurnemanz had always asked since Amfortas was the brashest of squires, and Gurnemanz his elder, assigned to whip him into shape. This time, though, the question came from a throat so tight that it was a wonder any sound could be forced out at all.

Amfortas nodded faintly, then realized that a gesture was not enough. It had not been enough when he was a youth to atone for sins that seemed momentous at the time, but were nothing to what he had done now.

"Yes, sir," he said. His tone was not the same, either. They would never again be as they had been—innocent.

He heard a laugh that was half sob above him. A large hand patted his head, smoothed the matted, close-cropped hair back from his sweaty face. Amfortas burned in an ecstasy of humiliation. Gurnemanz, that great knight, had already forgiven him, though this time Amfortas had broken his heart. But to hate the sin and love the sinner: Gurnemanz was perfect in that lesson.

"You, you, and you." Gurnemanz clearly was pointing at his chosen victims among the squires. "Burial detail. You and you—break off some of these boughs and build a stretcher. We'll sling it between the horses and bring our lord home."

Fierce chopping and digging ensued. Amfortas let his squire coax him to take some wine, then to lie back. He struggled with tears of shame. He had lost the Spear. He had stained his immortal soul. And he had endangered Montsalvasche and the treasure it had guarded since the Crucifixion. And yet his knights would follow him, as maimed, unworthy as he was.

He wanted to weep with remorse, but he clenched his fists and fought his tears, lest the men he betrayed think him a coward who could not bear his pain along with his guilt.

Behind him muttered the voices of knights and squires.

"That wench we met on the road, who guided us here . . ."

"You think she's the one—"

"Hush! He's not dead yet, not quite . . ."

"The woman betrayed him!" A younger, indignant voice, that of a squire.

"That's not the first time such things have happened," an older man reminded him dryly. "Why else were we expelled from Paradise?"

Some mutterings from the squire about going one worse than Eve, who never traveled with a wizard that *he'd* heard of, were quickly silenced with a box on the ear.

"Shall we send scouts out after the witch?"

Amfortas rolled his head back and forth on the coarse grass. Withering: as he was withered already. Montsalvasche would be a waste now, a citadel rearing up over barrenness.

"I don't think so," Gurnemanz muttered. "He doesn't seem to want it done, do you, my lord?" His voice grew louder, took on that too-hearty, almost bullying tone that is the hale man's most potent and annoying weapon against the sick. *Keep on talking like that, old friend; and, whether you know it or not,* Amfortas thought, *you'll have your vengeance.*

"Risk . . . no more . . ."

Gurnemanz turned away. "His Majesty doesn't want to risk any more of us. Personally, if that was the woman, I can't see what he fancied in her, but . . ."

Despite himself, Amfortas almost smiled. So Gurnemanz could not see the beauty and courtesy in his lady? No, perhaps not, not as she had been this dawn. *Kundry,* he thought. *Come back to me even now, and I would welcome you. Forgiveness? You would not even need to ask.* Were he the man he had been even the night before, he would hold her in his arms and shield her from her enemies, assuage the guilt he had seen in her eyes, protect her from all harm.

But she would not return, and he could not even guard himself. He had nothing to offer her, had never had aught to offer her—or she would have stayed.

"How's that litter coming?" Gurnemanz left his side to stride to the edge of the clearing and shout.

"Ready, sir!" four squires shouted at once.

When they lifted Amfortas onto it, the jarring of his wound caused him such pain that it almost rapt away his senses. Immediately, talk of a horse litter ceased; four men would carry him in turn.

"I am not worth these pains," he whispered.

"They think you are," Gurnemanz told him. "So you had better be, because right now, you are all they have, and all your father has. And I'm thinking he, at least, may still mean something to you."

Amfortas flinched away from the older man. He found himself staring into the sun, tears and sweat pouring down his face, until Gurnemanz shut his eyes, almost as if he were a dead man.

Then he stared at the dove on Gurnemanz's surcoat. Odd. He glanced around quickly. No, it wasn't just that blood tinged his sight. Each one of those once-pristine blazons was now charged and bordered gules—blood red to match his sin and his wound.

Face upturned to the cloudless sky as if he were already dead, Amfortas lay in a trance of pain as his men brought him softly through Broceliande, as softly as they could. From time to time, they must set the stretcher down, bind up blistered hands, report over his head to Gurnemanz, who would then relay their words to him as if he had not heard, or could care.

Amfortas did not know which would be worse, if the knights thought he had betrayed them because he no longer cared, or if they pitied him.

From time to time, he turned his head upon a rolled-up cloak, as if seeking ease. That gesture brought him tending: callused but gentle hands; words surprisingly tender from men he had known lifelong only as warriors; sips of watered wine and hyssop or an even more ancient drink, the vinegar and water of Rome's legions.

They thought he suffered, that he shifted in fever dreams. Instead, he scanned each thicket and each tree. His sword— but no Spear—lay beside him, close to his shaking hand. If

Klingsor's mamluks roamed Broceliande, he prayed to get in at least one good blow.

And always, his dimming sight sought his vanished lady. *She* might lie beneath some thornbush, not tended, but alone, despairing, in need of help. His knights had left her in just such a place, only he did not know where or when. Paths and trails in Broceliande, as none knew better than he, shifted. From time to time, he glanced down at his hand, where he still wore Kundry's token. He could not summon heart nor strength to toss it away.

He gazed up at the sun, turning orange now, the sky about it shimmering white with heat, as it began a slow descent toward the west. What was it that Kundry—ah God, how anguish and desire burnt him at the thought of her—had said about repentance? Till the sun rose in the West? Longer than that.

A shadow fell across him. "Looking for the girl?" Gurnemanz asked in an undertone. The shadow moved, and Amfortas knew that Gurnemanz shook his head in disbelief.

"I'll have the outriders keep an eye out for her. If she needs help, we'll give her what she needs, then get her away from here . . ." The fervor in *that* promise made Amfortas hope that Kundry would not, in fact, need their aid. They might find her, but she would not seek them out, he was abruptly certain. She was far too proud.

"Unless, of course"—Gurnemanz's voice was extremely doubtful—"you want to see her."

Amfortas shook his head. If she saw him now, perhaps she would laugh that bitter, shrieking laugh so different from the one with which she had seduced him. He feared he could not forgive that. She had cost him all he had—and yet, for his sake, she had hurled herself at Klingsor and his men.

For that alone, he told himself, he could have forgiven her, had he not done so already out of love. The one he could not forgive was himself.

How hot it was! Yet he shivered now, his teeth clattering. Surely ice formed on his wound. Or was it that he wanted ice laid upon his forehead or thrust in packs against him to cool a fever? Visions of fire and ice, more seductive than any woman, shimmered before his tearless eyes.

"Sweet Jesu, he's burning up and freezing, all at once!" Gurnemanz cried. "One of you, ride ahead. Tell Brother Infirmarer—yes, I know he is with the old king, but if he doesn't come, we may have no king at all by sunset! Tell him to meet us at the gates with *lign aloe* torches."

The wood that eased all wounds. Even that, even all the old healer's skill would not be enough, Amfortas wanted to tell him. He knew, with a sureness past human understanding, that only the weapon that had maimed him could heal him. Now it lay in Klingsor's hands, and he did not think that the wizard, out of the goodness of his heart, would give it back.

"It *is* ice," Gurnemanz said. "Caking on the wound. Set him down, you men. My lord, my lord, hold fast. I want to chip this away . . ."

Amfortas hissed, arching his back with the pain as Gurnemanz knocked away bloody ice from the blood-encrusted bandage on his thigh and cast it on the earth, where it surely would do no good. Saturn had been overhead when the wound was struck; and thus Saturn, in its wide course, ruled it: Saturn who had dominion over all types of violent death—drowning, or hanging, secret poisonings and public rebellions, and, above all, in its ruling aspects under the lion, vengeance and whatever atonement might be for treason. It was just that he shiver and burn.

His eyes burnt and his leg froze as they brought him past Lake Brumbane. The lake seemed a vision of Eden before the fall to him. *Just this time yesterday, I was . . . clean of sin.* Only, he knew now that he had not been; he had been rebellious, reluctant, the faith of his vows flickering like a dying lamp. Klingsor and Kundry, God help Amfortas for thinking of her with longing, had found fertile ground.

As he gazed at trees and grass and flowers that bordered the lake, he thought they looked tired and parched, as if it were autumn, not high summer, and they must wither and die.

Soon they would enter Montsalvasche itself. As Amfortas clenched his fists and vowed to endure, his finger felt something slick and cold—Kundry's ring. That could not enter Montsalvasche: harlots and their baubles—he forced himself to use the word—had no place within the hallows, he told himself. Yes, there was Magdalene; but he—it were blasphemy to think that *he* deserved a second Magdalene's devotion. He slid the ring off his finger and let it fall beneath a bramble.

"Soon you will fish again on that lake, Majesty," one of the squires told him, meaning it for comfort. He would never ride again, or hunt, or fight: he was certain of that.

They brought him past the lake and toward Montsalvasche itself, arriving just at sunset. As if report had run before him, the knights had formed up at the gate. The infirmarer's men strode forward, torches of *lign aloe* casting a mellow light upon his weary guards. The terrible, cramping chill began to ease. He drew a long breath and was instantly sorry.

He raised a hand, surprised at the effort it took. Immediately, he was set down. To all sides of him, his bearers stretched too-taut muscles, flexed sore hands.

"Set me straight," he whispered to Gurnemanz. He wore a knight's spurs, yet he was not too proud to do squire's duty as he took a fresh white tunic and mantle and laid them upon his king (looking away from the bloodstained bandages at thigh and groin) in place of the shameful indigo splendor of his seduction and fall.

"Are you ready?" Gurnemanz asked. "Courage!" he wished him. Amfortas had not the strength to thank him.

Now the ordeal would begin.

New bearers approached, draping the shameful litter with rich silk. *Am I the Pope, to be borne aloft in a throne?* Amfortas waved them away, but they ignored the protest, and he must submit to their will. Now they lifted the stretcher once more and bore him toward the walls carved from the living rock. Ahead of him, bells tolled. How had it come to be so close to noon? It was not: this service would be held out of the regular order of the day to succor Titurel's great need. The echoes of the bells trembled through the bodies of his bearers and into his own, and he shivered once again.

The massive gates of Montsalvasche swung wide, and its knights marched or rode through, Amfortas the flawed heart of their troop. Already, as the bells rang out and they trod the ancient, sacred ways, time and space were melding, and the light was changing. Montsalvasche was miles across, save when it came time to serve the Grail.

They passed from under the sun into a high-walled court, its ceiling the sky. A few stars had risen; Amfortas saw the Evening Star and glanced away: it was not for him, had never been. Now, neither was Al-Marrekh, he with the Spear. Always before he had thought of Al-Marrekh as a spearsman like himself, perhaps just a wilder aspect of the archangel Michael. Now that he had lost the Spear, his patron had turned his face aside. Only Saturn ruled him now, bringing the punishment of that grim sphere.

Then, as the bells laid down a rhythm for their feet, they marched toward the sanctuary of the Grail. Torches flared to life on either side the moment before they passed between them, and the great banners of Montsalvasche and every land in Christendom dipped in salute to him, unworthy as he was. Only a green banner hung stubbornly aloft, and would hang so until the stiff-necked heathen joined the companionship of the Grail.

Walls of gray stone rose higher and higher on either side of them, carved with figures whose hands rose in entreaty. Some of the carvings were very old. They had been Amfortas's earliest study: the tale of how his great ancestor, Joseph of Arimathea, had befriended Christ and His Mother; had been present at the Crucifixion; had comforted Mary when she swooned.

When darkness covered the noonday sun, Joseph had held firm. He had begged the Romans for leave to take down the Body and bury it in his own fine stone tomb. Nor was that all: for he had taken up the Cup from which Christ drank at the Last Supper, from which vinegar and water had been given Him as He hung on the cross and which had received His blood after the Lance had pierced Him.

I am not worthy, Amfortas thought in a passion of guilt. *Neither as celebrant nor as victim, I am not worthy to bear such wounds myself. God forgive me for the sin that caused them, because I cannot.*

Now the harmonics of plainsong from a thousand throats mingled with the bells like wine and water. The fabric of creation shifted as his knights brought the fallen master of Montsalvasche into the sanctuary of the Grail, where tables were set up for feasting in its presence. The tables were bare; the feast was still to come.

Thunder rumbled faintly overhead, trembled in the stone vault and caused its hanging lamps to flicker. Only the Presence light before the shrine that housed the Grail burnt steadily, a tiny replica of the fierce orange sun Amfortas had seen all day. Incense rose in sweet, pale clouds from burners set along the walls, each arranged along the points of the great cross incised in the floor of the circular chamber.

The altar, a tiered slab of plain gray stone surmounted by a curtained sanctuary, rose from the center of the cross, where the Corpus would have been. Near it, in a niche, was Amfortas's father Titurel. Amfortas knew what he would see if he entered there: a man so old that age had no meaning, stretched upon what looked like a bier. His hair was white, his skin wan, almost transparent, and he seemed to have aged a hundred years since yesterday. Let Amfortas look at him, and Titurel would turn his head on the white samite. There would be hope in his eyes, which were full of wisdom and welcome for the man who was his son as well as the celebrant who must ease his hunger and pain. Even now. He would not dare to look.

Amfortas lifted his hand. Down. He did not feel the jolt as the squires set the litter down. For a long moment, he lay there, absorbing the harmonies of chant and bells through his very bones. It shivered in the wound in his thigh. Levering himself up on stiffened arms, he swung his legs free of the litter and onto the tessellated floor, marked every few paces with the name of a hero of Montsalvasche and his arms, surmounted by the Dove.

Two squires bent and helped him rise from the stretcher, an arm about the neck of either man. Then Amfortas shook his head, and they stood clear of him.

Painfully, holding his breath lest the wound burst or the

agony grow worse, Amfortas walked across the floor to the niche where his father lay.

His voice faltered on the words, but he had determined what he must say, and forced himself to go on. "Father, I have sinned against heaven and in thy sight, and am no more worthy to be called thy son."

He was worse than the Prodigal Son: he had not only left his brother, he had profaned his memory.

Amfortas tried to sink to one knee, and the pain in his thigh felt as if he had just been stabbed again. To his astonishment, Titurel forced himself up, to catch Amfortas's shoulders and hold him where he was.

"For this my son was dead, and is alive again; he was lost, and is found."

Then the old man's lips turned blue. He fell back on his bier. "The fool made wise by pity . . . they told you?"

His father should save his breath, not waste it on a fool no one could make wise. But even his feeble old-man's voice had changed in that moment, took on the resonance of . . .

"Prophecy, Father?" Longing to believe it shook Amfortas.

Amfortas raised the old man's hand to his lips, then set it gently on his chest.

"My son, my son . . ." Titurel's eyes filled with the easy, piteous tears of age. "He *will* come; never fear it . . ." He coughed, a prolonged rattle in his chest terrifying Amfortas despite his own anguish. "He will come . . . but I beg you, my loyal son, make haste!"

Amfortas shut his eyes in fear and prayer. The son was lost, and now found? Well enough, unworthy as he was. It was time for the feast. *Not for my sake, Lord, but for this good old man.*

Get on with it! At Trachonitis, a desert so stark that vipers themselves could not live in its sun-seared furrows, Amfortas had taken an arrow in the leg once, and the wound had had to be burnt. He remembered the way the fire burned, so hot that it was only a shimmer in the dry, thin air, and how he had sweated and shivered on that day, impatient for the ordeal to be over so he would know how much pain was his to bear.

Now he would certainly know. He started up the shallow risers to the shrine. Overhead the lamps began to dim, and the bells to begin a soft, insistent pealing.

A silken cloth concealed the Grail from profane sight. It was soft, and it caught on his fingers as he laid it aside. The Grail began to pulse with a white light that turned steadily a deeper crimson as Amfortas raised his hands in entreaty toward it.

What would it do to him? The Grail could heal. But it could not raise the dead, like his brother, or the half-dead, like Titurel. And it would not heal one like himself, who had put himself beyond repentance.

Get it over with, fool!

He could feel the rapt eyes of the knights pierce his back as he stood before the Grail, could sense his father's desperate need for health and sustenance as an anguish that made the throbbing in his leg, the guilt in his soul, seem like nothing at all.

He extended his arms as if he hung on a cross, and the bells shivered and shuddered around him as space itself was transformed.

Come to me.

He raised his hands to grasp the Grail by its heavy stem. As always, he had the sense that it floated from its shelf into his hands.

Burning burning burning! Oh Lord, thou pluckest me out! Oh Lord! Burning!

Visions floated before him: a ram in a thicket, then lying in an altar, a blade drawn across its pulsing throat as rams' horns blared; a maid sacrificed by her own father, returning from the wars; at the world's dawn, Abel struck down by his brother, his blood flowing on the earth. The blade was piercing him, too; fire and sanctity struck him like a second spear blow.

The pain swept over him, and he was drowning, until, suddenly, it grew so great that he found himself borne up by it. His own survival awed him, no less a miracle than the Chalice he upheld, which glowed blood red.

Rapture lanced through his preoccupation with his anguish and his guilt. His scream of anguish and exaltation echoed in the great vaulted chamber as he elevated the Chalice and turned round to display it to all present there. His wound opened and bled down his thigh, pooling on the step; but a wild, exultant energy was on him, and he did not stagger as he felt an unseen spear pierce him anew.

Like the Grail, he was a vessel, albeit a flawed one. If the light took him, it was right and just that he suffer for what mortal flesh should never be asked to bear. He turned again, showing the Grail abrim with light that spilled down upon his hands and arms and set him to shining too.

The savory odors of rich food filled the chamber, mingling with the incense, as Amfortas set down the Chalice and shrouded it once more.

It could not heal him; it needed hope, repentance—and Amfortas had none. But it gave a cruel blessing. His wound would not rot, and he would live.

Released from the Grail's thrall, Amfortas collapsed. As if in prayer, he sank down on his knees. Then he sprawled facedown upon the cold altar stairs, and his blood stained the cold stone where the light of the Grail had faded.

6

KUNDRY staggered against a beech tree, rubbing her aching jaw. She glanced up through the leaves whose rustle sounded like the sighs of a woman exhausted after childbirth: bled out, bred out. The sun was already high overhead. She did not remember waking in Broceliande. One moment, a fist struck her jaw like a rock from a catapult; the next—which felt like quite a while later—she found herself wandering through the forest.

She had not intended to wake this way. Since she had never had a choice about it, she had assumed she would rise in Klingsor's palace, the usual bevy of veiled servingwomen about her to babble her into madness and torment her with offers of service she did not wish. They were spies, all of them, and they slept with Klingsor's mamluks. Not that she had any right to despise them on that ground.

What would she have wished? To her own horror, she knew. She would have chosen to wake beside Amfortas. The irony of it was that she had. Trapped in the trap she had set. But if the choice had truly been hers, she would not have slipped from his arms to betray him.

She had thought herself hardened. She had never dreamed it possible that she could sin worse than she had already done.

She stumbled toward a stream, and her legs collapsed under her. Her feet stung, and she brushed grit and pebbles from their soles. How long had it been since she had wandered, bare of foot? She was afraid to number the years; they had been centuries.

She cast about and within herself. What power she had slumbered, drained in her desperate race to find Amfortas his knights. Broceliande's inner ways would be closed to her: here she must remain until she grew stronger.

Whimpering a little, Kundry wet a tatter of her hem that looked less filthy than the rest and patted it against her bruised and aching face. She wished she dared peel off the wretched gown and let the cool waters of the stream wash the night away, but there was no telling who might ride by. Naked had been vulnerable since Eden, and she was afraid.

Already, the water's touch had stripped away too many of the years, and memories came rushing in unbidden. Once again, she was young, dazed, and sick of heart and body as she bathed, first her aching head, then the stained, sticky rest of herself in the water that bubbled up from the cleft in the rock. Finding it was the first lesson each child in her village learned before the elders entrusted valuable flocks to its care.

Mostly, it was boy children who were sent out with the flocks of sheep and goats; but Kundry had been the only child in her family to live; she was willful; and, after an outbreak of fever, her people needed every pair of hands and nimble feet.

The water stung her face, and the cloth, when she dipped it in the water again, showed traces of blood. The man who had struck her as she screamed and struggled—as they took Amfortas from her!—must have worn a ring. He could not have worn the mail mittens that armed knights often wore or the deadly cestus she had seen in her youth, or her jaw would have been pulped. Bad enough to go through the centuries, but to have to weather them with a scarred face—

The other time, there had been more blood, not only from her face. She had bled as if she were in her monthly courses. Kundry sank beside the water and tried to weep. Just so, she had sunk beside the cleft in the rock and demanded to know why the fever that had carried off her parents and her brothers had spared her only to meet shame.

Only that morning, when she had risen, the women who shared her home told her that her face shone and her mouth looked like scarlet threads. She had laughed; as much time in the hot sun as she spent, it was no wonder that she was

burned black. It was her kinswomen's kindness that made
them tell her how comely she was, with the long, long hair,
flowing loose only in the privacy of the tents, and the flashing eyes that reflected her high spirits and her confidence
that her world was a kindly one.

The girl Kundry was sure they loved her for herself, not
just for the flocks and tents and gold coins of her inheritance. They loved her and they let her run free, far beyond
the time that a daughter of her tribe should have been set
to hearth and cloth making. For pity of her losses in fever
season, they had even permitted her to remain unbe-
trothed.

From the men had come different stories. As the last of
her family, Kundry inherited. It was the law that she must
marry a man of her father's tribe "that the children of Israel
may enjoy every man the inheritance of his fathers."

Manlike, they would debate the law, as much for their
own enjoyment of its strength as to explore its truth. Voices
rose and fell; and then various groups of men would rise
and go out, to settle disputes elsewhere, if they must, or
consult other men, clustering in important-sounding
groups outside the rabbi's house, or—for the most serious
matters—spending hours in prayer. For a child, their disputes did not bear listening to, though she knew that the
elder women listened avidly when they could.

Sooner or later, she knew she would be told a name, and
the women of the tents would dress her in the special robe
dyed with a tiny hoard of rare indigo and laid away in a
cedar chest against such a day, would load upon her the
gold and jewels of her dowry until she in truth shone, and
would bring her, singing, to a new home. That too was the
law: she must be wed, and she was nearing the age by which
she must be a wife or a disgrace and a breach of law.

When Kundry bothered to think of it at all, she thought
only that one day this would happen. She supposed the
man would be one whose name and face she knew; someone young, she hoped; someone kind, she was certain they
would choose. Because they loved her.

But for now, it was more important that the flocks that

would be her gift to this as-yet-unnamed man be fed and watered; and, lacking brothers, she must do it.

Why had they ever let her out alone? A vastly older Kundry moaned, crouched beside that spring in Broceliande. They had done the best they knew how to do; she could see that now. After all, they had lost so many people. Still, for all her experience as a courtesan, she could still lament that girl-child's fate with a new keenness that rather surprised her. She had thought pity—even self-pity—to be a feeling that had been burnt out of her, but Amfortas must have touched her heart as deeply as he had her body. This, though, wasn't self-pity as much as compassion for that sunlit, untouched child who took her flocks up into the high summer fields that blossomed every year, watered as they often were with the rich blood of nations.

She climbed past a tumble of stones that had once been an altar. The children of Israel had toppled it when they claimed their land from the pagans who dwelt there. The Canaanites had been cast out . . . some of them. Many still lived nearby in Jericho, which had been cast down, too, but was now rebuilt.

She had never been there. It was a corrupt place, her older kinfolk said; her family lived on the land of their inheritance. If any idol worshipers came here, her family would have spit at them or hurled rocks. It was time to keep their fields free of enemies; too many enemies had passed by.

The Persians had marched through on their way to capture the Holy City. More recently—but still long before Kundry's birth—the Greeks of Antiochus's armies had passed through here, and heroes of the royal Hasmonean line had flung them out.

Now Romans built fortresses and walls to rival King Herod's buildings, wonders of the world that were almost as great as those of Solomon, son of David. These things had happened: battles had been fought, buildings flung up, and buildings destroyed. There had even been a time when Jerusalem and the Temple itself lay in ruins, to be rebuilt with rejoicing when the people returned in triumph from Babylon.

That Jerusalem and Israel would endure was assured. Grief might come in the night, but always, joy—and re-birth—would come in the morning. The land had been granted by God to the descendants of Abraham, Isaac, and Jacob; and they would be here after the last heathen soldiers marched away—as they always did—or till the land itself covered their unholy bones.

Kundry whistled, shrill as any boy, to her flocks. She had a promise about those buildings: once she was betrothed, the women told her, they would all go up to Jerusalem for the harvest, and she would dance with the maidens there before she was wed. By rights, they should have gone up every Passover, but it was a long journey from Jericho up winding cliffside roads that climbed up from heat to the high walls of Jerusalem; too high for the eldest of their families to manage safely.

Besides, some of the older women muttered darkly that Jerusalem itself was not what it had been in King David's time. Romans, harlots, and heathens flaunted themselves in its streets; Pharisees and Sadducees thrust dispute into the holy places; and the courts of the Temple rang as loudly with commerce as with prayer and sacrifice. Recently, too, the king had even allowed a gold eagle—almost an idol!—to be placed on the Temple gate. That was bad, not as bad as the time that gold shields were hung on the walls until the emperor himself had ordered their removal.

Rumor had it the streets had run red as the altars until they were removed, but Herod Antipas had shown himself a true son of his father, who had murdered the last of the Hasmoneans. They too had fought the building of images and the rule of Greece; *this* Herod ruled with the consent of Rome; and they were tyrants, the young men said, tyrants all of them. Usually then their fathers would hush them, and the mothers would twist their hands.

Up in caves in the hills, they whispered, lived bandits and heretics. Who knew? Perhaps one day, they would rise in revolt against Rome; and all would be destroyed as it had been before. The younger wives cried them down. Though it would be their husbands, and later their sons, who might suffer, day after day, they saw nothing but tents and fields, flocks and their children. Eager for a change, they longed to go up to the great city of David, to stand in the enclosed Court of the Women, and hear the chants and cries as priests sacrificed cattle and plumes of incense perfumed the sky. And the younger men, one eye on their elders, agreed. No doubt they dreamed of stranger girls from other towns or that other, darker lure of an uprising, like a second race of Maccabees, against Rome.

Kundry had her head in her hands now. She sat huddled and weeping by the water. Why must she remember this now? If she must remember only pain, she did not wish to remember anything at all—only to sleep and never wake. She had waked so briefly in the dead of night to find Amfortas's arms around her, as if he would shield her from the night air itself. Just for one precious instant, she had stolen a great luxury. She had pretended to herself that they were of an age (or even, that she was younger than he, and he her first man) and lovers in truth; and that, in the morning, they would look at each other and be glad they had given themselves away.

What right did Kundry have to wish for such happiness? She had no such fortune as a virgin daughter of her village. For even as she whistled to her sheep and dreamed of Jerusalem—the splendors of the City and of the Court of the Women; the white dress she would wear; and how the faces and jewels and long, curly hair of the maidens she would dance with would glow in the torchlight—a man rose from behind the huge red rock that Kundry had always avoided, thinking that vipers or scorpions laired beneath it.

She had been right.

At that moment, she did not even recoil. She was a fearless child, and she knew the man's face. He was a member of her father's tribe, a distant cousin, as indeed all were in that tribe. She even knew of his father—a poor man, quarrelsome in the matter of property, with many children to establish. The youth's name was Amnon—*no lucky name*, Kundry had thought then; and now, too late, she did shrink back.

For Amnon was also the name of that son of King David who had disgraced—she flinched away from *how* a prince of

Israel had despoiled a royal virgin, though she was his sister, then had flung her out the gates to mourn as if she had died.

Better Princess Tamar *had* died. For she had disgraced her family and caused war and death.

"I will not hurt you, little lamb, little dove," *this* Amnon promised her as she backed away. When she stopped, not wanting to be thought a coward, he laid hands on her. "You do not know how beautiful you are or what a man feels, seeing you alone like this. Come, let me show you. Arise, my love, my fair one . . ."

She screamed then, with all the shrill strength of her healthy body. Her healthy, untouched body.

Lying by the stream in the forest so far away in time and place, transfixed by her memories, Kundry screamed again, and the forest deadened the sound. Her nails tore up the unresisting grass as, so long ago, she had plowed furrows in Amnon's face. She had slapped and kicked and twisted with all the strength of a girl used to clambering through field and rock; but it had not been enough.

In the end, Amnon had had to strike her before he overpowered her. His fist had been the last pain she felt before waking in the fields with the sun high overhead searing into eyes that felt as if she had wept herself dry and turned the Dead Sea even more salt. Her body ached in places she knew should not have been touched. Her robes were torn asunder and stained with blood, and her flocks scattered this way, that way, and probably over cliffs and into the pastures of the neighboring tribes. For the first time, she did not worry for her flocks. She had lost, she knew, something more precious than flocks. Everyone said that virginity was a treasure, and now hers was gone. And, though she knew that she had done nothing wrong, she was suddenly, terribly afraid.

They would blame her, make it her fault. She had been betrayed. And if one man could betray her, they all could. She knew they would not listen.

There would be no indigo gown and heavy necklaces, now; no songs for a virgin bride; no bride at all—only whispers and shame. Yet she had done nothing wrong!

Whimpering, she had dragged herself over to the spring

and bathed, frantic to wash any traces of *him* off her. She wondered how the water could bubble up, sun-spotted, untouched. What had been done to her should cry out to heaven and earth. Why had the sky not darkened or the water dried up in its fountain?

Finally, when she saw no other way, she had knotted up the rags of her garments and assembled her flocks—she could not think of anything better to do than the tasks she had been assigned and that had brought her to destruction—and she returned home.

Women had been drawing water at the well when she staggered down the last slope. They surrounded her, appalled, and brought her inside, lamenting. Their wails as if for a death drowned out her cries that he had hurt her, forced her, and that she was so sorry! She had fought hard, but he was too strong; and now she did not know what to do.

They had given her wine, even put some of their precious, tiny store of myrrh in it—"as if I go to my death!" she had cried before the drug befuddled her. Finally, they had washed her once again and put her to bed, had stroked her hair and crooned to her; but she knew, somehow, they thought she had done something terrible—and she had done nothing!

And somewhere the men met with the rabbi. The next morning, when Kundry rose, she learned their decision.

"No!" she stormed. "I want him to die!"

The rabbi had shaken his head. Of course she felt that way. All good maids would feel that way. But such was not the law.

She had heard the law: if a man forced a maid in the fields, he would be slain. It was a good thing that they had not been in the city; for if Amnon had touched her there, and no one had heard them, the men of the city would have stoned her before the door of her father's house.

Would they stone Amnon? It was a pity that only men could participate in the execution. Otherwise, she would be the first to fling a rock as hard as she could, and she would pray to have the strength of David when he went up against Goliath.

But the rabbi shook his head again. That law did not apply, he told her. Not to her. His voice took on the chanting, hectoring tone that meant he would recite the actual words of the laws of Moses and she must set herself to listen.

"If a man finds a betrothed damsel in the field, and the man force her and lie with her: then the man only that lay with her shall die: But unto the damsel thou shalt do nothing; there is in the damsel no sin worthy of death: for as when a man riseth against his neighbor and slayeth him, even so is this matter: for he found her in the field, and the betrothed damsel cried, and there was none to save her."

The women about her rustled. Sorrow and apprehension rose like fumes from myrrh among them.

"This, my daughter, is the law that applies to you. 'If a man find a damsel that is a virgin, which is not betrothed, and lay hold on her, and lie with her, and they be found; then the man that lay with her shall give unto the damsel's father fifty shekels of silver, and she shall be his wife; because he hath humbled her, he may not put her away all his days.' "

Perhaps if she had not looked up in that moment, she might have been persuaded by the elder women that Amnon had been stricken mad by desire for her and would spend the rest of his life atoning for the madness that made her his.

They were nothing if not practical, those older women. They would din the benefits of the match in Kundry's ears. What if she conceived? Would she bring a bastard into the tribe? If a girl, it would have no husband. If a boy, it could never be called to read the law and stand as a man among its kin. Kundry owned the property; Kundry would have power of her own; and, best of all, she could not be put aside if she proved barren. Definitely, they told her as she raged, the match had its strong points.

"Why are there no more judges like Deborah in Israel!" she had screamed, frantic. Betrayed once by a man of her tribe, twice by the law, and three times by the people she most trusted, Kundry feared now to tell the women what she had seen: Amnon's face as he stood beside his father.

Under the scratches she had inflicted in her fight to save herself, he looked smug like a greedy man who expects a feast. Greed, not any beauty of hers, had been what drove him to the rape. Fifty shekels of silver—what was that, when Kundry would bring her husband herds and gold? Amnon had planned this all along, and his father had known of it. And because they had connived and knew how to twist the law, she, who had done nothing but enjoy the freedom in which she had been indulged, would be sentenced to a life in which, each night, Amnon could force her as he had done in the fields. And it would be lawful. If she resisted, she could be punished.

"That's not fair!" she had cried passionately.

Not fair, perhaps; but it was the law. And the punishment for a disobedient child was death. Unwed as she was, in law she still was a child and would be so till she married.

The women had led her away, had tried to persuade her, to remind her of the law.

"It's a bad law, an unjust law. I won't follow it, I won't! I spit at it!" she screamed.

The women paled. With a murmur of horror, they drew away from her as if she were unclean. Kundry understood that too; she had gone too far. Rebellion, grief they could understand, even share. With a new, bitter woman's knowledge, Kundry guessed that beneath some of those robes that swept away in horror were bodies that had not always consented to what men demanded of them. But blasphemy—what were they without the sanctity of the Law?

Whatever the women she trusted had been, whatever tears they had wept, they were wives together now; and they would not let a rebellious girl's acid fury at the laws that gave them their hard-won status erode the accommodations they had made. What was, was good because it had always been: it had to be. Who was Kundry to think it might be different for her?

Kundry's words scared her, too; but having said what she had, she would not go back on it. Someone murmured something about having to speak to the rabbi again, and they left her alone.

Dark as life had suddenly turned, it was sweet to her still.

I was a child, Kundry thought. *I thought that if I ran far enough, I could wake somewhere and be free of the entire coil.*

That night, she had bundled all her jewels into a blanket and run from the home of her fathers and mothers. Jerusalem had been a golden dream to her—surely, nothing could go wrong in the Holy City—so she had headed there. And been wrong again.

I wanted freedom, I wanted my body to myself—and look what I got! she told herself.

Once her jewels—the pride of her mother and grandmother—had been sold at bargain prices to sharp traders quick to see her youth, she had little else but high spirits, quick wits . . . and the body which had drawn hatred concealed as lust. She had used them all. She might have wound up outside the city walls with the other harlots, had her looks not brought her the attention of a stranger.

He was neither Pharisee nor Sadducee, Roman nor Greek. Persian, he called himself and hinted darkly that he was a magus, learned in herbs and in the paths of stars. He had given her herb brews that cramped her worse than eating unripe fruit, but brought on her monthly courses again. For that great gift, he had taken her gratitude, but nothing else. At least, not for a time.

That too had happened. It had not been pleasure, but Kundry had not expected pleasure. At least it had not been pain, and it had been a thing he wanted, a simple thing any woman could do: why should she be different? He would not, he explained, want such release often; as a magus, he must save his strength for his work, not consorting with women.

His eyes glinted with a hunger no food and no woman might satisfy.

Though that knowledge brought her relief of her own, Kundry had nevertheless thought herself lost in sin. If she went home now, the women would spit at her and draw their robes aside, and the men would gather rocks to hurl at her. Her protector had the right of it: once virtue was lost, it was lost forever. There was no repentance.

She wept and told the magus he was right: there was no going back, no pity for her. He consoled her, or so she thought he meant it, saying she had the looks and wits to be a hetaera, a courtesan in a villa, not a slut to be bargained for in the marketplace, or tossed to a greasy shepherd. He would bring her to clever people who could teach her. In return, she must remember only her master's name—Klingsor—obey him, and speak of him only what he told her that she might.

She had thrown herself into her new life with a kind of frantic gaiety that made her popular. Dark, intense women were the rage that year among the tribunes who sailed out from Rome to make their fortunes and, in the doing, collect stories of exotic women and strange arts to ponder at small dinner parties. To her master's ironic approval, she proved to have a quick mind, which his drugs and spells assisted; quickly she learned the languages and customs he prescribed for her—enough Greek to make credible her boast of time spent as a celebrated beauty in Alexandria; heavily accented Latin that the tribunes pronounced charming . . . thinking it charming that any Judaean proved willing to learn the language of the conquerors at all.

She read stories of forbidden gods and idols and found in them understanding and a guilty fascination. Her body had been sunk in sin; now her mind, too, was corrupted. From the stories, she knew why, despite his sleekness and the perfumes and incenses that Klingsor chose, she always scented an insatiable hunger and a foulness about him. He was like the Harpies who fouled their food and that of others, who hated and devoured and never rested. They were part woman, part eagle, and wholly vile; in his darkest moods, Klingsor reminded her of something misbegotten, like an Assyrian demon, an unholy composite of man and beast.

Others of her lessons were more pleasant, despite an initial vow not to allow herself to enjoy this luxurious degradation to which Klingsor had set her. She studied cosmetics and music, too, had sat in the white stone amphitheatre that had been but a whisper of scandal to her in her fields, and had learned to banter with the men who shaved their faces and spoke to her with laughter in their voices of their homes, of the fevers and the frenzies that they found in this land—*you have a plague of visions here*, they told her. *The prophets outnumber the locusts; and we cannot count even the locusts.* Laughing, she had poured wine for them herself, disdaining slaves. It was her people that they mocked. Mindful of Klingsor's commands not to betray herself, she was careful not to let her memories turn her laughter bitter as Dead Sea fruit.

From time to time, she would see a sleek man in Persian silks at the outskirts of the crowd, and she knew that Klingsor, as he had told her he would be, was watching her. Some of the younger women shuddered at the sight of him; the men squared their shoulders and talked of hinting him away. A fraud, they called him, with his boasts of digging in the Tophet of ruined Carthage, studying with the magi of Babylon and Sippar, even trying to draw the veils from the secret things of Israel.

He had told her not to speak of him, or to him. And she had obeyed her master. If she performed well, he would nod, ever so slightly, before slipping away, much to her relief. If, as occasionally happened when she was new to the trade of courtesan, Kundry made some tiny blunder, his lips would thin, his face would pale; and she would spend the night afraid of what he might send to chastise her. Sometimes it took the form of stomach gripes, sometimes of nightmares of Amnon's body thrusting above hers. And sometimes, most frightening of all, she would wake, wondering what would afflict her; and nothing would. When you had nothing and no one else, fear like that could rule you lifelong, even as long a life as Kundry had.

So here I am. Kundry broke off memories that were her oldest, though not her most painful. She flinched away from those as she would jerk aside from a leper.

She rose from the stream-bed, her bones protesting their true age. In all those years as a courtesan and the other things she had been, she had gone soft. She could not bear to think about it.

When had she realized that it did not matter?

It had all gone on too long: the fierce integrity of her childhood laws, the Greek witticisms, the Roman cynicisms, even the—what would you call it?—of the Franks, struggling to understand mysteries that were far removed from them in time and place, and which their race was not complicated enough to understand. She grimaced, knowing that thought to be one stolen from Klingsor.

At the thought of her old enemy and protector for these many centuries, Kundry ran from the stream and lost herself in the darkest thicket that she could find. Broceliande was all that mattered now. It did not care what she had been, what she was, or even what she wanted to be. She had no wants at all that it could not meet: it would feed her and give her the same clear water it gave the rest of its creatures. When she slept, it would cover her over with leaves; and when she slept for the last time, as, please the God she no longer was fit to pray to, she might one day be privileged to do, it would absorb her into itself.

Perhaps the time had come now that she might die. Kundry glanced about the dark wood. She had completely lost her bearings and did not care. She had power enough to shift time and space and forest paths about her and lose herself completely.

She dared not risk that Amfortas's men find her. It was not their anger or punishment she feared; it was that they might bring her before the man she had betrayed, and she would see forgiveness in his eyes. That would break her, drive her over the edge of madness as surely as eating the wrong weeds would drive a wise old sheep to leap from a rocky peak.

The day drew on, little of the sky as she could see through the dense cover of leaves in which she hid. They rustled; but they sounded tired . . . as tired as she.

It would be good to rest. She sank down.

Then she wailed in horror. Broceliande—leaf and bough—shifted about her.

I have not willed this! she wailed in horror. *No!*

For all her desperation, for all her haste in shifting place about her, Klingsor had found her and was hauling her back to his fortress.

He too was a part of her deadliest memories. She didn't want to see him. She didn't want to hear him gloat over his enemy or her, for grieving for her part in Amfortas's destruction, or scheme how best to steal the Grail. She didn't want to think of how he would use Lance and Grail . . . or her.

She tensed her will and fought to resist. Surely, in Broceliande's wizard shade, her powers must have come back. *Not this time, Klingsor. For once, my will, not yours.*

Amusement curdled about her as the leaves and branches shifted. She could not feel herself moving, yet she was being drawn.

She heard a voice borrowing power from the names it invoked; as the names of Samael, demon and destroyer, and Lilitu, who had confounded Eve, rang out in her head, she wondered why the air itself did not recoil, the earth did not shrink, to abandon her to some terrible limbo.

Nec saevior pestis ulla—nor is there any pest more foul. The Harpy's stench rose about her, and she staggered to her knees, gagging.

She retched herself dry as she had done when she was a shepherd girl a thousand years ago. *No!* Again she screamed it with voice and will, but now even the light shifted, grew darker, as it wrapped around her.

She cried and there was no one to save her. This was every bit as much a rape as Amnon had done on her, beginning the long, long tale of her curse.

The fist at her jaw again, the law at her throat, the anger in their eyes . . . it was all that again, hailing her from where she had gone to ground, pulling her back . . .

Blinding light exploded in her eyes, and before it faded, she thought she saw soldiers and three limp bodies hanging from crosses. Clouds hid them, and darkness. Klingsor had her now, was drawing her into his nets. She smelled incense masking foulness; she struggled and broke away for a precious second; here she was, though, where the earth was shaking—or she was moving; and people were screaming out oaths and prayers.

She recoiled from the hot sun, the stinks of sweat, death, urine, and vinegary wine . . . straight into the power that was drawing her away . . . she *had* to flee this place . . . she *wanted* to . . .

In that instant, Klingsor had her, just as he had so long ago.

And the horror vanished in blue light and smoke.

7

KUNDRY stepped through the swirls of light and smoke. Blue fumes of incense wreathed about her. Even after all these centuries, the familiar smell had not lost its power to outrage her. For his own unsanctified works, Klingsor used the formula of the incense used in the Temple in Jerusalem. That was bad enough; worse was how he got it. He had set Kundry to suborn a noblewoman of the priestly Avtina family bored with her ascetic life.

The peasant child she had once been protested—betray the daughter of generations of noble priests? Klingsor had reminded her that he was her master. By her own admission, he ruled her. When she still rebelled, he had used his smokes and drugs on her and whispered words that made her shake to hear them.

In the end, Kundry had done her work well. Too well, she had thought at the time, remembering her girlhood dream of praying in the Courtyard of the Women on the Day of Atonement or the Passover.

Now the scent, deceptively holy, of ground shells, Sodom salt, cyclamen, myrrh, frankincense, cinnamon, spikenard, saffron, and *maalah ashan*, the most secret ingredient of all, the one that made the smoke rise in impressive billows, wreathed about her. For a moment, it wafted her back in time. That illusion faded, but still the strong sweetness of the incense hid the dampness of mud and mold that clung to her and the musk with which Klingsor still perfumed himself after all these years. Still, she thought the stench of carrion pierced the sweetness of the incense, as in a badly kept tomb.

Blue light solidified behind her—Klingsor's mirror, used

in his most impressive workings. A glance at it showed her hair tumbled in wild elflocks almost to her knees. Her robe was rent and mud-stained; scratches and bruises covered her bare arms and feet and one cheek discolored from the blow that Amfortas's knight had given her as she had raved at him, trying to bring help for his lord.

Klingsor, reclining on a couch with cushions in the Persian fashion of *his* youth, daunted her by his very fastidiousness as well as the power he had used to hail her back. Not even faint shadows beneath his eyes showed that it had cost him aught. Instead he had gathered his toys about him: herbs, a model of the fixed and moving stars, stone tablets incised with wedge-shaped symbols, even a scroll or two from the oldest times.

On a table nearby were canopic jars with jackals' heads, a tiny jet statue of a demon that Kundry, with a thousand years' hatred of idols, flinched from, black candles in tarnished silver holders, murky fluids locked away from the air in glass beakers with walls so thick that they contained air bubbles.

> "*Ave formosissima, gemma preciosa,*
> *Ave decus virginum, virgo gloriosa*
> *Ave mundi luminar, ave mundi rosa,*
> *Blanziflor et Helena, Venus generosa!*"

Klingsor greeted her, hands upheld in mocking homage.

Kundry shook her head. She was none such, and knew it. No virgin, no light of the world; and if she were a rose, a canker lay at her heart.

Thanks to Klingsor and his circle of magi, she had even known Helena—not she who had fled with her lover to Troy, but Simon Magus's concubine, who had been hurled from the tower from which her master had leapt in a vain attempt to show that he could fly. It was like Klingsor to humiliate her, bedraggled and distraught as she was.

"Don't," she whispered. And when he glared, "Please don't." Each time, she promised herself she would ask for nothing; each time, she found herself forced to beg.

"How shall I greet you? As the Sabbath bride?" He began

to chant a song that still had power to bring tears to her eyes. He enjoyed blaspheming the traditions she had fled, if only to show her that they still had power to move her. As Klingsor would be the first to tell her, Kundry had no right to object. Had she not danced before Simon Magus and his guests? Had she not dressed Salome's hair the night the Baptist had been slain? Had she not done any one of a thousand things, up to and including the seduction of the Grail's protector just the night before?

No, as Klingsor would remind her, she was no virgin daughter, bride, or faithful adherent of the tradition that hailed the Sabbath bride as one of its most beloved manifestations. Apostate she was; and whore. She had forsaken her old loyalties when she fled the family that would have wed her to the man who raped her, abandoning the beauty of their law along with its rigor. Now, she wanted only to bathe and sleep, forever, if somehow that could be granted.

Perhaps she could dream of the man who loved her. *Amfortas.* Her thoughts faltered on the name, as if it were profanation even to think it in this place.

"Come here to me." His voice was gentle, making her hope for gentle treatment this time. She hated herself for the hope when she knew it was folly. Klingsor was most treacherous when he spoke most fair.

Kundry stepped from the mirror's frame onto a dais encircled by signs and letters that were older than she was. She hated passing through the arch here, with its broken pillars of black and white, mercy turned pitiless, severity turned to license.

Above Klingsor's head shone the blue and purple lights of his working, flashing up and down a tree she flinched from. Ancient words flashed through her head. "*Etz chayim* . . . It is a tree of life to them that hold fast to it. Its ways are ways of pleasantness, and all its paths are peace."

Klingsor, as she had learned in more than a millennium of this cruel partnership, close as a marriage but forged of hate, was interested not in a tree of life, but in its reverse; he had perverted the kingdom, the power, and the glory to his own studies and his own foul goals. And she was bound to them.

"No—stop right there," Klingsor commanded.

Willingly, Kundry stopped.

"Fah! Why did you not clean yourself in the forest? You had the time. You still reek of Frankish rut."

It had not been rape. Rape, she knew: had felt it in her flesh, had committed it herself on Amfortas's faith. She would not think of that. Permitting herself the small rebellion of contempt, she looked Klingsor up and down: a whore's scrutiny. Too-smooth skin, those plump lips, the hunger, the body slackening now that he no longer was a man. Then she let herself remember the lean strength of the man who had held her and fought for her.

Letting her disdain show in her face, she stiffened her shoulders and turned to leave him; after all, she knew quite well where the baths were here, but he held up a hand and the doorway grew opaque. She would not be permitted to leave, not yet. What horrible act would he demand of her now, as repentance for her pity? She could never repent; hadn't he realized that yet? Long ago, a better mage than he had warned it could be Judgment Day until her curse was laid to rest.

"Come here, you say," Kundry told him, sullen, her head down. "Then, 'stop!' you say. You play games. What is it you really want?"

"To look at you, wretched as you are. Have you been rolling in a midden, or just coupling with a swine?" Klingsor flung himself back upon his couch, laughing. "I cannot believe it. After all these years, I can still shock you by what the herd calls blasphemy."

"What is it you want of me now?" Kundry repeated.

"Must I want something? How petty of you. After all, how long is it that we've been together? Perhaps I simply missed you and yearned for your comforting words. I had to heal Ferris, and you know how healing always wearies me."

Kundry held up a hand. Checking him was always a risk, but left to his own appreciation of his wit, Klingsor could pile epigram on epigram, all neatly expressed in parallel clauses, for hours.

"Let us say I wish only the pleasure of your company. It

was I who had you taught how to make it a pleasure, though you seem to have forgotten your lessons."

"Let us say that you are a liar," Kundry retorted. "You miss no one because you care for no one. If you wanted the 'pleasure of my company,' you would allow me to *be* pleasant and let me bathe and rest. So, you must want something or you would not offend yourself with the sight and, as you say, the smell of me."

Klingsor's gibe gave her an absurd hope. Now she was eager to study herself in the bath. Perhaps Amfortas's hands or lips had left his mark on her, even a little one that she could smile over in the brief time before it faded.

"Now that you are done with walking up and down upon the earth . . ." Klingsor smiled to make certain she knew he was blaspheming again. "I have another task for you before I can allow you to rest. Perform it well and speedily, and I shall give you what will let you sleep for as long as you desire."

Kundry glared at him from beneath lowered brows. He had made that promise before, then had waked her to talk, to boast, almost babbling of his plans and accomplishments. He had a mirror wherein he could see his cleverness reflected, surely; why must he inflict it upon her? Clever, even brilliant, he was; but admiring his brilliance was a habit that had gotten old and stale long ago.

His fastness was full of women, most of whom attended her as willingly as she suffered their service. Surely, he must hate her as much as she hated him; why else use *her* for his plans?

"Now what?"

"You are my slave, Kundry. I could beat you for that sullen tone. Have I deserved ill will of you?"

Kundry shrugged. She didn't fear physical violence from Klingsor. A beating was soon healed, and she knew enough of him not to value his physical strength. The memories he could evoke, the pain he could wrap her in—those were things she feared, as he well knew. Soon, he would begin to tell her what she owed him, how bad, how mad she was to refuse to grant it smilingly. Soon, he would remind her of the many times he had spared her, the one time he had saved her from a brief, vile life; the other when he had rescued her—for so he called it—from Rome.

These games, these foolish, painful men's games of domination, fascinated him. Perhaps because he was no longer a man he needed the spice of dominion over a woman, especially one as passionate as she. All *her* passion had been burnt out; his work would be in vain. *Why not agree to what he says?* she asked herself. *It means nothing.*

Only she could not. Some fragments of law, of decency, must still matter to her, or she would not mourn her betrayal of the man she had fled.

"I know what you are thinking. Oh, I know every thought of yours, every care. You care so much, though you pretend not to. I think, sometimes, that you might even care for me as you did when you were just a frightened girl new come from Jericho. Even then, I knew how you felt. Didn't you know that?"

Say what you have to say and let me rest, she thought at him. Surely, if he were that clever, he would hear that too.

He gestured with a too-small, too-well-kept hand. He had held the Spear but awkwardly, Kundry remembered. He was no warrior, but a spy who fought with herbs and other people's strength. If Amfortas, wounded as he was, had gotten within grappling distance of the wizard, he . . . Klingsor had no second manhood to lose, but he had a neck, a spine, to be snapped.

"What do I want of you? Simply this. I am moderately pleased with your conduct in the matter of that Amfortas. So much so that . . ."

If Klingsor took her lover's name on those bloated lips of his again, she thought she would be sick all over the implements of his magecraft. Astonishing. She wouldn't have thought she had that sort of feeling in her.

Now, Kundry could see what Klingsor kept beside him, wrapped in a fold of iridescent silk. Bands of that same fabric covered his hand: so the Spear had seared that well-kept flesh of his when he had dared to pick it up and turn it on its rightful guardian, was that it? She suppressed a smile but let him watch her study his burnt hand.

"It will heal," he told her loftily. "Especially when you

have performed your little chore. You see, Amfortas is *not* the last of his line. He has no sons, that is true; and thanks to *our* good offices, is likely to have none."

Kundry shut her eyes. *Let the day perish wherein I was born, and the night in which it was said, "There is a man-child conceived."* She had heard Amfortas's voice, breathless with passion in her ear; she could imagine his laments now, if only he lived to weep. She would know if he were dead, she reassured herself. Somehow, she must break free of this wizard—she must!—and she would find the wounded man and serve him for the rest of his life or hers, whichever ended first.

"Pay attention, Kundry!" Klingsor snapped. "Amfortas has no sons, but there is a knight who could be called to be his heir. Gahmuret, a cadet of—Anjou, I think. He is much like your knight."

Kundry promised herself that she would snap Klingsor's spine herself. He raised his unburnt hand and his wards crackled into light about him.

"This Gahmuret is off playing knight-errant in the East. He has even spent time in the Holy Land. That should interest you. I believe he has just lifted the siege of Zazamanc. Its queen, Belacane, is quite taken with him, and he with her. Now, she really *is* black but comely. You should have no trouble overcoming any feeble competition on her part—or any feebler resistance on his. Call it a family failing. Or, let us say, you should have no trouble, once you are bathed and decently clad."

For "decent," he meant dressed like the whore she had been, scented and sent out to entice decent men to her bed and their own damnation. In the days of her whoredom, she had spent hours overlooking the Sea of Galilee, sipping chilled wine, eating the shellfish undreamed of and forbidden to the shepherd girl she had once been, listening to men recite the songs of Homer. A Siren was what she was, to lure men to their doom. Klingsor's Siren.

She shook her head.

"You succeeded with Amfortas."

Kundry winced. "That would not work again. He was . . ." Her voice almost broke and she controlled it brutally. "He was tired, almost in despair, ready to fall into my hands. This Gahmuret is in the pride of youth, achievement; he will not fall . . .''

"But he must, he must. I cannot rest easy without knowing that Sir Gahmuret is as helpless before me as Amfortas. I must destroy the line, dig up roots and branches. Bron is dead, Amfortas and his father worse than dead. And now this Gahmuret . . . Once all that line, the old line of David, are gone, Spear and Grail will finally yield to their real master."

She hoped that burn hurt every time he moved. She had not known that Amfortas and this new victim, Gahmuret, were of the old, kingly line of Jesse and David. Even now, it cast the old awe over her. Even now, she had but to close her eyes, remember an even, decent voice that never judged her for what she had made herself . . . *not till the end*. She flinched from the memory of the light that had speared over her as darkness overshadowed the noonday sun.

"Why stop with Amfortas and his kin?" She flung the words at his beardless face. "Why not wipe out every potent, decent man in Christendom? Do you hate them all that much? Because they have what you gave up. You wanted *power*, you thought, and *power*, you thought, is lost if you lie with a woman. Yet you could not restrain yourself, ever, not long enough to gain what you claim you wanted. So you told yourself the gift of your manhood would please the gods, and you went to the Temple . . .''

"Be still!" Klingsor reared from his couch.

"You went to the Temple of Cybele!" Kundry finished. "*I saw you do it!* You knelt at the altar and you bungled the cuts till the priestess had to come and help you. And even then, half stupefied as you were on wine and myrrh, you screamed and puked your guts up. And for what? Long life? Tell me what kind of life you've had! What *power* has it brought you that you couldn't have gained yourself?"

"I tell you, woman, shut that viper's mouth of yours!"

"I won't!" After all these centuries, Kundry saw her enemy flinch before her, and the sight made her drunk with glee. "You may be Persian, Klingsor, as you claim, and they say they do not despise eunuchs there, but I tell you, even now, you play with fire.

"Just look at your hand. You cannot be a half man and serve the Grail, no matter what magic you think you know. Amfortas, even as he is now, is more a man than you were before you traded what manhood you had for power you couldn't use. Could I reach him? It was because he was—he *is*—the man you never were.

"I tell *you*, Klingsor, when you were finished, and when they trussed you up like a capon for roasting, I went outside . . . and, yes, I laughed!"

Now she laughed again, her laughter that hurt as it tore from her throat. She hated her laughter, which had caught her in the curse she had borne for more than a millennium. Klingsor turned bone white. So she had stung him! She had never done that before. The knowledge made her reckless.

"Not," she added viciously, "that it made much difference given how it was the times you took me to your bed. No loss there, for all your blood and screams."

"I will have the Grail, I will! And when I do . . ."

Kundry stamped her foot at him like a mother imitating an angry child.

"You *will* have the Grail, will you? Stamp your feet and shout and say you will! And then what? Bid them make you a man again? Rule the world like Alexander? You cannot rule yourself!"

Do you see this, Amfortas? I fight him, I avenge you as best I can.

Klingsor's scream of fury at her taunts arched over her laughter, and the lights on the Tree on the wall began to flicker up and down the many paths of the dark kingdom. He stabbed out with both hands, whole and burnt, and power built up, crackling between the broken pillars of mercy denied and severity overthrown.

"Out of my sight! I may not rule the world . . . yet, Kundry, but I will rule you. I warned you, Kundry, and you forgot. You will not do that again. Do you hear me? You must *remember*! I will make you remember!"

Power thrust her back between the pillars, the mirror. She flung out her arms against its slick coolness. Klingsor's eyes were wild, maddened by the way she had defied him.

"I am master here. You will remember what you wish most to forget; you will remember and you will know that I am lord here. I promise you, you will relive what you hate most! Be gone! Back to your private hell!"

Fragrant gums wreathed her as if for her own funeral. The mists rose up. She could not see or smell . . . She was falling down the ages, back down the ages, down from a rotten tree of time . . . to a hot, sunlit place. Light, and the three crosses of her worst visions . . . exploded about her.

Her own flinty laughter rang out, the scream of a blasphemer hurled from a rock, trailing after her as the centuries toppled by. After untold years, she ceased laughing and began to scream. She screamed herself hoarse, though as she fell down the years toward her old damnation, she could not even hear herself.

Then there was nothing at all, except the rush of years and dust. Klingsor's triumphant invocations faded behind her, and she was alone.

8

". . . SO I told him, 'I would rather be Herod's pig than Herod's friend!' "

As if from a great distance, like sound almost overwhelmed by the surges of the tide as one rests on a beach, Kundry let the voices wash over her.

Loud male laughter and a shout, "By many-breasted Artemis, that's a fine story!" shocked Kundry awake as another woman, dark-haired and dark-eyed like herself, and dressed in the Greek fashion, tiptoed on fragile sandals away from the heavy doors and toward her past the merchant whose kneeling slaves laid out a rich tangle of filmy cloth.

Kundry glanced out over the terraces and froze, though, even at this height, the day was hot. Below where she reclined, the pale green leaves of poplars and olives panted for breath, and the gold stone of Jerusalem shone. Her eyes filled with tears. "If I forget thee, O Jerusalem, let my right hand forget her skill."

She raised her right hand, tanned and braceleted with heavy gold. Hurled back a thousand dusty, bloody years, her spirit had returned unerringly to the flesh it had walked in during that age. Kundry shut her eyes, dazzled by the sight of King David's city spread out four thousand feet above the plain. Vertigo seized her briefly as she remembered her first climb up the tortuous road. All her life, she had dreamed of going up to Jerusalem—but not of the manner in which that journey finally occurred. How young and frail this hand of hers felt! How young *she* felt, and so unfinished!

She had not, she remembered, been feeling young when

she had first entered the new Roman quarter of Jerusalem under the protection of the mage Klingsor. New in the arts of the hetaera, Kundry at the time had thought herself old and raddled. And yet now, after a thousand years' familiarity with her body, a thousand years' use, the lithe, healthy flesh of the young girl she had been seemed like a miracle of newness.

Klingsor had hurled her back in time. She was in Judaea once again, and she was young, little more than a few years removed from the rape that had exiled her from her home.

Surely, this villa—she had not thought of it for years, and yet, now, how quickly she remembered it!—had been built high on Mount Scopus. Below it and the new Roman quarter stretched King David's city. She craned her neck: could she see the great Temple from here? No; but she could see the splendid height of Herod's summer palace, with its three towers. She would rather have seen the Temple, with its facade a hundred and fifty Roman feet high and broad, facing eastward, glistening in the hot sun, its white marble adorned with gold like sunrise on the snow-tipped mountain passes of Klingsor's native Persia—or so he claimed.

Jerusalem! Oh, she was home. Even a thousand years later in an exile that looked all too likely to spell their deaths, the Jews who hurried through Europe on their way from shame to abuse dreamt of Jerusalem, praying at each Passover to be returned to it—and now she was here again. She laid her cheek against smooth wood and felt the brief heat of tears. *By the rivers of Babylon, there we sat down, yea, we wept, when we remembered Zion.* Below her, the olive groves blurred as she wept. Klingsor had meant to punish her by thrusting her back to the time of her damnation—a heavy blow. She would grieve later; but for this moment, she wept for joy. Lacking Jerusalem, she had forgotten how bereft she had been.

"Awake now and quite well?" The woman spoke gently to Kundry. "The men were just laughing again. It was an old story they were telling, about Herod the father, not Herod Antipas; but it is always better to listen when the men talk. You never know when they will throw away a pearl of information that one day may make the difference between prosperity in your old age and the street."

I remember her voice, too!

"Miriam?" she whispered.

"Kundry, your Greek should be better than that, after all your time in Alexandria! My name is Maria."

Kundry met Maria's mocking smile and wink with irony of her own. As they both knew, Kundry was no more from Alexandria than Maria was from the Tiberias where, she claimed, she owned a villa. Despite the patronage of a Persian mage (or so he had instructed her to say), Kundry was little more than a perfumed and painted version of a shepherdess from near Jericho, just as, not all that long ago, elegant Maria had been mere Miriam from Magdala.

To admit that, however, would be to drive down their price. Exotics were fashionable this year for the tribunes newly sent from Rome and seeking safe titillation, while Jewish women were not to be trusted, lest, like Jael or Judith, they turn on their conquerors and slay them at their most vulnerable moments.

"Do you have the flux? Any fever?" Maria's scented hand reached out to touch Kundry's brow. Maria was a great one for lectures on how a hetaera must protect herself from fevers and fluxes and youths who fancied themselves in love. Her advice usually involved watered wine, herb drenches, sponges, and unpleasant applications of vinegar. Usually, such medical advice was delivered in the same voice as her speeches on how a woman must save her money—Maria kept hers at Seuthes and Sons, and watched the bankers as if they were her kinsmen—and protect herself against the kinsmen who, like scorpions, leapt to hand whenever one turned over a rock.

"So lazy," Kundry sighed. Then, remembering her lessons at Klingsor's hands, "The day is so wearisome."

"You have not been well since you returned from Tiberias when the king came to live in his summer palace in Jerusalem," Maria said, the hetaera's languor gone from her voice. "What happened there? Any of the girls we know would have been delirious to have been invited to the pal-

ace there, even more eager to cap the rumors that we have
heard . . ."

Kundry shook her head, cast her eyes down in a way
Klingsor had assured her was sultry. She could not gaze
long enough at the Holy City below her. How long had it
been since she had seen it? So long: she had never dared to
return, not after the men of the West had returned with fire
and sword; and cross and crescent had met in blood in the
ancient narrow streets.

Those streets were not ancient now, but so new the stone
dust had barely had time to settle. The Romans were building again; they were always building, except when they were
tearing things down. As she gazed out on the shining city,
the newness of much of it struck her. Like his Roman
masters, Herod Antipas, who ruled as tetrarch where his
father had ruled as king, was a master builder—and a bri-
gand.

"Don't waste those bedroom eyes on your friend
Maria." That hand, strong for all its ornaments of pearl and
henna, tugged at her shoulders. "What happened . . ."

"The tribune has the right of it," Kundry muttered. "It
is better to be . . . a pig than a friend to Herod, father or son.
The girl danced; the man died; and then the girl died too."

"Salome?" whispered Maria. No one knew why Herod
had suddenly proclaimed his Herodias's daughter a traitor;
no one dared ask. But Kundry had seen; Kundry had helped
dress—or undress—the girl for her dance, and had cowered
horror-struck when she had asked not for gold or gems but
for a prisoner's head.

And so one of the madmen who stalked up and down
Jordan, rending the hot air with his prophecies, was dead
now; and Kundry had come, sickly and pallid, to Jerusalem
in Herod's train.

"Let be, I beg you, Maria," Kundry whispered. "I wish
I could forget."

"You need distraction. Look at the pretty silks." Maria
smiled as if urging a child to eat. "That color would make
them hurl rocks at us below; and that heavy, overwrought
stuff is only good for the *stolas* they will not let us wear . . ."

She pointed at a splendor of rose and gold that would

probably lure townswomen from their narrow houses and their water pitchers and cause the august rabbis of the Pharisee community in Jerusalem to reach for the nearest stone if they were so foolish as to venture into the Old City without the protection of their Roman or Sadduccee lovers. Thus it was all over the Dekapolis, the ten cities that most clearly showed the conquest by mind of Greece and that of the sword and nailed *caligae* of Rome.

"Are you buying that?" Maria asked Kundry, who nodded. Anything to take Maria's mind off Salome and relieve her own mind of the bulging eyes, the blackened tongue, the bleeding neck—stop it! A moment longer, and she would be gagging, fainting, perhaps, if she did no worse.

"I will wear it with pearls," she said. Not glass beads covered with fish scales. "Perhaps I should dissolve a pearl in vinegar this evening and drink it, as Cleopatra once did. Romans are always impressed with excess."

"No wig, though," Maria nodded sagely. "If they want blond tribeswomen, let them take themselves to Germania. I'd wager they wish they could."

"Seeing that it is cooler and that much closer to Rome . . ."

The merchant ventured to praise the estimable ladies' wits. The slaves clearly wished themselves elsewhere.

"We have said we shall purchase." Maria raised plucked eyebrows at the merchant. "Now take yourselves away.

"I could tell you were tiring," she said in a softer voice to Kundry. "Rest while you can. Tonight we will be expected to work hard, and tomorrow we will have our adventure. For now, though, we should listen to the men. I always say . . ."

Kundry laughed, delighted, though not for the proposed "adventure." *I could not have been that much of a fool when I was a girl. I had the brains to appreciate Maria.* Even after a thousand years, she relished her friend's wit. She knew it; she was about to hear another of Maria's homilies to the wise hetaera. "You cannot know enough about patrons. Knowledge protects you, and, in any case, they think they're helping to improve your mind, too." Maria laughed. "I ask you, do you truly think *they* think at all?"

"A whim in a *toga picta*, with a superstitious, arrogant whim of a wife . . ."

Laughter exploded again as the doors swung open.

"Ah, the noble Claudia, our beloved Pilate's lady. *Too* noble by far for our esteemed procurator, as she tells him, I have no doubt, every eve and morning . . . hey!"

Mutters about "mummeries and women's folly" died away as someone else hissed. Bored in Judaea, Claudia was known to be as easy a target for priests and prophets of all cults as a drunken merchant was at portside. And that was not safe knowledge to have: unsafe, and therefore necessary and desirable.

Maria and Kundry glanced at each other and leaned forward, intent. Listening to patrons had taught them both that the procurator of Judaea was a hard man to cross; he was hostile, vindictive, and fanatically exacting in his duties to Rome as well as to his own purse. Usually, he governed out of Caesarea; but when the king came to Jerusalem, Pontius Pilate came too—as much to watch Herod, rumor had it, as to escape the heat in the high citadel above the olive groves. Rumor also had it that his marriage to Claudia, daughter of the notorious Julia who had died, exiled from Rome by her immortal father Caesar Augustus, was at least as bitter as the Dead Sea fruit that so fascinated and disgusted Romans new to Judaea.

But where Dead Sea fruit could only turn to ashes in the mouth, rumor could—and had—turned poisonous. No wonder that demand—enforced by a push to the indiscreet man's shoulder—for quiet. Especially before hetaerae whose mouths could be bought for information as well as pleasure.

The two tribunes, their patrons for tonight and probably the next few days, walked in, other men of the Tenth Legion with them. Hearing Kundry and Maria laugh, they were quick to demand explanations. Only after the men were settled in chairs by the windows where the breeze of late afternoon could cool them—as much as anyone could ever *be* cooled, they swore, in this pestilential climate—did Kundry remember something else.

The last time she had stayed in this villa, the last time she had examined silks with Maria and the silk merchant, she had *not* purchased the rose and gold silk. This time, however, she had.

She had not lived with power for a thousand years not to know that such a change, even in so slight a thing, might be important.

The Romans had been drinking unwatered wine since the brutal sunlight of late afternoon had hammered down, then lengthened on the stone floor. Unwise in this heat; if they drank much more, they would lie prone, but noisier by far, alongside their shadows, Kundry thought.

More and more men had joined them: young officers and politicians, a few prematurely embittered elders counting the days until they could sail for Italy, a Sadduccee or three trying hard to convince the other guests that their hard-won overlay of Hellenic manners was natural, even a few Pharisees trying to adapt to Roman manners for some advantages they wished to win.

Kundry glanced beneath her lashes at the Sadduccees narrowly, then looked away. On several occasions, men of her people had called her "harlot" and "abomination;" the women were even more harsh, striking out for fear that one day they might find themselves brought as low as she. She remembered being young, the last time she was in Jerusalem, shamed by, cringing from, such accusations.

One of the Sadduccees was staring—was he minded to bargain for her when the Romans had done? Not that surely; the Sadduccees knew and kept the place that Rome had ordained for them. But surely, Kundry knew those dark brows, the hooked nose, and the black eyes. It was Klingsor—not the Klingsor of a thousand years' acquaintance, but just as deadly. Come to keep an eye on her, was he? He should see that Kundry, late of Alexandria, as he had ordered her to style herself, was as up to the niceties of a Roman dinner as any other woman present! A quick glance took in the other women, consorts of Empire. Like Kundry and Maria, most of them were native Judaeans trying hard to ape the manners of the capital. Some affected languor, others intensity; all were painted, depilated, and tricked out with varying degrees of successful elegance.

Sunset was exploding golden and orange in a haze of blue hills and dust when some fool declared that the evening was too beautiful for all of them to be pent up in the triclinium. A moment later, everyone was shouting it and congratulating himself on a magnificent scheme. Faced with the ruin of his dinner party, the host ordered his slaves to drag couches and cushions outside and bring the food—and, of course, more wine—out there. The women, whatever their status might be in the constantly shifting rankings of hetaerae, exchanged resigned glances. Veterans, veritable centurions of their trade, they suspected all too accurately that the feast would prove to be a debauch before too much longer.

Tomorrow's adventure—that is, if she remembered it aright—would come as a positive relief: even if it were to be no less raucous, it would hold no wine.

To Kundry's surprise, though, a shout did not go up for the flute girls or for pretty boys to come serve more wine. This was to be a serious symposium, another man declared thickly, at which politics would be discussed. In Judaea, that meant politics and religion, and probably another session of carping at Caiaphas, the Pharisee who was high priest, and Annas, his father-in-law. Klingsor leaned forward, like a lion scenting prey. At least three hetaerae yawned.

Maria leaned forward, however, attention divided with all her considerable tact between her escort and the men who blustered, schemed, and usually interrupted each other. Kundry flushed. Past and present seemed to overlay each other like two sheets of mica through which could be seen bright stone. She remembered this dinner as a test of her abilities to charm, even under Klingsor's critical study. Now, she found it more shameful than a barrage of insults from the Sadducees avoiding the sight of her across the room would have been. Here were the Romans, discussing affairs of state . . . the affairs not of their nation, but of *hers*. They were scavengers, plotting how best to dispose of the land's wealth and its people; laughing over unsuccessful attempts to dislodge Rome from the land it had stolen from the people to whom the Almighty (blessed be His name, Kundry added by instinct) promised it. Surely God would look down and pity the good people, if not herself. Surely, after all these centuries of hope and longing, God would send His redeemer to restore the Holy Land to Israel.

But hadn't that happened? Hadn't that been what Amfortas and his men had devoted their lives to affirming? That was why, for the past thousand years, this land lay under fortress after fortress, why people died in the name of God, and why she wandered, as much a victim of a curse as if she bore a visible Cain's mark.

Best not think of any of that, either now or as she had remembered. In defying the law of Israel, Kundry had turned her own face from the Almighty. She was as much to blame as any of the other women and the Pharisees and Sadduccees here. Skeletons at our masters' feast, she thought, eager for crumbs of food or information; and they trust us, they trust that we are so beaten down that we will not seek out those few rebels who survive.

No, she herself would not do so either. Those heroes' lives were far too precious to spill slaying fools like these.

Klingsor shook his head at her. Like a servant reproved, she bent to her task of being lovely and pleasant, the perfectly complaisant native mistress to a rising tribune.

But she wanted to spit in his wine.

"Kundry, a seat and wine for our friend here, the centurion Gaius Longinus, just in from Capernaum!"

What was this one's name, Servius Tullius, Gaius Claudius, Lucius Severus . . . ? What a bore it was, trying to keep straight the intricate, often repetitive series of Roman names! And yet, if one forgot, how dangerous!

Kundry rose quickly, as if to give the centurion her own seat. For a moment, she was a girl again, and the centurion any older man, therefore meriting respect. Then, remembering, she clapped her hands for slaves to bring and place another chair. When he did not immediately sit down in it, she glanced at him, and it took all her hetaera's arts of dissimulation to stifle the gasp of surprise. A white film coated the man's eyes, masked by their deep sun-creases.

His blindness gave him the look of a portrait bust set up along the road that had watched many caravans pass.

"This way, sir," she said, her voice going soft with what she hoped he would not hear as pity. "Allow me to guide you."

"I do well enough," he told her.

Kundry and Maria, occupied mixing wine with her own hands (though thin, the blind soldier was taut and fit; and she assumed he would not drink wine unwatered), flickered glances at each other again in that soundless language that the conquered use to protect themselves from their masters. *Observe: such knowledge could be to our advantage.* Gaius Longinus had spent so long in the Galilee that even his Latin bore the gutturals of the local speech. Blind or purblind as he seemed to be, it was a wonder he was still part of the legions. *Too valuable to be dismissed*, Kundry's experience, so much the senior of her body, told her. *Possibly a spy.*

"So many prophets in this accursed hot country," declared Lucius Severus. (Or was it Publius Tullius or Gaius Claudius? No, it *definitely* was not Gaius Claudius, which was a royal name; anyone who bore it would decidedly be spared the tedious, risky Judaean service.)

"I told"—the foolish young officer affected the lisp that Klingsor had told Kundry that Alcibiades, a famous and rich Greek dead three centuries ago, had affected—"our esteemed procurator that we might well group these prophets into teams. Assign them colors as if they were charioteers—Red, Blue, White, and Green. We could run them in the amphitheatre and bet on their points—like strength of voice, or smell, or the sheer quantity of madness they blat out."

Kundry shuddered. Those were holy men this fool ridiculed! Had she still been an innocent, she told herself, she would have been as shocked as she was the first time a Roman insisted she at least have a nibble of the pork. She had managed to choke it down it without gagging; a hetaera's training, clearly, was good at dinner, too.

"Have you seen the men all in white—tunic, cloak, head covering, the ones with little shovels at their waists. In case they must, ah, answer nature's call . . ."

A hiss of scandalized laughter from the tribune who definitely was *not* named Gaius Claudius . . .

"Let us simply say that Rome has its cloacae; Judaea and these Essenes their little shovels . . ."

"Lads—I mean, sirs—when you are as old as I . . ." Gaius Longinus cut in so smoothly that the interruption did not offend. In any case, tribunes though these young men were, a senior centurion, hardened in this land, familiar with every bandit or fanatic who might leap from a wadi to cut a Roman's throat, was a personage they would do well to heed.

The second tribune leaned forward.

"Well, what story have you to tell us now?"

Gaius Longinus's blank eyes appeared to glance from Kundry to Maria and back to the tribune's callow, sweating face.

"Why not before the ladies? They are of Judaea; perhaps there are other things they can share with us besides . . ."

Gaius Longinus did not join in the drunken laughter.

"I know him," Maria whispered. "He travels about the land, listening for stories of prophets, though he has never sought instruction, like some Romans."

"One of the *frumentarii?*" Kundry asked, dread chilling her, even old as she was now. The *frumentarii* truly were the adversary, walking to and fro upon the earth, determined to stir up trouble and torment honest folk.

Maria shook her head. "Hush!"

"Here is my tale," said Gaius Longinus. "Do you know Capernaum? You have not yet ridden there? Sirs, if you will hear the recommendation of an old fighting man, you will remedy that. It is a fair town. At its north end, near where the fast running waters of the Jordan pour into the lake, there is a small curving bay.

"Very pretty," the old man mused to himself. "I recall it from when my eyes were brighter than they are now. The hills are blue, far off. Very lush, too, with tamarisks and licorice trees, that dark green against white stone pavements, black basalt columns, and a broad staircase going up to the old synagogue there. You would not have thought the

Jews had money enough left to build such a synagogue or decorate it with lions and centaurs."

The tribunes cleared their throats with the abruptness of catapults snapping boulders into the air.

"I had gone to Capernaum because I heard a story of a new prophet."

"One of those wild-eyed types who live up in the caves and do funny rituals with bathing, like that . . ."

"Johanan." Gaius Longinus supplied the native form of the name. "He died a while back."

Kundry flushed, feeling the eyes of everyone in the room except the old centurion upon her. So the scandal had spread. What remained of the shamefast village girl she had once been burned to flee; Klingsor's glance pinned her where she sat.

"There's a tie between Johanan and this new prophet, Joshua ben Joseph. Johanan was—what is the word . . . one of you gentlemen help me, I never learned Greek. *Baptismus*, that's it. We would say *Baptizatus*, I guess, though I am no philosopher. The sprinkling of water over a willing person to purify him. You do know," asked the blind centurion, "that the Jews use bathing in their rituals?"

"First civilized thing I've heard of them," muttered someone. Maria of Magdala's dark eyes flared, heat lightning in the cool of the evening. Ostentatiously, she sniffed at the man, who smelled now of sweat and wine, and the people nearby laughed.

Protected by Maria's diversion, Kundry shut her eyes again in absolute anguish. Now it would begin again. Now, once again, she would see the Lance pierce his side, see the cup fill first with vinegar, then with blood and water . . . and she would laugh.

Fool. This time you bought the silk. You changed things. What else can you change?

"This Joshua came to Johanan and asked him to dunk him in the Jordan. Under the circumstances, that was a logical request . . ."

"So Jews are capable of logic."

"My servant"—Longinus persevered in his story as if he had not heard the tribune's interruption—"told me that

Joshua had been spending time in the desert, and that was what made me decide to watch him. What was interesting, though, was that Johanan didn't *want* to baptize—ah, that's the word!—him; Johanan wanted *Joshua* to sprinkle *him*. They argued about it for a while—all these Jews love to argue—and finally the Baptist saw it this new prophet's way. Once the thing was done, this Joshua headed straight back into the desert.

"That gave me some time to check up on him. He could be a problem. For one thing, he's not just from the back of beyond, a struggling carpenter from a village called Nazareth."

"Can any good come out of Nazareth?" One of the Pharisees, a man named Simon, called that out to a scatter of half-scandalized laughter.

"You tell me, sir," replied Gaius Longinus, his blind eyes effortlessly turning as his ears told him where the speaker had shouted from. "Only this: I must tell you that this Joshua ben Joseph claims descent from the Jews' King David."

A low, thoughtful whistle rose from somewhere behind her, with the mutter, "Wouldn't Herod be overjoyed to hear of a *real* king of the Jews?"

A crawling sensation at the back of her brain brought her attention back to the two Romans, Longinus and her own lover-for-the-night, who discussed prophets with the owl-eyed solemnity of the half drunk. At least, *her* patron was half drunk. For all the film that clouded Longinus's eyes, he saw more clearly than the young Romans.

"Capernaum is in the tetrarch's territory anyhow, so I thought I had better check. After all, they say Judaea is a hotbed of insurrection, though it has been a good home to me and I propose to take my land here when it is time to receive my wooden sword . . ."

He laughed at an old joke. He was a centurion, not a manumitted gladiator. Fields and a mule, not a wooden sword, would be the sign of his release from service.

"Let me introduce a brother in arms," said Longinus. He clapped his hand and spoke long and intently to the slave who answered the summons. "No," he replied to a question Kundry did not hear, "he chose not to join the feast and asks your pardon for it. I don't know if that makes him a Jew or not. You must ask their Sanhedrin. I do know that he is a good soldier and, if he swears by whatever gods he reveres these days, he will answer honestly."

The man who strode into the center of the feast—a lost battlefield of crumpled cloths, spilled wine cups, and the carcasses of countless doves—could have passed for Longinus's son, coin stamped by the Legions into faith and endurance.

"Tell us, lad," Longinus said gently, "what happened when your son's nurse took sick. He is married . . ." A buzz rose; legionaries were not permitted formal marriage vows, such as the patrician *conferratio*; but the associations formed were often far more binding than those of divorce-riddled Rome. ". . . to a woman of Capernaum, and his son's nurse is—"

"She is my wife's aunt, sir," said the centurion. "And dear to both of us. When Hadassah, my wife, was ill last winter and like to miscarry, this woman pulled her and the boy through." He shook his head, simultaneously wondering and bewildered.

Look at your leaders, lad. Aren't they just stunningly worthy of service?

"Are you a Jew?" came the question. Kundry flinched, but there had been no sarcasm, no threat in it . . . yet.

"No, Excellency. But I honor them for my wife's sake. You may have heard it said that I have caused a synagogue to be built. That can hardly be true, seeing as I am a son of Rome and have only my pay to live upon. But I made what small contributions I could when my son was born."

Of course he would. Roman though he was, if the mother was Jewish, the child was Jewish; and as a firstborn son, it must be redeemed from temple service.

Longinus walked over to the younger centurion as surely as if he could see. "Tell them what happened. I promise you they'll hear you out."

"My wife's aunt grew very sick. Oh, I know, old women blow hot and cold, push away their food, or eat everything in sight; but this wasn't one of those cases. She simply went to bed and shook. Then my wife came running to me, weeping; said her aunt had a high fever and was like to die, and I must send for the elders, the new prophet, anyone, only . . ."

Someone laughed.

"Sirs," the centurion appealed to the half-drunken crowd, "my wife is still nursing, and I would not have my firstborn son stinted." He shrugged. "So I *invited* the elders of Capernaum to visit me and asked them if they could speak to this Joshua. I had him looked into; I knew no harm of him, and . . ." Again he shook his head.

Kundry shivered. The centurion tried to be judicious, skeptical, to appeal to like-minded men; but she sensed that he, as much as his wife, had wanted to appeal to the new prophet. She remembered this story—but she did not remember hearing it. *Another thing that is changed.*

"They told me they would bring me to him. They were very kind; they even told him I had served them right, had given them a synagogue. It isn't true, but that's what they said. Then they set me in front of him. You should have seen his eyes . . ."

"Shooting fire?" Someone asked that, then was elbowed into temporary decorum.

"Nothing like that. Just calm. Like seeing your father when you're three and knowing that there's nothing he cannot do. The minute I saw him, that's how I felt. My wife had told me . . . I mean, I had meant to ask him to come to look at my wife's aunt. But the minute I saw him, I said, 'I can't talk with him. You talk for me, and tell him, I am not worthy you should come under my roof. For that reason, I did not think myself worthy to come to you; but say a word, and my servant, my son's nurse, shall be healed.' For I also am a man set under authority. I have soldiers under me. If I should say to one, 'Go,' he goes; if I tell another, 'Come,' he comes; and if I say to my servant, 'Do this,' of course he does.

"I watched him, and he turned straight around and told the elders, 'You are of Israel, and he is of Rome; and truly, I tell you, I have not found so great faith anywhere in Israel.'"

The centurion shivered, and Maria rose and handed him
a cup of unwatered wine. He nodded thanks to her and
drank it off. He raised one hand to wipe his mouth—an
unmannerly gesture, but Kundry saw him dab at his eyes
before he stood at attention, as if facing his general.

"When I returned home"—the centurion's voice was
hoarse—"my wife brought me to see. There was my son,
laughing in his nurse's arms; and she looked twenty years
younger."

"Thank you, centurion," said a man who had not spoken
before. Kundry did not know—or did not remember—
him; but the centurion saluted gravely.

"He is a good man, sir. No menace to Rome, my honor
on it." With that, he walked within the house, clearly wondering if he had helped or hurt his benefactor. Longinus
followed him. It was clear that both were eager to be gone.

For a long time, the dinner guests remained silent. Much
to Kundry's surprise, Simon, the Pharisee, invited Kundry's patron to dine; also to her surprise, he accepted for
them both. She glanced at Simon. Would he withdraw his
invitation—and his befouled presence—from them now
that he had been forced to recognize a harlot?

It would not be easy for Kundry either. She would have
to go, would have to enter a house where no woman would
permit herself to be seen as long as Kundry was present and
which such a woman would probably scour, not just to
prepare for Passover, but to cleanse it of the contaminated
dust that the whore's skirts had swept in. She did not want
to go.

Had she gone before? She could not remember.

Then a howl went up for wine, torches, a *buccinator*, if no
better horn player were available, and, to crown the evening, someone to dance the dance that had so stirred Herod
that summer.

A scandalized whisper went up, and Kundry shivered.
Salome had worn seven veils and no more; the evening was
chill. But it was not for cold that Kundry shivered; it was
for danger. Once Salome had finished her dance, there had
been blood on the paving: she remembered. It was danger-

ous to play with the passions of princes—as none knew better than she.

In the thousand years gone by, she had trained herself to stillness. Stillness was not what this younger Klingsor would expect, but protest and appeal. She manufactured a begging glance, cast it at him, and saw him repudiate it with a raised brow. The Klingsor of this time, still a man, though young in malice; and the Klingsor who had hurled her back to Judaea to punish her—no man, and expert in the malice of his thwarted hunger. She must separate them in her mind.

Hysterical laughter threatened, but she forced herself ruthlessly to calm. Given the mood of the men here, she was not likely to be allowed to remain that way for long.

"Kundry saw it! Let Kundry show us!" came the cry; and Kundry found herself pushed to the center of the panting, drunken crowd.

For a moment, panic ripped through her as one young man tugged at her gown. The silk ripped with a scream. She had screamed too, long ago on that hillside outside Jericho, but no one had come to rescue her; and no one came now.

Klingsor, easing his way to the outskirts of the group, showed Kundry a wry twist to his mouth. But as the torches sputtered into violent life, his eyes showed naked hunger. It was not the lust that any normal man would show at the prospect of seeing a woman dance naked before a crowd, but a desire for power that made Kundry shiver, old as she was. She wondered how Kundry the girl, whose flesh she now wore, could have missed seeing it.

Yet it was something she remembered, and it called back to her her centuries of experience: she was no girl to be devastated by a smutty dance. She tugged the torn silk out of the drunken Roman's sweaty hands, then pushed him away almost coyly (though she longed to backhand him across the garden). He staggered back, lolling across his couch and the woman who shared it, his mouth slack; and Kundry, loathing the need, summoned a laugh.

"At Tiberias, as I recall, the veils *dropped*, sir; they were not torn from the dancer. Do I make myself understood?"

Laughter and ribald shouts wreathed about her. The

Roman pretended to be abashed and buried his flushed face in his companion's bosom. She squealed, pushing him away, which he allowed, eager to see the dance.

"Then let half of these torches be removed!" Kundry clapped her hands to call the slaves.

Flute and high taut drum were summoned, and began to play, a shrill wail of passion encompassed by drum sound as fast and hard as a heart laboring in passion. She turned her anger into ice, then into sinuous movement. As the torches flickered and men laughed, sharp and excited, she dropped her veils one by one, long, long after they had undressed her in their minds and lewd comments.

Maria had the grace to look away. Kundry was glad that the centurion of Capernaum had not stayed to see, gladder yet the elder man could not see her. It was bad enough to dance before these men and women whom she despised, worse to posture and writhe before Klingsor, smug at the success of his toy.

Kundry's steps grew wilder. Tears mixed with the sweat that slid down face and throat and breasts until a young tribune snatched her off the table and bore her into the darkness of the garden.

Despite her training, Kundry resisted. Her life had taught her resistance was futile, and yet, this older Kundry had to try: the young man was not Amfortas. Her struggles excited the young man above her to a frenzy of puppyish lust that drew cries of approval from other men as they sought the shadows with the women they had brought.

Kundry moaned and hid her face from the moon.

9

KUNDRY wrapped her head in the coarse fabric that Maria had decreed for their "adventure." Such as it was: for a chaste woman, safe in the care of her family, it was no adventure but a right and duty to go to the Temple and pray. But for hetaerae to venture thus—one single, outraged shout of "Harlot!", one rock flung, could start a riot. This close to the Passover—with Pilate resident in Jerusalem—even a small riot, such as flourished daily in the twisty ways of the lower city, could have drastic consequences.

"Kundry, come *on!*" Maria hissed and tugged at her robe.

They could not descend to the lower city unguarded; both women knew that. It would be all too easy for one of the Sicarii to edge up to them and stab them in the back or throat for consorting with Rome, or to follow them to where they had agreed to meet their patrons.

What if I did die? I would not have to relive the next thousand years. It would be so much easier . . .

Ahead of her, stonework reared up, and Kundry's thoughts stilled. Once again, she was awed, despite herself. Casting her memories back a thousand years to this time, she recalled how the girl she had been wept when *she* had seen the Temple; the immensely older woman, tenant now in that lithe flesh, found it all new and wonderful.

It was not, of course, the Temple of the great Solomon, son of David. That Temple had fallen with Jerusalem before the exile to Babylon. This one . . . After fifty years, the first Herod's plans for the Temple were still not yet complete, but they bode fair to make Solomon's shrine seem a rustic waystation by comparison. Even now, as the holiday approached, workers and supervising priests thronged the scaffolds and the entryways.

Rome made straight what had been crooked, not necessarily to the advantage of what it wrought its changes upon. The bridge and even the roads leading to the Temple Mount were straight, as if built on ruled lines, imposing the arrogance of human will on an ancient city.

"For we were strangers in the land of Egypt," Kundry murmured to Maria. "Tyrant's gold and Jewish sweat, whether we build for Herod or for Pharaoh."

Maria hissed. Kundry peered into the swathings of wool that proclaimed their wearers' respectability and saw that the other woman was honestly afraid. Let someone hear and raise a shout of "Blasphemy!"; and far too many stones lay close to hand.

"That is new," Maria pointed out as they crossed a bridge from the upper city toward the portico that led to the forecourt. Kundry glanced where Maria pointed, then looked away. In any place and time, she would know Klingsor. Surely, that was he, but . . .

"Who is that he speaks to? Is that Annas . . ."

"Hush!"

Maria bent her head and pushed forward, joining a small covey of women waddling like hoopoes toward the Court of the Women. Suddenly, she choked—with amusement, Kundry was glad to see. The women, the respectable family women in whose midst they sought to hide, were not singing the traditional psalms of ascent; they were gossiping.

"My husband says that the sanctuary is almost barren and that the Holy of Holies is bare . . ."

"Bare gold! What would he know? There are no priests in his family or yours . . ."

"They will *hear* you," squealed a younger woman, awkward with a pregnancy the size of a melon.

"Ahhhh," an old woman smiled, her gums ruddy, her eyes almost as milky as those of Gaius Longinus. "Even I can see it . . . walls of gold and silver like fire . . . I shall die happy now."

Walls loomed up before them, wrought of white stone that had never felt the bite of forbidden iron. Gold and silver shimmered on the gates, and polished bronze gleamed on the crests and gear of the legionaries. They stood far enough away that none of the Hakamim, those very pious Jews who still lived in the world, but whose word could cause riots, might take offense, yet close enough that thieves and Sicarii could take nothing else.

The eagle that had once hung on the gates and that had been removed at the cost of riots and the protracted executions of young students was long gone. Now the enormous stones glowed, polished almost to the luster of fine marble. Some of them were as much as forty-five cubits long. Kundry's first thoughts had been right; with such stones, you could build pyramids and sphinxes—*or Christian cathedrals*—as well as synagogues.

In all those years of Christendom, during which Kundry had lived as temptress and renegade, how often had she thought of herself as a Jew? How often had she thought herself akin to the exiled descendants of the crowds who flocked into the Temple they now possessed? Remembering, she shuddered despite the day's heat. Less than a generation from now, Israel would lose its Temple again, never to be rebuilt till the Messiah came. *If* ever the Messiah came.

They passed through the gates and into a forest of intricately carved Corinthian pillars. Kundry glanced down. Below, an immense distance below, was the great stair that led from the lower city to the Temple Mount. Maria pulled her back.

"If you fall . . . So many people coming up, all at once . . . they'll trample you!"

A middle-aged woman glared at them, and they fell silent. After a moment, Kundry raised her voice again, singing, "I was glad when they said unto me, let us go into the house of the Lord . . ."

She had not sung it for more than a thousand years, not even in the darkest, loneliest watches of the night, but her voice rang out true, and tears she could not shed stood in her eyes.

The woman turned away. Maria drew a breath of pure relief.

Now they walked through the cloisters. Though women were permitted to see no more of the Temple than the Court of the Women, these cloisters were open to all. Here doves were sold, and here money changers thrived, changing coins from all over the world for the "Holy Shekels" that must be used within the Temple to pay for sacrifices of beasts and incense.

"Looks as if a riot has already happened," Maria commented from the corner of her mouth between lines of the psalm. "They're sweeping up, but they're shaken."

Kundry turned her head slightly, the better to overhear.

"Madman!" snorted one fat money changer. "Probably one of those madmen from the caves!"

"He didn't wear white like they do," protested his fellow, as he directed three assistants to move the tables *there* and a younger man, almost as fat and probably his son, to place the cashbox—no, not like *that*, you nameless fool!

"Since the days of Solomon, money has been changed in the Temple, but no, this young madman from Nazareth has to come in and disrupt our business like a rampaging lion. The strength of him! I thought he'd broken Mordecai's leg when that table went over, but no, he was well enough to get up and run after the young hothead, cursing . . ."

"Do you think he'll come back?" a seller of doves asked as he stared ruefully at the clutter of shattered cages and feathers that had once been a profitable stall.

"Someone said he's at Olivet this morning. Prophesying again." The word was spat out like a blasphemy. "More trouble than they are worth, these prophets. It's a bad day when they bar a man from his living."

"Calling us a den of thieves! He must have been out in the sun too long."

"They're all mad in the Galilee. No wonder the *kittim* . . ."

"Quiet! You'll have the Romans in here."

"Calling the *Temple* a den of thieves," the fat money changer corrected him. "Has anyone thought to bring charges of blasphemy?"

Kundry shivered. *My house shall be called the house of prayer; but ye have made it a den of thieves.* Maria tugged at her robes, and they went toward the gate. Behind them, they could hear people sounding out the warnings in Latin and Greek that no non-Jews should enter, on pain of death. A veritable tide of women, chaste bundles of woolen folds, thrust them past the gate and into the huge Court of the Women.

It had a special court for Nazarites and one for lepers, which everyone else avoided even glancing at. No provision was made, of course, for whores. *They would shrink from us if they knew*, Kundry thought. The great wave rolled on, depositing the women on the carved stone as their men proceeded further to the stairs leading to the Court of the Israelites. Though Kundry could not see it, she remembered that yet other flights of stairs led to the Court of the Priests, where the actual sacrifices took place, and the sanctuary within.

Billows of smoke, sweet with the smell of burning flesh and incense, wafted from the Court of the Priests. Animals screamed in panic and sudden agony, mercifully cut short by the practiced strokes of the priests. Kundry remembered how, in her earliest days with Klingsor, he had compared the Temple with the rites he had seen in Moab and Carthage; she had been horrified, but not for long. Someone muttered something about how "even Gentiles could sacrifice" and the story, fifty years old, but still enthralling, of how old King Herod's friend, the Roman Marcus Agrippa, had offered a hecatomb. The teller almost spat at the name of one of the *kittim*, the hated Roman overlords, then recollected her place.

Fire roared up and refreshed the smoke. Now it covered the heads of the men who climbed the stairs as if they walked through cloud to the peak of Sinai. They were so thickly clustered that she could not see the stairs, only bobbing, covered heads. Deep-throated chanting began once more, with the sweet voices of choristers soaring above it to the music of a double-pipe, a twelve-stringed harp, a ten-stringed lyre, and bronze cymbals. From time to time the silver trumpet and the ram's horn compelled attention.

"Surely there is no greater glory," whispered Maria. "The whole earth is full of this glory."

Her eyes looked huge, as if she had swallowed some drug to make them very deep and black. She watched the other women, who pressed and jostled as thousands thronged the court, as if a distance vast as the Wilderness of Zin separated them. The women, the chaste women and righteous women who would rejoice at seeing her brought low. Who would turn away from her as unclean—indeed, as worse than the lepers who huddled in their isolation, away from other worshipers. Lepers had a place reserved for them in God's Temple; harlots did not.

What else could Kundry or Maria expect? The women who had kissed and cosseted her in the days of her innocence had turned to scolding, bullying, and silence when Kundry had begged for their protection. Being a harlot gave one great experience, but no great opinion of people—men or women.

But there was Maria, shrewd, cynical Maria. For her the sight of the Women's Court had been enough to strip courage from her as easily as a Roman lover might strip away her garments.

Shocked into compassion, Kundry leaned forward to embrace her friend. Maria jerked away and bent to her prayers. In an instant, courtesan resembled wife resembled crone, swathed in wool and piety.

Kundry saw Maria beat her breast, "for the sin that we have sinned against thee . . ." That was not the appropriate prayer for this season. The last time Kundry had been here, she had thought Maria resigned to her lot. The visit to the Temple had been, pure and simple, an adventure, just as Maria had presented it to her. Kundry had longed to see it; very well, hetaera though she was, Kundry should see it, should enter into the Court of the Women and pray if she could.

Then, as now, she could not. Her eyes scanned the restless crowd of women, through which the men passed on their way toward the Court of the Israelites, looking for other faces that she might recognize—an old man carrying a silver cup, a young man with a sun-parched face, surrounded by friends, even the too-crafty darkness that meant Klingsor. Theatres she attended came to her mind.

The tragedy could not take place, could not turn comic until all the players were gathered, now, could it?

Beside her Maria sobbed. Kundry shook her head, thrust from her self-absorption to grief for her friend, admiration for her courage, and perhaps—who knew?—even envy. For well Kundry knew that repentance was barred to her; and she knew why.

The Passover approached. Already *he* had been here; *he* had passed like avenging fire through the Temple: *he*, whom she would see again and mock before he died.

Leaving Maria lost in her self-accusation, momentarily one with the women from whom she knew herself outcast, Kundry edged toward the stairs. As a girl, she had been lost in wonder at this place. As a woman a thousand years inured to power, experienced in shifting its times and tides as she moved through the Broceliande that had yet to be, she quivered to the power that clung even to Herod's newest stones.

And even this power, made fearsome by its association with her earliest memories, was something that she had learned in her centuries of wandering how to use. This time she would see further, she decided. She too must pass up those steps and see the players in the drama that Klingsor willed would cost her her soul once again.

She stood, rooting herself into the paving stones, drawing their strength into herself. There was power in this place, the second Temple built in Jerusalem, hallowed by the strength of the faith that generations of priests and pilgrims had brought here. She reached within herself for the core of fire that she had thought of as her own power. In this life, and in this place, she had had none: but the Kundry who lived and walked a thousand years from now had learned much sorcery. She hoped to draw on it now.

Stronger for her presence on holy ground, power tingled in the newness of the flesh she wore, cutting the necessary channels up along the centers that flowered in groin, in spine, in heart, and in throat until it pulsed behind her eyes and bloomed, ready for use, in her brain.

It was blasphemy for a woman to enter the inner Temple courts. Blasphemy was punished by death. She doubted she could die, and she must see. But there was no reason why anyone should see her. No reason why anyone could. She drew power up from the gleaming stones of the Temple. Wrapping herself in it, concealing herself in it like a veil, as if clad in an extra robe, she insinuated herself into the tide of pilgrims and let it bear her up the steps to the Court of the Israelites and past them to the Court of the Priests.

The sanctuary's gates yawned wide. Light shone within, a light that had very little to do with the gold of the vessels and fittings that Herod, father and son, had lavished on the hallows. *Put off thy shoes from off thy feet.* The compulsion was almost irresistible. It had Kundry on her knees, tears streaming down her face from the light. It was not the brightness of the eternal flame that blinded her. That was like the hour before the dawn, compared with the blaze of sanctity that it concealed.

She glanced away. A man jostled her and glared at the man next to her, who shrugged and turned away: Kundry passed unnoticed.

And then her eyes flinched away from another source of light.

This time, it was not the sanctuary nor the altar where constantly renewed streams of water sluiced away the blood of sacrifice. It was a man.

In a quiet corner, a group of men sat, studying Torah. Younger men, boys and unwed lads, stood on the periphery, listening. At the center, though, it was the center of that circle from which the light had come. It concealed the face of the tall man who sat in the midst of the scholars and travelers.

How could they not see it? Kundry wanted to demand.

They could not see her, either. They lacked her power, just as she lacked their sanctity and their hope.

Others about him fidgeted and shifted position, but not he. His very stillness compelled first attention, then respect.

The rams' horns blared. As if that were their cue, men headed for the circle of students; important men in the robes of the Pharisees or the special garments of the scribes. They bustled and shoved as if a riot went on in their midst, and were shoved back until the man who sat so still gestured: give them place.

Kundry heard the sounds of a blow, a cry of pain. Panting somewhat, the newcomers subsided.

Kundry gasped, then glanced about. No one had heard her; no one could. In their midst, a woman staggered, fighting to keep on her feet. Her garments were wrapped hastily about her, a bruise darkened one eye, and her olive skin was dark with grime and humiliation. She had fought not to be dragged to this place. Now that she was here, she sank down, the fight draining out of her with the hope. It was blasphemy for a woman to stand where she stood. And against that charge there was no appeal.

The teacher looked up. Kundry could still not make out his features, but she knew who he was. Joshua ben Joseph. The madman of the Galilee. Klingsor's enemy. The centurion's benefactor, Amfortas's king, and the magus whose death had cursed her to wander until she might repent.

She could not see his face, but she sensed stillness and calm inquiry.

"Master, a judgment, a judgment!" one of the Pharisees cried.

The quiet man tilted his head slightly.

"A woman, here? And you have brought her to me?" He looked quizzically at the sweating, self-important men, then shrugged. "By bringing her here, you seem to have condemned her already. To death for sacrilege, if nothing else."

"This woman's husband found her taken in adultery, in the very act . . ."

So? Intrigued, Kundry raised an eyebrow. The woman did not look brazen . . . *did not look like a harlot, like herself,* she might as well say. There was a scar on her chin; one eye was blackened; and she held herself like someone who has been beaten hard and often and has learned to expect no better. Kundry listened to the righteous clamor below her, then tuned it out. She knew what the Pharisees and scribes were saying: the laws of Moses commanded that a woman taken in adultery within the city walls should be taken and stoned before her father's house. She knew that too well.

Such a punishment had all but been meted out to her as well—and she had been a virgin daughter.

"You are a learned man." The most indignant man confronted the seated teacher, who did not even raise his head to acknowledge him. "What is your judgment? By the laws of Moses . . ."

It was a trap, Kundry wanted to shout. Any way the man answered, they would twist what he said and trap him.

Kundry studied the woman. She stood hopeless, like a beast of burden whose strength is outworn, who can expect now only a death blow, and who retains only the hope, in the darkness of its beast mind, that it not take too long nor hurt too much.

How could such a one sin? Kundry thought she knew. Perhaps someone had been kind to her, had smiled at her, and in simple gratitude, she had granted the one thing for which a man had ever wanted her. Taken in the act, eh? The woman's clothes did not look particularly fine; perhaps her husband preferred to be a widower, betrayed by a faithless wife, to divorcement and return of a (probably) scanty dowry.

She was certain that this Joshua could see the signs of hard use, testimony to the fact that this woman was no wanton. She was equally certain that if he said so, he was as lost as she.

He leaned forward, stooping down with the ease of a man long used to sitting around fires in the desert, and he wrote upon the paving stones as if that were the most important activity in the world.

"Did you hear us? What is to be done?"

The voices, querulous in their virtue, beat upon the man's bowed shoulders, but he ignored them. As they rose, as their description of the woman and her act grew more inventive, their victim flinched.

At that, the teacher looked up, mildly as if asked a simple question by a child. "A judgment? This is my judgment," he said calmly. "Wise men all, you know the law. He that is without sin among you, let him cast the first stone."

He looked from Pharisee to scribe, from scribe to Pharisee to outraged, sweating husband, who stood with jaw clenched. Then, as if releasing them all, he bent and returned to writing with a fingertip upon the paving.

The husband muttered, growling like a dog balked of his meat by a larger beast. A scribe, averting his eyes from the bare skin of the woman's shoulder, followed him. Gradually, the crowd dispersed the way ink, dropped into a bowl of water, dissipates and vanishes. Finally, only the woman stood in the center of the students, facing the silent man who wrote upon the ground.

He looked up, as if bemused that the tide of angry men had ebbed away. "Woman," he asked, his voice gentle, "where are the men who were your accusers? Has no man condemned you?"

She swallowed, tried for speech, and swallowed again. Glancing round, she saw herself alone, and her face lit with a wild relief. "None, lord," she faltered.

He caught and held her eyes with his own. Though Kundry could not see his expression for the light of power that shimmered about him, the woman could; and what she saw reassured her. She would not die for adultery nor for the crime of being forced to stand where she now stood.

"Then go," he told her. "Quickly. And sin no more."

She stood incredulous in the midst of men who gaped, then began to mutter among themselves, and might have stood there until they took action, had her rescuer not gestured, a tiny movement of his hand: Go. Be gone. Sin no more.

Then knowledge of her freedom released her feet. Drawing her robes about her, she fled.

Kundry could bear to watch no further. She dodged away and ran back the way she had come, down toward the Court of the Women.

From the corner of her eye she saw a flash of darkness—Klingsor, again, talking to the same richly garbed man she had seen him with earlier. He gestured behind him at the man who now sat alone, concentrating on the invisible words that he still wrote. Then Klingsor jerked his head, almost as if he sensed Kundry's presence.

She gasped and fled. On the steps, she met the woman whose life had been spared. She grasped her hand and, in the instant when the woman gasped with fear and the gasp could have become a wail of grief—*to be stopped now just when I was sure I was safe!*—flung the mantle of her power over her until they were safely down the stairs forbidden to their sex.

Releasing them both, she pressed coins into the woman's work-worn hand. "I know you," she said. "Your husband beats you. I should return to my father's house, if I were you." Command underlay the simple words, and she did not turn aside until she saw the woman nod, thrust the coins into her breast, and vanish.

That too did not happen before, Kundry told herself. *How many changes can I make in my past life, before time itself changes?*

Drained of power, Kundry felt curiously limp and sweaty. She wanted a bath and fragrant oils, chilled wine to drink, and fruit. Instead she turned to find Maria, who huddled on the pavement, still as a rock with water streaming down its face toward a deep pool.

"Maria?" Kundry touched her shoulder, a gesture that Maria allowed this time. More than that: she flung herself into Kundry's arms as if in sore need of a woman's comfort. About her, women murmured sympathy: weeping at prayers was not that uncommon. Look at Hannah; and God rewarded her with a son who became a prophet. This woman too prayed and wept, and surely now, all would be well.

Maria drank in the consolation as thirstily, surely, as the Israelites must have drunk when Moses struck the rock in the wilderness and sweet water sprang forth. They did not know, they did not know; and still, their words comforted her.

Kundry felt the same urge to laugh that had always damned her. But this had all happened before, as she remembered. Last time, she had not laughed. She could restrain herself this time, too.

Finally, Maria rested quiescent on her shoulder.

"Are you well? We should go."

Maria remained silent for a moment, then nodded. Something danced at the corner of her mouth, and Kundry knew that whatever grief had seized her, it was under control for now. Taking her friend's arm, she guided her down from the Court of the Women, out across the bridge, and toward the arrogant geometry of the Roman road that ran from north to south in the upper city.

"Do you still want to go to the Cardo?" Kundry asked.

"We left our gowns in the silk shop there, didn't we?" Now, Maria's earlier tears might never have occurred; the other woman flung back the folds of her robe from her glossy hair, earning a scandalized glare from passers-by. She tossed her head, resuming her old role, her old bravado with as much ease as she would shift these sober, heavy garments for lavish silks. "We have to get our clothes. This wool is chafing me raw."

10

FROM the hideous days when Klingsor was teaching her Latin, Kundry remembered a description of a creature that rendered her nights equally hideous: Rumor clacking away with its thousand tongues about a queen who was soon to lose life and reputation. Still guilt-ridden at her flight from home and law, Kundry had dreamt repeatedly of an unclean bird swooping down to snatch her away. The story of how the latest of the prophets to emerge from the desert and stun Jerusalem saved a woman from being stoned spread so rapidly that Kundry all but thought that Rumor, that foul thing, had to be involved.

By the time that Maria and Kundry had reached the Cardo, the Roman road that divided the New City like the hinge for which it was named, the story was being whispered. They strolled down the paved road, carefully, casually peering into the arcade of expensive shops that lined it on either side; and the story buzzed from man to man, growing with the teller. By the time they reached the silk merchant who would willingly allow hetaerae with money to toss away on a prank (as they told him) to change clothes in the upper loft of his shop, the story had grown so wild that Kundry, who had seen it take place, could barely recognize it.

Maria, however, turned pensive. "When you . . . when you came here," she said, "didn't you think it was for always and that . . ."

"I felt as if I had fallen into Gehenna," Kundry agreed. "Pain everlasting, and no way out."

"What if . . . ?" She shook her head. "Never mind. Let

us dress and be about our business. I take it that you could
not avoid dining with this Simon either?"

Kundry, matching her courage, also matched her grimace
of distaste.

"Well, then, let us dazzle him—and his womenfolk, who
will doubtless peer at us and profess themselves shocked at
anything we do!"

For the lower city, fish-scale pearls were good enough.
Kundry tossed strands of them over throat and wrist, hung
them from her ears until she shimmered, then posed before
her friend.

"Well?"

"You look as if you want to cause a riot," Maria commented. "Put on your cloak."

She did the same, and they walked past the bowing shop-
keeper into the street. Though long shafts of light fell from
overhead, gilding even the filthiest detail as it touched it, the
Cardo was still thronged with people eager for the best
bargain, the loudest dispute, the most scandalous rumor.
Jew rubbed shoulders with pagan, local, Greek, or Roman.
Wealthy merchants kept one hand upon their purses and
looked anxiously about for their servants. Ladies constantly touched their jewelry to make certain that no one
had snatched it; as cloaks and veils shifted under anxious
fingers, thieves closed in, studying the wares offered by
pedestrians.

This being holiday time, the shops, too, brought forth
their choicest wares—gold from Ophir, opals and tur-
quoise, fine papyrus, silks and cottons brought by caravan
from the very-far-away, and, from the incense routes of
North Africa, jars and beakers of balm: frankincense,
myrrh, and spikenard. Taken by the fine alabaster of a box
of ointment, Maria bargained briefly, then bore her prize
off.

A sudden uproar whirled Kundry and Maria around.

"A plague upon the house of Boethus, a plague upon
their clubs! A plague on the house of Annas, a plague on
their spying!"

A group of students, too poor, really, to frequent the

Cardo, formed a wedge and charged down its center, chanting of plagues and confusion.

Maria groaned. "Do you see your tribune? If those fools keep it up, there'll be a riot."

They stepped up their pace. Maria's cloak fell open, and a splendor of indigo silk brought a disapproving hiss from two women who passed, unattractively hunched over.

"There!" Kundry said. "At the corner." She had always hated litters, claimed they made her as sick as a woman bearing a three-months' child; in that moment, she would have welcomed one.

A shriek made everyone stop.

"Sicarii!" Impossible that the twisted street could grow more crowded, but at once, the tiny street boiled as men sought escape.

"Quick!" Kundry's tribune and Maria's latest protector leapt forward, with a rasp of steel as their guards drew short swords. Togas were draped for dignity, not speed, and conquerors, in any case, should not flee; but all Jerusalem feared the Sicarii.

Someone else screamed, a death shout, freeing them from their stillness. A copper stink of blood rose in the street. Once again the street erupted into frenzy, then cleared just as suddenly—except for the tangle of robes, stained across the back where a dagger's hilt showed.

"Let's move!" It took two guards to shock Maria from the stillness into which she had fallen. Someone darted forward, and she swung at him with the alabaster box of ointment she had bought just a short while ago. Her assailant darted back, and someone jerked thumbs up at her in compliment.

Kundry drew a pin from her hair and brandished it at a street youth who had reached out to seize her necklace. It was not real, but suddenly it took on unreal significance: she would not lose even fish scales to thugs, no! Spitting and swearing in languages that she should not have known—for they had yet to come into use—she ran at the boy. Faced with more than he bargained for, he backed up; and by that time, their path was clear and one of the Romans had even extricated a dagger from the folds of his toga.

"No time to fight! Run!"

They hastened through the darkening twists of the Lower City until they brought up sharply before the house of Simon, the wealthy Pharisee who had watched Kundry dance the night before. Behind them, the screams, clatters, and crashes of riot swelled, accompanied by outraged howls that told Kundry, at least, that the local thief population had not let the opportunity to loot slip by them.

The street had grown silent. Outside the house, the Romans adjusted the folds of their white togas, each bearing the narrow stripe, crimson or purple, that boasted the birth—respectable or noble—of its wearer. The women pinched their cheeks and reddened their lips. To Kundry's surprise, Maria still held the box she had purchased. Seeing Kundry's eyes upon it, she shrugged and tucked it into her gown. Trust Maria not to lose something of value!

"Good man, this Simon, for a Jew," Kundry's consort said. "For a Pharisee, he's amazingly easy to deal with."

"Don't let any of them fool you by moaning he can't wear a toga or by quoting Virgil," said Maria's tribune. "Pharisee or Sadduccee, all these Jews hate Romans. Some are just better at hiding it, that's all."

Neither of the Romans glanced at the women with them. A *wonder, to carp about a man, then eat his food,* Kundry thought. She thought forward in time, remembering Saracens who would not betray a guest, a king who would not dine till he had heard of some wonder, a king whose men could not dine until he had performed a wonder. She had lain in that king's arms, then betrayed him. How could he perform that wonder now?

This Pharisee, for all his birth and place, was Romanized enough to have set a slave at the door, greeting them and exhorting them to step high over the threshold, right foot first, and thus avoid bad luck.

If only you knew, fool, Kundry thought at the slave, but lifted a careful foot in any case. Ideas had begun to glimmer in her thoughts, like the first glimpse of golden shore after a long sea voyage.

11

SIMON the Pharisee greeted them, or at least the two tribunes, with an awkward obeisance. Kundry, schooled in a thousand years of such gestures, found the attempt to combine a Roman salute with the more supple obeisances of the East ludicrous, accompanied as it was by staring eyes, a sweaty face, and apologies for the riot.

Of course, no women from the house were present. She heard a whisper from a gallery, and firmly suppressed the urge to glance upward and raise an ironic brow.

From the dining room (which Simon referred to with a flourish as his triclinium) came voices discussing that very thing. Rumor again, Kundry thought, exercising its thousand clattering tongues. Some of them were probably waiting to lap at dinner right now: savory smells reminded her how long it had been since she had eaten.

Simon held his newest guests outside the dining room, clapping his hands for bustling servants with towels and water, offering Kundry and Maria rooms in which to recover from their ordeal, clothes . . . Kundry caught Maria's eye. If Simon's womenfolk heard that offer, he would be in more danger from them than anyone in the house was from the Sicarii.

Then a voice brought Kundry up short. Ignoring Simon's laments about the parlous state of the city these days, this close to the Passover, she edged into the dining room. Immediately, she saw that Simon's calling it a triclinium was more than the boast of an assimilationist; though it was not yet Passover, Simon had all his guests reclining. Places on the couches had been set even for the women, though at more austere, "old" Roman houses, women sat upright.

Leaning in the place of honor was an old man. Beside him . . . it was the voice of the man beside him that had drawn her. She had heard that voice only that morning in the Court of the Israelites; but that had been when she herself walked veiled in power, and a stronger force had hidden his face from her.

"That is Joseph from Arimathea, a tin merchant, newly come from journeying."

"Who?" She had thought she had more control than to breathe that out like a Roman daughter at her first games, enamored of her first fighter. Simon flushed beneath his beard at having to speak directly to a woman, let alone one such as she. Nevertheless, he was answering.

"At his right is . . ." Simon shook his head. "The guest of my guest must be my guest as well." Clearly, the idea discomfited him, though he fought against anger or embarrassment. "You may have heard him on Olivet, or heard *of* him. Joshua ben Joseph."

Now, at last, Kundry could study the man. He was taller than the average Judaean. He wore his dark hair long as befit a man of Nazareth, even if he were not a Nazarene; he had long features, well cut, but with a hint of melancholy; eyes deep-set in sockets around which the flesh was creased as if he had stared too long into the desert sun. It was the eyes that held her. Though debate crackled and waged war about him, Joshua ben Joseph's eyes were serene, though filled with light, like water running fast over smooth stones.

Where had she seen such a face before? Add age, a beard, a look of discontent amounting nigh to anguish; and she had her answer: Amfortas. He too was of King David's line, though far removed and all too fallible.

Time flickered before Kundry's eyes, replacing the confident ascetic who sat beside the old merchant with a creature that could barely be called human. Its shoulders were torn and bleeding, its face swollen and congested with blood, and its hair matted with sweat. It was impossible that one should become the other: and yet they were the same. She shuddered, and quickly accepted wine.

"A priest, is he not?" Maria had joined Kundry at the door and appeared to study the young man with the cool

hauteur of her trade, as if she meant to bargain for him. "Is
he very rich, too?"

Simon laughed awkwardly. "Lady, he is the merchant's
guest, and rich only in blood. Though he is the son of a
carpenter, he is of King David's line, or so they say."

"They say a lot," muttered Kundry's escort.

"I beg you, bring us within." Maria swayed up to Simon
and widened great dark eyes. "I am very hungry."

The man recoiled and led them within.

As they entered, the talk of riot rose and swelled. Simon
listened for a moment to the calmest voice in the room.
Visibly, he swelled, as if angry, but recollected himself.
Asserting his prerogative as host, he stepped forward and
interjected, "Surely, if men die, you too, Joshua, you must
accept part of the blame—and you a man of peace. How do
you reconcile the two?"

Joshua leaned forward. Just thus, he had leaned forward
and written on the ground as men had brought before him
a woman whose blood they hoped to shed. When he finally
spoke, his voice was the one Kundry remembered. "Men
think, perhaps, that it is peace that I have come to cast upon
the world. They do not know that it is dissension that I have
come to cast upon the earth: fire, sword, and war."

His voice was very calm, very soft, as if he were more
used to speaking his thoughts to sand and stars than to
human beings. Yet it carried, just as the sound of a human
voice carries over the desert at night, stunning the unwary
listener or reassuring a wanderer that help is at hand.

He glanced over at Simon. His host was sweating by now
and glancing nervously at the two Romans. Joseph of Arimathea watched the byplay with sardonic amusement. They
indeed were nodding at the quality of the wine, which was
Falernian rather than the product of the land, a product
most Romans characterized as rough swill. It was being
poured into silver goblets which Simon, with an attempt at
too-elaborate Latin, asked his guests to keep.

The Romans nodded at each other at this attempt to ape
their ways. Surreptitiously, one hefted a silver cup: of good
weight. In the wealthiest—therefore most sought-after—
Roman households, the cups given as presents would have

been more elaborate, and cupbearers, pretty boys or girls, would have accompanied them. Simon was neither as Romanized nor, to his credit, as corrupt as he affected. Despite the rumors that flocked through Jerusalem, befouling all they touched, some Pharisees were not.

Servants brought in the various courses: dishes of pigeons, doves, fish baked in peppers, and the golden, crusty breads that would soon be replaced by the flat, unleavened rounds used at Passover ever since the Flight from Egypt to commemorate the Jews' haste and wandering.

As host, Simon tore off bread from a loaf and passed it to his guests, a sign that the meal might start.

Murmuring words that Kundry remembered from her girlhood (Maria's lips moved in agreement, and he smiled encouragement at her as he would to a child), Joshua drank and nodded. "I have had this wine before," he replied to a question. "At my friend Zacchaeus's. It is too fine for a poor man to drink often. But the cup"—he raised it appreciatively, and light glistened from its polished, perfect curves—"I thank you for this offering."

There was a long, embarrassing pause, embarrassing, that was, for some of the Jewish guests because murmurs brought home the fact that Zacchaeus was a publican. If Kundry might judge from Joseph of Arimathea's tolerant smile, such awkward pauses were nothing new.

"I thought men of Nazareth never drank wine," one of Simon's guests put in.

Joshua shook his head gently. "Only those of us under vows to abstain. Some will refuse to eat with people who do not share those vows. As you can see, I do not agree. Surely, overindulgence has been bad, since the time of Noah, when it led to his disgrace; but surely, too, there is no harm in a cup of wine at a wedding or a feast."

"Still debating, are you?" Joseph commented with a warm chuckle that made Kundry abandon her wariness and decide she liked him. "I mind that in Thule, he was ever speaking to the people, arguing even with the priests . . ."

"Especially with the priests," Joshua put in with a smile.

"You were in Thule?" demanded a tribune. "How was it?"

"Cold, cold and rainy as your own historians say. But the tin is there, and the trade for wine is very good."

Joseph reached out and touched the silver cup that stood at his place and that he had refused to allow to be filled.

"I hope my host will forgive me," the old merchant said. "But this is a fine gift. By your leave, I shall save it to use on the Passover."

Light glinted off the empty cup as it had all the others, yet it drew Kundry's attention. *That* cup. Kundry had seen it in her dreams. She had followed it as she hurtled down the centuries. It did not glow, as she had expected, with a supernal red flame. In this time and place, it was still just a cup. Nonetheless, she could not take her eyes from the way light glanced off its smooth surfaces and pooled in its depths.

"You are a scrupulous guest," Joshua told the older man. "As taxing as I am myself."

"Still, drinking and dining with those publicans!" Simon drew a laugh with the wordplay, somewhat to his relief.

"And why not? They are sons of Israel. Surely, they too can feel love, and remorse . . ."

"At least this time you washed your hands," Joseph cut in deftly. "I mind the time you told that old—the one who reproached you and your students for not washing before breaking bread, and you accused him too of breaking commandments."

A laugh went round the table, though Joseph had implied that the man who had reproached the young teacher had been a Pharisee, possibly even a kinsman of Simon. Simon shrugged and gestured for more food to be brought. Kundry wondered if he could afford to discard the plates, cups, bowls, and platters that had been used by outsiders: somehow, she thought not.

"We were all very hungry, and no basins had been provided," Joshua replied.

"I understood"—Maria's voice had a breathy hesitance that Kundry had never before heard from her lips—"that your father is a carpenter. And yet you left his workbench for Thule?"

"My mother's husband is dead now. Here in Judaea, or

far away, even as a youth, I have ever been about my father's business. To rebuke a man overly secure in his own righteousness or to sail with Master Joseph here north to what you of Rome call Thule—it is all the same."

"What did you do in Thule?" one of the tribunes asked. He sat up still, and when he was offered wine, he took it as if in a daze.

"Earned my bread and that of my mother and brothers, whom Master Joseph's firm supported while I was away. Though I am a landsman, I learned to assist the shipwrights when they needed woodwork. When we reached Thule, I helped to build a shelter that we could live in—much as we do during the Feasts of Tabernacles. I warrant," he added with pardonable craftsman's pride, "that it will still be livable when you return."

Joseph nodded as if to say, "No doubt."

"As has been said, I spent much time speaking to the priests of that realm. They are not just in Thule . . . you would call it Britannia." He turned courteously to address the Romans. "I found them wise and welcoming to strangers, as is our host."

One of the tribunes muttered that Caesar had found the "wise and welcoming" priests of Britannia to be maniacs who howled at his ships from the beachheads.

"*Pagan* priests," Simon put in with the Israelite's longtime disgust with the local pagans.

"Priests and priestesses, strange as it may seem."

A muttering rose from about the table, and Joshua fell silent for a moment. Then, "They are wise men and women, though, and I learned a good deal. After all, is it not written, 'Wisdom, where shall it be found?' "

The Romans shifted, not at all eager for a lesson in Jewish scripture during a feast.

"Their power stretches down almost to the Middle Sea. There is a great forest in that land, and they are wise in its ways."

Broceliande with its waving branches, its patterns of sun and shadow, stirring up ripples of time, flickered in Kundry's memory. This man had seen the one place she thought of as home! She smiled warmly at Joshua, despite her consort's restraining hand. He smiled back as one might at a child.

Kundry's plate was heaped with all manner of rich food, food unlike anything she might have imagined in the days when she remained a maid, in the home of her family; but she had little appetite for it.

"Pagans, nonetheless," another harsh voice accused from across the table.

Joshua shrugged. "Pagans too may be righteous. There was Alexander, who spared this City as"—his eyes went blank, opening onto distances so vast that they reminded Kundry of that pit of time down which she had hurtled—"some others may not. We have the words of Jeremiah and Ezekiel to remind us. And sometimes, it is our enemies, not ourselves, who follow our laws the best. I remember coming upon an inn near Jericho . . ."

Kundry started. That was her old country. Did this Joshua's eyes rest upon her? She felt as if they had pierced the careful defenses of false gems, of silk, of a courtesan's makeup to expose a frightened country girl.

"In it, I found a man. He had been beaten by thieves, he told me, stripped and left for dead on the road. But he was strong, that man, and he cried out. A priest and a Levite, from whom he had every right to expect help, averted their eyes and passed him by. It was, believe it or not, a Samaritan who saw him, bound up his wounds, picked him up in his arms, and carried him to the inn, where he made provision for the innkeeper to provide for the man until he was fit to travel.

"Who of the three men who saw the wounded man do you think was the best neighbor?"

The silence grew oppressive. None of the Jewish guests wanted to admit that one of the hated Samaritans had bested men of the priestly families; and yet it was undeniable.

Joseph of Arimathea looked pained, and the younger man held up a hand, shapely and well kept except for the scars of his trade. "It shows you that there is mercy, like a sweet spring in the wilderness, even in our enemies."

"It is true, then?" Maria broke in, though her escort

frowned. Entertainment should wait until it is called for. "There can be repentance, forgiveness for even such as I?"

Kundry fought an urge to the wild laughter that had always heralded disaster for her. The expression on Simon's face! Here he had succeeded in bringing actual Romans of no mean birth or position to his house, and conversation at his dinner had turned from one awkwardness to another until now, when even one of the hetaerae imported for mirth and pleasure had turned to the very religious excesses that men like he tried to conceal from their conquerors.

For a long moment, Joshua merely studied Maria. In a moment, Kundry thought wildly, he would lean forward, dip his finger in the wine cup at Joseph of Arimathea's place, and write upon the table. His eyes brightened, and he smiled: the same bright haze that Kundry had seen becloud his features shone over them and hid them once more.

"You wear my mother's name," he told her. "It is wisely asked, 'Who can find a virtuous woman? For her worth is far above rubies.'" Those were the old words, the beloved words that each Jewish woman dreamed one day of hearing her husband say to her in the presence of her family. They were words that Maria, and Kundry too, had given up all hope of ever hearing, save as a reproach.

They brought tears to Maria's eyes and down her painted cheeks. Unabashed, she wiped them with her hands, and bravely met the man's eyes. "I beg you, do not mock me," she whispered.

"I mock you? You asked me if there were forgiveness. And I tell you that there is forgiveness, not just enough for one, but for seven; for seven times seven. Nay, more; for seventy times seven."

Joshua looked at Maria, really looked at her as if seeing the woman beneath the hetaera's garb and now-blotched cosmetics. "And I offer you yet more: whatever you have done, no matter how scarlet your sins, let them be as white as snow. It is all forgotten, sister."

"If I believed that . . ." Maria whispered to herself, her eyes as enormous as they had been that morning in the Court of the Women, when she had stared at the mothers, wives, and daughters of families and, Kundry realized, broken her heart knowing that she could nevermore blend into their midst and be accepted. "Oh, if I believed that . . ." Her voice broke as a child's voice breaks after punishment when it is called back to eat its dinner, forgiven, and restored to grace.

"Believe it," said Joshua. His eyes widened too, and Kundry had the sensation of staring into vast space where fire and comfort mingled. She shuddered. Once again, she had the sensation of being flung, as Klingsor had thrust her, into a whirlwind of hundreds of years. Her breath came fast. Then, it eased. This was different. This ocean of time that she saw revealed could only comfort her; it was power, moving upon the deeps of time and bringing forth a new birth.

That new birth, though, was for Maria, not Kundry.

The older hetaera rose. With trembling fingers she plucked the pins, some with heads of amber, some of fine Egyptian faience, from her hair and stripped it free of its plaits and curls. It hung almost to her knees. A fluke of the lamplight allowed Kundry to see the streaks of gray that henna usually concealed.

She stripped gems from her ears, wrists, fingers, and throat and set them quietly down at her place—a gesture more matter-of-fact than dramatic. A fat pearl earring spun and rolled across the table, and Joseph of Arimathea caught it and put it back.

"I had not known until now," she said to Joshua. "These are real. I beg you, sell them, and buy food. Redeem girls lest, like me, they . . ."

"You shall do that for me," Joshua said.

Maria's fragile composure shattered. She went around the couches and crouched behind Joshua, at his feet, clutching them, looking like Klingsor's descriptions of slaves in Persia or the nomes of Egypt, privileged to salute Pharaoh by kissing his feet.

Weeping, she laid her face against the man's feet. They were dusty from the street; believing he had to do only with Romans and renegades, Simon or his servants had neglected to provide the customary basins of water for washing.

From a fold in her robe—all its tawdry elaboration picked out cruelly by the lamps—she pulled out the alabaster box she had bought only that day. A tinge of blood still sullied it from when Maria had used it to strike out during the riot. She wiped it away on indigo silk and cracked the wax of its seal.

Fragrance filled the room, cleansing it of the smells of food and oil and sweat. Still she crouched at Joshua ben Joseph's feet and wept until they were clean. Then she dried them with her hair and poured the ointment—all of it—over them.

How could she repent so easily and know that forgiveness was hers? Kundry fought back burning envy.

Then the faces—dumbfounded, appalled, or totally confused—in the dining room drew her attention, and she struggled once again to fight back laughter.

12

HIS patience at an end, Simon rose from his couch, muttering into his beard. Trained to catch nuances of voice and manner, Kundry made out his words. "I have borne with Joseph and his follies long enough. If this man truly were a prophet, he would have known who and what manner of woman this is who touches him. She is a harlot."

Maria's weeping neither increased nor abated. Her sorrows could not be worsened by any words of Simon's.

As he had in the Temple, Joshua looked unperturbed, either by Maria's actions or Simon's accusations. He glanced down at the table, as if collecting his words from the broken fragments of bread and fishes that had not yet been removed, then turned to his host.

"Simon," he said finally, "I have somewhat to say to you."

"Say on, *Master*," Simon replied.

Joseph of Arimathea flickered a warning glare at his young guest, but shrugged when Joshua disregarded it.

"You are a man of business," he began—perhaps an insult in itself. "So you will understand this. There was a certain creditor who had two debtors. The one owed five hundred shekels, the other fifty.

"And when they had nothing to pay, he frankly forgave them both."

Simon muttered into his beard that that was poor practice, for the first time during the whole disastrous meal in complete sympathy with the Romans.

"Wish I could find a banker like that!" one exclaimed.

"Do you recall the time Marcus Brutus charged almost

fifty percent to—I forget what city?" said another, who was already flushed with wine.

Disregarding the interruption, Joshua went on. "He forgave them their debts. Now, tell me therefore, which of them will love him most?"

Simon chewed his lip, clearly displeased at being back in the schoolroom. "I suppose," he muttered, as if the words were coins paid to a creditor, "the one to whom he forgave most."

Joshua nodded. "You have judged rightly."

Then he turned to Maria and raised her. "Do you see this woman?" he demanded of Simon. "I came as a guest into your house, but you gave me no water to wash my feet."

Joseph of Arimathea put out a hand as if to stop Joshua, and even one of the Romans pursed his lips to whistle.

"This woman has washed my feet with tears and wiped them with her hair. You gave me no kiss of greeting, but she has not ceased to kiss my feet. You did not anoint my head with oil, but this woman has anointed my feet with precious ointment.

"So it is as I told her, and I tell you. Her sins, which are many, are forgiven, for she loved much. But I also tell you: those to whom little is forgiven love little."

Maria's face shone with almost the luster Kundry had seen on Joshua's face at the Temple. The same light flickered above it now, transforming both of them, setting them apart from the other guests in the room, though a shadow of that light cast a gleam on the old merchant's hair.

"Your sins are forgiven," he said gently to Maria.

"Who do you think you are, to forgive sins?" Simon's confusion was building up into a full-throated roar. Maria's abandoned escort made a gesture acknowledging a shrewd blow in the Games.

Joshua turned his shoulder on the indignant Pharisee.

"Your faith has saved you," he told Maria. "Go and sin no more."

She gathered up the gems that she had placed upon the table and thrust them into her robe. "These for the poor," she said.

"As you yourself decided."

A twist or two of the dark fabric secured it about her: already she looked less like a courtesan and more like a woman who had been caught and disheveled in a riot.

Without being told, Kundry knew that Maria would sell her trinkets now, sell them to buy food. So much for her lectures on thrift! Now, her savings would go the same way as her gems. And then what? There were orders outside the city, settlements where people who hungered and thirsted for God lived apart from the world. Perhaps she would go to one of them.

"There is a need . . ." Kundry heard Joshua's voice, yet did not see him move his lips. The words sounded like an assignation, and Maria's eyes gleamed as if a long-awaited lover summoned her; yet Kundry would have wagered her own soul, had it not been lost already, that no such meaning was meant.

"Enough!" Simon shouted.

Quickly, all rose, the Romans laughing to themselves. This would provide high entertainment in the upper city— the Pharisee rebuked by a madman and a harlot in his own home. She abandoned any thought of reclaiming her cloak from the confused servants, and followed Maria out into the night.

"Where will you go?" she asked.

Maria's face still glowed, though her tears had washed the cosmetics from it and she looked her full age. Her eyes went strange, and she mumbled words Kundry could not understand.

She understood their import, though. Maria had ceased to be a whore. This very day, a new prophet had risen up.

She could only imagine what the Pharisees would say to that. It would be like hounds yapping at the hunt—with Simon leading the pack.

Maria's hands fluttered and her body twitched. "Possessed!" someone cried from the back of the dining room and made a pagan sign against demons that would certainly have earned a beating if Simon had not been so busy withdrawing himself from contagion. His hands made shooing motions incongruous in a man of his age, robes, and girth; even the Romans hastened to leave, and the heavy door of his house shut as if it were the gates of the Temple itself against the unrighteous.

Kundry stifled a shriek of laughter. Best not think that way. Compunction seized her; Maria had always been a friend, and so Kundry owed something to the man who had restored her to the self she had always wanted.

She slipped past Maria to Joshua where he stood outside Simon's house, its door now most firmly closed against them all. From the shadows, several young men, then more, emerged. Though they wore the coarse robes of the poorest Galileans, they stood about him like a guard of honor.

One, whose red hair and black beard glinted in the torchlight, made as if to stop her as she came up to his leader. With a headshake, Joshua forestalled the man.

"She means no harm, Judas," he told him.

You would not say that if you knew me.

The man Judas stepped back, slowly. Kundry had to brush against him to approach his leader.

After all, Joshua had called her harmless before and been wrong. He had been wrong last time, as she remembered; when this fearless young man, finer than any she had ever met, struggled and sagged on the cross, his face battered past any human semblance, she had laughed.

But he could not know that; it had yet to happen.

Only she could not shake from her mind the idea—wrought upon her by the centuries between her laughter and the punishment that returned her to relive her sin—that this man could see not just the past and the future, but all possible futures.

"Rabbi," she began, then could not go on. After mocking him, after so long unredeemed, impenitent, how dared she?

He smiled at her, and she forgot her despair for a greater need.

"You have made an enemy," she warned Joshua.

He shook his head as if amused by a child. "No. I have merely caused an enemy to reveal himself."

To the accompaniment of scandalized hisses, he held out a hand. "And you? Maria shall be one of my companions, my disciples, as people are fond enough to call them. She would be glad of a sister's presence, I am certain."

Light seemed to fill that hand, light and all the hope and trust in the world. If she took it, if she could bring herself to take it, there might be forgiveness, even for her. It had been so easy for Maria to be forgiven.

Maria does not bear my weight of sins.

Joshua's words, "Her sins, which are many, are forgiven; for she loved much," resonated in her ears.

She had loved Amfortas, whom she knew to lie in torment and dishonor because she had allowed herself to love where she had been ordered only to entrap.

What good was love if it betrayed you?

A cough came from the shadows, where a darker shadow stood, like an assassin choosing his moment. Night wrapped it like a shroud, a darkness so opaque that it turned aside the light that spilled from this Joshua's hand and face and shone in Maria's eyes.

Klingsor . . . he had followed her, and he would expect her now to follow him. What rites would he expect her to perform—or what boasts must she listen to this time?

If he laid a hand on her, for lust or for power, she thought she would slay herself.

Still that outstretched hand . . . oh God, if only she dared take it.

What right have you to call on God? You laughed! Was that her voice in her head or Klingsor's? She shook her head, as if the demons Maria was accused of harboring had gotten into her mind and heart and spun poisonous webs over her wits and senses.

Her Roman moved as if to retrieve her, but she repudiated him with a glance of pure hate. "Crazy women, these Jews," he muttered. "Sure you won't change your mind?"

Kundry spat after him.

He shook his head and disappeared into the night.

"Child . . . " began Joseph of Arimathea. "You know where to find us. Do you need help? You could sell this . . ."

What he drew from his dark robe had the glint of silver—the cup Simon had given him, that he pledged to save for the Passover, and that Kundry had seen every night in her guiltiest fancies for more years than this Joseph could comprehend.

That least of all!

Kundry recoiled with a scream that was part laugh, part sob.

"What ails you, woman?" Joseph approached her, unafraid, even though Kundry herself would have said that a woman who screamed so because a man wished to help her was probably possessed by a devil—or had reason to fear all men.

He was an old man, a kind man. He deserved better of her than shrieks and madness. She forced herself to composure.

"It is none of your worry, Master," Kundry spoke huskily. "I am not worth your efforts. No!" she cried when he moved toward her. "I beg you, leave me alone!"

"You will come back to us," Joseph said. "All the world knows where to find me. Seek me out, if you need me. Or ask my friend Lazarus for aid. He owes our friend Joshua his life, and his sisters would succor you."

The idea that other women, women who were not Maria (now barred from her forever), would help her, rather than spit on her and drive her away, almost threw her into another paroxysm of laughter. But she remembered: Joseph had traveled far. He had met and liked men and women of all kinds. If he said he would accept her, he would.

And she could go. She had been offered, and she could go; and it would all happen anew—*not* as it had happened before.

Sensing refusal in her abstraction, Joseph turned, walking after Joshua and his friends and leaving Kundry alone outside Simon's house.

She stared after him until the shadows had swallowed up even the hem of his garment.

The Roman had left her to her own stubbornness and such safety as she could provide herself. And in the shadows, Klingsor and his hungers waited. So many people, each with his ideas of how to rule her life; and she herself, with her hard-won knowledge of how it had been, how it must be again, and again, and again . . .

Must it?

A familiar charnel stink made her lunge back.

Even as Klingsor reached out a pale hand to draw her close to him, Kundry screamed. Insatiable hunger gave his face the look of a maddened jackal.

She tore free and ran down the twisted streets, steep as stairs, into the lower city.

That also *did not happen before*, she thought in wonder. Then a beast's fear, a beast's speed, and a beast's will to survive though hunters pursue it closely possessed her.

13

BENEATH the disapproving gaze of the moon, Kundry ran through Jerusalem, looking for a lair. She feared the light. Behind her, as she ran, came cries.

"Thief!" Did they mean her? She ran faster, terror-stricken by the deadly old cry, though she had stolen nothing.

"Fire!" She had set no flame, save in men's hearts, nor ever would, but in a city as crowded as Jerusalem, the cry of "fire" could mean a death sentence for the accused.

"Help!" But it was not for her.

Help *had* been offered her, but to take it, to take any of the hands outstretched to control her, would set her on a path she would rather die than walk again. Panting, she brought up against a rough stone wall. When the pain in her chest from her rush down through the city subsided, a sharper pang remained in mind and heart: help had been offered even her by people who might see her only as someone needing help, deserving it—not as a pawn or victim.

Joseph of Arimathea's face with its smile and its web of lines shone before her eyes, followed by Maria's and Joshua's. Joseph would help her out of kindness; but the other two, she feared the other two worse than she feared Klingsor. Their power was greater. If she took their outstretched hands, if she let them touch her, that power would flow into her, and the *Kundry* she was, that she had suffered with for all these years, would fly upward from trouble like a spark until it darkened into ash and vanished on the night wind. She would be something else, not herself; and she had spent too long in the mold she knew to break it and change.

Again she fled, more afraid of gentleness and offers of
help than of Rome or even Klingsor.

This close to the Passover, power quivered throughout
Jerusalem the way she had sensed it the day before in the
Temple. Even now, in the night, people crowded the narrow streets, newcomers to the city in search of food and
family and shelter, either their accustomed lodgings or what
hovels they could find. It took all Kundry's strength to hide
herself in their midst; and the power helped.

No woman dressed like her, in the sweaty tatters of finery
once fit for the upper city, might wander its underside safe
from thieves, or from the law that sought to protect the
humble against the vicious. Once, she was spotted by a
group of herdsmen still reeking of their flocks, but alert
enough to raise a cry of "Harlot!" Whether they hoped to
turn her in or use her, she did not stay to learn.

Another time, she was almost taken as a thief; one of the
stones that a boy flung bloodied her nose. A third time, and
a daggerman with spittle-moistened chin lunged at her. She
leapt aside, but lost the necklace she had worn. The pearls
spattered over the streets, and Kundry ran, lest her attacker
discover that they were false and kill her in his rage.

Thereafter, panic abated and cunning returned. The
power that Jerusalem shed, almost as a quarry sheds dust,
lay before her to be taken, and she wished insignificance
upon herself until, in truth, she became the thief she had
been called and stole a robe much like the one she had worn
into the Court of the Women. A waterskin lay unwatched,
ready for the taking; and she washed her face and drank,
lapping from the palm of her hand.

Trading her earrings for a sum only large enough to avoid
suspicion that she had stolen them bought her bread.
Dressed decently enough and fed well enough to keep her
belly from crying out, she crept through the city. Joshua's
name seemed to be on the lips of almost every newcomer—
stories of his driving out demons, of raising the dead, even
of setting traps in words for Pharisees who took an uncertain voice and a rough robe for rustic wits.

Does he want to die? Kundry demanded, and knew that
question for one she had asked of herself. It was getting

hard to tell, now, what had and what had not happened before, just in the way that a goldsmith draws out fine gold into a wire, spinning and pulling it out incredibly fine and long. The metal responds and the wire loops round itself and round, shining—until the moment when it reaches its limit and it snaps asunder.

At any moment, had Kundry taken the help that was offered, would she now be released from the shackles of cause and effect, set free of her punishment? Would simply grasping Joshua's hand or Joseph's, accepting the help and the pity offered, have released her from the curse set on her before? Or from Klingsor's power, for that matter? Trembling with weariness now, on stone-bruised feet, she crouched in a doorway, struggling desperately to think.

It was late. She was tired. Perhaps if she sought it out, sought *them* out, the change that Maria had undergone would not hurt too badly.

Tendrils of another power crept out, seeking her, and she drew her mantle and her own will about her, crouching until the search passed by. Joshua would not use such means to hunt her down; he had all but said that she must come to him. But Klingsor had no such scruples, and he, of all beings, was the one she must avoid.

Kundry crouched, waiting for the dawn.

Banners unfurled at the horizon, showing their edges over the high walls of the city. The golden stone from which they were hewn was still black, solid, as the color at the horizon crept above walls and arches to touch the towers of the upper city. The lower city still cowered, locked in shadow, imprisoned even from the light, and Kundry cowered too, trapped within it.

She had longed, as all her people did, for Jerusalem; and now she had it. Where would she find her freedom, if not in Jerusalem? Yet now she saw that Jerusalem was yet another trap.

She kicked off her battered sandals, gilt and leather trinkets fit only for indoors or a walk from villa to litter to a feast. *Put off thy shoes from off thy feet, for the place whereon thou standest is holy ground.*

This land was *all* holy ground. Yet, it was also all a

prison, penned in by the cities and fortresses and palaces thrust upon it from the rose walls of pagan Jericho, cast down by that first Joshua and rebuilt now, to the Antonia Tower of Herod, and Masada of the old kings. Kundry hid her face from the sun. Her knowledge of the years ahead oppressed her worse than the dawn, worse than any other punishment. Jericho would fall once more, its walls cast into rubble, the rubble mounded into an anonymous hillside on which goats and sheep would graze, as ignorant as the prisoners of the countryside of what lay beneath. The Antonia Tower would be cast down and—she moaned quietly—the Temple with it. And at Masada, more than stone would fall.

Arrogant in their eagles and their arms, the fortresses of Rome would tower over the ruins of those built by Israel itself. They would fall in their turn and be replaced by stonework bearing the crescent of the Prophet and the massive towers and keeps of Outremer. Iron would shatter the holy stone that no iron should touch to secure the land for its new masters, no matter for how brief a time. And it would kill, as if a guard sought to secure a prisoner by driving a spear through his body into the land itself.

The land would groan and wither under all of them as the descendants of Abraham, Isaac, and Jacob had groaned when Pharaoh's overseers demanded that they build treasure cities at Pithom and Ramses. The very stonework was mortared with their blood and tears.

And the land bled, too. The very altars of its highest Temple were sluiced with the blood of beasts; worse hecatombs watered the land itself like the Nile in flood. Judaea was not just soil and river and rock: it was bones. All the peoples had left their bones in this place—Amalekites and Moabites and Israelites—who had even *brought* the bones of Jacob from Egypt to lie in this earth. Babylonians, Greeks, Romans, Muslims, and men from the lands Kundry knew would ride out to conquer Judaea more than a thousand years from now. And their blood and bones would lie in the land too.

Again, that questing tendril of power reached out to capture her. Demons went in when the sun came up, she thought, harking back to stories she had heard in her days on the land when she had dreamt she ran free. If the stories were true, why was Klingsor free to walk in the daylight?

The stories were all lies, just like the lie that her people had cared about her when they had punished her for her own violation by sentencing her—on pain of death—to marry her attacker.

She bit her arm, lest she wail and betray herself.

It would be better to stop it all now, she thought. When full light came, she would return to the upper city and cast herself from the heights.

And if she did not fall? In all the years she had known him, Klingsor had been obsessed with flight, had followed Simon Magus practically to his death because the little madman, charlatan as he had been, had one spark of the true art about him and boasted that one day, he would fly. Klingsor might well prevent her death—and what then?

She did not think she could die with these burdens upon her and bear them forever in Gehenna or wherever it was suicides were sent.

But her idea of stopping it, stopping it all had been a good one. All her girlhood, she had been taught to wait for the Messiah; and now, throughout Jerusalem and Judaea itself, people whispered that the long, long night of waiting was over, that Joshua ben Joseph, of the line of David, had come.

What if they *went on* waiting? What if this Joshua lived out whatever life the Almighty might otherwise have decreed for him: as a rabbi rich in years, learning, and grandchildren, please God—or whatever other life he might otherwise have had? What if the silver cup she had averted her eyes from when Joseph of Arimathea had shown it to her in the street was just a cup? Or, if you had a taste for fancy, old-fashioned words, you could call it a grail; it would just not be *the* Grail, but a silver vessel of good workmanship and adequate size, to be used in a comfortable household until it was battered and dented and could be sold for scrap.

Would any of that be so terrible?

Of course, it would mean that there would be no cult of

the risen Christos and no search for the Grail of his Passover and death. His followers would no longer enrich Judaea with their blood and bones—and those to come would
no longer slaughter her people for the sin, as they perceived
it, of being stiff-necked.

There would be no such followers. There would be no
order of Grail knights. There would be—she drew out a
long, shuddering breath as a new loss struck her—no Amfortas; no hand touching hers, no loving, astonished voice
murmuring in her ear, showing her the joy of what had been
stolen from her a thousand years before.

But better so, she insisted to herself. Better so. She had
dishonored him, and she had known enough of the man to
know that he would have preferred death. This way, he
would never taste either, and she would have made restitu-
tion. One thing she had learned from him—how to fight.
Had she ever fought before? She had just cowered, raged,
and run, from her rapist, from her people, from Klingsor,
and even—and especially—from her own guilt.

Never again, she vowed, and hoped she could keep her
vow. This time, she must stand her ground and even advance if she were to win her desire.

Some fought with swords and banners; she must fight
with guile and will.

But how? Already, in her few days back in Judaea, she
had seen—she had lived—a life different from the one she
remembered. She might have forgotten some of her earlier
life; some of this more recent one was not forgetfulness but
genuine change.

Knowing what she did, by how much *could* she change
the here and now? Enough to allow Joshua a normal length
of days with his workbench and a family? Enough to reduce
the Grail to just an ordinary drinking cup? *Dayenu*, she
thought. Any of that would be enough—more than enough.
Maybe even enough to end her curse? That was beyond
praying for—even if she could pray.

She would, she vowed, trembling. She would expunge
the future. She would smooth it out as if it were what the
Romans called a *tabula rasa*—wax from which all previous
marks have been erased and which waits for the next stylus

and the next, please God, more peaceful story. There would be trouble, of course, and sorrow; there would even be wars. But it would be different trouble, different sorrow, and different wars.

And with the history in which she had doomed herself scratched out, she would not have to see what would lie ahead. She would not have to watch the Romans beat Joshua until the *plumbatae* slashed bloody furrows in him and each step he took came only in mortal pain. She would not have to watch him, battered and beaten, carry a cross to the barren ground where the rock itself was shaped like a skull, hear the impact of hammer driving spikes through flesh and bone, or watch his ribs struggle so he could draw one more anguished breath.

She would not have to laugh. That alone would save her. That would be her victory and her final penance.

Once again, her life span would dwindle to that of a normal woman, and she could die then, spared this damnable foreknowledge that would have driven her mad had she not already been accursed.

Dawn exploded over Jerusalem like a ball hurled from a catapult, igniting into flame as it arced into the sky. Rising from the doorway which no sun would probably warm for hours yet, she pulled her mantle and the shreds of her power about her and advanced toward her battle.

14

IN the short time Kundry had known Maria, she had learned the older woman's detestation for the older, poorer quarters of Jerusalem. But now she found her not just in the lower city, but in a quarter so low, a room so poor, so surrounded by stews and alleys of the sort that King David (said the Pharisees, though Kundry had rather a more sanguine notion of his adaptability) would have wept to find in his city, that she went guarded by several of the young men of Joshua's circle.

The room was dingy, an odd setting for a woman who had relished color and luxury. But in it, Maria shone as she had never bothered to shine at the dinners, theatres, and symposia at which she had exhibited herself as a courtesan. She had her dream now, of rescuing young girls from a life that might—if they were very lucky—resemble her own. For that dream, all her years of careful savings, all her lovingly hoarded fabrics and jewels would pay. She looked so happy that Kundry, for once, wanted to weep, not laugh, with joy.

Her escort hovered in the background. One of them, despite joking complaints about doing a woman's work, laid out a meal of wrinkled olives, hard bread sprinkled with sesame, a fish or two, and sour watered wine, scarcely one step up from vinegar. All of them moved quietly, careful not to frighten the people who clustered around Maria. With one hand, she passed out the coarse bread. With the other, she smoothed back the hair of the young girl who wept on her shoulder, while she pleaded with another young woman, this one with an infant in her arms, to allow her to contact her father; see, one of the men (they were friends and wouldn't hurt her) would write a letter if she didn't know how, or walk her to safety, or—if she really felt that she must—return her to her home. Still, if she would take Maria's advice, she would stay here overnight and think about what she ought to do.

Kundry saw the woman's blackened eye and swollen jaw and flinched. She had looked thus after Amnon had walked off and just left her lying on the hillside, wondering what, in God's name, became of a girl no longer virgin, no longer eligible for a family's protection . . .

Across the room, Maria saw Kundry. Her dark eyes widened, warmed, then flashed with welcome. Kundry shook her head briefly, a remnant of the language they had used when "working" parties and young, patrician Romans as a team: *You're right, but let me play this my way.* Maria nodded, and permitted the crowd around her—it hardly seemed possible—to thicken.

Kundry drifted into the crowd, one woman in a throng, each talking at once, many weeping, a few thanking God. Had there been a Maria for Kundry, she might never have sunk to being a pawn of Klingsor and the temporary bedmate of Romans able to pay.

Most of the women gave the men of Maria's escort a wide berth, afraid of the red-haired man with the black beard who watched everything as if calculating costs or the big, burly man who tried to soften a voice more accustomed to booming at sailors across wind and wave than soothing frightened women.

Kundry slipped by them, trying to work closer to Maria. Then the door was flung wide, and a girl—scarcely more than a child—in robes almost shredded from ill-usage rushed in and flung herself at Maria's feet, weeping, trying to clutch her ankles. Immediately, women surrounded her, comforting, cajoling, crooning until the girl could look up at the woman responsible for her rescue.

Maria bent and whispered to the girl while the room fell silent.

"Who *are* you?" the girl asked in return.

That was the wrong question.

Immediately, Maria's eyes rolled up in her head, and she

raised her hands. The hot air in the little room quivered with the onset of her prophecy.

> *"I am the first and the last.*
> *I am the honored one and the scorned one.*
> *I am the whore and the holy one.*
> *I am the wife and the virgin.*
> *I am she whose wedding is great,*
> *and I have not taken a husband.*
> *I am the midwife and she who does not bear."*

The girl collapsed, weeping, as the others told her, see, things were not so bad; see, she had come to a safe place where she would not be judged harshly—that was the meaning of the prophetess's words. That was all she meant; prophetesses just spoke strangely, that was all. And she had to remember that there had been prophetesses in Israel before—Moses's own sister, named Miriam just like their benefactor, the judge Deborah.

Maria went on.

> *"In my weakness, do not forsake me,*
> *and do not be afraid of my power.*
> *For why do you despise my fear*
> *and curse my pride?*
> *But I am she who exists in all fears*
> *and strength in trembling.*
> *I am she who is weak,*
> *and I am a well in a pleasant place."*

The red-haired man muttered something, to which the man with the look of a sailor about him grimaced and rumbled something that Kundry could not hear, but that Maria clearly did, even in her trance.

"Why have you belittled me in your counsels?" she demanded. "I am the one who is honored, and who is praised, and who is despised scornfully."

The red-haired man grimaced, as if he wanted to jeer, but did not quite dare. A third man entered the conversation.

"Say what you wish about her words. I at least do not

believe that Joshua has said these things to her. For certainly, her teachings are strange ideas."

His skepticism stopped Maria's prophecy as if someone had hurled Jordan water over her. She drew a deep breath and began to shake, as if waked too rapidly from too deep a sleep.

The sailor asked, as if speaking to the whole room, "Did Joshua really speak with a woman without all of us knowing it and not openly? Are we to turn about and all listen to her?"

"Did he prefer her to us?" asked the red-haired man.

Maria wept then, and was immediately embraced by the woman with blackened eyes and the newcomer. She pushed free of the weak arms that, nevertheless, sought to offer shelter and consolation, to stand before the men and demand of the sailor, "My brother Peter, what do you think? Do you think I thought this up myself in my heart, or that I am lying?"

"You have always been hot-tempered," a younger man said to the sailor Maria had called Peter. "Now I see you contending against this woman like her enemy. If Joshua considers her worthy, who are you indeed to reject her? Surely he knows her very well, which is why he loves her more than he loves us . . ."

The red-haired man grinned, and Kundry moved in closer. Just a little closer, and Master Red Hair was likely to find himself sprawling on the ground without knowing why. And if he persisted in leering, someone would not be able to resist temptation to kick him in the gut once he had fallen. Regardless of her high resolves to fight and not to yield, Kundry would take positive pleasure in doing that much to protect a friend's newly purified name.

"Rather, we should be ashamed that we pretend to be perfect . . ."

Peter grumbled and threw up a hand, almost a gladiator's acknowledgment of a shrewd blow.

"Mercy *must* be weighed equal with severity," Maria said. "That may not be the law, but it is Truth. And it will come," Maria whispered to Kundry. "It will take some time, but if all goes as I pray, there will be no more little girls like you in this city; and, who knows, perhaps in all Israel, all over the world!"

Her voice took on the incantatory tone of her prophecies, and Kundry grasped her shoulders.

"Now what?" she demanded. She had to know where Joshua was, had to keep sight of him to protect him.

"Joshua has left Jerusalem. But he will return, and we prepare for it," Maria said. "He will enter the Holy City after the Sabbath, and we shall all wave palms and sing as he rides in. It will be our own festival before the Passover. Will you come?"

If Maria knew Kundry as Kundry knew herself, she would not trust her, would not ask that with such childlike assurance that Kundry would not betray her. They were on the same side now, in one sense: Kundry earnestly wished Joshua to be safe.

At the same time, she earnestly wished for him *not* to be the Messiah—or to be hailed as the Son of David. There, their ambitions diverged.

Still, she thought that none of the people who now circled her—not Maria nor the young men zealous as any of the Sicarii—wished his death, either.

"I shall stay with you."

Maria's eyes lit, then surveyed Kundry with growing enthusiasm. In that moment, Kundry became not just friend and ally, but one of the women whom Maria had made it her mission to help.

"I am sorry. But the sun will rise in the west before it is time for you to write *my* family."

"Yet, you came here, you sought me out . . ."

"So I did. But my presence here will do you no credit." *And if Klingsor finds us, God—whatever God, assuming one exists—help us all.*

The red-haired man shifted uncomfortably.

"Be still, Judas, for once in your life," said Peter, the sailor. A Galilean, judging from his accent.

"An unrepentant harlot." Judas's eyes scanned her as if they could see beneath the coarse robe she had assumed for her flight into the lower city. "And penniless."

I was never *a harlot; at least, I didn't sit by the roadside for long before I met Klingsor,* Kundry thought. Laughter welled up and was suppressed; she had sold her body for money— foolishness to argue that selling it for gold made her more virtuous than selling it for copper or just a night's lodging.

"Ever since Joshua let you carry the bag with the money in it . . ."

"Quiet!" Seasoned by years of calming dinner-party quarrels, Maria did not even have to raise her voice to silence the men. At least, these men were sober.

"My dear," she whispered to Kundry, "do not judge Judas too harshly. His is a sad story. His father was a tribune in Damascus . . ."

Part Roman, then? That would account for his skill with money and his anger and his resentment of the women here.

". . . and he was raised by an uncle. Joshua is the first *kind* teacher he has ever had."

Roman father or not, *patria potestas* or not, they were in Judaea now, and Jewish law decreed that the child followed the mother, the one parent of whom there could be no doubt. Yet Jewish law had been hard on bastards since the Decalogue visited the sins of the parents upon the children. This Judas would bear scars, and Kundry had learned— unfair as it was—to distrust such people, starting with herself.

Kundry glanced at Judas out of the corner of her eye. Seeing a red brow flicker up, she allowed her eyes to cool and raised an eyebrow. What was he doing here, with these penitent girls, if that was how he stared at them? Or was that look reserved for *Kundry,* now that Joshua's favor and Maria's prophetic frenzies lifted Maria out of the orbit of possible bedmates?

But Maria was speaking again. "I know you missed your family. We will keep you from . . ."

Kundry held up a hand. *Don't even speak his name.* What would Maria have said if Kundry had blurted that out? She was a prophet now; more surely than any magus or what-have-you like herself, Maria must sense power as it twisted through the cool night air of the city. She shivered, and Maria's face grew compassionate.

"We must find you a place. You have been harshly treated."

"Do you say that to all the girls who come here?" The question, with its crude echo of thousands of crude introductory flirtations, slipped out. Instantly, Kundry was sorry.

"You see? Your life—the life we shared—has hardened you. Give yourself time, gentle treatment, good teaching, and you will no longer have to defend yourself thus. And we may hope . . ."

There is no hope, Kundry had been fond of saying. Now, though, it was the work of a second to allow the hope she harbored in her heart for the first time that she could remember since her rape to shine in her eyes. It was not the hope that shone in the eyes of the women Maria had gathered here. They hoped only for lives in which fathers or husbands would not hit them or revile them or their children. Kundry hoped for all of them.

What if there were hope? Daring to believe, she allowed to grow the wildest hope of all: to change history, to wipe out the memories of a land impaled by fortresses and spears. Even the Holy Spear itself was one weapon too many. Let Kundry have her way, and it would be holy no more—just legionary issue. And the Grail would be just a silver cup.

And finally she would be at peace.

"But you will stay with us, will you not?" Maria asked. At Kundry's nod, she smiled with a child's delight. "And we shall both pray that you too will be penitent. Come, walk with me; help these poor girls . . ."

Thus began the strangest part of Kundry's life since she had come to Jerusalem. Effortlessly, she slipped from the role of harlot to those of penitent and zealot. Her resistance might appear peaceful, but it was as zealous as that of any Sicarius. And it brought her what she had never before known: acceptance and respect.

"Not for what you are, but for what you would be." Maria repeated Joshua's words to Kundry and took the tears that sprang to her eyes as a sign that she was softening.

The words only confirmed her resistance. What would she be? She would be free; Judaea would be free; and even the so-beloved Joshua and all of his disciples would be free to live long and healthy lives, deprived of a martyrdom no one could possibly wish on them.

But she had the semblance of a respectable woman now—provided she stayed away from the upper city where someone might recognize her, even disheveled as she was. And it brought her into places she never dreamed that she would go. Joshua's people made a great point of going among all people, Roman, Pharisee, Sadduccee, countryfolk, Samarian, even lepers. One hour, Kundry might be speaking to women who had fled a caravan. The next, she might be braiding her hair and washing her face before a dinner in a private house of the sort where no courtesan—and no raw country girl—would ever be welcome.

Kundry could almost regret that a philosophy that would lower the barriers between class and class, between man and woman, would never come fully to fruition. Then she reminded herself of women, sequestered more ruthlessly than any girl in Judaea, of men bending the knee to other men, some wearing the Cross that had yet to become a mystery (and never would, if she proved victorious), yet smiting them with fire and sword in the name of simple people who earnestly wished to escape fire and sword. It was better so, she told herself. *This time*, she had truly chosen the better part.

The days passed. The men who guarded Maria came and went, frequently muttering among themselves about this Pharisee, or that Roman, or the threat to a friend, Lazarus, who lived in Bethany. Kundry strained to hear any news that might trickle down from the upper city, but heard nothing.

She was roused from sleep one night by a pounding at the door. Rising quickly and flinging a cloak about herself, she ran toward it, but Maria was faster.

"Put that *away!*" she hissed at Peter, who had acquired—only a sailor would know where—a legionary's sword.

With ill grace he complied and opened the door. A

Roman in legionary's gear entered, carrying a woman muffled head and foot in a cloak—his.

"I found her in an alley," he told Maria. "She must have been late going home from market, and thieves . . . they were not just thieves . . ." He glanced away, and Kundry thought briefly of the soldier wed to a Jewish girl in Capernaum. "I give you my word, I shall report this . . . this incident to my centurion."

Maria took the woman from him and folded back the cloak from her face. A bruise discolored her jaw.

"She ran from me. I caught her, and she struggled . . ."

"So you had to hit her to subdue her," Maria sighed.

And one of Caesar's own looked down, embarrassed and downcast as a boy caught in a crime.

"I thought she might flee from one harm to worse. Then I thought to bring her here."

"So people know of 'here'?" Maria asked.

"All over the marketplace. Even in barracks, we hear, those of us with . . ." He flushed brick red, and Kundry knew he meant those men who lived with native women. Rome did not recognize such liaisons and forbade her legionaries to wed; but that did not stop them, or stop the best of the men who entered them from calling them true marriages.

"You have done well," Maria said almost absently. "I will be happy to help in any such cases. Tell that to your comrades. You men—Peter, Johanan, Levi—out! When this child wakes, she is going to be afraid, and I will not have men looking at her then!"

Hearing the tone of an order, the legionary all but saluted and began to withdraw before he caught himself. "Lady . . ."

Maria shook her head kindly at him.

He pulled out a few small coins. "All I have, but take care of the poor maid."

She smiled and gestured at a scar on the man's brow. "You follow the god of the legions, do you not? Yes? In that case, you will not want my blessing. But accept my thanks. Mithras has a good servant in you."

This time, as he left, the legionary did salute.

Then the girl woke and began to wail and gag. Kundry

was kept busy, but she could still hear one or two of the men in the outer room grumbling, again, about the Pharisees, who had complained when Joshua gathered food or had worked healings on the Sabbath.

"Tell them to be quiet out there!" Maria ordered, and Kundry obeyed. The sight of women commanding men seemed to stop their patient's initial panic long enough for her to tell them her name was Ruth. But the next questions—had she any family in the city, could they be contacted to help her—made her tremble.

"How can I ever leave this room?" The woman shook in Kundry's arms. She had not yet wept, though, and that was a bad sign. "How do I dare go home and tell them, beg them, 'Take me back, used thing . . .' "

Maria fixed Kundry with a demanding gaze, as intense as anything Klingsor had ever used on her. *Tell her*, she was ordering; but she used no force. Kundry might share her own story, or might not. It was her choice.

"As I did, sister." Kundry lowered her voice to the croon she would have used to her children, had she ever borne any. "What happened is a thing that was done to you. It is not your sin, not your guilt."

"You too?"

Kundry nodded. A lump rose in her throat.

"And could you go home?" Ruth asked.

Kundry was mute, unable to reassure the woman: her family had welcomed her, but only on terms that she could not submit to.

"It is all right," Maria was there, insisting softly. "If your family casts you out, you will have a family here." Her eyes lit with that glow of faith that made Kundry's heart sink because, sooner or later, she was probably going to outrage it. "Have you heard of Joshua ben Joseph, whom some are calling Christos, the anointed one?"

The woman nodded. "They say he is the one prophesied in Isaiah. Surely, it must be time now for him to come. How could things get any worse?"

Easily, Kundry thought.

"Oh, we need help, help . . . and I screamed, but no one came." Finally, the unnatural calm that had gripped Ruth broke, and she wept. Maria took her from Kundry, held her on her shoulder, and stroked her hair, promising her that, the next day, she would come to Bethany with them and meet the man who could bring her to peace and happiness that would last forever.

There was no peace for Kundry. She could not accept it. Yet, she too must go to Bethany and pretend. Dear God, did anyone have any idea how tired your face could grow from beatific smiles? It was like being a courtesan, always pretending, always adjusting your face to please the people around you.

Abruptly, she rose and left the room. The men had questions for her, but she shook them off, not gently.

15

THE house to which they were bidden in Bethany was a
solid one, the type of respectable place that Kundry as a
shepherdess would have regarded with awe of the rich folks
and that Kundry as a courtesan would have been driven
from. It was owned by a man named Lazarus, long a friend
of Joshua's and now, with his sisters, a great supporter.
Much to Kundry's surprise, the house was guarded—not
against Romans, but against men in the town who were
Lazarus's enemies. Judging from the watchfulness of
Joshua's followers, Lazarus was in some danger because he
had always been a faithful friend to the little band.

The women were met by Lazarus's sisters, who kept
house for him. Kundry sized them up. There was Mary,
who embraced Maria without hesitation and who had a
glint of the same madness in her eyes that Maria got when
she was about to prophesy. Elder than she was her sister
Martha, who cast a shrewd eye on all of them before welcoming them with a warmth and practical attention to de-
tails of washing water, clean linen, and unguents for the
woman who had accompanied them that reminded Kundry—

There was no point in thinking of home. Home was
barred to her. And if Martha knew what she was, this house
too would be barred to her and the threshhold scrubbed to
remove the taint of her footsteps.

Martha might have had some doubts about women like
Kundry, but none at all about the man they came to meet.

"He brought my brother Lazarus back to life," she insisted. "Anything he wants, anyone he wants welcomed, I
will welcome, and I will defend."

A fever, perhaps, Kundry thought. People fell into fevers that resembled death. She said as much, but Martha shook her head with such vigor that even the weeping woman wiped her eyes and smiled.

"He was *dead*. I myself"—her eyes filled at the memory—"washed him and spread the shroud that I had woven over his limbs. *Those fools* said he was sleeping." Martha jerked her chin at the door to indicate the men who sat with her brother. "But I knew, and so did Joshua and my sister. I was weeping—everyone complained that the bread was too salty that day—yet when I heard that Joshua was here, I went out to see him. Joshua came here, and I told him, I said, 'Lord, if you had been here, my brother would not have died.' "

For a moment, Martha's eyes took on the visionary sheen of Mary's and Maria's. She was such a practical body, yet she believed, Kundry marveled, that this young man had the power to repeal death.

He *had*, Kundry recalled. In so much, history had not changed. Lazarus had been raised from the dead. She could not wish him dead again; but the fact remained. His return to life was a major element in the story she hoped to change. Every event that happened just as it had before was a strike against her.

"So Joshua told me, 'Your brother will rise again.' Now, I know that. I may not be a scholar like Mary here, but I do know that, come the last days, we all shall rise in a great resurrection; and that I told him.

"Then he said, 'I am the resurrection and the life: he that believes in me, though he were dead, yet shall he live; and whosoever lives and believes in me shall never die. Do you believe this?' "

Martha nodded emphatically, reliving the moment. "What else could be said? I believe that he is the anointed one, the Christos, come to redeem us, so I said so, and went to call my sister. She couldn't bear to sit with the people who had come to the house, and had run out to our brother's"—Martha swallowed heavily before she could say the word—"grave, weeping, and Joshua came to her there. He wept too. Then he told us to roll back the stone that covered the tomb. I said, I told him, 'Lord, he has to stink by now, he has been in the tomb four whole days,' but no one listened, and the stone was rolled back."

"And . . ." Ruth prompted.

"All he did was pray and call, 'Lazarus, come forth.' And he did, oh, he did, with the very napkin I had used to keep his jaw from sagging coming half off!" Martha wept, joyous this time. "I tell you, I rushed back to the house and told the servants, 'Your master is coming, get a bath ready, and I have got to prepare such a dinner!' I tell you, it was good fortune that the neighbors had brought in so much food; after my brother came home, they ate and ate until not a scrap was left."

"So you serve this Joshua," Kundry put in softly.

"*This* Joshua? What is this '*this* Joshua'? He is family to us as well as . . . as what I said he was, even though I am a foolish woman."

"Even though he makes extra work for you and I give you no help?" her sister Mary asked mischievously.

"You listen. I cook. *Someone* has to," Martha said.

"Could I help?" asked Ruth, whom Martha was trying to bathe and compel to lie down. "I am not sick, truly, and if I work . . ."

"Work is healthy," Martha agreed. "I always say that if you cannot find a physician, find a good cook!"

Lucas, a physician who often traveled with Joshua, smiled as he packed away his phials. " 'Who can find a virtuous woman? For her worth is far above rubies.' I think we have one here. If you could keep this woman Ruth here among you . . ."

Martha flicked a towel at him, though her plump face flushed a richer olive at the praise. "And who will provide her dowry, eh?" She sighed. "Never give a thought to that, do you? Leave her here, and I shall be as a mother to her. Come along. You shall help serve, and if you are too shy to speak to Joshua—as I am certain you should not be—you shall at least see him."

In the end, they all sat down to dine. Martha bustled about with great contentment, grumbling happily that many men made for dirty dishes that they felt themselves too good to wash, while Ruth looked shocked, and Lazarus exchanged smiles . . .

. . . with Joshua. Kundry had forgotten the unique impact of his eyes, his stillness. She could not take her eyes off him. In the upper city, she had been a beauty, had seen men and boys acclaimed as beautiful at the games or at the theatres, but this man, with his scarred hands, his eyes wrinkling at the corners from his time in the desert, made them seem as tawdry as she herself felt next to Martha. He looked like his kinsman who had yet to be born, who would never *be* born, if Kundry had her way. She studied him beneath her lashes, but her blood was cool, as it had not been when she looked on Amfortas. No desire, but the same . . . she had no right, had never any right to call it love.

It was more than Kundry could bear. She murmured something about helping Martha, and slipped from the room.

Mary followed her. "My brother has just asked Martha to stop fussing about and sit down and *eat!*" She laughed. "And *he* has nodded at her, so she is complaining that she is not fit for company. But she will do as he asks; she always does."

"Will you take over now?" Kundry asked. "I can help . . ."

Mary looked at her hard, as if seeing more than an older woman and guest offering to help a woman of the house in the kitchen. Prophecy was a gift. Regardless of what else he might be, or might have done, Joshua had the gift of waking it. Power quivered in the air, and Kundry snatched at it as a woman, surprised in the street, might draw a veil over her face.

Mary sighed, and her eyes returned to normal.

"Actually, I am not going to the kitchen, but to fetch a present I had saved to give him the next time he came here." She opened a chest and from it drew an alabaster box. When she opened it, spikenard filled the air.

Marveling, Kundry put out a finger to touch the box. This was a prosperous house, but still, not one in which one would expect a younger daughter to have . . . "There must be a pound of ointment there!" Kundry said.

Mary laughed, the happy laugh of a generous child. "I

have been saving and saving." She shut the box before the fragrance of the ointment could alert the diners, then gestured Kundry back toward the dining room. As she entered, Joshua looked up, and his gaze halted Kundry where she stood. It seemed to pierce her, to know and understand what she was, what she dreamed of doing, even to fathom her weariness at seeing him thus *a second time? So it is. Blessings on you, daughter, and peace.* His face shone, and Kundry staggered.

Mary caught her.

"You really care too, don't you?"

Kundry nodded, mute.

"I have an idea!" Mary whispered. "Do you want to be the one to anoint his head with it?"

"But it is *your* gift to him!"

"He'll know . . . he always does." Then Mary blushed. "The gift is what matters—that he receive it, not that I have my little moment of pride. You do it . . . don't be afraid of him." She gave Kundry a gentle push.

Terror gripped Kundry. How could she go up to this man, regardless of what he might be, and actually touch him, lay her hands, which had touched so many men, on his head and rub costly ointment into his hair and beard? It was too like and too unlike anything she had done before. Her heart hammered and her eyes swam; power rose like music, when the voice of the flute rises intoxicatingly with the breath of a master player, soaring up to the high, half-heard pitch of bat song.

The comfortable room glowed, from lime-washed walls to the indigos and whites and ochres of tableware and cushions; all at once, the faces of the diners altered subtly, becoming more truly themselves as weariness, age, and trivial thoughts were revealed as illusions, to be stripped away and leave . . . not what they were, but what they wished to be. Martha's face glowed like a hearth on a cold night, while Maria's eyes gleamed like fire kindled afresh on an ancient altar. And the men's faces looked tranquil, or as tranquil as they could. Peter's intrinsic, rocklike strength all but held up the room, while Lucas's compassion and capability radiated from eyes and hands. Even Judas's shrewdness and restless energy seemed to be harnessed, for once, in the service of a goal larger than his own ambitions.

And Joshua's face . . . Kundry glanced away. As in the Temple, it was too bright for her to look upon. Abruptly, that brightness faded, and what she gazed at was only a very human face after all, lit by a smile that invited and reassured her as one might reassure the youngest child, who must speak before all his elders on Passover. That he looked, or that he reminded her of Amfortas, whom she had betrayed, did not matter. Mary had offered her the best honor in her power, and she must not spurn the gift. Besides, if she accomplished her will, she would have brought this man life, not death; and Amfortas would never be betrayed.

Drawing a deep breath, Kundry entered the dining room. The coolness of the alabaster was blessed relief to her sweaty hands. As she opened the box of ointment, the rich fragrance of spikenard filled the air, spilling out the door of the dining room to perfume the whole house. Kundry wanted to tell Mary to open the doors so the fragrance could intoxicate the desert and spread out over the whole world.

Instead, she approached Joshua. *Pour the ointment on his head*, Mary had said. That was foolishness. Kundry barely dared go near him, much less touch him.

Then Joshua nodded at her, Maria tilted her head and smiled wryly, and Kundry knew her path.

She knelt before Joshua, unbound her hair (a clatter to one side showed that Judas had almost jumped to his feet in shock—*and what did he think I was going to do?*), and anointed his feet. He sighed, his body relaxing as she rubbed the ointment in and the soreness of too-long travel away. Just so, she had eased Amfortas—and not just so. This was atonement; if it could not be worship, it was respect, it was devotion, and it even might be love. She finished rubbing in the precious ointment, and Joshua laid a hand on her head in thanks. She shivered at the strength she felt in that touch. Then she wiped his feet with her hair and backed away into the darkened doorway.

"You didn't have to do it that way," Mary whispered.

Kundry shook her head violently. "You don't know what I had to do."

Judas half rose from the table. "That ointment could have been sold and the money used to feed the poor! If you really cared about us, you'd have left your extravagance behind along with . . ."

Had he remembered the flaunting hetaera he had seen outside Simon's house so long ago? Or was he simply a man who liked correcting women and who accused them all of wasting the money that men earned?

"It was *my* gift!" Mary protested, acknowledging it to defend Kundry. Lucas whispered urgently in Judas's ear, and he recoiled. Kundry glanced at Maria, who simply eyed Judas as if she were a Roman patrician and he a street idler who had accosted her. Yet he had flinched as if he had been kicked. Surely no prophetess would descend to kicking someone under a table.

Kundry glanced over and saw Martha firm her lips. "No one talks that way to my guests," she muttered, her voice rising with her indignation. "What do you care about the poor?" she demanded of Judas. "You're the one who keeps the money! Do you have gambling debts, or something else, that you begrudge my sister a gift? It was well done, sweetheart, and Martha is proud of you!" she called to Mary.

Lazarus shook his head, clearly distressed at the quarrel. Joshua held up a hand.

"Let her alone. She kept this against the day of my burying. The poor will always be with you, but you will not always have me."

He held out a hand for Mary to come and sit by him. She tried to tug Kundry to come with her, but Kundry retreated to the kitchen to help Ruth scour pots with the servants. Let him be wrong this time, she begged, but she did not know whom she begged.

Looking at Ruth's face hurt; adoration shone bright upon her. Kundry stifled a pang of resentment. Ruth's life had been wrenched awry and then, almost as quickly, restored to her.

"But you are not safe!" That was Martha's voice. Once persuaded to abandon what she considered to be her place, she was quick enough to argue with the men. "Will you just throw your life away now that it has been given back to you? You have a family. You cannot go on as if nothing could happen?"

"I tell you, sister, as I have told you before." Lazarus tried for patience, but his voice rose. "I do not scorn the rabbi's help, but a man who has died once does not fear death twice. It is in God's hands. And I would rather suffer death again than ask Roman protection against other Jews."

The talk turned to the coming Passover in Jerusalem. Lazarus had a white donkey he wanted to give Joshua for his entry. Remembering, Kundry clashed the pots, trying to deafen herself.

But the odor of spikenard penetrated even to the kitchen.

16

KUNDRY stared down the winding road. It was choked with dust from the feet of men and beasts hastening into Jerusalem for the Passover, which would begin tomorrow. They were late, but it was not for them that Kundry kept watch.

The palm fronds in her hand felt harsh, like something someone else held. She had not wanted to come here. She had argued against *anyone's* coming here, against the whole idea of Joshua's entering Jerusalem so conspicuously. His disciples had thought she argued prudence; she had hoped to change events as she remembered them, and as they were written. Yet, here she was—as she had not been the last time—with palms in her hand.

"It is too like Rome, too like a triumph," she had pleaded. "They have a law, the *Lex Juliana*. It is death for a man to make himself king. You know the Romans will take that seriously, especially in Judaea. Especially," she added with a sense of venturing out across a quagmire, "when the Romans accord divine honors to their emperors."

"What is this women's foolishness?" demanded Peter. "We are not afraid, no more than the Maccabees before us."

"They *killed* the Maccabees." Kundry's voice throbbed low.

"And you would have us cower lest they kill us? I suppose your way is better—*Rahab!*" Judas interrupted with the old, insulting cry of "harlot." "You come among us with your talk of Roman law. What do you know of

Roman law? Where did you learn it? And what right do you have to speak out among us?"

"They will kill him," Kundry repeated over a buzz of comment and reproof.

"It is written in Isaiah, 'I gave my back to the smiters,'" Judas replied. "What is prophesied will happen, and if we die for it, we will be remembered forever. Better to sacrifice all than to grow old in a little village and be forgotten."

Reddish glints kindled in his eyes, and Kundry forced herself not to recoil. Once, she imagined, Klingsor must have been just such a man.

You *will never be forgotten*, Kundry wanted to snap. For a brief, mad moment she thought of telling him precisely how he would be remembered, but horror blocked her tongue. She had *not* been here before. She had not sat among Joshua and his disciples, had not argued with them for their leader's life, had not been shouted down by one who would commit worse betrayal than she. This was a new thing, a new time. Any new word, any action that had not been done before might tip the scales in which Joshua's life—and the whole future she sought to undo—hung.

She covered her mouth and nose with a corner of her veil, as if concealing herself from someone unacceptable. For an instant, she had sniffed the same carrion reek with which she associated Klingsor.

Maria jumped in, silencing Judas with a deft phrase, and Kundry let herself fade into the background.

Which was why she stood outside Jerusalem, palm fronds pricking at her hands, waiting for the victim to ride up on a white donkey colt, caparisoned with the most lavish cloths they could find.

At least her pleas had borne fruit in this much: the men, women, and children who followed Joshua but who were not in his inmost circle were sent on ahead. If the Romans dispatched cohorts with their deadly short swords, the innocent might be spared.

They were *all* innocent, a cry had gone up.

But not in the eyes of Rome.

"Is he coming?" Ruth demanded eagerly. When Kundry had been attacked, she had hidden in her house for days.

One glimpse of Joshua, though, and Ruth was hale, willing to brave a frenzied crowd in which men and women jockeyed for a place along the road that led up to the city.

"I see a cloud of dust!" someone cried. The people lining the way tensed. Ringing out thinly from below came a psalm, then three families, obviously worn out with their haste to enter Jerusalem that day. Seeing the crowd, they tried to straighten their backs, to walk with pride. They were fulfilling the ancient laws; they would worship in Jerusalem; they had no cause to shrink. Feeling no such pride, their pack beasts strained to keep up. Their heads drooped under heavy loads, and they panted until their owners took pity upon them and slowed their pace.

The crowd subsided. The sun beat down, hot even at this height. A child cried thinly somewhere behind Kundry, then quieted as its mother gave it the breast. A youth fainted from the heat or from excitement and was loaded on a groaning beast. And the wait dragged on. They were good at waiting, these people of Judaea, survivors of one conquest after another. *Please God*, Kundry prayed as she had not prayed for a thousand years, *let them wait yet longer for their redeemer*. They could bear it.

And that would be all the redemption Kundry herself craved.

A rumble came from below. Kundry tensed. Had her thoughts been so vile that the earth would open to swallow her up?

"They're coming!"

Kundry felt the approach of Joshua and his followers first as a rumble of feet and deep-throated voices singing. "I will bring a seed out of Jacob, and out of Judah, an inheritor of my mountains; and my elect shall inherit it." It was no psalm Kundry had ever heard; it was part of the prophecies of Isaiah that had whispered round Judaea faster than rumor itself.

Beside her Ruth raised the ululating cry that women gave in the deep desert. It was picked up by a thousand throats, high, sweet, and shrill.

The wind blew shriek and prophecy away together. Now a new cry rose. "Hosanna! *Hosanna!*"

"Blessed is he that comes in the name of the Lord!"

"The king, the king of Israel!"

"Hosanna!"

She had not wanted this parade, had counseled against it. And yet, when the crowd cheered, she cheered too.

A veritable thicket of palm fronds and branches stirred up a second wind. Dust whirled up in miniature storms, then blew away as a huge gust swept across the road. It was the *ruach*, the breath of God, of prophecy itself. Did its appearance mean that Joshua was indeed the redeemer for whom her people waited—or that her attempts to spare him from what she knew awaited him would fail? The wind stiffened, forcing many to their knees. Kundry forced herself to withstand it.

Thus she was standing when Joshua came into view. He was such a tall man that his mount was too short for him. Kundry would have thought that he would look incongruous, his legs practically dragging on the ground as he sat on the white colt, caparisoned with motley attempts at finery. But no Roman general could have looked more at ease— and Joshua had no one whispering at his back, "Remember, thou art mortal."

Joshua's students and friends walked alongside him. Johanan kept a hand near the colt's reins lest the cheering make it spook and bolt. Lucas walked staring into the crowd, as if seeking patients, while Peter marched stolidly ahead with a just-let-them-dare expression on his flushed face. Judas looked almost intoxicated by the excitement; did he think these cheers were for him?

Far behind them came Lazarus and Maria, who had one arm around Martha. She paused, looking down at the shorter, heavier woman who struggled to keep pace. But Martha shook her head as if this were all madness, but she was delighted to be thought insane. Beside them walked Martha's sister Mary, tears streaming down her cheeks. As the crowd screamed "Hosanna!" her eyes grew rapt, and Kundry knew that she sensed the power in the air.

Kundry's determination wavered. She thought of what must come to pass if she failed—splendors of cathedrals, of knightly orders, all rising because a young man rode a white

colt into Jerusalem for Passover and waved at friends who
had come to greet him. She thought of the blood that would
be spilled in the name of that young man, who smiled as if
he wished that all the harm in the world could be wished
onto the head of one goat and that goat driven into the
desert. She shuddered, mastered by the power that quivered in the blue sky and overhung the dusty road and the
puny, cheering creatures that lined it to welcome another.

"Hosanna, hosanna!" The ragged chant rose from the
weary crowd, forgetful now of Rome, of the daily fears and
struggles of their lives. Their hope that the long night of
waiting had ended beat at Kundry. For a moment, she met
Joshua's eyes, and he smiled at her, glad for every friend
that he saw. She wavered, tempted.

Just kneel. Cry out. Accept it. He may die, but you will
weep, not laugh—and will that be so bad?

She would be one of them, one of the breed that had
murdered her people for the next twelve hundred years.
She would not kneel.

She began to edge through the crowd, which jostled and
shoved with a total absence of malice.

A hand grasped her arm, strong fingers pressing in against
a nerve. She gasped.

"Don't scream," came an angry whisper. Klingsor's whisper. "Samael take you, bitch, for an ingrate runaway." The
thumb pressure against her forearm grew stronger, and the
pain was enough to make her writhe.

"Let me go!" she hissed.

"You're coming with me now!"

She could stop him, of course. If she screamed "Thief!"
or "Assassin!" there would be a panic—and armed men
would be dispatched from the garrisons to stop the riot.
Blood would be spilt, and Klingsor could probably draw
power from the life it held.

That is, if he hadn't power enough already to draw on
and blast an innocent crowd this close to their holiday.
Now that would truly be a betrayal.

Kundry let herself be drawn through the crowd, through
the gates, into the house he had made his own. It looked
like a face with its eyes shut, the face of an enemy—or like

a fortress. She had stayed here when he had plucked her off
the street. If she had had a home in Jerusalem, this was it.

The idea made her shudder. So did the statues, the colors, even the incense with which he had furnished this
place. The girl Kundry had not known enough to fear them;
Kundry the woman not only feared them, she knew why.
For her own lost soul's sake, she had to get out of here.

Klingsor threw off his hooded robe. With his long black
hair and beard, he looked like some Assyrian tyrant, come
to cast down her people's shrines and thrust them once
again into exile.

"Is this the thanks I get for helping you, for introducing
you to important men able to help you rise in the world?"
he demanded. "You vanish, and all I hear is that you ran
away from a patron at a dinner party to join a group of
Zealots."

"They're *not* Zealots," Kundry snapped.

"Then what are they?" Klingsor demanded, grabbing
Kundry's shoulders and wrenching her around. "What is
he?"

Kundry gasped for breath and sense. In this time and
place, *this* Klingsor was younger than she. No matter how
long he had lived before; no matter that he would live the
next thousand years, the man who stood before her had not
yet lived them—and she had. He might have more power,
even now, than she did; but the Klingsor of this age was
used to a younger, weaker Kundry. That might provide her,
given her greater knowledge and experience, with a weapon.

"What do you think he is?" she asked, gaining control of
her voice.

"I don't know! But he has power, power such as I would
give my soul for."

Lost already, she thought, *bartered for length of life and a
passion for dominion he would never satisfy.*

"Listen to me!" His black eyes were wild. Kundry flicked
a glance at the incense burners. What, besides fragrant
gums, burned in them? She stifled a cough at the sudden
reek of something long dead and unholy.

"When I was a student in the great school of Sippar, I
heard of such as he. Our astrologers mounted the ziggurats

to study the stars. They prophesied that when two great stars conjoined, there would be born such a mighty one that kings would bow before him. And kings did—magi and adepts of Sippar, at whose very names my teachers prostrated themselves, journeyed out into the desert into the back alleys of Bethlehem to bring a beggar brat myrrh and gold and bow before him.

"I had been searching for that power all my life. When *he* was born, I sensed it from far off. I searched for him when he was a baby, determined to kill every man-child in this wretched land until I found the one who held it. But he escaped me.

"So I waited till he was a man, and I went to him, I sought him out where he fasted in the wilderness, and I looked at him. He could fly, I know he could. So I tempted him: step off that cliff; see if your Father's power will bear you up. If you truly have faith, you will do it."

Joshua had probably looked at him as he would stare at a madman, wondering whether to exorcise him or reason with him or just to pity him. Klingsor would accept none of it, Kundry knew: it was his curse never to be sated with what he had.

"Did he laugh in your face?"

"He repulsed me with the words you would use to a demon. Me, a demon!"

Kundry laughed. "He is a wise man to know what he speaks to." She braced herself for a slap that never came. The magician looked distracted, tormented by a vision of power he had sought but was unfit to touch.

"He has power," Klingsor went on. "You can see it shimmering from his skin in gold and white lights. Why has *he* the power? It should be mine. It must be mine—or no one's."

"And if it is not yours, you would destroy it?" Kundry asked.

"Not it! But if its vessel is gone, it can fill another. It could come to me. It must come to me. I have spoken to Annas, Caiaphas's father-in-law. He will tell the other priests that this man is a dangerous heretic. And there must be some power I can invoke—"

Kundry gagged. "Call on Azazel or Samael, then, or on your vile Ereshkigal or Typhon! Go ahead," she screamed, "call on them! Surely they will answer one so much like them. You are a pestilence, *my master*."

The last time she had reviled him, he had cast her back in time. She waited now for Klingsor to scream, to call up his demons and annihilate her. He glared at her, and she realized that she had spoken as the older Kundry, the woman weary of her whoredom, a sorcerer's familiar who had become, of necessity, a sorcerer herself. He was too astonished to strike her.

Instead, he shoved her against a wall where Cybele with her heavy breasts, her lion-drawn chariot, raised hands to bless them. There was a dagger in his belt. She had only to draw it and slash it across his throat—

—but could he die? Some unholy pact had already extended his life far beyond the normal threescore and ten, and she knew how much longer he had yet to live.

"I will have my vengeance on you," he promised. "Though it take a thousand years, I will be revenged."

That much of his ranting she knew for truth.

"And you will see my vengeance on you and on him and all of the fools that do not acknowledge me. Go to the baths now. Wash off the stink of the streets and those foolish peasants. Anoint yourself." She would have sworn that the pupils of his eyes could have expanded no further, but now they gaped wide to devour her. "I need you for my rituals . . ."

He would put his hands on her, would chant and burn his noisome incenses, and God only knew what powers would answer, would enter her so soon, so soon after she had touched what she knew now was genuine holiness, whether she chose to bow to it or not. She recoiled from him. One thing she would choose—not to be touched by Klingsor or his tamed demons.

With a cry of pure fury, she hurled herself at him, seizing the dagger in his belt, and slashing it down across the hand that numbed her arm.

He screamed with the pain and his hand released her. Panting, Kundry held the dagger before her. Klingsor flung blood from the wound she had given him in her face. With more control than she would have believed possible, he held out his wounded arm and began to drip dark blood onto the floor in a pattern she recognized.

"I will have my revenge," he promised.

That much of his ranting she knew for truth. But she would have to try to oppose him, even though she had failed in every such attempt during her long and misspent life.

A spell set with a magician's own blood would be doubly, trebly powerful. She spat bile at the thought that he cast such a thing in Jerusalem and hurled herself at him again, the bloody dagger outthrust with her determination to kill him before he summoned up whatever evil he wished. But the air had already thickened around him, and tiny glints of fire shone in the air. It began to stir, aroused by the taint of magic in the house.

If she screamed, no one would hear her, just as no one had heard her when Amnon laid hands on her. No one would hear Klingsor's chanting either: a pity, that. Pharisee and Sadduccee alike would order him stoned for sorcery.

> "Huesemigadon, Ortho Baubo, neo odere soire soire
> Kanthara, Ereshkigal, sankiste, dodekakiste . . ."

Klingsor was chanting, many-syllabled words rising and swirling about him like so many snakes.

"Stop it!" she shrieked. She raised her hand, attempting to cast wards about herself as she invoked the archangels.

> "anchor anchor achachach ptoumi chancho . . ."

Damn herself for a fool, for taunting him with the idea of raising Typhon! With her own fledgling skills, she could not hope to withstand such powers for long. She cast protection about herself and felt Klingsor's rage and pain begin almost immediately to erode it.

Kundry ran. She darted into her room—her room in the sense that Klingsor had let her call it that—and seized what she could of silks, of gold and jewels. If he were speaking to the Romans or the high priests, she would need treasure to combat him. But if he were speaking to demons, there was no protection in gold, no protection in aught but power.

Liar, something told her.

Nevertheless, she fled. Her Roman patrons would call it a tactical retreat. She called it cowardice.

17

WITH her jewelry and the gown she had snatched up wadded about the glass and alabaster phials of cosmetics and bundled beneath her rough cloak, Kundry slipped down to the lower city. Just let her find Maria's shelter, and it would be the work of a moment to change back—no, not change back—to become a new thing. A great lady.

The girl Kundry could not have done that at all. The woman?

She had convinced Amfortas, hadn't she?

And then, wearing the armaments of unguents, paints, and fine gems, she would do battle for Joshua's life.

Abruptly, the need to make sure of that life obsessed her. She had to find him, to find his friends. But the shadows were lengthening, and the few people who had not already withdrawn into their homes or booths for the Passover feast were walking more rapidly, eager to get home before sundown.

A great lady would offer silver. But no great lady would wander down here in the lower city, so poorly dressed. She drew a deep breath and widened eyes with fear she had no need to simulate.

"I beg you, master," she called, with a fair assumption of timidity, to a man hastening in the opposite direction. "The teacher who entered the city today. Do you know where he is?"

"After he threw down the money changers' tables in the Temple once more, little one? No, I do not; and if you are wiser than you seem, being out so late, you will not, either. The priests have been out to question him and ask why he should not be taken up on charges of blasphemy. It is no subject for a girl to think of. Get to your home and help your mother with the cooking."

He was gone.

A boy child raced by, yet stopped to stare at her.

"Boy!" She held out a coin so he could see the glint of silver against the setting sun.

"Have you seen Joshua ben Joseph?"

"The teacher from Nazareth, who caused the riots today?"

Not daring to answer, Kundry nodded.

"He is sharing the Passover with Joseph of Arimathea."

"Where is that?" She had no expectation that he could tell her.

But the air thrummed with the sweet sound of power correctly used.

"I can take you there. I heard it, me. There was a man carrying a pitcher of water, wearing the clothes of Joseph's household; and they came up to him and asked, 'Where is the guestchamber where I shall eat the Passover with my disciples?' "

"And you followed them?"

The boy shrugged. Kundry pulled out another coin, thought better of it, and tugged out a necklace. "Do you have a sister?" she asked.

Wide-eyed and more than a little afraid, the boy nodded. "I will give you this for her dowry if you take me to this guestchamber and tell no one about it—not ever."

The boy held out a hand for the necklace. She let him touch it: massy gold, enough to marry off the daughter of a poor family more prosperously than even the most hopeful mother would dare to dream.

He swallowed. "Follow me."

The guestchamber was on the second floor of a large, well-kept building. Lights the color of golden oil shone from the narrow windows, a welcome that she knew better than to attempt. Right now, Joseph as eldest would—no, Kundry thought. Tonight of all nights, Joseph would resign the privilege to Joshua. He would hold up the unleavened bread and proclaim, "Lo, this is the bread of affliction." He would rehearse the flight from Egypt. And he would hold up the silver cup that Joseph had vowed to reserve until Passover. It would shimmer in the lamplight, filled with rich red wine. And then Joshua would pray over it. Would the wine change under the men's eyes? she wondered. She almost thought she could see, piercing through the honey-colored lamplight, the red and silver radiance of the Grail.

The women, under the lash of Martha's orders, would be adding the last, anxious stirrings to the feast that would follow the retelling of the Exodus. She would find a welcome there, and Martha would thank her for providing two more hands. She would be grumbling that her sister and Maria sat as idle as the men, but she would be proud of them. But Martha had little Ruth, no longer lost now; she would not need Kundry with her fears and fits of vision.

Magic unlike any she was used to shimmered over the olives and the poplars, glistened on the gates and high walls of Jerusalem. It was a magic of memory in which all the pain had been transmuted for the moment to joy. It was a magic that she had been entitled since birth to share in; but she would not go in.

For a long time, she stood staring at the windows. A blot of shadows slipped down the twisted street. One opened the door to the guesthouse, and light glinted off his red hair—Judas, late to the Passover service and meal. Kundry narrowed her eyes and saw another blot—the absence, actually—of light pad away toward the upper city. The shadow drifted past a lit torch, but not before Kundry saw that one of its arms was bandaged.

In a moment, the tendrils of Klingsor's power would search her out. *You do not see me; you do not hear me; I am too strong for you,* she thought and hid herself beneath those thoughts just as Roman soldiers would escape the battering of rocks flung from a city wall by advancing beneath a tortoise wrought from their sturdy shields. *I am secure.*

The shadow darkened, then disappeared round the bend. There was betrayal in the air tonight; God forbid that she be a part of it.

Amid the betrayals and the magics in the night air, Kundry could feel her own growing strength like a dark cloak, concealing her. Best to sneak away, not to contaminate the feast.

The moon rose over the city's abandoned, darkened streets as its people kept watch and celebrated a feast Kundry dared not partake of. She wandered past homes from which rose singing and laughter, more alone than she had felt for centuries. She knew there was an end to this exile: the feast might not last beyond midnight.

But the pavements were hard under her feet—so much for Jerusalem the golden and all that milk and honey. She might be a sorceress; still, she was tired and lonely. And she had begun to despair. Wind sang through nearby trees, and a brook (doubly miraculous in this dry land) rippled in the shadows of a garden. Grateful for the wind on her eyes, hot with unshed tears, she slipped within, sank down on a rock and set aside the burden she had carried from the upper city. The thought wandered through her mind that she might do well to hide the silks, the jewels: there was nothing could stop Klingsor from reporting their loss as a theft, and she knew no one during this holy season would want to take the word of a common whore.

She bent to conceal her plunder beneath the shadow of the rock on which she sat, then froze. What she had thought to be saplings were moving now, darker shadows that, as the moon broke through the clouds, she could see as bodies and faces that she knew. Her wanderings had drawn her full circle, back toward the guesthouse in which Joshua had celebrated the Passover and from which he had led his friends out into the garden.

They were dancing. Moonlight glinted on their eyes as they circled, hands joined, around their leader, who stood in the center.

"Answer 'Amen' to me," Joshua commanded, then began to sing.

Kundry flung herself down on the earth. Was it betrayal, profanation for her to be here? Then let it be so, she told herself; this time, she would not flee. Her heartbeat pounded so loudly in her ears that she caught only fragments of the chant. "To the Universe belongs the dancer . . ."

"Amen." Stamp, clap, and circle.

"He who does not dance does not know what is happening . . ."

"Amen." Countercircle, weave back and forth.

"Now, if you follow my dance, see yourself in Me who am speaking . . ." Weave, circle, grand chain, and so, each man back to his original place.

"You who dance, consider what I do . . ."

The rhythm of the dance overtook her, smothered her senses, and she sank down with her head upon the ground.

Someone groaned, and Kundry stirred.

"What, could you not watch with me one hour?" She had heard that voice singing; she had heard that voice praying, chiding. But she had never heard that voice so sad, yet so affectionate before. She rose with a guilty start. The sorrowful words were not addressed to her, but to the men who lay not ten feet from her, sleeping after the exhaustions of a triumphal entry into the city, the long feast, and that eerie dance.

Joshua moved silently away from them, sandaled feet silent in the grasses and stones, and Kundry followed him to where he knelt and groaned again. "Abba, Father," he prayed, "all things are possible unto you. Take away this cup from me."

Let it be so, Kundry prayed, seeing a different cup altogether. All her rebellion and, yes, her love rose in that prayer. Would it be so bad if the strength and kindness welling from him made some young girl a happy wife, if he taught not multitudes, but children of his own, if his children—and not he—took up the burden of dealing with Rome-in-Judaea? It would not be an easy life, though easier by far than what he faced: and he would be happy.

Let one of the men of that line be happy, Kundry wished.

"Nevertheless, not what I will, but what thou wilt."

He knelt, his head bowed, for a long time. When he looked up, his eyes rested on her with a total absence of surprise.

"You were not at the feast," he said.

"I was not worthy."

He shook his head. "Worthy? It is not a case of 'worthy'

when one is alone. The meanest stranger at the gates would have been welcome; and you have been our companion. My own disciples, my friends and brothers, are all *worthy*. I washed their feet tonight. I gave them the unleavened bread and the wine, and I felt as if I tore my own flesh and blood asunder and gave it them to eat." He raised his eyes to the dark sky from which no word came, no order that the cup be dashed from his lips, then he sighed heavily.

"My very dear, my worthy friends. Yet tonight, one of them will betray me, while another, the very strongest of them all, will deny three times before dawn that he knows me. He blusters, that Peter, and yet I love him well. And the others . . . they have not been tested in battle, and they will run. So, I do not want to hear you call yourself unworthy."

Kundry raised a hand, started to protest, but he shook his head, silencing her.

"Stay with me, just a little. It is hard to look ahead and know, to see my own . . ."

"Lord," Kundry broke in, "perhaps it will not be so."

"I have prayed for that," Joshua said simply.

"I cannot worship you," she told him. "I am sorry."

"I do not want your worship. Leave it be. If you need to be forgiven that, it is forgiven, or aught else you need—if you can accept it. It does not matter. Leave it be."

"What does matter?" she asked gently.

"Life matters. I have prayed to be permitted to return to Nazareth and my workbench there, to divide up my life as a normal man would—among my work, study, and my family. Even to wed a girl, perhaps one of the lost ones our Maria cares for. My mother would rejoice; she has a special love for weddings. But . . ."

Again, he groaned. "I am," he whispered into the quiet night, as if testing the sound of the words. Then, more boldly, as if gathering courage for the admission, "I am afraid."

Kundry had heard Romans laugh at fear and weaklings who confessed to it. But weakness lay not in Joshua's admission, but in the denial of the truth.

"Not of death, for we are all creatures of light, and death will not chain us forever. But *knowing*; of the fear and the pain, of the foulness that must come at the last, and of breaking under the test: those things I do fear, yet I must know every burden that men and women face. Oh, Father, must I?"

His eyes flashed upward, wild and not quite human. Then he sighed, lowering them again to earth.

"I know what is to come. If I could only be sure that my life and death, the lives and deaths of those to come, were not just so much water poured out onto the sand . . ."

He bent his head, and the dark, unshorn hair fell onto his bowed shoulders.

This is your chance, Kundry ordered herself. *Tell him, fool.* Had she not sworn to change the times, to make the world a place in which the Grail was just a silver cup, Joshua ben Joseph merely a carpenter with mildly risky political friends, and Amfortas of Montsalvasche not even a thought? All she had to do was speak to that bent head, those bowed shoulders. Speak the words only: tell him of the thousands upon thousands of people of his blood cast from their homes or dead—all in his name; the boots kicking the life from children; the horses riding down fleeing men; the fire wrapping about whole towns; the voices, ruthless as any Roman's or Pharisee's, demanding, "Kill them all. Heaven will know her own."

He would weep, rise, and go his way. He might thank her, come morning; might even find in her the bride he hoped to bring to Nazareth.

She opened her mouth to speak.

Lord, I am not worthy.

Joshua raised his head. Once again, their glances met. Once again, she saw—exhausted, disheveled, worn by living on the run—the face of the man who would never be born if she now spoke. Amfortas.

Speak the word only and my servant shall be healed. But he would know it if she spoke half-truths. Amfortas's face blurred before her: she had lied to him with silence, if nothing else. At the last, she had betrayed him, yet he had hurled himself naked to her defense.

If she spoke now, he would never live, never be betrayed. And yet he—or what he might become—was he not worth the pain she had endured? Could she add to it with yet another lie?

Kundry could not do it. Better to betray herself and all her hopes instead, and have that, too, as a reproach upon herself. "You would be the one, Lord, to know that: not I."

She put out a tentative hand, then drew it back. She had touched too many men to touch this one, even in comfort.

Absence was the best gift she could give him, she determined, and retreated to the concealment of a rock.

After a time, Joshua raised his head. His face, white in the spectral light, was calm as he returned to his sleeping men. He had resolved, then. There would be no workbench, no happy bride, no well-fed children. There would be war, death, and exile. But there would be faith kept, too.

"Rise up," he urged as he walked among them, nudging and shaking them. "Let us go."

Kundry tensed and cowered. She heard footsteps, voices, almost a growl that a thousand years had told her was the cry of a hunting mob.

"Let us go!" Joshua urged. "He who is to betray me is at hand."

It was happening. For all her hopes, for all her attempts, they were coming, the priests, their guards, and their traitor; and he would be arrested once again, once again led down through the city bearing the instrument of his own execution on his bleeding back.

If she shrieked a warning, would he run? Or would she simply betray herself, too? She bit her lip as the crowd entered the garden. A most august mob, armed with staves and swords and the presence of the chief priest and scribes and elders, and in their midst, black-bearded, red-haired Judas. Kundry stared longingly at the weapons. Once she had seized a blade from Klingsor. What were her chances of stealing another and striking Judas down as he told the chief priest, "The one I shall kiss, that is the leader"?

But Judas was too quick for her. He hastened to Joshua as if he were a loyal man rejoining his leader after too long an absence. "Master," he greeted him, and kissed his cheek.

That was the signal for the priest's guards to surge forward and surround him.

Joshua's men woke in confusion. Peter bellowed, a sound more suited to a ship's deck in a storm than a garden on the first night of Passover. Drawing his sword, he struck at the head of one of the high priest's servants. The man turned, and a trick of the moonlight misdirected the blade. Blood sheeted down his face as the sword sheared his ear off, and he screamed.

"Put up that sword," Joshua said. "All you that take the sword will perish by it. Have you come out with swords and staves to take me like you would take a thief?"

The men fell back as he turned his back on Judas and walked toward them. "I sat daily with you teaching in the Temple, and you never laid a hand on me," he reminded them.

He laid a hand on the wounded man's head, and the air shimmered around it. When the light died away, the gaping wound was healed and the man collapsed, his sword clanging on the ground.

Joshua's disciples had seen him heal the sick or raise the dead before; but this miracle in the midst of battle shocked them all. Someone screamed and ran—a man no one had seen before, the cloth in which he had wrapped himself for the night dropping from his pale limbs as he fled. Panic fell like a deadly mist upon the garden, and all Joshua's disciples fled as the priest's guards bore their leader off.

She had failed then. All her plans, all her hopes had gone awry. She would have wailed aloud, only she feared to be discovered. She pressed fingers against her eyes until lights exploded behind them, just such lights as she had flinched from in her long fall down the centuries back to Judaea. But she was a victim no longer; she was Kundry, and she had not yet given up all her hopes.

She tugged loose her bundle of garments, gems, and fine lotions, and hastened into the deepest part of the garden. Secluded by the trees, she began to throw on the delicate bright silk, to paint her face, to toss necklaces over her head in just the way that a soldier flings on his armor and his weapons when an alarm comes in the night. She too was going to fight, and there were other weapons than the sword. Time to admit defeat when she could no longer wield them.

Glinting in the moonlight, Kundry raced out of the privacy of the trees. Peter would have understood how she felt. A great wave had swept over her and, even when she bobbed gasping and flailing to the surface, she knew that the undertow had her trapped and would drag her out to sea.

18

RISKING a riot later on, the Romans had posted guards. Their torches spat and smoked, dimming the tiara of starlight high above even Herod's citadel. Kundry raced by one guard point. A soldier reached out to stop her, but she swerved and leapt away, leaving him to hold her dark cloak like a shed skin. She saw herself reflected in the shining metal of his harness—dark tangles of hair catching in the elaboration of necklace and earrings; darker eyes, enormous with fear in their kohl circles; skin chalky under a death mask of cosmetics, distracting curves of hip and breast to which her garments clung as she ran.

He shouted, and she ran faster. A few idlers, released now after midnight of the Passover, hooted and threw stones halfheartedly. She called the shreds of her power to cloak her. She had failed, she had failed utterly. Yet there was still a hope, if she could only reach the upper city.

The guards would have taken Joshua to Annas and Caiaphas; and they were all Klingsor's creatures. Nor would they dare, themselves, to have him put to death. Death was Rome's province, and the priests would remand Joshua to Pilate to answer to Rome on the trumped-up charges of breaking the *Lex Juliana* and seeking to be the King of the Jews. *That* would have Herod shaking in his sandals, wouldn't it? Joshua was of King David's old line. Though his ancestors had not ruled for centuries, she had no doubt that he was fit to rule, that he would do a far better job of it than Herod.

What *Pilate* would think of any of that made her shudder. From party after party, she knew what the tribunes whispered of him: a *novus homo*, therefore more Roman than the Caesars, and rigid in his hatred of the Jews.

It was not Pilate she was bound for; she was not fool enough to hurl herself, in elaborate gems and makeup, into the midst of a group of men. No, she would use her jewels to bribe her way to Claudia, Pilate's wife. Fallen on hard times—if she had been married off to *him*—Claudia was known to make a hobby of religions. A new prophet might intrigue her, and she might intervene.

Gasping, Kundry ran, always upward toward Roman Jerusalem. She flashed around a corner and into—no, walls were not swathed in coarse wool, did not reel back, then catch her.

"*You*, Kundry!"

"*You!*"

It was Judas who held her.

"Let go of me!" Kundry tried to twist free, but he held her with more strength than she had thought he possessed. Then she saw his eyes. Even in the starlight, she could see reddish glints as if some madness held him enthralled. Some madness—or some demon. Even on this holy night, Samael walked, summoned by Klingsor with his own blood, seeking a host to work his evil.

And here he was.

"Don't flee me. I have silver . . . see? Thirty pieces. They gave it to me . . ." He babbled worse than a man who had eaten poppy or mandragora before he falls into a stupor. He boasted of fame, of power, of how she must not fear him, he had money, and she must come with him now—he had always wanted her, and she had never known a man like him.

She was sure that last was true. And had no desire to change it.

Kundry spat at him, struck his thirty pieces of silver from his hand where it rolled and rang on the stone.

"I do not have to go with you or any man."

"But you are a harlot, it is your trade, and I can pay . . ."

"With the money paid you for a friend's blood! Joshua . . ." She spat at him. "You are not fit to hear his name. He trusted you. He let you carry the money to feed him and his friends. And you betrayed him with a kiss! And am I to let that same mouth touch . . ."

Judas reached out again, firmly blocking Kundry's way.

She summoned power, poised it, then stopped. If a demon indeed possessed Judas, that power could recoil threefold upon her head. She would never have this last chance to save Joshua and prevent herself from having to relive twelve hundred years of torment.

"You want fame?" Kundry whispered. Spittle flew from her lips and glinted before it vanished. "I'll tell you your fame. For the next thousand years, you'll be remembered as the man who betrayed his friend to shameful death. My God, do you know how they'll think of him? You've heard him called King of the Jews and Son of God. What do you think they'll call the man who turned *that* over to the courts?"

Judas gasped and recoiled. This time, Kundry followed him.

"Scholars will forget the words for 'traitor' and call such men 'Judas' instead—after you! And all for thirty paltry coins! Ha! In my hungriest days, I would not accept so little as a gift from a man. You want me? Go off, little man, and think who else you can betray—Pilate, perhaps, or Caesar himself. And get a better price this time."

Judas hunched down against the wall, muttering. Though every moment wasted made Kundry sweat with the knowledge that men die in prison, under questioning, some compulsion made her lean over him.

"I said, 'I will give it back,' " Judas mumbled, "but they laughed at me and hurled me out of doors. The man with the black beard said Joshua could cheat death, that he could *fly* out of prison. He could fly? I went up to the city and I looked out over it; but all I saw was a pit with flame in it forever." He raised his hands to his face and gnawed at his fingers. Spittle trailed down into his black beard. "Is that my fame?" The whites showed around Judas's eyes, and the redness of possession began to fade and be replaced by fear.

"That is your fame. To be despised as a traitor and to burn evermore. There is a gallows in your face and eyes. Go find it!"

Kundry fled, ignoring the despairing cry from behind her. Fool, she told herself an instant later, remembering. The demon that rode him would let him feel enough guilt, enough despair—enough purpose that he would hang himself, thus fulfilling another element in the story and driving another nail into the cross that Kundry hoped would never be raised. This one was her fault. She should have taken time to comfort him, to remind him that Joshua had said, "Go and sin no more," that he had always forgiven people, that he would forgive even Judas.

After all, had Joshua not suffered the man's kiss, hoping to the last that Judas would not do what prophecy had shown him that he would?

Joshua could do that. She was only Kundry.

Kundry sobbed as she ran, and felt the kohl sting her eyes. She must look like a drunk, a wanderer; they would never let her come in, much less see the Procurator's most excellent wife, the Imperial Lady Claudia. They would probably not even believe that the jewels she wore were good enough to bribe them with. With trembling hands, she sought to pat her long hair into order, to smooth her silken dress so that its folds did not wrinkle on her sweaty body and expose every curve, to wipe the worst of the smears from cheeks and eyes.

Rome, or Rome-in-Judaea, was stone and iron and brass; it nullified any power she had beyond her wits, and even those had wandered far tonight. Already a crowd had gathered by the walls and gates. Even as Kundry slipped by, the crowd was thickening. She recognized faces in it—some were priests disguised as common men, breathing outrageous lies of blasphemies, of Sabbath-breaking, of proscribed deeds in ears too easily inflamed and mouths too free to pass them on. Others whose faces Kundry knew from her wanderings about the city, her work in its poorest quarters, listened and were outraged: three times, fights broke out. Others in the crowd were wastrels, while a few men moved as quietly as shadows, their arms cocked in a way that meant they were not just armed, but adept.

"You're a liar!" A countryman shouted and drove his fist

into the falsely confiding face of—one of Klingsor's servants! Kundry realized with outrage.

Just as she herself was sighted, she came up to the gate she sought. She might not look like a great lady, but she no longer looked like a madwoman or something tossed from a feast as if unfit to roll on the dining couches with drunken officials.

Even in that, she did wrong. The Imperial Lady Claudia might well have had her curiosity piqued by a madwoman, a Jewish Sybil. Her earrings bought her admittance through the gate; a bracelet an audience with a servant who might have been a slave but who bore himself with all the arrogance of a victorious general. Not all her rings and necklaces could convince him to bring her before the Lady Claudia— "who is not to be spoken of by the likes of you"—but they *might*, mind you, *might* encourage him to mention her story to his mistress. That is, if she were not sleeping or bathing or doing any of a myriad of more important things.

With that, Kundry must be content. And with that, she was escorted out the gate. She wanted to hope that the Lady Claudia would intervene, but she desperately feared that she had spent her last treasures in vain.

The crowd had thickened. Kundry huddled into herself and waited for the sky to pale into dawn. A stupor of exhaustion was creeping over her, making it, in a curious way, easier for her to endure this time. Before it claimed her, she wondered why the sky did not darken instead.

When the sun had climbed halfway to its zenith, she came to herself. The crowd had shifted, and she half stood, half leaned against a wall, which could mean her death if a mob decided to surge forward. Some charitable soul had draped a robe over her, hiding clothes that could have gotten her stoned as a harlot.

Rumor ebbed and flowed around her with its thousand clattering mouths. Joshua was alone; even his friend the fisherman had denied knowing him when one of the high priest's servants had recognized him for a fellow Galilean by his accent. Joshua had been sent to Pilate with a great outcry of priests and sycophants.

"They're quick enough to hand him over to Rome," one man whispered, "but they sent others to do it, rather than risk being unclean during the Passover by actually setting foot onto Gabbatha."

Once, Kundry had seen the place of which the man spoke. Gabbatha was not its name, but the name of the immense stone pavement from which the Procurator rendered judgment.

"His lordship wasn't at all pleased at having this man brought in front of him, so he asked what charges they had against him."

" 'If he weren't a criminal, would we have brought him to you?' they asked. They had a bunch of trumped-up charges, like he'd said he could destroy the Temple and rebuild it in three days, or that he'd sit at the right hand of God. Right away, Pilate's face changed. 'You judge him,' Pilate said— you could see he doesn't want to get his hands any deeper into a local problem than he has to and he hates the priests—but, no, the priests said that our law forbids putting people to death."

"Not true," another man cut in. Kundry cowered into the folds of her robe. The heat from the sun and the bodies pressing so closely together was beginning to stifle her.

"Things went back and forth, and Herod got into the game. At first Pilate said that if this Joshua were a Galilean, that was Herod's jurisdiction, so he sent him over. They haven't been getting along well. Someone said he was probably happy to interrupt Herod's Passover."

An old man spat. "He's superstitious, like his father. Probably had a list of miracles as long as his arm he wanted to see performed."

"They didn't get done. Herod lost his temper, finally, and made Joshua get into one of his purple robes, then sent him back to Pilate dressed up as the 'King of the Jews.' "

"If he had any respect for himself . . ."

"Quiet! They can stone you for that."

"Someone said that this Joshua was preaching against giving tribute to Caesar and he wanted to be King of the Jews. You could see that that really hit the worthy Procurator—Rome doesn't like it when its officials let riots happen in the lands it's swarmed all over. And some man I hadn't seen before, big one with a black beard, all but said that if Pilate didn't have Joshua crucified, he was no friend to Caesar.

"So he asked them to bring Joshua in. He saw the robe, and you could tell he thought that was a laugh on Herod. Then he asked, 'Are you the King of the Jews?' You could see Joshua didn't want to answer; he just said, 'Do you ask this, or did other people tell you this about me?' Someone hit him for speaking that way to the Procurator.

"Whatever you want to say about him, Pilate's no fool, and he doesn't like Caiaphas and Annas . . ."

"Quiet, or you'll be in there *with* him!" someone hissed fiercely.

"Go on, man, I want to hear."

"So he asked, '*Are* you a king?' So then Joshua says, 'You say I am a king. To this end, I was born and for this cause, I came into the world, that I should bear witness to the truth. Everyone who is of the truth hears me.' You could see that this really annoyed Pilate. Here he is, hauled away from a feast just to talk to what he thinks is another of the madmen from the hills. So, he asks, 'What is truth?' to shut up what he thinks is another crazy prophet."

"That never works. You ask a prophet what is truth, he'll *tell* you till you wish you were deaf—"

"Then, Pilate goes out to talk to the priests and tell them that he finds no fault in this man Joshua."

"Kundry, is that you?"

Kundry turned around. It was Peter. The burly ship captain's eyes were red, and he hunched over as if he couldn't bear to be seen.

"You heard," he stated. "I could kill myself for denying that I know him. But that Judas has killed himself already, and I'm damned if I want to put myself in the same boat as him. Let's get you away from here. Any moment, Pilate's going to come out, and there could be a riot."

Tears filled Kundry's eyes. Peter was treating her as if she had a perfect right to condemn him. More than that, he seemed to think she was a sheltered family woman, concerned about her presence in a crowd. "I can take care of myself," she heard herself saying. "What are you going to do?"

"I'm going to wait till he comes out, and then I'm going to say, 'He is my friend, and I'll stand with him.' "

"You'll get killed!" she hissed. "Don't throw away your life. Go to Joseph of Arimathea; he's got money and influence. Maybe he can—"

A higher-pitched voice blurted out, "I'll wager Pilate is counting the days till he's recalled. We're making him crazy, him and his wife. I heard she sent him a message that he was to have nothing to do with Joshua ben Joseph because she'd had bad dreams . . ."

So the slave had been an honest slave, and Claudia had heard her message—for all the good it did. No matter what Kundry did to break the pattern, it seemed to snap back into its former order. She could act, weep, or curse; she could even pray—if she knew to whom—but it would do no good. Hope drained out of her with the remnants of her strength, and she pulled a fold of her robe over her head until she stood in darkness.

Several men laughed. "Roman or Jewish, they're all the same about religion. Keeps them busy."

Someone whispered and pointed at her.

"Come on!" Peter tugged at her garments.

"Why are you bothering that woman?"

"She shouldn't be here. Kundry, come on!"

"I will be all right here," Kundry whispered urgently. "These men look like decent sorts. You get to Joseph. Now, go!"

The crowd swelled throughout the morning. Several people fainted from the heat and were carried away. Inside, the Romans were feasting.

"It is the custom that the Procurator will release a prisoner after this feast," the man who had warned Peter not to bother Kundry told her kindly. He had told her that his name was Simon, and that he had two sons, Alexander and Rufus. Nervously, he talked about his family. He was from Cyrene, he said, and he wished he had never left. "The story was that Pilate had a criminal ready and waiting. He's stirred up a great deal of trouble, and he's killed someone—definitely a bad lot that no one wants walking around until his next crime. Everyone thought that Pilate would release *him*.

"He's angry at the priests. What odds will you give that he releases Joshua ben Joseph instead just to watch them sputter? You know they want him dead."

Under her robe, Kundry clasped her hands together. Maybe *that* would be the change in the pattern.

A roar went up—not cheers for the hated Romans, but a yell of gratified excitement like Kundry had heard at the games. Pilate appeared outside. The place where he stood was built like a good theatre so that his voice carried. "I see no harm in him," he said to someone remaining within the hall. "We can have him . . . chastised and released."

Kundry's nails bit into her palms and she felt the warm wetness of blood.

Pilate looked out over the crowd. "Well, do you want me to release the King of the Jews to you?"

A cry of assent went up, then was immediately drowned by the voices of men who thrust to the forefront of the crowd. They wore the clothes of farmers or merchants, but had the carriage of armed men. "Give us Barabbas instead!" they shouted.

Above them, standing at a cautious distance from Pilate, the high priest and Annas, his father-in-law, nodded. Behind them—Kundry tensed, for behind them was a black-bearded man dressed like a man of good family and proper upbringing—Klingsor!

Pilate thinned his mouth in distaste. All his Roman distaste for lawbreaking urged him not to release a plotter and a killer—especially if it would oblige a man he detested. "I ask you, what evil has this man done? I have examined him and found nothing worthy of death. Therefore, I will punish him and release him."

"Crucify him!" one of the newcomers shouted, and his fellows took up the cry.

Pilate looked as if he wanted to spit. Instead, he spoke too softly to be heard to a younger man, who went out and returned with a servant who bore a bowl of water. He waited till all was quiet, then dipped his hands into the basin. "I am innocent of the blood of this just man; do you see that?"

"His blood is on *our* heads and on our children's!"

Kundry gasped. That was Klingsor's voice. But when she looked up, she saw that he had not moved his lips at all. She had not realized that he could cast it so that it would sound as if it came from the crowd.

"So be it," said the Roman, chill with disgust. He thrust the bowl of water from the servant's hands to shatter on the stone and splash the nearest onlookers. "Give them Barabbas. And get ready . . . Jupiter Optimus Maximus, *gods*, what a people!"

He turned his back on the mob in a swirl of white toga folds and went into the hall.

"There's a mob been put in charge," whispered her friend. "Come along out of here. This is no place for decent folk."

The crowd seemed to have thinned out. Most of the onlookers had been people of the city, harmless folk caught up in a rush of anger and excitement; now, as if ashamed, they left the square to the rule of Klingsor's bought guards.

A roar of laughter came from the doors as they were flung open, and soldiers stamped out, dragging a bundle with them.

"God of Abraham . . . don't look, woman!"

A roar, as of bloodlust sated at the games, went up. Kundry had not thought there was that much cruelty anywhere in the world. Then the legionaries propped Joshua up before the mob, and she knew she was wrong.

"Behold your king!" shouted a centurion. Two of his men pretended to salute, abasing themselves in mimicry of an Oriental prostration, then rising hastily before Joshua could slump down onto the stone.

He could barely stand. They had not been content just to "chastise" him, but had beaten him with the *plumbatae*, the deadly whip with hooks of lead worked into its many strands. Many men had died under its lethal kiss: unfortunately, Joshua was too strong. He had been a handsome man, straight and strong. Now, it was impossible to tell what he had been; it was even hard to know that once he had been a man. The soldiers had wrapped him in the robe that had been Herod's ironic gift; it was almost the color of the driest of the bloodstains or of the bruises that covered what could be seen of Joshua's flesh.

Spit glistened on his battered face. One eye was swollen shut, and the other covered with blood. More blood sheeted down his face from . . .

"Don't look, I'm telling you! Dear God, they've driven those thorns into his head!" Simon tried to stand between Kundry and the battered near-corpse to whom the Romans pretended to bow. He gagged, then got control of himself. Around him, some people were not as fortunate. Others were weeping. "King of the Jews, they called him. So they made him a crown!"

Kundry sank to her knees. She hurled off her cloak and rent her gown. The silk tore with a shrill scream. "Woe, woe!" she wailed.

"Come on!" Simon of Cyrene grabbed her by one arm and wrapped the dark cloak about her with his other. "You can't get away like that. I'm getting you out of here."

"You don't need to . . ."

"I'd do the same for one of my sons' wives, and I'd hope anyone would."

"Bring me . . . where will he pass? I must see him . . ." Kundry gasped between sobs.

"Do you have people in the city? Is there anyone who can help you?"

"You saw. That Galilean. The sailor. Others, too. Leave me with them. I'll be all right."

"Will you?" asked Simon. "I don't think that anyone will ever be all right again."

He led her away. Another shout went up; the crossbeam had been brought out and loaded onto Joshua's back. And it was a long, long walk to the place of execution. Golgotha, it was called. The hill of skulls.

19

"I TELL you, there is no safety for any of us! Go back to the city," Simon implored for at least the fifth time.

"Is it any safer there?" Kundry asked him quietly.

"Jerusalem? The Holy City?" He wiped his forehead and scrubbed his hand across his beard. "We must be coming to the end of things if Jerusalem the Golden is not safe. Perhaps God will send us . . ."

"Then you think . . ."

"I *fear*," he admitted. "What if he *were* sent, and we did not know it? And let the Romans . . ."

She held up a warning hand: Simon's doubts could be the death of him.

Guiltily, he fell silent, swallowed, and glanced at the road as if he saw Romans escorting Joshua to Golgotha. He sweated and started like a spooked horse, clearly anxious to be away and just as clearly ashamed not to stand his ground and to leave a woman unprotected and alone.

"I won't be quite alone," she told him gently. "Look!" Down the road, she saw Peter and some of Joshua's other friends, muffled in heavy robes that would not conceal them from the Romans' sharp eyes: not for a moment. She hoped they were not planning something heroic, and therefore foolish. Last time, they had not, but in small things—a roll of silk, a life here, a wound there—the pattern of time and events did not change . . . as she had cause to know.

"Thank God!" he said. "Let me take you to them."

She shook her head and knew to the instant when he would try to overawe her with a show of male authority: she could see his shoulders twitch as he rehearsed gestures of taking her by the arm, escorting her—whether she would or not—over to the sturdy-looking men into whose hands he could honorably resign her. It would not have worked, but Kundry might have given much had she been able to dwindle to a maid on whom such might have worked.

Simon saw only a young woman fallen on fearful circumstances; but Kundry knew her level of experience and her age.

Just as obviously, he abandoned authority for persuasion. He would fail, but not because she did not respect his attempts.

"I beg you, just go over and stand near them," he asked her. She could read his thoughts. Just let her stand over by Joshua's disciples, Simon told her, and the danger might not feel as great. Even the pain could be kept in bounds.

"I have no place among them and will not presume," she insisted.

To her relief, she saw Martha shepherding a group of the women Maria had tended. Maria was up ahead, her arm around an older woman of immense beauty and dignity.

"Leave me with these women," she told Simon. She thanked him. If she had had even a single jewel left, she would have tried to give it to him. She did not think he would accept.

"I am sorry to leave you," he told her repeatedly. "But if this is the end of all things, I must get back to Cyrene."

"You," Kundry asked almost shyly. "What you started to say earlier . . . Do you believe that he is King of the Jews or . . . or the man of sorrows that Isaiah foretold?"

"I do not know what I believe. But I believe in my family, and I believe there is danger. So I must leave you. I beg you to forgive me . . ." His eyes went a little wild.

Promise me that you will be all right, that I need not fear for you, his eyes seemed to plead.

"Look after her," he told Martha before he left. *Watch her!* As if so much of this were not her fault. She was not used to such kindness.

Kundry began to speak, but "Hush, child," Martha said, stroking her hair.

"Thank you for bringing her to her friends," she told Simon, who gestured, indecisive, reluctant to leave the women where they crouched beside the road to Golgotha.

"We'll all manage," Martha promised him and gestured with one hand, almost a dismissal.

He seemed relieved to go as he hastened back to the city where he had money and affairs to wind up before he could return home. He did not look back, ashamed to flee before the women, who stationed themselves by the road along which convicted men were led to their deaths. Martha's heavy figure seemed to radiate calm. But her lips trembled, and she had to force a reassuring smile out for the man in case he did turn back.

A sheltered woman of the house, much cherished, much occupied with little things: where had she learned such courage and such calm?

"I saw my brother die and be reborn," Martha whispered to Kundry. "I didn't want to learn but I did. Nothing good is ever lost, no matter what it feels like.

"We will wait here. My sister will come with your friend Maria, and the men. My brother, too. They are bringing his mother; she came in for the Passover with us."

Kundry looked up into Martha's face.

"She will bear it because she must. And she can. You will know that the instant you see her." Then Martha's control cracked. "Oh God, dear God, child, this is hard. But we go on . . . is that really our Joshua? Who is that walking beside him?"

A howl of jeers and grief swept down from the city as Joshua plodded to his own death, urged on by legionaries. The howl shrieked up.

"He's fallen!" Ruth cried and huddled weeping.

"*Quiet!*" Martha demanded. "Control yourself. He was your teacher, not some trashy Greek actor. When he passes, you will greet him calmly and with respect. What's happening now?"

Kundry darted forward. "He rose and fell again—oh, it's heavy for him, he can't carry it! Who's that . . . the soldiers dragged someone off the road . . ." She began to laugh, her voice arching up into hysteria. Martha slapped her.

"Behave yourself! What is it?"

"It's *Simon!*" Kundry cried. "He was so afraid, and they

pulled him from the road to help Joshua carry . . ." Her mouth ran dry and she could not say the words.

"Here it is," panted one of Martha's servingwomen. "Ran . . . ran as hard . . ."

Martha took cup and phials from her hands. Removing the cloth that covered it, she sniffed. "Quite right," she said. "Here, Kundry. I've watched you. You move like a flash of lightning. When he"—her lips fluttered on Joshua's name, and her self-control faltered—"passes by, run out and raise this to his lips."

She handed the cup to Kundry.

"Don't drop it! That is all the myrrh we could find, and it costs the sky!"

The wine was unmixed, thick with sweetness and the heaviness of the drug, which would cloud a man's senses and stand between him and his pain. Enough myrrh and a man lost consciousness; more, and he died. Kundry did not think the cup held that much myrrh. It tingled in her hands—simple, silver, a shape of coolness and relief. Her own thirst swelled in her throat. If her belly had not been so empty, she would swear that she had been eating sand; but no, her eyes scratched so that, surely, she must have been rubbing it in her eyes instead.

Abruptly, the cup's curves and luster became familiar.

"Where did you get this?"

"The myrrh? I had it; and this balm, it was part of my mother's dowry, brought her from the spice routes. Tuck the little phial into your gown, so. Yes, that is good. And here is another, too. We may, God willing, need it yet.

"This morning, Joseph of Arimathea brought us the cup to use in case, in case they released Joshua and we could hold the feast . . . Oh my dear Lord, there he comes!" Martha wailed, forgetful of her own counsel. "Look at his poor face! Kundry, give him the wine!"

From the hollow blue sky, wind swirled down the road and hurled dust onto the women where they waited. Simon trudged forward, sweat matting his hair and brow as he bowed under the weight of the crossbeam. He would not see Cyrene now as soon as he wished; if the Romans took a fancy to question him, he might never see it at all. But

there was no rancor in his face, just the steadiness Kundry
had relied on in him. In the face of Joshua's mortal pain, he
had put aside even his fear.

"Steady, man," he muttered to Joshua as he had obviously muttered many times before. "Show those Romans
how a *man* does it. Let's go, brother. One more step . . ."

"No talking!" A legionary prodded him, and Simon
pushed on, taking pains to look down and hide the anger in
his face.

For ye were strangers in the land of Egypt. This *was* the
Passover for him. Once again, Jews labored for masters who
brought them only anguish; it was tears and sweat that
made the herbs bitter.

Joshua struggled forward, his head down, matted with
stinging flies that lit on his hair, the thorns that crowned his
head, and the oozing sores. They buzzed about his eyes,
coating them like a living mask. He blinked, but it did not
help.

Kundry ran forward. Her skirts cumbered her, and she
staggered to her knees. Yet still she raised the cup, and
Joshua smelled it over the reek of blood and sweat, dust and
fear.

He shook his head. Kundry thought he sought to rid
himself of the flies. She struck at them, wiping his face with
a corner of her cloak. Two soldiers came forward and she
glared at them, holding up the cup again.

"This is one cup I may not drink," he told her, though
his lips quivered with need for it.

Kundry turned the cup upside down, letting the wine and
costly myrrh mingle with the dust. She thought her thirst
would choke her, and she swallowed hard. If he was not to
drink it, no one should.

Behind her, the assembled women wailed and tore their
clothing. Kundry forbore. If she tore hers any more, she
would be naked. She dried the cup on the nearest tatter of
cloak and handed it back to Martha.

"Move on, 'Your Majesty,' " urged the nearest legionary; but Joshua wet his bitten lips and spoke.

"Don't cry for me, daughters of Jerusalem, but for yourselves and your children." His voice was stronger than it

had a right to be. "Soon, the days will come in which people will say, 'Blessed are the barren and the wombs that never bore fruit, and the breasts that never suckled.' Then they will begin—"

"Quit your babbling, and move it, Jew!" A Roman pushed at him.

"—to say to the mountains, 'Fall on us'; and to the hills, 'Cover us.' For if they do these things in a green tree, what shall be done in the dry?"

We shall thirst. Kundry bowed her head. Perhaps there would be a final mercy for her, if for no one else, at Golgotha. She could not imagine how she could have been callous enough to laugh at suffering and courage such as this. No, this time, since she must, she would watch, and she would weep. *She* might go free—but in that instant, she thought she might trade her freedom for Joshua's life.

Joshua and the surrogate who carried his cross trudged on. Behind him came another swirl of dust, two more, as soldiers herded up two robbers who would also be executed that day.

Weeping, the women fell in behind the grisly march toward Golgotha.

"You—the king there—you're going to have the place of honor. Right there in the center of the hill. King of the Jews." One of the guards laughed. Another made some jest about being the middle one in a group of three men; it made all the guards laugh even harder. They trudged up Golgotha. From all the comings and goings upon it, it was gray and sere; and it jutted up from the ground like the dome of a skull. On it lay three beams of wood and three coils of rope, waiting.

"Let's get them planted. Get those clothes off them," ordered the leader of the execution detail. Quickly, they stripped the three men to be executed. The two thieves were scarred, scrawny, of mixed nation and little shame. What was the point? They were going to die anyhow. Kundry suspected that they had been drugged; they staggered as the soldiers pushed them this way and that, and moved as if they had no idea what was happening to them.

But Joshua was conscious. He had lived among the Essenes, a modest people indeed. Stripping him in public was a violation, Kundry thought. So he must suffer that, too? They tugged the robe from his back and shoulders, and he flinched as they pulled the stained robe away from the flesh it had stuck to and thrust him down on the wood of the cross. She had seen many men's bodies, and she could have wept for the ruin of what had been almost sculptural beauty.

"Don't look, child." Martha urged. Numbly, Kundry looked away. But the chunk and splat of a hammer driving spikes into human flesh and bone made her cower into herself. Despite the drugs, one of the thieves screamed.

"This one gets a special sign. Procurator's orders. Got it right here, do you see? You don't read? It says, 'Joshua of Nazareth, King of the Jews.' Just looks it, don't he?" The sound of a nail hammered into wood, not flesh, this time came almost as a relief.

"All right, my lads, on the count of three, heave 'em up! And one . . . and two . . . and *three! Lift*, you bastards! All right, that ought to hold. Count off for guard duty. And you on guard, keep that pack of men at a distance. They could be trouble."

Behind her Ruth was mumbling, "Oh God. Oh God."

"Someone make her be quiet," Kundry whispered desperately to Martha, who would. Why was this happening again? She had tried so hard; surely, she was accursed. By rights, she ought to find where Judas had hanged himself and join him.

Kundry glanced up. The sun was near its height. And here she was, here Joshua was, again. All her planning, all her hope, and it had come to naught, except to stand on a skull-shaped hill before a dying man whom she earnestly believed *not* to be the Son of God, but who had reached her in a way that no one else had ever done.

"All you women—if you won't go home, trot yourselves over there!" One of the soldiers swung a spear at them. Painfully, they levered themselves up and moved to the spot that the legionary pointed out.

"Can't we stay here? He looks so *alone*," Ruth whispered

to Martha, who shook her head. Her round cheeks were wrinkled; she had aged years in a single morning.

"Pray, little one," Martha told her.

The women settled down to wait for the deaths. The sun crawled toward noon. Kundry had not remembered how harsh a thought it was: to die at noon.

The crucified men, their hands and feet bleeding from the spikes, tossed heads back and forth. The two thieves hardly seemed conscious; Joshua, though, was all too aware. All three moved in the fatal dance of the crucified. First, slump down till all the air was gone. Then rise as high as you could on the part of the cross called the horn or even, ironically, the seat, despite the tearing pain in hands and feet as torn flesh pressed against the nails that impaled it. *Steal* as much air for cracking ribs and struggling lungs as you could; suck it in till your ribs cracked. Then sink down and breathe it out in a spasm of pain or forgetfulness, while the blood and the sweat trickled out of you, and the flies buzzed, and the guards bet on how long you could last. Then rise to snatch at the air again until strength or will gave out and the body sagged against the spikes, against the wood; and into death.

"If you *are* King, why can't you save us?" one of the thieves wasted precious breath to demand.

"Shut your face!" the other told him. "Lord, remember me."

"Today," Joshua gasped and used precious strength to turn his face toward the second thief. "Today, you will be with me."

Around the sixth hour, the sky darkened.

"Going to be quite a storm," muttered a legionary. "By the breasts of Artemis, this is boring work. Anyone got any dice?"

"What you got to wager?"

"Me? Nothing. But *they've* got robes, and I don't think they're going to be using them again. That's not much, but it's the best stakes we've got."

"This one's bloodstained."

"All right, I'll give you odds on it."

"Who'll play?"

If Kundry could have cursed them for the clatter of dice and gossip, she would have.

The darkness grew. The women wept silently. Nearer their leader's cross, the men kept guard. The legionaries diced. And the men on their crosses writhed up and down, fighting for their next breath. With a groan, one sagged, his body dangling from his pierced hands.

"Marcus! That's one!" a man off guard called out.

"No guts, these Greeks. Whole world's going to Hades. You have a wineskin there?"

"Just the usual."

"Pass it over."

Gradually, Kundry fell into a kind of numbed waiting. You could never tell how long anyone would last on the cross. If a man's will was strong, stronger even than his body, he could last more than a day. That was the reason for the *crurifragium*. Break the victim's legs, make it impossible for him to rise up and strain for breath, and he would die more quickly. If you counted any shortening of pain as mercy, you could almost call it kind. Kundry did not.

Clouds unusual for Judaea massed over the hill, and the day's heat grew oppressive. Kundry found herself listening for thunder.

A rumble made the ground tremble. Standing as near the cross as they dared, Joshua's disciples tensed. Hoofbeats rang out. Two Roman officers accompanied a guard detachment and some officials from the Temple. Their robes were clean and bright, despite the dust of the roads, and they looked like they had never suffered even as much as an upset stomach. With them, but looking as if he wished he had come by himself, was Joseph of Arimathea.

"Say what?" asked one of the soldiers standing watch. He looked up from his dice at a man drinking vinegar and water. "They want to break the men's legs. Early for that."

"Weaklings," spat the man, who set down the cup. "This lot hasn't been up there all that long. What cowards those priests are. Can't wait for us to nail them, but once they're up, the damned priests whine about blood and their laws."

"It's something about their religion," the gamer said.

"They have a holiday coming on tonight. Their Sabbath, you know, when the City closes down?"

"*Everything* shuts down—except the assassins."

"In any case, it's their Sabbath. What's more, it's also this Passover, the festival that's made for all the crowding in the city lately."

"Made for more crime," snorted his fellow.

"The law is that bodies of executed men cannot hang overnight. So they have to help these fellows along. Why not let them? Those bastards'll be glad to be out of it."

"They can't break his bones," muttered Peter. "I won't let them. It's written in Isaiah that his bones . . ." He began to close in on the newcomers, his eyes on the spears that the guards carried.

The two mounted officers closed in. One of them, Kundry realized, was Longinus, the blind centurion. His companion kept a hand on his reins. Both held aloof, wearing the impassive face of official Rome.

"We can't let this happen," Kundry said. "Not a riot. They'll all die."

"It won't if we're down there." She never heard who made that suggestion. But in a flurry of skirts, Martha leading, the women ran to Golgotha and, abandoning propriety, stood among the disciples, restraining them by their presence.

Joshua looked down and saw his mother standing among the others, next to Johanan the younger. She had dropped her veil to let her son have the comfort of her face. Of middle age, she would have been beautiful, had she not been so worn; the blue cloak she wore seemed to fold in about itself, so slight she was.

"Woman," he said, his voice hoarse, "there is your . . . your son." And when Johanan looked up, "Your mother is standing there." Immediately, Johanan went over and put his arm around her. He started to lead her away, but she refused to go.

Longinus's fellow officer leaned close and muttered something into the older man's ear. On two of the crosses, the lethal dance for breath continued. Joshua whispered something.

"What is it, Lord? What did you say?"

"Thirst . . . I thirst."

"Where is that cup?" Martha looked around frantically. "None of their dirty things for him, even now."

She pulled out the silver cup that Kundry had given back to her. With a speed she would have denied having, and before Kundry could give her the second phial of myrrh, she set the cup down at the base of the cross and reached for the vinegar and water. A Roman gestured her away. "Go home, mother. This is no place for you."

And, when Martha would have poured the drink anyhow, "Go on! Move! Infernal gods, these women are as stubborn as the ones on Tiber bank!"

He snapped his fingers at the guard from the Temple. "Give me that spear, you." From a pack, he took out a sponge and soaked it in the drink. Taking the spear, he impaled the sponge on it and lifted it to Joshua's mouth. He touched it, but only for a moment, and the soldier took it away.

"My God, why . . . why . . ." Joshua's voice trailed off.

"What's that?"

"He's calling on Elias," a soldier said. "Some sort of wizard. Thinks he's been abandoned."

"Can't save him now, can he?"

"That's one bad storm, a real ship crasher, brewing. Odd this time of year. Do you hear the thunder? Ought to put these men out of their misery before we all drown."

The thunder rumbled and rumbled again, drawing closer. Lightning shone dimly within the darkening clouds. The guards moved closer, reaching for hammers heavy enough to break the dying men's legs.

"No, don't, don't!" Kundry broke and ran forward. Exhaustion and grief as cruel as death shattered her control, and she flung herself down at the foot of the cross. "Don't!"

"I'll take charge of this one." Hands caught her by the shoulders and jerked her up against a body she knew too well. Klingsor shook her, and her robe fell open where she had torn it. One of the Romans smacked his lips.

"Save a piece for me!"

It was all too much. Kundry sobbed. She should have

known better. Was this—to try and fail to save the man whose death had damned her before—part of her punishment? The worst of it was that she had dared to hope, she, who should have known better. She could not believe that Klingsor was that clever; yet he had known enough to come here, to be in at the death and to lay possession to her in a way none of the people here could dispute without endangering themselves. Certainly, she dared not protest for her companions' sake. Joseph of Arimathea started forward to defend her, but Kundry warned him away with a quick flash of her eyes.

Kundry flung up her head to look at the death throes of the man she had fought to save. Exhaustion and fear, compassion, and an absolute conviction of her own uselessness crushed her will. She had never been fit to bear the weight of such grief; if there were a God, why had He brought her here?

Silence fell over the hill of skulls. It was not to be borne. She could not bear it. She could bear nothing further.

In that moment, it spewed out of her like poison from a wound—*just as it had the last time*. Kundry laughed. Laughed till the women recoiled and the Romans made warding-off gestures. Maria started toward her, but Joshua's mother collapsed in the arms of two of the women, and Maria had to tend her.

"Quiet, you bitch!" Klingsor slapped her. But still Kundry laughed, laughed till she gagged and sobbed.

"Enough of this!" The growl came from Longinus. "Are you men and soldiers, or a cat playing with a mouse? You'd kill a pig with more decency!"

He tore his reins free of his companion's grasp. Guiding his horse by sound as well as by his all-but-useless eyes, he rode toward the man who held the spear. He tore it from his hand, then raised it as if he would use it as a lance.

Joshua looked up.

"It's finished," he said simply, as if something surprised him. He sighed with relief, then sagged against the cross. He was dead before Longinus's spear pierced him. Blood and water gushed from his side. Some trickled into the cup set by the cross.

A flight of birds darted overhead. Two soldiers fumbled for their luck-pieces. For a moment, all was silent. Not even the Romans seemed to breathe.

Lightning lashed down from the sky, crackling with a smell like garlic and fresh blood. With a glare that lit up all Golgotha, it struck the spear Longinus bore aloft. For an instant, the old centurion went rigid. A blue haze enveloped him, and he shook. Drops from the spear spattered onto his face, and he cried out.

Then his horse screamed and bucked, and he fell. His aide flung himself from his own horse and was at his side, supporting the older man's head against his shoulder. He struggled to get free.

"Get back," he shouted at the others. Then his voice changed. "Sweet . . ." It trailed off. "I can *see!*"

Longinus's eyes, unclouded now, glanced over at the cross and the cup that stood at its base. "It *glows!* Look at the cup! It's shining crimson!"

Above him, Joshua's ruined face almost seemed to smile.

At the same moment, all of Kundry's muscles locked. She felt as if she were kneeling in a violent light, impaled on it by hands and feet and side. She thought she had never seen anything so wonderful; she feared that if it went on, she would be reduced to ash; she *remembered* how this had happened before. She hung suspended in that light. For the moment it took for her to hear her doom, she was absolutely calm. Her laughter was over. For now.

Again, again, the judgment and the sentence. To wander, a voice echoed in her tortured mind. To wander until a fool made wise through pity would appear and she could find forgiveness. It was not a curse, save that she heard it so. The man who died had been kind to her; even at the last, he would not curse her.

The curse lay in her own mind and how Klingsor twisted it. Joshua meant only a blessing—time to work out her own salvation, since she would not accept the help he offered. For an instant, hope fluttered, white-winged, overhead, and her heart rose toward it . . .

The light died away, and she was bereft, except for the

crimson gleam that rose from the silver cup at the base of the cross.

Kundry felt Klingsor's body tense. He didn't know whether to drop her and steal the cup, with the promise of power that that blood and water might hold, or to clutch the victim he had found again. As the crimson flame faded from about the cup, Joseph of Arimathea stepped forward. Gently, with the care he would have given to an infant son, he lifted it and wrapped his dusty cloak about it. A hint of white light appeared to form around him, then to dissipate.

"They say I can take his body down for burial," he said to Joshua's friends and his mother. "Don't worry about a funeral. My tomb has long been ready."

Balked of the cup in the instant of its transformation, Klingsor tightened his hands on Kundry. She would pay for that loss.

She drew another breath. She felt another laugh coming. What could she lose by it this time? Her life? That would be a blessing, not a curse. Despite her battle, it had all happened all over again. Maybe she should laugh, should scream something that would condemn herself and Klingsor, and then they could both be dead.

That would save him the centuries of frustration, of emasculation, of hatred. Too good for him, she thought. Just too good.

Klingsor's hand smashed against her jaw and she tasted the flat, coppery sweetness of her own blood. "Now, you come with me . . ." he hissed.

Kundry wailed. Dear God—no, she had no right to call on God. But she would *not* live through it again, not watch Klingsor pin their fortunes to those of Simon Magus, not see him scream as he traded manhood for power; and, God help her, she would die before she relived the thousand years of bloodshed she had suffered through before. It was just: this time, she had not only laughed, she had *made* this death happen. But she was weak, she was wicked, and she could not bear this.

"I *won't!*" she wailed as the full horror exploded in her mind: once again, she would betray Amfortas.

"Oh yes, you will," Klingsor muttered. *He* had not been

cast free in time. In this time and place, he had no idea of what Kundry was ranting about. All he knew was that his creature, his tame female toy and lure had broken free and fled, and he would punish her for that.

Again, and again, and again . . . for more than a thousand years. What had started as a laugh came out as a wail. Then the earth shuddered and split asunder . . .

. . . and Kundry cast herself free of the body of Kundry-the-girl, following the crimson track of light cast by the Grail. Like a swimmer escaping a foundered ship and cutting through gray water toward a light far in the distance, she hurled herself after that light, back up the toll of years and decades and centuries. She had laughed again. She had fled again. She was hopeless again and she hated herself.

Bells rang out, teasing at her consciousness. She had heard such bells before, but she did not know where. Their somber cadence drew her even as the crimson light faded. Blind and screaming, she flew past the centuries.

Then her head cracked against something hard, and for a long time, even her guilt and hatred vanished.

20

KUNDRY awoke. She was lying on crumbling rock and lichen. Her hands clutched rough wood. Where her face rested against it, the wood was wet.

She tensed, but refused to open her eyes. Joshua's mother had fainted. Maria had caught her, while Kundry, the coward, had hurled herself forward to embrace the base of Joshua's cross. Her fingers tightened on the wood, preparing for the moment when Klingsor would haul upon her shoulders, dragging her away, as he had done the last time. She wondered he had not kicked her already.

Kundry shuddered. Oh God, Joshua had died again. Again, she had watched. Again, she had laughed. And once again, she had been doomed to live and to wander again until a fool made wise by pity could pardon her. She wanted to die, but there was no death for her.

That would never happen. She too was a fool; her own pity had simply worsened her vice and folly.

Look at the costs of folly, she ordered herself. She made herself raise her head. She drew a deep, shuddering breath. No dust crusted her mouth or filled her hands. Lush green and black shadows rustled overhead. Nearby, a stream rippled like Cedron in Gethsemane, the night Joshua and his friends danced together.

Every muscle in her body ached as if she, and not Joshua, had been beaten by Rome's soldiers. Hands so pale and wrinkled that she had difficulty recognizing them as her own clutched a thick, gnarled root where it forced itself up from the rocky ground and into the trunk of the huge oak whose leaves whispered overhead. A breeze stroked her hair like

a mother consoling a daughter who had wept herself sick
over her betrothed's death.

She lay on rocky ground, entwined in the oak's roots as
if in a mother's arms, cushioned by moss and some hardy
grasses. Piercing the leaf shadows, sun warmed the rocky
ground on which she lay. Her face rested in long blades of
soft green grass that had grown up where it had cracked and
soil had formed. A rhythmic beat-beat-beat like the heartbeat of the earth itself lulled her.

The whisper of leaf and water and the rustle of the wind
melded with that steady throbbing and another sound altogether. A voice? She shuddered against the oak roots. Then
truly, she had run mad. Perhaps Klingsor had dragged her
out into the desert to die, and this was all a thirst-dream
before the end. It was too much to bear. She whimpered.
Fear, mercifully brief, overpowered her, and she fainted.

Overhead, green leaves dropped from the vast branches
to cover her.

Instinct pricked her awake. Even with her eyes closed,
she knew she was being watched. Awareness returned, not
with a quick snap back to alertness, ready to fight or run,
but languidly. She raised her head. It was feverish, as if she
lay in the desert in the blinding heat of noon. Still, it was
shadowy here: merciful, seductive, shadows she did not
deserve. And the leaves, stream, and heartbeat from the
earth had not gone away.

Now she saw she had companions. Even as she watched,
a squirrel chittered anxiously and moved in to snuffle at her
hair. A fawn and a cat, both dappled for concealment in the
woods, stood watch. The cat padded forward, ignoring the
squirrel, and extended a fastidious paw to touch her face.
Claws prickled out, then were withdrawn. She tried to out-
stare it, but it blinked and yawned. Not a cat for lap or
hearth; though it forebore to attack, it was quite at home in
the wild.

"Time to wake, is it?" she muttered. Her voice, rasping
in a dry throat, sounded like a crow boasting of its thefts.
The cat hissed and backed up. The squirrel and the fawn
fled. Overhead, the leaves rustled more loudly. Kundry
drew a deep breath.

The beasts . . . the gentle beasts of Broceliande, a kind of living heraldry, flanked her. Her fate had brought her full circle, out of Klingsor's castle, back to Judaea, then away, back to Broceliande—and when? How many years had passed?

She thought she had been thirsty for all of them. Abruptly, the ripple of the nearby brook became intolerable. Scrabbling against the oak tree for handholds, she forced herself up by stages and staggered to the stream. The cat followed, much more decorously. Flinging herself down by the bank, Kundry lapped at water so cold it made her teeth ache. It tasted rich, of earth and iron, not like the stale, muddy stuff of the Judaean lowlands or what you drew from the wells in Jerusalem, where the water blinded you as the sun struck it. She drank for a long time, then wiped her chin. Her hand still was pale, the color of dust, but it seemed less wrinkled, as if the water had restored fullness and flesh that she must have lost in the long flight across the years. Sighing, she rolled over onto her back and blinked at the play of sun shadow on leaves until the cat extended its paw again to tap her cheek.

"Turn that way?" she whispered. Fool, going to a cat for counsel. It would betray her: but how much better did she deserve? She had flung herself down on a little spit of land that jutted into the stream and separated the water into two parts. One continued to flow swiftly; the other was a pool. Given the winds that constantly whispered through Broceliande, its surface was almost unnaturally still and clear.

Kundry recoiled at what she saw in it—an old woman, withered like the beggars outside the gates of the Temple, her eyes wild, her face sagging with age and exhaustion. Her hair was matted, dark, but almost as dead as the fabric that unravelled about her shoulders and breast, showing collarbones and ribs almost as ridged as the roots of the nearby oak tree, and her breasts were the merest flaps of drooping skin.

Why hadn't she heard the footsteps of such a creature? What was it doing in Broceliande? Her hands flew before her to ward it off; the creature in the pool flung up its hands, reflecting her fear.

Klingsor's power had flung her back in time, costing her
nothing but the pain of having to relive her own damnation.
That pain had forced her to draw on power of her own to
escape a place and a time she could no longer bear to live
in. She had not believed such a power was hers, to hurl her
from Golgotha to Broceliande.

How long had it been? Judging from the face and body
reflected before her, hundreds and hundreds of years.

Poorly trained as she was, drained as she had been before
some instinct made her summon it, there was a price for
such power. Here it was. The strength of her body. The
vigor of her protracted youth. The beauty that had been a
snare and a delusion for Amfortas. She had scorned that
beauty, and now it too was gone, extinguished with the
power she had drained to thrust herself away from Golgotha. She was appalled that she mourned it.

Her hands clasped upon the coolness of crystal, concealed within the rags she had worn. A phial. She had thrust
it there, and the balm it held was as useless as she herself.

With a low moan, she rose from the too-revealing pool
and retreated to the oak tree. Cowering against its roots, she
shut her eyes and willed the world to go away. The earth-
beat rose comfortingly against her. After a while, light and
sound subsided.

How long she slept, she did not know. Intervals of sleep
and dream and wakefulness flowed past each other. There
was food, there was water, there was moss to lie on. There
would be darkness—well and good; after a time, there
would be sunlight again. If flashes of lightning, violent
faces—a red-haired man with fire in his eyes, a black-
bearded man with white teeth, or the sad, sad faces of the
dead or maimed—brought her awake moaning, the forest's
heartbeat and the trees' voice lulled her to rest.

No beasts awaited her when she woke again. Her mind
was as clear as the attention of the old and dying. She felt
as likely as they to dream dreams or see visions. What *was*
truth? The last person she had heard ask that had doomed
a holy man to death. Truth? It was a word; and then it was
nothing at all compared with the whirling in her brain, the
hunger in her belly, the loneliness in her heart.

But she had not, it seemed, been altogether alone as she slept.

A pile of fruit, windfalls carefully borne in jaws or fore-paws and left here, awaited her. She seized an apple and rubbed it on her cloak. So, those rags had come forward in time with her? How long had she come—and how long had she lain here? Judging from her hunger, quite some time. She bit into the apple, and juice ran down her chin. The pulp and sweetness made her think she might be drunk—but on one apple?

"Easy . . . easy . . . slowly now . . ."

Decidedly, she was drunk. She had always heard that old people grew drunk quickly, and she was old now; she had seen that in the pool. Drunk or mad to hear voices and heartbeats coming from the ground and the oak tree. She dragged herself up to rest against its trunk, in a convenient, sun-warmed hollow that felt like leaning against an old friend's back.

"Daughter . . ."

She whimpered and dropped the apple.

"No fear, daughter. Rest . . ."

Any peasant knew that Broceliande was filled with voices, filled with spirits that flew between heaven and earth and were neither human nor demon. In her last life here, she had ignored them or moved through the woods, confident that they would stand aside or do as she bid them. Now, though, she was helpless against any revenge such a being might take. She tried to think of the invocations Klingsor had used to command and control such beings, but her mind flinched from that knowledge as if she had tried to raise herself on a broken leg.

Names were power. If this creature knew her name, he could destroy her. She could not trick its name from it or command it to surrender it. She could but ask.

"Who are you?" Such a feeble reed of a voice to come from a withered throat. She did not expect an answer, much less the one that came.

"I am . . . I was . . . Merlin."

Shadows crept within her mind as if a physician probed a wound. Merlin! Arthur's mage, bound to fight the dark as

surely as she had been Klingsor's slave. If he had seen her
in the noontime of her power, flaunting her beauty and her
magics, he would have struck her down in defense of his
lord. Perhaps he would do so now. Appalling: she found
herself unwilling to die thus.

She flung up her head, sought deep within herself for the
traces of the power that had hurled her from Golgotha.
Lightnings exploded behind her eyes. Then darkness over-
powered her.

That she woke again at all surprised her. She lay still,
unable to move: when she was a child, she had had such
dreams in which her enemies compassed her about, and still
she could not move. She opened her mouth to call out—*she
had screamed over and over again, but no one came, no one
would come*—but no sound emerged.

I am dreaming this, too, she thought. *A waking dream.*
Then dream and waking engulfed her reeling consciousness,
overwhelming truth and lie alike.

Moisture beaded her forehead. It could not be dawn yet;
she could not remember seeing a sunset. Even as she tried
to puzzle out the time, the cat returned, carrying a leaf wet
by the stream. It dropped it on her forehead, then retreated,
fastidiously cleaning its paws with its tongue.

"Forgive . . . I tried too hard, but it has been so long . . ."

Again the voice of the entity that called itself Merlin. It
was true that Merlin was a master in Broceliande, more
aware of its secrets than any other man or woman who
journeyed in its shadows or spent a mage's lifetime studying
it.

But Merlin was a man, Arthur the king's adviser, not a
disembodied voice and heartbeat located in an oak tree and
a rock. That told her. She had returned to the time from
which she had been exiled—or close enough. How odd it
seemed to think of Arthur, not Herod, as king again.

There were other kings in the world. She wanted to think
of none of them. And she was afraid of the voice that spoke
to her out of Broceliande's heart.

"How can you be? Merlin is a mage, not a spirit; he
dwells in Camelot with Arthur the king."

Her voice was sharp with fear.

The heartbeat seemed to speed up. "Ahhh . . ." A sigh that Kundry, even weakened as she was, could tell held deep sorrow. "No longer, child, no longer . . ." A branch snapped and fell to the ground. Kundry reached out and picked it up. Sap trickled from the break.

"Did my limb hit you? I am sorry." Already, as if heartened by the simple fact of someone to talk with, the voice took on increased vigor.

"You didn't mean to. What happened to you?"

"I was betrayed," the voice breathed with a swaying of leaves and branches as if the oak tree groaned in a high wind. "She was so lovely, but she was of the dark, and I could not resist . . ."

"How can you tell *me* this?" Kundry demanded. "Do you know who I am—what I am and where I came from? My name is Kundry!"

Leaves fell, covering her, and she waited to be engulfed as the ground beneath her shivered and some of the mosses split asunder.

"Do you not *know?*" she asked. She was too feeble to sustain her rage, and her voice broke. She did not wish to die with her mind shattered by madness, but she could no longer bear the truth in silence. "I lured Amfortas of Montsalvasche, your great king's ally, not to his death, but to worse. He lost the holy spear and was wounded where . . . where he most offended. I fought not to submit, but I am weak, useless."

She remembered now: since the defeat that cast her from her home, she had always fought, but she had always failed.

"Betrayer and betrayed," came the voice. "We are alike, you and I. It is all failing. Camelot will fall; Arthur has sinned and will fail, and I cannot be there to help him. Oh woe . . ."

Merlin's anguish reached out like a high wind and caught Kundry into its core. Betrayer and betrayed. Kundry remembered now Klingsor's words. *Some say Merlin is the devil's son. No need to turn on Camelot; it will rot from within soon enough.*

What had happened to snare a victorious mage within

the wood that he knew better than any other man or wizard? Why did he call himself betrayer and betrayed?

She huddled against the trunk of his oak tree, laying her wrinkled cheek against the bark. For a moment she was a child again, sick of a fever in bed and tucked up in blankets. *Tell me a story, Father. See, I am listening.* She was a babe again in that moment. Then the moment passed, and she shuddered.

"Tell me," she whispered.

The branches soughed for a long time, and Kundry shivered. Beasts drew near and crept up against her, warming her. Old as she was, she slept easily; and though she meant to lend Merlin whatever ease an old woman's listening could provide, once again, she slept. This time she dreamed. And as she slept, she dreamed and trembled as she dreamed: of a slim minx in a green gown, a court turned knowing, though not greatly wise, and of how a lonely magus turned to folly and was betrayed, shut up beneath the stone to die for daring to try to love. For after all, who was Merlin to dare to try?

Klingsor would have laughed. Kundry wept.

"Master," she cried, who had called no man "master" even under compulsion, "you know I too am a betrayer!"

The branches of Merlin's oak rustled, and twigs snapped. *And are you not punished?*

"I was sent back by Klingsor . . ."

"Do not speak that name!" The branches of Merlin's oak rustled feverishly, then were stilled too silently. Kundry thought of a sentry, halting the better to hear what might be the footsteps of his enemy.

"He—best you do not name him here—watches this place. Any untoward use of magic could draw him and force me to spend my powers. I beg you"—the trapped mage's voice was hoarse—"help me save my strength."

"I promise . . . if I can."

"Go on."

"I must. Sharing Amfortas's guilt, I share his punishment. I must wander until a fool made wise by sorrow heals me."

Joy and a sudden wild surmise kindled her heart.

Could Merlin be that fool?

An answer came.

Not I, child. I have spent too long in being Wise.

Kundry's head spun. She laid it back and sank fully into her dream. Merlin's arts were deep enough that he knew their value: he had no escape from the trap he had devised and blurted out the secret of. If he could not turn his arts to freedom, he turned them to what freedom he could have. He learned patience, how to use his art to bear what he must bear. Learning that, he learned how best to learn in his changed life. The years taught him how to speak again, how to spread his power through the woods like a vast tree's latticework of roots. His power brought him knowledge, his knowledge a greater sadness.

For Camelot waned. It grew knowing and clever, where once it was content to be good. Even the road to Montsalvasche grew narrow, raided by Klingsor's mamluks and even by bandits pretending to serve the wizard, whose castle preyed upon travelers in Broceliande. Camelot withdrew, then Montsalvasche. Finally, the road between the two cities closed altogether.

Arthur's men clustered around their king at his Round Table and spent their skills on feasting, on the crafting of glorious robes like a snake's new skin and shimmering tail, not on weapons. Now, the tales of wonders they heard as they dined were slurs upon the ladies whose virtue they should have fought to protect.

But the knights no longer believed in virtue: they had become sophisticated. Firelight glittered on brocades and gems plundered worldwide. Guinevere laughed as she presided over the wine, her red mouth bitter. And she too was a betrayer and a wrecker.

Half waking, Kundry flung herself forward. It was the Grail that could redeem Camelot as it nourished Montsalvasche; and she had turned upon its dearest hope.

Resting her cheek on the arching roots of Merlin's oak, she wept, and the falling leaves touched her matted hair. As well that she had been . . . elsewhere. Her mind recoiled from the memory as if she had touched velvet and found it warm and moist with blood.

This is my kingdom now, Merlin whispered. *The beasts are my students and my care. And you . . . I would heal you if I could.*

"There is no balm for me," Kundry told the wistful voice. "None save the coming of the fool."

"Fool yourself!" came a crisp voice that reminded Kundry of Maria for its pragmatic compassion. "What is that you bear against your heart?"

An alabaster phial, iridescent with great age, lay beneath her eyes.

"No? Broceliande itself can heal the spirit. If it has not taught me peace, it has taught me patience. I shall lie here, and I shall wait.

"But now, Monsalvasche is waning. When the power fails, the wood will truly become a waste, devoid of magic or even health."

Leaves rustled overhead. As Kundry looked up, a green leaf fell upon her withered cheek like a benediction.

"For now, though, and here, there is peace," the voice told her. "*I* ward this place. To the limits of my strength, I will protect those whom God put in my care. And I believe that even my soul will rise again. *I* shall rise again when Arthur wakes and calls me back to his side. Sleep, child. Heal as much as you can."

21

CAST out from the mercy of the world, Kundry flung herself on the charity of Broceliande. Day slipped into night, wake-time into dreaming almost imperceptibly: and whether Kundry heard a voice in truth or madness ascribed wisdom to the leaves, she did not care to know. It was enough that the beasts of the wood brought her food, the nearby stream provided her drink. The rustle of leaf and branch taught her patience, if not wisdom.

Lying on her back, cushioned by the grass and fallen leaves, she stared up at the sky until her eyes dazzled, her mind reeled, and she thought she would have to look away. Clouds scudded across the sun; in those instants of restful dimness, her battered mind thrust free of her body. She found herself now able to summon the beasts. A fawn, its dam watching, would hold still as she touched it. A bear might drop a honeycomb at her feet. As she lay on the earth, she learned the earth's wisdom: patience, the way time and events flowed, and how—although feebly—to tap that great stream and fill her few needs.

She might have reviewed old spells: she thought to. But when she tried, dizziness exploded behind her eyes. Not yet, then? Best to sleep. Once again, her consciousness escaped the mind and body abused by the plunge through time and ranged the limits of the forest.

It was embattled land now, though guarded still against the ills that plagued its neighbors. Camelot's Arthur sat upon his throne and pondered the decline of his realm. Too many knights died in foreign lands, fighting for no cause but the joy of fighting. Some had even allied not with Christian princes from afar, but with heathen lords. Now, all had been recalled.

And the fortress of Montsalvasche seemed waiting only for the last attack that must inevitably come to cast it down. Titurel was scarce more than a breath of life in ancient bones, while Amfortas—

The name struck her like a blow to a half-healed wound, bringing her from her trance.

"Sweet God, how long have I wandered?" How long had the Grail king survived, betrayed by her, wounded, yet kept alive by the miracle he must still perform each day?

Each day that she had strayed and he had suffered lay upon her soul.

She wept. Her tears brought her no comfort. Merlin's voice whispered in her ears. It was madness: she was mad. Perhaps she had never been aught else.

The weather turned cooler. By night, the beasts huddled by her side. How good she felt that her body warmth could comfort them, providing some recompense for the food they brought her. Often they whimpered, as if the bad dreams that haunted her stalked them too.

On a gray morning, she awoke and found the branches bare. No cats or fawns answered her calls. No bears brought her late-summer fruits. For a while, she drifted as beasts drift from an abandoned farm, foraging as she must, but returning to the place she felt was safe. Her lair. The growing cold impelled her, and she snatched up what she could find to augment her tattered dress: a snakeskin cast in the spring; an abandoned strip of cloth. Fewer and fewer beasts crouched at her side for warmth; still, none menaced her. The colder nights made her briefly lucid. She longed for fire, but lacked flint and steel.

Autumn was dying; winter was drawing near. Even the rippling of the stream sounded chill and subdued; its water when she drank had a tinge of ice, of iron in it.

Like a child seeking its parents lost in war, not wanting to believe they cannot return, Kundry wandered, but always returned to her accustomed oak as a child whose village is destroyed by a war will return to the charred timbers of what had been its home. She sat there for hours, though she might better have spent the time gathering food. She listened for the voices that had whispered in her mind all summer, waiting for instructions.

Merlin's voice came no more. Instead, as if she listened now to Broceliande itself, Kundry gathered herbs, roots, and leaves in her small wanderings, and marveled at the wealth she found in such a small compass of ground. Sniffing and tasting, she remembered the properties of what she had harvested: this for aches, this for fever, and this to make a wound heal clean.

She was a beast of Broceliande, she thought; and like a wise mother, it taught her what she must know to hunt its depths and survive.

The dawn she woke to find rime stiffening the rags she wore, she woke as well from her long dream and took stock. Broceliande was no longer the lush realm she had invaded with her perfumes and her flaunting crimson silks, to corrupt a king so long ago. Nor was it still the refuge of a frightened woman, who learned what she could of power from an old man. Winter was coming, and the wood lay waste.

The wonder was she had not noticed it till now. She had a sense of an outside, hostile intelligence scanning the wood, as might a guard stand on some high platform, looking for a hint of smoke, a flicker of movement that was not what he knew to expect. Frantic, she flung up what defense she had: *Abandon consciousness . . . sink, like the beasts, like the trees in the cold, into the depths of their being and rest.* She could feel that, and more—and then it died; or her power to perceive it did.

It was time, and past time, to go.

She turned her back and set off.

Evening brought with it violet shadows and something more: the rhythmic lure of deep-voiced bells. Their songs and echoes tempted her out of her frozen stupor. Where there were bells, there were other people. They might have weapons—but they also might have food and fire. They might even be willing to share.

With her? Dimly, she recalled she was accursed. All that night, she forced herself to stillness: if she were accursed, she must not approach the bells. She would be driven off.

But the peal resumed in the morning, and hunger over-powered her fear. She broke the skin of ice on the stream and drank her fill. If she were accursed, surely her face would bear the mark. All she saw was a face hollowed by cold and hunger, scratched from low-hanging branches, wary with fear: no Cain's mark.

All that day, Kundry followed the solemn voices of the bells. Broceliande's tall trees rose in aisles about her. Dark-ness swirled into dawn, into noon, and darkness again: how many times, she did not know. Snow fell, and the forest's tracks shifted and doubled back upon themselves. She wan-dered where once she had known all the ways and possessed the art to meld them, one road upon another.

With a beast's cunning, she dodged beasts as eager as she to find food and a place out of the wind to sleep. She stared into the eyes of a hungry wolf, and it whined and backed away from the fire in hers: she saw it, reflected in the beast's eyes, and was frightened herself at its strength. What small power she had, now that her body had healed, had turned the threat aside. The danger past, she forgot her strength.

This and this alone she remembered. She had always been cold. She had always been hungry. She had always dwelt in the wild. Her name was Kundry. Anyone else could have succumbed and died, but not she; for she—though she bore no mark—was accursed.

Now only the bells kept her to that resolve. When they sounded, she knew her course. Her feet bled a little on the snow on paths she was the first to walk. The sad clangor of the bells grew louder. She pressed on. A compulsion to flee mingled with their dirge, but she had followed the bells for too long to reason out that she neared a place where she was not wanted.

With cunning she had not known she owned, she waited, as a bear waits who seeks a fish. All things flowed through the paths of Broceliande: the wolf she had warned off af-frighted a young horse. Kundry stripped off her ancient, ragged gown and the phial that had lain in its bosom. Scrab-bling up the icy earth with a pointed rock, she buried them beneath an oak tree as naked now as she. It looked like the tree she thought of as Merlin's oak.

From the horse's blanket she made herself a tunic, girdled with the cast-off snakeskin she had found and carried with her. She breathed into the horse's nostrils. When its eyes ceased rolling in fear, she stroked its mane and neck until she could lead it to a rock and there clamber to its lathered back.

Its hooves rang on the rock and frozen ground, and she rode toward sunset.

Before her shone a lake, glazed over with ice. Beyond it lay towers that glimmered like mountains at the horizon. She whimpered a little: there would be warmth and food in those towers, but she could not reach them unless she crossed the lake. She slid from the horse's back. Slipping on the icy reeds, grasping at the sturdiest of them for balance with the hand that did not hold her horse's mane, she struggled to the shore. A boat lay there, but someone had beaten in its sides with its oars, which lay half buried under the snow.

She took up one and tested the ice. Perhaps she could walk across it to those towers. If the ice were strong enough, perhaps she could lead the horse across it, too.

The sense of wrongness, of being an intruder, grew. So did the sense that some enemy was watching her. For an instant, wrongness and watcher clashed, all but freeing her.

Almost, Kundry remembered this lake, this place, those towers. She felt like a beast, sniffing at the trap that had maimed her the previous season. To cross the lake, to cross upon its surface—how could she dare?

Because I must! A beast's compulsion pierced her, awaking hunger and cold. Unless she had fire and shelter, she might die tonight. With fear came anger. *Because I will!*

She set foot upon the thick ice. Water pulsed black beneath its surface. The horse screamed and reared, tearing its mane free of her hand. A violent burst of light and sound exploded about her. Something *reached* for her. She tried to fling herself back, after her fleeing horse; but she was caught.

As if she had hurled herself through a sheet of glass and

down a wall, Kundry lay stunned in the snow. She lacked even the will to close her eyes. A figure shining red and silver walked toward her, an old man's face glowing above a long cloak that hid his form. Did a crown gleam over his head?

She felt herself lifted and borne some distance, then brought into light and warmth. Fire crackled, and she lay under a pile of coarse, warm fabric. Voices muttered as hands tended her. Her cracked lips formed names that were breath without sound.

"She will live." A deep, man's voice. "I told you it was a woman, not a woodwose."

"The wards struck her down."

"The wards strike down all outsiders, as our king commands."

"Woman, spirit—think you she will last the night?" That was a lighter, younger voice that Kundry did not like. She raised her gummed eyelids the width of a lash. Too many men stood around her. That could mean no good. Where were Martha and Maria? Maria would not let men cluster round her as she lay. Martha would chase them away and promise them a meal.

"Martha?" The old man bent closer. "Is that your name?"

She shook her head, back and forth, feebly, on the coarse pillow.

"Kundry . . ." Her voice trailed into a sigh of pain and exhaustion. The old man stiffened. Behind him, someone cried out, and too many faces pressed forward. They were warriors' faces, and she fell back with a weak scream.

"Out of here, all of you. *Yes*, I shall report this to the king. Now, out!"

His voice, when he turned back to her, held a deliberate gentleness.

"So . . . so . . . I am sorry you were troubled. That is no fortunate name for us here. Could there be two? *She* was young and vilely fair," muttered the old man. "This wreck . . . But my king, if he were himself, would say I owed her charity. Even that other one, if she repented . . ."

Kundry stirred and cried out.

"Sleep, woman. No one will harm you here. I am Gurne-manz." He spoke as if to a child. "Can you say that?"

She tried, but her mouth would not work, and her head fell back. She had come to Montsalvasche, and Montsalvasche did not know who she was.

Not yet, a voice warned her through the half-sleep, half-stupor in which she lay. She whimpered, and the old man came back with a cup.

Kundry flinched away from it. But it was battered wood, not silver, not the cup she feared. What it held was warm. She remembered drinking it before.

Something wet fell on her face. Footsteps left the room, all but those of the old man, her protector, who knelt heavily and pleaded with the air.

She remembered now: times had been when she too had pleaded with the air.

"It . . . doesn't help," she muttered, her voice rusty.

The old man turned.

"Do you know what I am doing?" he asked. "I am *praying*. Do you know that word? No? Sweet lord, is this the fool we seek?"

For a moment, his eyes kindled like coals, spilling from a hearth fire to burn as they would.

"I . . . called. No one answered."

Gurnemanz sighed. "I see. You do know. And you despair. Child, sometimes, so do I."

He rose from his knees and put more wood on the fire.

"Soon it will be spring. But unless help comes, it may be a spring more bitter than this cold."

22

LIGHT followed darkness, like a pattern of sunlight and columns down which Kundry roved until, finally, she woke with a sense she had wandered in her mind far enough, and far too long. Opening her eyes as little as she dared, she glanced around. She was alone. Safe enough, for now.

She rose from her pallet and flung out a hand, seeking the blanket she had worn. Instead, she found rough garments—a heavy cloak, a coarse gown—on a peg and put them on. Beside the peg was a tall shield in a canvas cover that looked like it needed stitching. A quick hunt found needle and thread. She removed the cover, marveled at the dove blazoned upon the great shield, and mended the canvas. That task done, she found brown bread and milk, and basked beside the fire. When it died, she slept beside its ashes.

Fire and ashes alternated like night and day. She found a broom beside the hearth. It was poorly swept; in fact, the whole room needed care. She swept the ashes; she drew water. When the old man whom she remembered finally appeared, a sack of food on his back, he seemed surprised and pleased.

"So, you find yourself well," he said.

"Well enough, Lord Gurnemanz."

"I am lord of no one and nothing," he told her. "I rejoice to see you awake." He studied her.

Gradually, her world widened. She met the other men who shared the forest watches with Gurnemanz. Younger than he, they were dressed like him, in long tunics blazoned with a dove, though theirs were less shabby and they wore them as if somehow that garb showed they served a sterner, higher fate than the rest of the world. He frowned when they laughed at her or muttered when she spoke. One squire told her the old man's title ought to be "my lord." Gurnemanz reprimanded him and waved aside her mumbled apologies.

She expected no better. The youths reminded her—she could not remember the names of what they reminded her. Sleek, powerful, even deadly, these young men, scarcely more than boys, who laughed a little too loudly when her protector's back was turned.

They were quick to quarrel, quicker to spar with weapons in play that drove her from the clearing outside Gurnemanz's hut. They talked enthusiastically of war and wonders, but bore no scars. They spoke boldly of the enemy whose castle full of evil sorceries and lewd wonders loomed at the very boundaries of Montsalvasche, yet they seldom ventured beyond the clearing.

They wore their armor as if it were a costume in some noble drama, not as a daily burden, the way that Gurnemanz donned it each morning and took it off with a sigh of relief every night. Untested, unsure, Kundry thought; and wondered how she knew.

All at once, she recalled a face, a man who had borne scars. Unlike these men, he had spoken her fair and had not talked of war at all. And he had fallen. Where he had faltered, how could these youths hope to prevail?

They might jeer at her, but day by day, they became accustomed to an extra pair of hands, a willing pair of feet, a woman's voice that would yield a point rather than argue it. Gradually, her service became theirs by right.

Day by day, her body strengthened. The sun rose in the sky; the days drew out as winter turned toward spring. The ice on the lake thinned. One day, it rang like a bell, flawed in its casting, and then cracked. The days warmed, and flowers gleamed like small suns in the snow that lingered beneath the pines. In her moments of leisure, Kundry basked like a worn-out cat in the sun, almost at peace.

Yet names she almost remembered haunted her nights. And she trembled at the voice of the bells.

Spring waxed, and the voices of the men she served grew

sad, then hopeful. Though the king was no better, when it grew warm, said Gurnemanz, the king would bathe in the lake. Its holy waters could restore and lull even him.

Today, the king would hunt. The younger men smiled as they said it. Gurnemanz shook his head. His eyes brightened, and he blinked.

Kundry cowered at the thought of the king. Was this king Gurnemanz served the one she sought? Sick, in pain, he might well be.

Gurnemanz laid a hand upon her head. "You have not seen him, yet you mourn his pain? Ah, lass, we will save you from your madness yet. My poor king. I mind when he could outride any man of Montsalvasche," he said. "Ride or fight all day, then aid the healers and the priests all night."

"Must have got damned tired," muttered a squire. His fellows laughed.

Kundry shot a glance at him, and he flung up a hand in exaggerated horror. "Call off your pet witch, my lord!"

"Witch?" Gurnemanz demanded. "She is no witch, but my guest and our charge."

"Your servant merely," Kundry whispered. She crept away to think, but dropped into fitful sleep instead.

Yet, the thought troubled her. How would a man worn out with illness hunt?

The next day, Kundry had answers to her questions. Swathed in furs and cloaks, borne in a litter on the shoulders of his strongest knights, Amfortas the king came down to the lake. Four infirmarers bearing torches made of *lign aloe* wood guarded him, the smoke of the precious wood casting balm and heat into the chill air.

"To ease his pain," Gurnemanz whispered. With an effort he forbore to look at the torches.

"How shall he hunt?" Kundry whispered to Gurnemanz. No horse fit to bear a king pawed or arched his neck, and she was glad. She would hate to see the beasts, such as those who befriended her in her madness, slain. And she remembered with regret the young horse that had borne her to the lake. Perhaps he had not slipped as he fled and broken a slender leg; perhaps he wandered still; perhaps he had found a stall, and grain, and a kindly master . . . just as she had.

"Our king fishes." Gurnemanz pointed at the boat that lay at anchor. "They will carry him out to his boat. There he will spend the day, until it is time . . ." He silenced himself. "He claims it gives him strength. But look! He beckons to us! You must see the king."

Kundry hung back, but Gurnemanz laid a kindly hand upon her shoulder, and the strength in it could not be withstood.

Gurnemanz paced forward slowly and knelt with ancient, ceremonial practice.

"How is my liege today?" he asked. When Kundry had been recovering from the cold, he had knelt beside her to tend her, had asked her a thousand times how she felt, but voice and actions had never held this formal ring.

"No better," said the king. "Never better this side of the Resurrection. I shiver and I burn. Each night I long for the peace of the grave; each day, I raise aloft . . ." He broke off. "But who is this?"

He motioned Kundry forward, his eyes compelling her as she had forced the wolf to turn aside from prey, while his knights whispered.

"Bow as best you can," Gurnemanz muttered. His hand pressed against her shoulder, forcing her into a crouch that would pass for a curtsy and spare her having to gaze up into the king's face.

"And who might this be?"

"A hewer of wood, a drawer of water," Kundry wanted to say, but her voice died. She remembered that voice, a warm breath against her throat and ear. It lulled her, let her raise her head and look upon the man who spoke.

A thousand times she had seen that face in her dreams. A thousand times she had dreamed of it. As in her dreams, the face of the king shifted aspect. One moment, its eyes kindled into warmth. The severe planes of cheekbones and jaw were relaxed, and its lips were warm, taut with desire as they brushed hers and, often as not, woke her from her scanty rest till she sighed and prayed to dream again. Then she would see the face again, the anguished eyes, the lines

of cheek and jaw that she had stroked now gaunt with the
pain of wounds and betrayal. From time to time, a spasm of
worse pain jolted across them. His lips were thin and dry,
bitten at times with a pain that sought relief in enduring an
easier discomfort.

She had caused that pain, marred that face. She forced
herself to look upon her work. Amfortas. She saw not just
the king, but the man who had been her lover, and the
wreck that she and time had made of him.

And now she knelt before him. Once he had trembled at
the sight of her.

Not to let him see me like this!

She thrust clawed fingers into her braids and drew matted
hair across her face. No need, though. No recognition
chilled his eyes: nothing but pity. How should it? The waters of Broceliande had shown her what a hag she had
become while, wasted as he was, weak as he was, she still
remembered the knight who had fought for her in the forest. Now he put out a thin hand, gracious even to a madwoman, offering his hand to her.

"Has this poor wretch friends, family to go to, Gurnemanz? It is not meet she live among so many men."

What about the queen an ardent fool once hoped to bring here?
Kundry thought. The knights who muttered behind her
back would have bowed before her, while at her side . . .
Laughter tore loose from her throat, ending in a moan.

Amfortas flicked a question with his brow at Gurnemanz, who shook his head minutely. *Not like little Ruth,*
Kundry thought. The last man who had touched her now
lay before her in his litter, in no shape to threaten or delight
any woman.

"As you can see, my liege," Gurnemanz said, "she is
quite mad. When I found her, she was near death from
cold. She had nothing, nothing but a few rags and her name.
Now she earns her keep. She . . . cooks, cleans, builds
fires."

The old man threw up a blind of words. Even Kundry
could hear that. Amfortas merely raised a brow and waited.
"Does she also speak?"

Kundry cast down her eyes and let Gurnemanz answer for her.

The king bent forward. "What is your name?"

I should have asked before; I am at fault. But may I beg to know my lady's name?

Last time, she had not feared to yield her name; this time, despite the king's familiar voice, she dared not. She hung her head and wished that Gurnemanz's voice was not so clear.

How would Amfortas take the sound of her name?

"Her name is Kundry, lord. Forgive it."

The king stared a moment, then flinched as if someone had brought a fist down upon an old injury.

As bad as that? She moaned, drawing a wary glance and surreptitious gestures against ill luck from the squires.

"Your wound, sire?"

"No," he muttered. "It is well—as well as it will ever be. Kundry." He sighed, and something in Kundry quivered, then grew warm. It was not a sigh of pain. "That is not she. Poor thing, to bear that name."

He pitied her. Old as she was, old, mad, and worn, he pitied her, and he sighed at the sound of her name. How it hurt to see the hollows in his cheeks, the gauntness round his eyes, like a living skull. She knew herbs, balms that might ease him; more than *lign aloe*, such herbs might stanch the bleeding, melt the ice that clung to his wound. She wanted to stroke his face and beg his forgiveness.

And she would do none of it. Let that be another part of her punishment. Until the fool made wise by pity should arrive—if such a creature ever came—she would live within sight and even touch of Amfortas, and she would never tell him. Unless, of course, she gained the courage to tell him and watch his face chill with disgust. Now *that* would be a real punishment. But how much pain would it inflict on Amfortas?

Tears rolled down Kundry's face. The king put out a hand to wipe them away. He moved as if he would trace a sign upon her brow, but she flung up her hand, as if warding off a blow. *Lord, I am not worthy!*

Amfortas flinched at the gesture, then fell back.

"I but meant to ease your sorrow," he whispered. He turned to Gurnemanz, who stood with a hand on Kundry's arm, ready to lead her away. "Has she been blessed?"

"She has no reason: how then could she be blessed?"

"A fool . . . Oh, Gurnemanz, if this were . . ."

It was Gurnemanz's turn to flinch as if he had taken his death wound. His glance flashed about the king's guard as if he numbered even them as enemies.

With a slash of his hand, he motioned them to stand back. They shifted as if they would stand their ground, but finally obeyed.

"*She* is privileged to hear?"

"A wose of the forest, come to curse or snare us? Perhaps even sent by . . ."

"Silence!"

"The fool made wise by pity?" Sorrow sharpened Gurnemanz's voice. "I do not think so."

Amfortas sighed. "It was too much to hope." He beckoned. "Bring me to the lake. It always eases me. Sometimes, I can even rest. Merciful God, what I would give for one night of sweet, unbroken sleep!"

Picking their steps over the round rocks, Amfortas's bearers brought him to the lake. His fingers clutched their shoulders and he tensed in anticipation of familiar pain. Tenderly, they lowered him into the boat. Once down, he lay in the bow, panting from the effort. They tucked silk robes about him, careful not to disturb his legs.

Two knights kilted up their long surcoats. Each taking a rope, they drew the boat out from the shallows and pushed it toward the center of the lake.

There it drifted across the reflection of the ancient forest and the gray walls of Montsalvasche. All day long, the king sat in his boat, neither asleep nor yet quite awake. The fishing rods in the boat went unused. All day long, Kundry watched the lover who had known her name, but not her face. A silver cord seemed to link them. When the sun grew warm at noon, she drowsed and dreamt of the greater heat of desire. Fear jerked her awake too quickly.

On the lake, the boat rocked. King Amfortas flinched,

and she felt the pain in her own body as if, once again, they lay body against body.

Gradually the day passed and the light waned. Slowly, as if obedient to an unheard command, the boat drifted back toward shore. The king's hunting day was done. Amfortas lay amid his wrappings, his head lolling to one side, brief peace upon the too-taut brow.

"He is no better, never any better," muttered one knight with red hair and a restless eye. "I must try my skill at finding some drug that can ease his pain before I return to my uncle's court."

"God grant you succeed!" One man clapped another on the shoulder, then slipped away to a mutter of "Good luck and blessings, Gawain."

The knight slipped away, but the king and elder knight did not notice, and Kundry did not care.

From the tower in the fortress of Montsalvasche, the bells began to toll. The young men drew near, like hounds let slip from their leashes; but not to run, these hounds: to return to Montsalvasche. Kundry had seen such looks before—usually before something died on the sands of the arena, and the crowds cheered . . .

Sands? She could not remember all; but she remembered sitting high above a place where creatures died in pain, men with the look of warriors looked on, while women with bright eyes bet gems, gazed upon the blood as if on silks, and inhaled the smells of combat as if they were fine oils.

Amfortas raised his head.

"It is time for my penance," sighed the king. "You will not spare me?"

"My lord, the old king, your father . . . You are in pain, yet to deny him what will keep him alive . . ."

"It is no great blessing to be alive!" Amfortas burst out. "Who will take this cup from me?"

The question echoed across the lake as if it would provide its own answer. But no fool made wise by pity appeared.

A peal of bells drowned out the echoes. The young knights and squires pressed forward with Amfortas's litter. The king looked toward Gurnemanz, who turned away.

Amfortas sighed. "Bring me before the altar." He suffered himself to be lifted into the litter.

"You will not come?" one asked her protector.

"And leave her as she is, alone and unhallowed?"

"It might do her good to witness." That brought Gurnemanz's heavy eyebrow up. He surveyed Kundry as if she were a fortress he planned to storm, and she crouched down, earnestly wishing him not to agree. She thought she could not bear to watch her lover impaled on the power of his own faith.

"Or," a voice whispered, "she might turn into a demon and fly up out the window when the king reveals the . . ."

Gurnemanz whirled and stared down the man who whispered.

"Quiet! He is sick, guilty, but he is still the king! Take yourself away from here. I will come, and I will bring mistress Kundry when I decide it is time. When I decide. And not before!"

The knights raised the litter and started forward toward the sound of the bells. One stepped wrong, and the litter jolted. Amfortas bit his lip, and blood ran down his chin.

There had been other blood, a crimson tide that reeked of copper and betrayal: too much blood to stanch, and no time or charity to try. This time . . . Kundry fumbled at the neck of her new kirtle. She had balm: designed to soothe a prophet, there was none finer in all Arabia, Martha had said, a thousand years ago.

She had none. Now, she remembered. She had buried her Judaean rags and with them, the glass phial of balm.

He should have it! She could not atone. That took repentance, and she had none. That took forgiveness, and she did not dare. But in this tiny thing, she should make amends.

The force of her desire built up until she could feel it, crying out within her. She sank down on the ground, her head on her knees, wailing. About her, knights and squires scuffed their elegant boots in the grass, waiting for the madwoman to have done.

A scream erupted from behind her: not man, that shout, but beast. A horse trumpeted its rage at the squires who sought to turn it from its path toward the king's litter.

It was the horse Kundry had found. Her need, her longing had drawn it here. It would bear her back to the oak to find the balm, then return her to ease, if she might, the maimed king's pain.

Passionately glad to see it, she hurled herself forward, clambering with the vitality an old man's care had given her onto the horse's back. It flung up its head, menacing two squires with teeth. She clung to its neck as it curvetted and ran from the clearing.

Shouts rang out behind her. The horse stumbled, and Kundry fell forward, feeling the spear that one fool threw only as a breath of wind that stirred her hair.

"No!" Gurnemanz was shouting in the voice he must have used to sack towns. "She is our charge, not our enemy."

But the squires surged forward. Kundry shivered at the shouts of "Demon!" and the whine of spears. *Could* she be killed? She knew she could not die.

"Hold! Is this your obedience?" demanded another voice. Kundry had heard it in the dark, calling men to account for assaulting the lady she had seemed to be. "Stop!"

The command broke off into a stifled scream of pain, almost a retching sound. From the safety of a thicket, Kundry turned to look. The men had frozen where they stood. Sunlight limned them, picked out the gules encircling the silver dove upon their surcoats and tinged their faces with crimson, like silk held before a lamp or blood flowing.

"Now you've done it, lads." Gurnemanz cursed in a most unsaintly fashion. "Opened the King's wound. You and you, run forward for the infirmarer. Tell him to bring bandages and *lign aloe*. Sweet lord, my king, *hold on!*"

"For God's sake, keep order," came a strangled voice Kundry would have known anywhere as Amfortas's. "Go past the wards and K—" The king shut teeth upon the name. "Our enemy could strike you from behind."

"We should attack!"

"How can he lead? Sweet Jesu, look at the blood! How can he *live* with that?"

"The Grail will not let him die," cried a younger voice, husky with tears.

"Better if it could. Then . . ."

"Silence!"

"Never mind the infirmarer." Amfortas's voice had sunk to a harsh whisper. "Bring me . . . bring me before the Grail."

He braced himself as his men picked up the litter. Kundry paused. Amfortas had better look to himself if he cared to go on ruling. She would fear for his life but, such as it was, it was safe. The Grail would not let him die, but it could not heal him, either. Not as long as he did not repent. *Why* could he not repent?

You call that life? Kundry, who endured it, knew better.

The horse gathered its legs beneath it and stood, trembling. Kundry forced herself to calm, then thrust her thoughts out, as she had with the hungry wolf. She did not take possession of the horse's mind—it was not hers to command. Instead, she urged calm, comfort, the welcome knowledge that a rider would protect it. She touched bare heels to its heaving flanks, and it set off.

The sky darkened toward night. The horse's run slowed to a walk. Then the beast stopped, thinking, no doubt, of grain, fresh water, and shelter, among the smells of other beasts.

Kundry whistled to hearten the beast. A nightingale echoed the sound. The horse flung up its head. Beyond the clearing, the wood lured them, trees and branches seeming to shift even as she watched.

She extended her senses as she had learned to do and took counsel of the moon. It was as mad as she. Merlin, said the face within its disk, might know where lay her tree. After all, it was spring now. Perhaps, as the sap rose, Merlin too suffered a resurrection. She could ask him.

She could compel. The thought rose dark within her mind, and she crushed it. Something flickered, interested, at the perimeter of the clearing. Kundry stifled a scream, forced calm upon herself, and reassured the horse. She made her consciousness a blank. Best not stir up curiosity she might not be able to counter. What was it Amfortas had said at the last? Pass beyond the wards, and she might draw the watcher's—best not even *think* of his name—attention?

You could stop now, Kundry told herself. Cease and remain a hewer of wood, a drawer of water, turning away the jeers of the knights and squires with soft words. Is that all you would be?

She had seen Amfortas smile, had flung her arms about his neck and seen his features relax from rapture into rest. *He is the* king! *Why could he not withstand me?*

Now his face, restless with ancient, flickering pain, rose before her. Laughter welled up in her throat, left bile upon her tongue. She would do anything to stop that laughter, as she would have done anything to stop the crucifixion at which she had laughed.

You had your chance to stop that, but you quailed.

Compared with such cowardice, such betrayal, it was a small thing to risk being Klingsor's captive once again.

23

BRANCHES and fronds swirled about Kundry as she rode through Broceliande, and starlight shone upon her path. She would not have been surprised to see answering gleams from her horse's eyes. The way twisted and shortened, and the ways of Broceliande shifted about her as they used to do when she had the full use of her youth and powers. The night wind tossed her hair about her like dark banners. She crooned to her horse. Her hands on its neck sent strength into its body. Any destrier or palfrey she had ever seen would be lathered and snorting now, but she had need for speed and was willing to pay the price later for the strength she expended now. On her mount ran, and on.

Tonight's ride was a far cry from her ordeal of the past winter. She must find balm for Amfortas to ease the wound she had caused.

A white hart leapt across the path. Her horse reared and screamed. Kundry clung to its back, wrapping arms about its neck. For a moment, beasts peered out from trees and thickets to stare at the live heraldry of leaping hart and pawing horse beneath the moon. The moment broke, the path shifted, and on Kundry rode past the hulks of distant keeps where narrow lights gleamed in windows gouged from their massive rock.

Distance was annihilated as Kundry looked at hart and castle.

Her horse's hooves struck sparks from the rock, then were muffled in thick grass. Now Kundry rode through a clearing. Here a boy knelt before a woman whose fine, thin features wore beauty as if it were the deepest mourning. She laid her hands upon his head, and her lips moved sound-

lessly. Names she had never heard before—"Herzeloyde
. . . Gahmuret, your father . . . fair son, dear son, my
Parsifal"—flicked across Kundry's consciousness, and she
whimpered at the intrusion. Then the sorrow rising from
the mother's mind and heart struck her as a second, greater
pain. Herzeloyde, or heart's love, the woman's name might
be; but that heart was breaking because her son was leaving
her.

No such sorrow troubled the features of the boy who
rose from his blessing, only joy so unmixed with any other
feeling that his features scarcely seemed human. Taking up
a bow, he strode from the clearing. Behind him, her long
fingers laid on trembling lips to stop them from crying out,
the lady sank to her knees, then onto her face, and lay
motionless.

Another look; another window, this one stained the pur-
ples and gold that meant it must belong to a chapel. Now
she beheld the body of a woman who lay on a bier before
the altar. The woman's face was serene, its sorrow relieved
by death. It seemed to shine with holiness, and Kundry all
but found it in her heart to envy her. She glanced up at the
figure nailed to the cross that loomed above the altar.
Crowned and polychromed, it did not have the face she
remembered.

She would have liked to remain, but the horse leapt, the
forest shifted, and on she rode.

Another darkness behind the trees, another dwelling,
another window, this one to a lady's chamber. Carpets and
tapestries of rich silk brought from the East softened the
stone walls; velvets curtained the bed. A man pushed aside
the bed curtains and walked to the window. The moonlight
was so bright that it picked out the battle scars upon his
naked body, the tousle of his hair, and the wry beauty of his
face.

Gawain! She did not wish to see this. She *knew* she did
not wish to see this, but her horse slowed to a walk.

"How sweet the air is!" Gawain whispered. "And how
sweet my freedom from that holy tomb! Yet to think I must
return to those walking ghosts at Montsalvasche now that

you have given me what I sought . . . and more than I dared
to dream of . . .''

Gawain tilted his head as if at a question. "What of
Arthur, you ask, my heart? What *of* him? He is king, he is
my uncle, but when I visit Camelot, I feel like a bug trapped
in a particularly stifling amber. And Montsalvasche is
worse. Your gift has raised me from that tomb. But let us
not talk of kings and crowns . . . let us not talk at all!"

Even as Kundry gasped, he turned eagerly back to the
bed, drawing aside its curtains long enough for Kundry to
see the dark-haired woman who held out arms to her lover.
A flask of balm lay upon a chest; moonlight gleamed on it
and illuminated the bodies of the knight and lady as they
twined together.

No hope for the king there! Even Kundry shuddered at
the harshness of her laughter. Gawain broke from his lady's
embrace. His hand flashed to his sword and he stared out
into the night. And Kundry's horse plunged on.

As if she flew above her path, knowledge of the earth
stretched out before her. At the end of this road lay Camelot. No trust, no faith remained there, save in an aged,
grieving king who looked himself toward Montsalvasche
for help.

She eased forward so that she lay against the horse's
arched neck. Her hands in its mane tensed as she turned its
head: not this way. Not back to the great cities of the south,
with their dark-eyed, silk-clad physicians and their faith in
crescent and blade. The horse veered. She dared a glance
down at hooves, rising and falling, shining as if polished
from obsidian on which the starlight fell. Horse and woman
seemed poised on a wheel that turned beneath them. Kundry cast about her, seeking for the place where, a winter
ago, she had buried rags and balm from more than a thousand years ago. She could not find it. She shook her head,
removing one hand from her mount's neck, diverting
strength to herself. The horse snorted, then stumbled. Hastily, Kundry replaced her hand upon it, feeding it her
strength with a speed she feared she would pay for later. She
had seen nothing.

Abruptly, another vision slashed across the first, as lightning blinds the fool who stares at it: flasks of crystal, alabaster, and rainbow glass standing upon a chest, reflected in the watery gleam of a huge silver mirror. A thousand years of physicians' and courtesans' arts lay in those flasks. Lying as they did in her old rooms in Klingsor's castle, they were as far from her as she was from the Mercy.

Do not say that name! Amfortas's warning to the knights rang in her ears.

Wind tore down from the sky, threatening to overset horse and rider. The horse withstood the gusts. Kundry thought to stop and wait out the sudden blow, but the winds only intensified. Laughter threatened to overpower her. By that laughter, Kundry knew her peril. The power rising in her had sufficed to activate her curse. And even the single thought of Klingsor outside the sterile safety of Montsalvasche had been enough to draw the winds down around her head.

The thought, a voice whispered in her mind, *and the free use of your power.*

Klingsor could ignore a woman crazed and half frozen to focus his powers upon Montsalvasche. A woman who could summon a horse and take the inner ways of Broceliande, though—such a woman could be an enemy, even if her powers were still weak. She could imagine Klingsor lounging in his tower, gazing into the great mirror he had used to summon her the last time.

Even now, was he leaning forward, his black eyes intent on his feeble prey? Did he blow gently against the mirror? And did the demons that he had invoked in its making call up the winds and hurl them against her, not to stop till she lay senseless, easy pickings?

He must not find me again! Terror made her sweat, made the laughter start to well up again; and she forced her mind into a kind of blankness as a beast might go to ground when the hunter stalks it. Kundry flung herself forward on her mount's neck and tried to invoke nothingness. Wind battered her and her mount.

After a while, dark clouds hid the starlight, and thunder played a drumbeat to the shrieking of the gales. Purple fire crackled down, and Kundry had time to wince at the light and the stench of burning before her horse bucked and curvetted. With a wail, she was flung from its back to lie beneath a tree, and the wind howled a triumph song about her.

Overhead, branches creaked and swayed. Then, they stilled, as if coming under a new master's control, to move again and form a canopy held over her to shield her.

"Go back," Kundry heard a voice intone. "You shall not prevail this time, nor any other."

Merlin? Kundry raised her head, seeking to find the oak that must be the source of her protector's voice. There was no oak, no wizard: only herself.

"Go back!" Again the command. As the echo blended with the rumble of the nearing storm, she recognized the voice. It was not Merlin's, had probably never been Merlin's. It was her own.

Kundry rose into a crouch. Words whispered across her consciousness: spells she had heard for a thousand years, returning to her memory as if to a long-forgotten home. Her power, drained by the ride across Broceliande, glittered like a coal buried overnight in the ashes, then breathed upon and brought back to glowing life. Fire kindled in her spine and rose along it, coursing along a webwork of power until Kundry saw it pulse in her fingers. For an instant, the thin bones glowed in her hands, and her flesh looked briefly young and pink. Then light stabbed from her fingertips into the curdled darkness.

It did not hurt. That was the wonder. She had used her power against a hated master, and it had not pained her.

Overhead, the oak's leaves rustled, heartening Kundry. She found herself laughing, and for the first time in a thousand years, her laughter held only exultation.

The storm paused, then returned with new fury. She held up her hands and watched the light gush and gout from them into the storm, tearing at its cloudy substance. She held. The light flickered, then crackled, darkening from its pure white. Now sustaining the flow of power hurt and she wanted to whimper, but she forced the fire up from the base of her spine and out against her ancient enemy. Now there was pain, forcing from her not a scream, but laughter.

Lightning exploded and flung her against the nearest tree. Before its afterglow would fade, the storm died. Something heavy fell, and the great tree quivered.

Daylight had assaulted the clearing some time ago, and Kundry had tried more or less successfully to hide from it. But now someone was whimpering back to awareness.

"Must help . . . must heal . . . must serve . . ." she moaned.

The whimpering stopped. She had been the one who wept. Her hands ached, so tightly had they clutched the gnarled roots of the tree against which she had curled. She was not surprised to find that it was an oak. A massive branch lay nearby, and Kundry knew what had struck her down.

Sunlight caught her eyes and dazzled them into tears. She told herself it was only the light, only a trick of the light on eyes shocked by Klingsor's fury. She blinked fiercely and looked up again. She tried to lever herself up on her elbow, to rise and find her horse, but dizziness seized her and hurled her onto her back.

The oak bore no crown. That last bolt of lightning had rived branches from bole and split the massive trunk for a third of its height. Smoke still coiled lazily as it does above a town after it has been sacked and the raiders have withdrawn, leaving the dead to their own company and the circling birds.

The day drew out. The remains of the oak cast their shadow over her and marked the passage of the hours like a sundial no one would ever see again.

No other shadows crossed it, and, when no dark mage or his servants came, Kundry rose shakily. She was thirsty, and her thirst seemed a worse torment than last night's storm. Nearby, as she recalled as if from another life, lay a spring. Yes, that was right. Now that the dinning in her ears and the stupid monotony of her own keening had died, she could hear its rippling.

Muffled hoofbeats in front of her told her that her horse had survived the storm and was drawn, as she was, toward water. The horse and she were all that moved in the clearing. With Merlin's death, the spell that had drawn the beasts there to live together in peace had vanished, and they had fled.

The lure of sleep faded as her thirst woke. Her feet stumbled on the rock that bordered the stream. As well ask it for comfort as anything else, she thought. Just a few feet more. The water poured over round rocks. She remembered how cold, how sweet it was, an ache in the teeth, a relief in the throat. Right here was where she had lain the first time she had drunk from this stream and seen herself changed from hetaera into hag; right here, she would slake her thirst again. She forced herself down, first on aching knees, then onto a hollow belly, and drank until she was full. Water poured down her face, a substitute for the tears she had not shed for so long.

The light dappling the water and the rock dazzled her when she glanced up. Surely . . . Kundry scrabbled up into an ungainly crouch, her hands hugging herself rather than daring to reach out to what she saw.

She had told herself: ask the rock for comfort. She had not, yet comfort was provided. It was a flat rock, lying almost on its side as if it had once lain flat, but the earth had heaved it up. Beneath it lay a tangle of old cloth. And in the midst of the mouldering tangle was a phial, shimmering with the rainbows of glass that had lain buried for years in the desert, capped with fine wrought gold stamped with the seal of Solomon.

She remembered that phial, its warmth in her bosom once her body had heated it, and how useless she had felt when Joshua refused it. Coming to a quick resolve, she pulled out the cap. Myrrh and frankincense filled the air.

Kundry laid her cheek against the smooth glass, imagining that she could feel the sun and sand of its native desert. As she had not done for centuries, she wept until her eyes and throat ached. She might have wept yet longer, but a wet nose nudged her. Her horse. It had found grass and water; let it now find a rider and its world would be restored.

Kundry bent to drink again. Then, shaking like a crone, she mounted. Drained as she yet felt, it would be a long ride back to Montsalvasche.

24

ALL that afternoon Kundry rode, and into evening. From time to time, she walked to rest the horse. When she could go no further, she would crouch upon the ground and let the beast graze. The horse's head drooped. Kundry hated to burden it, but her feet were raw and sore, and she had no strength now to shift the endless, winding paths of Broceliande.

Night came, then paled toward daylight. Kundry's feet bled now into the undergrowth, and she paused to bind them up with strips torn from her gown. Her shoulders slumped; when she dismounted to walk the horse, it was all she could do not to drop to the ground and sleep.

Sleep? Kundry wished she could sleep forever. Her eyes burned; she thought of sleep as cool water to drink, to bathe in, to listen to as it lulled her . . . to sleep . . . She jolted herself back upright. Sleep was not safe; dreams might come, sent by . . . She shook her head fiercely, to clear her thoughts of the name of her ancient master and enemy. Her matted hair whipped about her shoulders, stinging where a matted elflock caught her cheek. The last pool she had passed had been shrunken, but still wide enough to show her her semblance: demon and hag.

Kundry sniffed the air. Almost dawn. She could tell that the day would be calm, even hot for this time of year. Such days, Kundry recalled, had always been called the king's "hunting days" at Montsalvasche. Before his wounding, Amfortas had fished; now, he would rest in his boat and pray for release.

Perhaps ease for his pain, even so little as an hour's dreamless sleep, lay in the flask. She must give it to him now, before his boat drifted to the center of the lake where she would not be allowed to follow.

She kicked at the horse for speed. It broke into a trot, stumbled, then gained speed as it drew on what Kundry feared was the last of its strength. Ropes of froth blew from its jaws and onto her arms. From her grip around the mare's neck, she could tell how mortally weary it was. Once again, she dared to will it strength. Slow fire crept up her spine, and the horse's pace steadied. But the fire died soon enough, and Kundry knew she dared not repeat it. Even the smallest show of power, like a plume of smoke to a forester watching from a tower, could alert her enemy.

The horse snorted, then broke into a gallop. Still too slow! Kundry closed her eyes, breathed a brief prayer—she who had not prayed for centuries—and summoned yet more strength to twist and shorten the ways of Broceliande. The horse's apparent speed slowed; once again, woman and mare rode at the still point of the turning world, as the sun rose in triumph.

A sudden nostalgia for her life as a hewer of wood, a drawer of water outside the fortress of Montsalvasche almost brought tears to her eyes. She could see the clearing in which Gurnemanz had his poor hut. Sometimes, he did not even bother sleeping in it, but spent the night outside in prayer, under the huge tree that overhung much of the free space. The clearing sloped down toward the shore of the holy lake Brumbane, in which—on his good days— Amfortas would bathe or perhaps drift in a little boat, too pain-wracked even to fish. She thought she could see the swans, floating in stately circles.

A solemn clamor of horns rang out from the fortress she had never dared approach. It echoed, flung back by the trees arrayed across Lake Brumbane. Kundry remembered that as the signal that summoned Gurnemanz and the squires he taught to another day of prayer and disillusionment.

The horse staggered. Kundry leaned forward and patted its lathered neck. "Not much farther," she whispered. Already she could see familiar trees and, beyond them, light glancing off Lake Brumbane.

The air was sweet; the day would be sultry. Amfortas would certainly venture from the citadel today. Even now, the knights and squires must be preparing the king's bath.

She wondered if Gawain had returned with the balm, or if it had aided Amfortas at all. That thought bore with it a pang of shame, as if by witnessing Gawain's faithlessness, she had shared it. She was no better—and she had sinned with a nobler man. The phial she bore against her heart: would it help that man at all?

Her horse faltered. Kundry heard voices up ahead, a chorus that died into a murmur. The horse nickered. Not much longer now! Just a few steps more! It stumbled and broke into a desperate gallop.

Over the sound of wind, water, and hoofbeats rose Gurnemanz's familiar voice, just as she had heard it when she woke to life in the clearing.

"There is only one cure, only one healer!" Gurnemanz was saying to his assembled squires.

To her horror, Kundry felt her heart warm to the stalwart old man, so careful to tell the old stories just as they had always been told. She did not want to love Gurnemanz. She did not want to love anyone. Where she loved, she betrayed and slew and cursed. She wanted . . .

The squires were demanding the name of this unknown savior. No doubt, they were all on fire to ride and seek him right now. Kundry clenched her teeth against laughter. And here *she* was riding in. They would think . . . if they thought at all . . .

"A rider! Look, the madwoman comes riding in!"

Steel clashed as two squires whirled, one seizing his sword. Kundry's horse tossed its head. Its coarse, wet mane struck her in the face and tangled with her own hair.

"Is that a horse she's got or a broom?"

"A rack of bones! How could she treat a beast so?"

"She's a beast herself!"

"Look, the mane of the devil's horse is streaming!"

"Ha! Devil's mane, devil's mare! It's that Kundry we thought was safely fled, clinging to the poor beast's back like an ugly burr."

Gurnemanz turned toward her, one hand out to quiet the

squires. At that moment, the mare stumbled and went to her knees. Kundry tumbled from its back and landed hard on the coarse grass. Her hair tumbled over her face in the dirt. For a moment, she lay stunned where she had fallen. She wanted nothing more than to lie there forever, or at least for an hour of sleep. How long had it been since she had truly slept?

She had not rested since her last night here, in Gurnemanz's care, she remembered. Thought of the doughty old man reminded her. She forced herself to her feet, ignoring the shrieks of joints and saddle sores, and rushed to his side. A squire tried to stop her, but she glared at him till he fell back. His fingers moved in the sign against evil.

"Never mind that!" Gurnemanz snapped at him. "Walther, Ulrich, see to the horse. Walk it till it cools, then a blanket, hot mash for its wind . . ."

The squires nodded obedience and waited till Gurnemanz's back was turned before they tapped their heads.

"Daughter, where have you been?" His arms held out to her, Gurnemanz started forward.

Kundry waved off support and comfort. Thrusting her dirty hand into her gown, she drew out the phial she had recovered.

"Take it!" She had meant that to be a plea, but it ripped out like a caw from a crow. "Balm . . . it may help . . ."

The phial was lost in Gurnemanz's scarred hand. He examined it as if it might suddenly vanish in a wail and a puff of foul smoke. "Tell me where you got this."

You don't want to know, Kundry thought. How could she tell him of the battle for her soul, deep in the forest, or aught else she had seen? He stared at her as if prepared to hear wonders.

"From further off than you can imagine," she spoke at last. "If this balm fails, there is nothing in Arabia itself that could soothe the king's pain."

She hurled herself onto the grass. Strength flowed from the earth into her body. If only she could lie like that forever and wake strong once more! "Ask me no more. Just let me rest!"

She felt Gurnemanz's shadow cross her body as if he

wanted to speak privately to her. Confession tempted her; she feigned exhausted sleep.

Then the ground trembled as a procession approached. Each footstep brought pain, piercing her body like a lance. The moment of her weakness past, Kundry raised her head.

The shadow across her stiffened as Gurnemanz braced himself to stand before his lord.

Pain hollowed the king's temples and cheeks. Though the day was yet cool, sweat ran down his face.

"Now he can't even walk this far," Gurnemanz muttered to himself. "God, God, once he was a man and a hero. I don't know how long I can stand to see him like this, chained to that damned litter."

One of his bearers stumbled. Agony lashed across Amfortas's face, and his lips went white.

"Careful!" Gurnemanz snapped. "Do you have to hear our lord cry out before you know you're hurting him?"

The ground itself ached with the pain of the maimed king and the faithful old man. Kundry curled in upon herself like a hideous infant. With infinite care, the knights set the litter down. Amfortas lay back against his cushions for a moment. Kundry could practically feel him turn his will against his body. His panting breath slowed and grew steady. He sat up. And he smiled at the old man who went to one knee before him.

"So, a moment's rest. It is easier now, and I thank you."

"Was the night bad, my lord?" Gurnemanz asked in a low voice. He put his hand out as if to touch his king's shoulder, then withdrew it.

Amfortas shut his eyes briefly. "The night is past. When the sky finally cleared, I was glad to see that the dawn was fair. The holy lake always gives me some rest. The lake and . . . what, is Gawain with you? I would thank him . . ."

Kundry pressed her burning face against the grass.

A knight came forward and knelt. Dress and armor were precise; equally so was his face, smoothed of all personality into a mask of loyalty. "Sire, Gawain is not here. When the herbs he labored so hard to bring you gave you no ease, he set out again upon another search."

Kundry's mouth opened against the ground. Bite grass;

eat earth; do anything but let loose the shriek of laughter that threatened, she commanded herself. The spasm passed, just as pain flickered and faded on Amfortas's face. Kundry lay limp upon the earth. Behind her, the squires muttered and chuckled.

"Without my blessing?"

Kundry saw the look two men exchanged—*for whatever your blessing is worth.*

Amfortas raised himself a little further and almost managed not to flinch at what it cost him. "I pray he does not regret leaving before the Grail commands. He is a bold man, a rash man; and Klingsor sets snares for such as he." The king's voice trailed off. Did he remember another snare, the fairest of all?

"My lord?" Gurnemanz leaned forward, as if to shake his king back into life.

"Let none presume to help me," Amfortas murmured. "I am fine, old friend, as good as I can ever be. But I mean that: no more quests to bring me herbs and salves! I wait for my appointed healer. Isn't that so, old friend? The fool made wise through pity, they say . . ."

"You told us . . . it was so." Gurnemanz bent his head, where the gray hair was rapidly turning white. Amfortas rested his hand on it briefly, blessing and comfort from a man who had none to offer himself. Kundry wanted to kiss that hand. She took hold of the grass as if it had power to restrain her.

" 'The blameless fool,' " Amfortas went on. "As I get older, I think I begin to know his name. And when I finally meet him, I think I will greet him, 'Hail, Lord Death! Accept my sword and my breath!' "

His eyes glittered and his cheeks bore a hectic flush.

Gurnemanz fell back somewhat, then held forth the phial he had received from Kundry. "My lord, before you swear fealty to death, I beg you see if this will help you."

Amfortas took it, long fingers curious as he held the glass up to the rising sun. A beam of light struck it and cast rainbows over the king's face and his white tunic. He almost smiled. "Where did this mysterious flask come from?"

"From far Arabia." Gurnemanz fell back on Kundry's story.

"And who brought it?"

"Our wild girl, over there. Up, Kundry! Come here!"

It took all the will Kundry had left to refuse the summons.

"You, Kundry?" Did his voice linger on the sound of her name? "Again, I have to thank you. You will not come and greet me?" She remembered that voice, his old gentleness with injured creatures—except himself. He held up the phial, delighting in the play of light on cap and glass. "I mean to try this balsam of yours, and I thank you."

She laid her head upon the ground. But, "Answer our master, witch," a squire muttered as he pressed his toe into her side.

She twisted away. "Don't thank me." A laugh escaped, but she choked it off. "How can I help? How can that help? I can hear no thanks—be off, quick . . ."

To her astonishment, Amfortas chuckled. "So, my best thanks is obedience?" He gestured, and his bearers picked up his litter once again. The figures of the procession dwindled, then disappeared as they started downhill toward Lake Brumbane. Swans formed a ring upon the dock, as if awaiting the king.

Now, Kundry was free to rest. She stretched out upon the ground, sensing footsteps coming and going about her. The sun was blessedly warm upon her back and head. Then a shadow blocked its path.

"Hey, you there! What are you doing, crouched there like a wild beast?"

Kundry turned her face up to look at the squire who confronted her. "Are all the beasts here not holy?"

"Of course they are. Are you holy, though? We're not as sure of that."

Another young man joined him, leaning an arm across his shoulder. "You know, with that magic balm she brought, she could hurt our master, maybe even poison him."

Their shadows touched and blotted out the sun. Other shadows, a muttering wolf pack of them, joined them.

Kundry put her head down and flung her arms over it. *Just so she had seen a woman running, her hair streaming behind her and her belly swollen with child. Knights had seized her by her hair and flung her down. She had time for one scream of* "Sh'ma Yisroel . . . Abba! Help!" *Then they kicked her till the screaming stopped and the thick blood pooled out from under her.*

Memories uncoiled like a burning scroll: families slaughtered by mothers; wives slain by husbands; and, at the end, friends slaying friends, then turning, with the same prayer on their lips, to fall upon their swords lest their enemies drive them as a shame through the burning streets of their homes. She had seen these horrors in Gethsemane; she had not been the only one to see them. One word from her to Joshua might have averted them all. She had not spoken that word.

So, it was just. As it had been done to them, let it be done to her.

She forced her body to relax. So many years ago her faith was broken, yet Kundry still recalled the rest of the prayer . . . "Adonoi elohenu, adonoi echod." Where would the first boot strike *her*—in the head or ribs?

Warmth slashed across her hair as Gurnemanz pushed into the pack of squires. "Get back, you! I said stand back! *We* do not do such things, not even in war. Kundry is not our enemy. I ask you, what harm has she ever done you? You want messages borne, and she bears them; you command, and she obeys. You do not house her, you do not feed her—she has nothing in common with you, not even kindness. But when you need her, she gives her aid and asks no word of thanks or aught at all.

"You are sworn to protect—does your oath mean you protect all souls but this one? Is she outside the Mercy as well as your oath?"

The young men muttered and shifted, but Gurnemanz would not let them off. "Let me ask *you* if your confessors will not: are you sunk so low that you would return ill for good?"

Tears filmed Kundry's eyes and turned the gold dappling of sun filtered through leaves upon the grass into a haze in which Gurnemanz glowed. How long had it been since she had heard someone—some mortal man—speak words in her defense? She wanted to put out a hand and touch Gurnemanz's foot, lay her head across it in thanks like the beast they had called her, but her sinews failed her.

"She hates us." The first squire fell back, though grudgingly; and he still protested. "Look how those black eyes of hers flash hate!"

"You insulted her, made her fear," Gurnemanz pointed out. "When she is less afraid, she will be herself again. Look what she did for the king. She can be kind."

"A woodwose—here in the heart of Montsalvasche!"

Gurnemanz stood between her and the young men. From the shore of Lake Brumbane, a cry of pain tore from an unwilling throat, and the old man flinched as if the pain had been his.

"Yes, I think that our Kundry may wander under a curse. Perhaps her service here is penance for some guilt. And"— he stressed each word—"as nobles and knights, *we are grateful* for her service, in which, perhaps, she helps herself as well."

A squire edging toward the safety of the trees muttered, "And this guilt of hers has brought on our distress, too."

"Are we not all, all under a curse?" Gurnemanz burst out. "From the Fall itself to . . ." Again, a cry rose from where the king was bathing.

Gurnemanz looked down at Kundry. "The old King Titurel told me that he saw a maid like her once, when he first built our castle. She lay numb and lifeless, and he sent for healers; but she disappeared. I myself found Kundry much like that this winter, and once before, when that unholy schemer who has built his lair across the pass attacked . . ."

He broke off, his head tilted toward the lakeshore. Clearly, he wavered between protecting her and running to aid his king. When no further outcry came, he knelt beside Kundry. "You, woman! Yes, listen to me! Where were you wandering the day the Spear was lost?" He raised her by the shoulders and shook her. His eyes were anguished with doubts he probably did not admit even to his confessor. "Why did you not help us that day?"

Kundry's mouth opened and shut. Blessedly, she did not laugh. She locked her eyes on Gurnemanz and waited till his own remorse made him release her.

"I never help anyone," she whispered, and turned her face toward the ground. Still, she could not help glancing up.

"You heard what she said." A squire folded his arms over the dove emblazoned on his chest.

"Let *her* seek the Spear if she is so helpful."

"That is not our task, or hers," Gurnemanz reminded them. "Oh my dear God, the holy Spear! When the old king held it, it worked miracles. In the wrong hand, though . . . it is an abomination that that damned wizard, may his name be blotted out, possess it." He sighed. "To think the Klingsor once sought to join our fellowship."

"My lord, you *knew* Klingsor?" The squires hunkered at Gurnemanz's side, their rage at Kundry gone for now.

Gurnemanz looked past them toward the men who came up from the lakeshore. "How fares our lord?"

"Somewhat refreshed. He rests before we return to the citadel."

"He cried out when the bandages were removed, but the balsam eased his pain." Surprisingly, one of the squires sketched a bow in Kundry's direction.

"It doesn't heal; it doesn't close: how long, Lord God, how long?" Gurnemanz looked up at the birds flying overhead. He twisted his hands, then forced himself back to impassivity before the squires.

"Gurnemanz, say on. How did you know Klingsor?"

Kundry flinched. The mere thought of that name in Broceliande had brought wind and lightning down upon her. But this was Montsalvasche: holy ground. No lightnings would strike here—for now.

"Our lord's father Titurel knew him well. When *he* defended the realms of faith, angels came to him and brought him wonders—the cup used at the Last Supper and that received Christ's blood when He died on the Cross, and the Spear that shed that blood. Think of it, they *gave* these relics to Titurel to guard. For them, he built our citadel and bid you all to its service. No evil may enter here, no knight, save he is willing to be our brother.

"Klingsor was denied that fellowship, eagerly as he pressed for it." Gurnemanz leaned forward, and the squires drew closer. "He had to be denied. I saw him, and I tell you, brothers, there was a wrongness about him. And that wasn't all. We are not all a brethren of priests, but that is our failing, not by any prohibition. And to be a priest . . . a man must be a man. A whole man." He looked at each of the squires, his gaze testing for levity or lewdness, then nodded, before going on.

"Klingsor sought for purity but could not restrain himself. Rather than fight and fail, repent and fight for a purer life as a man must, he . . . turned his hand upon himself and became less than a man. He was even heard to say that this would bring him power. Titurel scorned him, not for his maiming (which could happen, God forbid, to any man in battle), but for his cowardice.

"Being dismissed so enraged Klingsor that he vowed to destroy Montsalvasche. He had begged for power, had unmanned himself to seek it. Well, he got his heart's desire and his bane all in one—but from no godly source. Now, across the mountains, he has made the desert bloom, built a high keep, and filled it with she-demons who sleep on silk and sweat perfumes—much good it does him to keep them. Lacking a natural use for such ladies, he sends them to lure our brothers away to defilement and death."

She remembered how Klingsor had sent her forth to tempt Amfortas, a troop of mamluks at the ready. At that time, she had not seen Amfortas. All she knew was that he served the Grail, he led the knights who slaughtered her people and occupied their holy places. The ruse had been a good one; Kundry was to scream as if she were being ravished by invaders. She had even laughed with Klingsor as they planned it.

But when she had put it into play, had seen Amfortas come running, all unarmored to her aid—"No, no . . ." she moaned, twisting back and forth as if in a hideous dream. Gurnemanz and the squires sitting at his feet ignored her, and she thanked God for that small grace, if nothing else.

"When Titurel resigned his crown to Amfortas, our own dear lord planned to wipe out Klingsor's threat," Gurnemanz continued, intent on his story. "Instead, what happened, you know. Klingsor has the Spear and covets the Grail. And with our king so stricken, he boasts that he will win it soon!"

"Then first of all, we must win the Spear back!" cried the squire who had kicked Kundry.

"Whoever does that would win lasting glory . . ." His fellow leapt up as if he saw Klingsor brandishing the sacred Lance right then and there.

Gurnemanz held up his hand. "Easy, easy! You heard our lord Amfortas just this morning. No one, *no one* is to help him. He knows. He had a vision. The night after our king was wounded, he forced the infirmarians to bear him to the sanctuary. All night long, he lay before the Grail, pleading for pardon. (I knelt at the back, in case he might need help, and he never knew.) An angel, like the ones who came to Titurel, appeared to him. The chapel glowed as bright as noon, and the angel spoke: 'Wait for the man I choose, the blameless fool made wise through pity.' "

The squire who had leapt up knelt and crossed himself. "Made wise through pity, the blameless fool . . ."

"God send he come soon and heal our king."

"Amen," wished Gurnemanz. Kundry wished it too, though it had been long since she had prayed, and her prayers had not been answered.

Shouts and horn calls erupted from where, by the lake, the knights attended Amfortas.

"My lord, my lord!" Gurnemanz rose like a man a third his age. Even as the squires dispersed, each to go on guard, the old man's sword rasped out from its sheath. Gurnemanz started toward the lake.

"My God, what's that?" He clapped a hand to his cheek and brought it away bloody.

He looked up, and gouts of blood spattered him. Birdsong such as Kundry had never heard rang out from overhead.

Shouts of outrage came from the knights who attended Amfortas on the lakeshore. Then a great swan, its plumage glinting except where blood dripped from its breast, plummeted into the clearing, singing even as it died.

25

"SOMEONE shot one of our forest swans, and the arrow's weight is bringing it down!" cried a knight.

Terribly, the bird had not yet died; and still it sang, bequeathing surpassingly beautiful music to the world. A poem she had heard once and never forgotten flitted through her memory like a shade: *When shall I become like the swallow and cease to be mute?*

Then, silence. The dead swan's wings extended on either side of its crimsoned body. Even the squires who had reviled her had tears in their eyes. First of the men, Gurnemanz reached the swan and took it on his knees. His gnarled hands were surpassingly gentle as he smoothed its plumage.

"Shameful," he whispered. "Who shot this swan?"

He drew the arrow that had slain it from its breast. Poorly fletched, the arrow's feathers loosened and fell off even as the shaft was drawn from the wound.

The squires crowded around, to be waved off by Gurnemanz. The younger ones, barely out of boyhood, loved the swans and all but made pets of them; the elder squires and young knights guarded them, intent on keeping faith in this, if little else.

One of the king's attendants ran from the shore. "You found the swan, then? King Amfortas saw it and hailed it as a happy omen. It circled the lake. Then an arrow . . . We feared assassins and sent out men . . ."

"We found something else—the wretch who shot the swan!"

A pack of knights and squires, their sword blades bared, surrounded the man . . . no, he was no man grown, but scarcely more than a youth. He was poorly dressed, in a cap, tunic, and roughly cobbled shoes that resembled a rustic attempt at a court fool's garb. The bow he bore was crude and looked as if he had whittled it himself out of whatever wood he could find.

"Here's the arrow that slew our swan. See if it matches those in his quiver!"

A shout of assent.

The knights tugged and pushed the archer to stand before Gurnemanz. They tried to shove him to his knees, but he resisted, his eyes flashing. He tossed his head as they jerked him about, and his cap fell off. The sun filtering in long shafts through the leaves that overhung the clearing picked ruddy highlights from his hair. It was so ruddy that in some lights it resembled red gold. As the light struck him, it glowed as if the boy were a figure in one of the mosaics Kundry had seen in Constantinopolis.

Had the angels of God been female and seen the sons of man before the Flood, they might well have abandoned heaven for a lad like this, Kundry thought. He was so fair her vision almost blurred as she looked at him. So fair, so carefree, and so heartless, more like a statue than a creature with a vulnerable soul. Her memory cast her back to her night ride through Broceliande: a boy leaving his mother, who watched him, hands to her mouth and heart breaking, then pitched forward. In a dead faint, Kundry had thought; and she had not thought nor been able to turn aside to aid her.

This boy who had abandoned the woman Herzeloyde: was he cruel or was he a fool? His blue eyes glinted in the sunlight like pools undisturbed by a single flicker of thought. He was beautiful. For that beauty, people might forgive him anything. For that beauty, his way would be made smooth, while others had to struggle and plead even for a civil word.

"Did you kill our swan?" Gurnemanz asked the boy. Even now, his fingers stroked its plumage. Tears glistened on his cheeks, and he did not bother to wipe them away.

The boy nodded, his eyes dancing with glee. "Of course! I shoot at all things that fly!"

"Give him a good thrashing!" cried a squire still young

enough to be thrashed himself. Kundry remembered that one: he had stood closest to her and menaced her ribs with his elegant boot, so ill suited to the Grail knights' austere life.

"It was cruelly done," Gurnemanz told the boy. "This wood, this clearing—these are holy ground. What harm did our faithful swan do you when he was seeking his mate? Had you been a kind lad, you might even have admired them, circling over the lake; wouldn't it have amazed you?

"But no, you just saw a target. The swan was our friend; what was he to you but a moment's sport?"

Gurnemanz lifted the limp, heavy bird and showed him to the boy. "Look at what you did. He will never fly again, and the people who might have rejoiced at the sunlight on his wings will never see him now. Can't you find the grace to repent what you did?"

Blood from the swan was smeared across Gurnemanz's tunic just where the embroidery of the emblazoned dove frayed across the breast.

Blue, blue eyes blinked, and the boy passed a hand over them. His lips trembled, then thinned. In a move as rapid as it was unexpected, he broke his bow over an upthrust knee, then tossed his arrows passionately away.

The boy looked down at his feet in their coarse boots. "I did not know . . . then."

Gurnemanz shook his head. "How could you not have known? Where are you from?"

"I do not know." One of the younger knights tapped his forehead.

"Who was your father?"

"I do not know."

"Who sent you to seek this forest?"

"I do not know."

Gurnemanz shook his head again. "At least tell me what your name is."

"I used to have many names," the boy replied. Distress showed in his face, but like a picture wrought by a master's hand, not like honest human bewilderment. "But they are all gone, too. I have forgotten."

"Then you know nothing?" Gurnemanz reached out to

grasp the boy's shoulders. His eyes met Kundry's in a painful question. She had to shake her head, but regretted the motion; her temples felt caught in a vise.

"Never have I met anyone so dull, so removed from the world . . . except Kundry here," Gurnemanz mused. When two squires ventured to laugh, though, he glared at them.

"Be off with you!" he ordered. "The king needs you; I do not."

Two squires broke off low-hanging branches and wove them into a rough bier for the swan. Tenderly, they carried it away, as if they bore a wounded king on his litter.

A fool this boy surely was. But a fool made wise by pity? Childish tears and a snapped bow over the death of a swan were hardly wisdom. Kundry's head throbbed. She put it down and drew up her knees as if she were a babe in the womb. Hiding brought no relief. Something in her mind struggled to be born. She moaned, but Gurnemanz did not hear her, so intent he was on the fool.

"You can speak now," he reassured the boy. "I know you cannot answer my questions, but tell me what you can. There must be something you remember."

The boy scuffed in the leaf mold, like a child who had forgotten his lessons. Clearly, he was trying to remember. The effort sent pangs of light shooting through Kundry's eyes, but shutting them only made the pain worse.

"I have a mother!" the boy brought out in triumph. "Her name is Herzeloyde, and we lived in woods and lonely meadows." Again that radiant, fool's smile. It renewed the waning day and seemed to restore Gurnemanz to early middle age.

"Who gave you your weapons?" He almost chuckled.

"I made them myself to frighten the savage eagles from the forest."

And yet you shot the swan. Gurnemanz left that unsaid. "You seem like an eaglet yourself, and nobly born, too, or I am no judge. Why didn't your mother find you worthier weapons?"

The question exhausted the boy's paltry store of remembrances, but it caused Kundry to twist and cry out as the prophecies that had afflicted her tore free of her consciousness and out her throat.

"Weapons? How should his mother give him weapons? Fatherless, he was born after Gahmuret lay treacherously slain on the field of honor. To save her son from dying as his father had, his mother raised him as a fool, far from deeds of arms and all people—the more fool she!"

Kundry laughed until her breath caught and she gagged on her own laughter.

The boy turned to her, his eyes wide and glittering in the sunlight, his whole demeanor changed.

"Yes! I remember now! Once, I saw a whole troop of noble men on great horses riding by the forest's edge. They could not be men, I thought then. They must be God's own angels. But when I asked, they laughed and rode away; and my mother wept. I pursued them, but I could never catch up."

He gestured, his tanned, long-fingered hands waving this way and that in his enthusiasm. "I wandered through savage places, over hills and dales, day and night, defending myself with my bow and arrows . . ." He cast a regretful look at the snapped arrows, the broken bow.

Kundry rose. The pain in her head was gone, replaced by compulsion that made her draw near the boy. He was young, innocent, fearless as she had been more than a thousand years ago. She wanted to touch him, but would not dare. She watched him as a beast that went to ground might watch a hunter. And then she was made to laugh again.

"Yes! Robbers and giants fell to his might and soon learned to fear the fearless child!"

"Feared me? Who fears me?" The boy's voice almost broke in astonishment as he demanded, fierce as any emperor, "Tell me!"

Kundry bowed deeply and came up laughing again. Gurnemanz was shaking his head.

"The wicked!"

"So those robbers and giants who fought me—were they wicked?"

Gurnemanz chuckled.

"Who is good, then?"

The old knight was instantly sober. Kundry knew he saw his duty: instruct this lad even in the nature of good and evil. "Your dear mother is good. But she mourns and grieves because you deserted her."

Kundry's laughter turned into a wail. Her vision in the ride through Broceliande, this boy whom Gurnemanz was prepared to cherish as a new son, the king who suffered by the shore fused into a totality of anguish. "His mother grieves no longer because she is dead."

"My mother? She's dead?" the boy cried. "Who says so, you witch?"

Kundry crouched over, her dirt-stained hands clenched into fists. Herzeloyde had had a son who had left her, and she had died of it. Mary had a son, who died in torment before her. Amfortas had been a son and had destroyed the edifice his father had spent his life building. Even Kundry—she had been someone's child, and just look at the pride and joy she had brought on her family. It was just as well she had had no children. They brought only anguish. She glared at the child and spat out her words.

"I say so. As I rode by, I saw her dying. But she sent you her greeting, *fool!*"

The boy hurled himself forward and seized Kundry by the throat. Such strength in those slender hands! Each finger felt like a dart pressing into her body. Her vision darkened, except for flashes of lightning in which she saw Gurnemanz's face twist with amazement. Slowly, too slowly, he rose, pulled the boy's hands away, and held him while he shouted and kicked.

Blessedly, the pressure lifted, and she gasped, sucking at the air like a child at the breast.

"Violent again? Brutal again? I thought you had learned your lesson."

The boy's eyes rolled up as Gurnemanz shook him. He trembled, then sagged in the old knight's grasp. Gurnemanz eased him to the ground and began to open the throat of his garment.

A horn hung on a nail driven into the wall of his hut. Kundry ran to seize it and fetch water from the spring in the woods that supplied them. She was staggering as she re-

turned to Gurnemanz, the air rasping and burning down
her throat. The boy who lay before her was in worse case—
almost bluish-pale beneath the hearty tan his life in the
wilds had given him.

Kundry bent forward and sprinkled the boy with water,
while Gurnemanz chafed his hands and slapped his face. He
moaned and stirred, then struggled upward until Gurnemanz could support him, one arm beneath his head as a
prop, the other wrapped loosely round him in case he
attacked again. Kundry knelt and held the horn to his lips,
and the boy drank avidly. His hands came up to take the
horn and hold it himself.

Gurnemanz rested a hand on Kundry's head. "This is the
Grail's compassion. Bless you, child."

Warmth flowed from the big hand as the knight blessed
her. A moment longer, and Kundry would rub her face
against it, kiss it, and proclaim herself Gurnemanz's grateful
slave. From the corner of her eye she saw knights passing
back and forth, arranging for Amfortas's return to the citadel.

She twitched away, lowering her head lest she see the
disappointment she caused Gurnemanz. "I never do good.
All I want is rest."

Gurnemanz sighed, but released her. She was free now,
free to creep into the shelter of a thicket that would hide her
and that would shield her from the sight of Gurnemanz
lavishing a father's care upon a fool. She was sinking, sinking into sleep now, but a chill seized her.

"Not now! No! Get back from me . . . oh God, help!" She
shook and burrowed deeper into the bushes. "I . . . can't
fight . . . so tired of fighting."

Glitter and sound rose from the lakeshore as his knights
escorted Amfortas home. All Kundry had to do was rise
onto her knees, and she could see his face, remember how
his eyes had warmed at the sight of her, how the heavy lids
had closed in pleasure . . . and how that had all turned to
lashes.

She could not bear to see it or remember. Her eyes
burned from the rides through the shifting paths of Broceliande, the battle at Merlin's clearing, and her grief at the

trapped old mage's final death. Her throat ached from the blond fool's attack. It was time she rested. Even *she* deserved to rest at some point.

Just this once, let her be weak. In the way a man falling from a cliff clutches the branch he hopes might save him, Kundry fell into the pit of sleep she had fought off so long.

26

INTO the pit Kundry sank. Voices ebbed and rose about her, and strands of power, like fishing lines, angled to snare her. With a flick of her tired mind, she evaded them: a time would come, she knew, when she could no longer do so. Then *he* would come, in the guise of a shark, and devour her. The water of her thoughts grew turbid, troubled. Escape . . . Kundry floundered, seeking minds in which she might find escape, if not an anchor.

She found one in Gurnemanz. Even as her thoughts brushed that sturdy, faithful consciousness, the old man rose. He eased the fool to his feet and draped the boy's arm about his neck. Taller than he, more slender by far and more feeble, the fool leaned heavily upon him for support as, step by painstaking step, Gurnemanz led him toward Montsalvasche.

"You saw the procession," Gurnemanz told the fool, using the same steady voice he had once used to school war-horses. "Our king is returned from the holy lake. The sun is high now. Let me lead you to him. If you are pure, now that you have repented, the Grail will comfort and refresh you."

Gurnemanz looked over his shoulder, half afraid that Klingsor might appear from behind a tree and demand possession of Grail as well as Spear. Not for the first time, he wanted to curse Amfortas; and yet, how dared he? *Let him who is without sin among you* . . . Besides, Amfortas was his lord.

Curse God and die. At any point, Amfortas might have done just that. Instead, he clung to his post; served the

Grail; preserved his father, his old lord Titurel in life; and insured for himself an endless life of pain.

Gurnemanz sighed. It wasn't enough that his king was an invalid and a sinner, that the land roundabouts withered, and that Montsalvasche, such as it was, stood in a constant posture of guard. Now, he had to be wet nurse to a fool. And naturally, the fool could not restrain his folly in decent silence.

"Who is the Grail?"

Sweet Jesu, listen to the lad!

Had the boy been taught nothing? Was he not only simple, but perfect in his idiocy? *Mea culpa*, he chastised himself and vowed to spend the night on his knees, which were no better than they should be, Grail or no Grail.

"The Grail"—he suppressed a sigh—"isn't a *who*, it's a *what*; but I cannot tell you what because that's a mystery. Do you understand 'mystery'?"

Blue innocence, its good cheer returning, met his eyes.

"Mystery," Gurnemanz repeated. "Like the sacraments." A terrible thought struck him. "You *have* had instructions, haven't you?" Lord have mercy upon him, the lad was probably a perfect pagan, among everything else; and here Gurnemanz was, leading him before the Grail.

The cheerfulness faded. "The bread. The blood. My mother said . . . Can you tell me why . . ."

This time, Gurnemanz could not suppress a sigh of pure relief. "That's better. Well, if you know that, then you know what a mystery is. The Grail is another such mystery. I cannot tell you what it is yet, but if you are chosen to serve it, you'll learn what it is. There is no one way to the Grail unless It calls you Itself."

They had their feet upon the way to the citadel now. Broceliande's shadows shifted and rustled as they walked, their path shortened. Even the boy's weight upon Gurnemanz's shoulders seemed to be lightened.

He glanced around with delight. "How does this happen? We seem scarcely to be moving, yet the trees dance by. Will you tell me?"

So he could perceive the shifts in time and place? That was hopeful. *Don't think it yet*, Gurnemanz warned himself.

Don't dare to hope. He patted the boy's hand where it rested on his shoulder.

"This much I can tell you, and then you must not ask so many questions, especially not where we are bound. Here, my son, time blends here with space, lest we be tardy to serve the Grail."

Then the times and paths of Broceliande wrapped about the old knight and the young fool, sweeping them closer to the citadel. Overhead, the sky dimmed to the sacred twilight of Montsalvasche, lifted only when the Grail was borne out and held aloft by the man who was more sufferer than celebrant these days.

Kundry, hidden in her thicket, felt her consciousness caught up along with Gurnemanz and his charge. She had time for a moment of panic—*I cannot go in there!*—before the other minds overwhelmed her resistance.

They are getting weaker, my two kings, Gurnemanz thought. Once, in Egypt, he had seen a mummy stripped of its yellowed bands. Titurel, too weak these days even to raise his head, had that look. On any decent battlefield a man that feeble would have the mercy stroke without having to beg for . . . but what was he thinking of? Old men didn't ride the battlefields. Titurel was a holy man; his death would come in God's time, and no one else's.

Not even Amfortas's? That thought, too, insinuated itself. No longer his "young king," Amfortas wore the look of a man whose life had long been a waking agony. The knights would never have worked a horse so hard; any horse they rode—in the days when they still rode out on missions— would have been honorably retired to its pasture ten years ago. But they burdened their king. Needing him, they burdened him to the point where he longed for death. And even his own father denied him that.

The young fool quivered beside Gurnemanz, his earlier faintness gone. There was no guessing what he might be thinking, or if indeed he thought. At least, Gurnemanz had seen to it that the lad wouldn't interrupt the celebration with some freakish question. Then, well, if the Grail called him, fools could leave their folly and become wise—though whether this particular fool *could* be made wise through

pity was probably as much beyond Gurnemanz's understanding as transubstantiation.

Never mind. God knows, there were fools enough in the
world; and if this were not the fool of the prophecy, another fool would come . . . one of these decades.

In the glimmer near Montsalvasche, the branches began
to resemble the leading of colossal windows, wrought all in
greens. Then trees yielded to gray stone and to enormous
gates, by which two knights stood with bare blades that
shone as if bespelled by the radiance of what they guarded.
Restraining the fool with a heavy pressure of his hand upon
the boy's shoulder, Gurnemanz strode forward, his free
hand wide of his body: quite defenseless as one must be
before the Grail. Bells rang out, the gates swung wide, and
Gurnemanz entered. It was a foretaste of the welcome he
prayed he might receive when he died, when the Gates of
Heaven admitted him and he could finally kneel before
Saint Peter and hear him say, *"Well done, thou good and
faithful servant."*

They walked along a passageway wrought all of stone,
pierced with lancet windows. Along the walls, torches
flickered in their holders. The flames quivered as the deep-
toned bells rang out to summon the knights to prayer.
Other footsteps, steel-shod or bare, depending on whether
the knight went garbed these days as fighter or penitent,
joined theirs. The boy tried to crane his neck to see these
newcomers, but Gurnemanz restrained him.

Just when it seemed, as it had always seemed, that the
passageway had become a tunnel from which there was no
escape, they reached the feasting hall. Other doors at the
end of the vast hall opened, and the knights filed in, wearing
the shabby grandeur of their order. In the twilight broken
only by torches and the Presence light, the doves emblazoned on their worn surcoats looked as if they might take
wing at any moment and fly up into the dome.

Squires passed behind the knights. Some took up their
own stations. Others laid baskets of bread and flagons of
wine upon the altar, then stood waiting.

As if in formation, the knights moved swiftly to their
assigned tables where they remained standing. The habit of

more than half a lifetime overcoming him, Gurnemanz took his place, too. His guest followed, uncertain.

The dome soared high overhead, a chalice to catch the cries of the bells and the songs of the youngest pages and blend them into the harmony that Gurnemanz prayed daily would be the last thing he would ever hear. He could ask no better than to die here, his brothers about him, on holy ground. His king shared that prayer . . . and, oh God, though Amfortas was far younger than Gurnemanz, he had a better right to pray it.

Then four squires, marching slow, brought in the Tabernacle of the Grail, gold curtained by white linen. They placed it upon the broad stone altar at the back of the room, then withdrew to its sides, hands folded. Following the Tabernacle came the king.

The familiar anguish of seeing his king borne in by serving brothers and the strongest of the Order's squires caught Gurnemanz by the throat. He winced at each step. Any unsteadiness might cause Amfortas hideous pain; just setting down the litter and resettling the wounded king upon the couch made him bite his lip till the blood ran.

Gurnemanz's fool looked troubled, and Gurnemanz shook his head minutely: *no questions.* Blast the lad. At this moment, when his mind and heart should be enraptured, was this any time to be training unlicked cubs?

Stationed in the clerestory that ran just beneath the dome, a choir of youths sang of the joyful sacrifice of blood. A boys' choir, their pure high voices arching up almost to the edges of hearing, sang of the dove that signified grace and the banquet that brought life to soul as well as body.

Then silence. Waiting replaced the song of boys and bells; and the dome caught the silence and cast it down upon the knights who prayed to feast in the hall of Montsalvasche.

(Kundry, cowering at the fringes of the old knight's thoughts, writhed in her troubled sleep. Amfortas! There he lay, the wound in his thigh reminding him of guilt and desire, even in this holy place. *Lord, I am not worthy.* But there was no other. Not for the Grail. Or for either of them.)

From a vaulted niche wrapped in shadows came the voice, echoing like the horn announcing the last days and startling the celebrants as it always did.

"My son Amfortas, are you prepared?"

The man lying on the couch did not reply.

"Shall I see the Grail once again and live?" The voice rose with the force of a king.

The silence drew out. Like the others, Gurnemanz might crave the sight of the Grail, crave it as he craved communion, and strive mightily to deserve both. But the presence of the uncovered Grail was all that preserved Titurel from the grave.

"Must I die then without its light to guide me?" Though Titurel's voice broke, it bore the force of a command. The silence that followed it, hovering like a bat's shriek on the very edges of consciousness, compelled obedience.

Once again, pain speared through Amfortas's thigh as he thrust himself up from his couch.

"God, God, God, the burning," Amfortas cried. "This eternal grief. My father, oh God, just once more, take up the holy task and let me perish."

Let the old man, the ancient tyrant, take up the duties his son had been too weak to bear. Why must Titurel insist? Was this also part of his punishment?

Silence drew out as it always did. God forgive Amfortas, but he could almost hate the old man, trying to demand his son's strength, draining him almost unto death so he might live to see another dawn and again force him to reveal the Grail. You could not even call what Titurel had life: call it some lust for sanctity or some urge to test Amfortas as Job had been tested.

How long, oh God, must this go on? How long must he expiate his guilt?

Till the ache in his body reminded him only of his sin and not how it was caused. Till the fool made wise through pity appeared to redeem him.

He had long ago decided the fool would never come. That was too much to hope for.

All his hopes right now were bounded in a single wish:

just once let Titurel rise to serve the Grail; just once let him rest.

The silence drew out until that voice pierced it once again. "Entombed, I live here by our Savior's grace, too weak to serve. You, now, make atonement for your guilt. Reveal the Grail!"

Obedient to the king in his tomb, the four Grail bearers paced forward, hands raised to unveil it.

"No!" Amfortas mourned. "Leave it dark. Pray God that none of you ever knows how the sight of its holiness burns me alive. Even the spear wound is nothing beside having to serve, the sinful guardian, who holds the Grail for you and begs it to bless you. You're pure, you're chaste, you're blessed already. Is there no mercy ever? My God, I am heartily sorry . . ."

His voice broke into a sob. (Kundry shuddered. Amfortas *was* heartily sorry for his sin, for his own pain, for the sorrow he caused the men of Montsalvasche. But he could not repent because he had never, in all the years he had suffered, rejected what had caused his fall.)

As if his tears had released them, the four Grail bearers approached the altar.

"Too late for me," Amfortas cried. He levered himself up, feverish, the way a man got after fighting and being wounded, and having to rise again before the healers approved. "The blood within that holy cup is glowing, shining with light. Make it stop! Have mercy, God! Even here, I freeze and burn before you!"

Now it was the Grail itself that drew him. At the very moment he was most conscious of his own shame, his blood surged with desire to unveil it, to look upon it, to touch it. Once again, he thought of his wound and of the blood tide that had caused it. *"Behold thou art fair, thou art fair . . ."* he had whispered, but she had been vile, a witch.

He lunged away from the couch as if his very posture were sinful. Wet heat and tearing warned him his wound had reopened. Blood stained the white of his robes and congealed quickly, hardened by the ice that formed at the unhealing wound.

Christ had bled for others' sin; Amfortas bled only for

his own. No repentance could control the heat of his thoughts, the memories of fire, and sword, and lust that flooded through him as his blood gushed forth. He thrust himself upward again as the frenzy seized him.

"Take back my birthright," he screamed, whether to his father or his God, he did not know. "Take it back and end this curse upon me."

Soft voices dropped down like manna from the clerestory, reminding Amfortas of the holy fool, made wise by pity, the chosen one—who had not come yet.

"You were promised," Gurnemanz had told him once, in the darkest watch of the night. "Hopelessness is the only deadly sin," the old man had advised him, in blithe ignorance of his own heresy. "Wait on—but fulfill your task today."

"Reveal the Grail!" Titurel commanded.

Today, there would be no fool, no hope for Amfortas. The cup would not be lifted from him. Carefully, as every man in the hall held his breath (and Kundry, lying in the wild, forced herself to lie still), the Grail bearers lifted the Grail from the tabernacle and drew the last fine veil to reveal a silver chalice embedded in fine crystal.

It was not a particularly large chalice or a massive one; nor was it ornately wrought like some cups Amfortas had seen on his campaigns in the East. But it was the Grail. It accepted him as it always had. And at that instant, it was the only thing in the world for him. A corona of reddish light, intensifying to white, enveloped it and reached out to embrace him.

"Take here my blood," sang the choir. "Take here my life and eat and drink."

Beneath the dome, the chorus drew out the words as a plea. There was no triumph here. Christ had not scrupled to wash the feet of the poor or walk among lepers. Could Amfortas begrudge his knights—his brothers and his father and his spiritual sons—what his own pain could provide them?

Amfortas flung himself to his knees. The ice on his wound thickened; but he was conscious only of the warmth of the Grail, the sight of the Grail, the promise of the Grail.

Each day, the sight of it restored him, so he would never die. Each day, the sight of it drained him, so he could never die. None of that mattered now for the moments he could bow his head before the Grail and be one with it.

The hall darkened even as the Grail's light grew stronger, as if it drew sustenance from the man prostrate before it, the men kneeling at their tables, even the young stranger who stood with mouth agape and one hand over his heart.

Amfortas prayed. He felt himself sprawled at the foot of a cross, mind and heart open in a wordless plea, blood pouring from a wound that was the dark twin to the one dealt Christ so long ago.

The Grail's light pulsed like a living heart.

Finally, the king rose. Pain subdued for that moment by prayer, his face was calm, his brow clear. Closing his hands upon the carved, cold crystal stem, he raised the Chalice aloft. The Grail's radiance surged out to embrace him until he wore a cope of light, dark only with his blood.

He stood motionless, celebrating his achievement. Then, as if he were a thurifer scattering incense, he gestured with the Grail to the four cardinal points, consecrating the sacrifice of bread and wine that lay upon the altar.

"How radiantly God greets us today!" Titurel's voice rose, vibrant and joyous as the choir's song. It rang from the clerestory, arched up into the dome, and poured forth, redoubled, upon the praying knights.

Amfortas set the Grail down in its tabernacle with such tenderness that the crystal of its reliquary did not even click against the gold.

Immediately, the squires stepped forth, more briskly now. Gradually, the room brightened. Sunlight poured in from the windows beneath the dome. The servers passed among the tables, distributing bread and pouring wine—a simple feast, but a joyous one.

(*Can you not see?* Kundry wanted to cry out to them. *The life is pouring out of your king. Go help him!* But she was mute, mute as the beautiful fool who stood behind the tables at which the knights were now seating themselves. Gurnemanz beckoned to the boy, who stood as if nails had been pounded through his boots to the stone beneath them.

Once, twice, he beckoned, then had to turn aside to attend to the blessing and the meal. *Go to him!* Kundry thought now, though the fool was no friend to her, now, was he? Her neck still ached from his clumsy attempt to strangle her into silence about his mother. Yet she had forgiven him, had eased his faintness . . . It was getting hard to think, hard to remember . . . so sleepy . . . *No rest for the wicked, Kundry.)*

When the meal was over, the knights rose and embraced. Gurnemanz, clasping arms and shoulders with the rest, did not even turn toward the fool; his anger and disappointment could have made Kundry laugh had she but the strength. She could no longer postpone the sleep that comes after a sorcerer draws heavily upon power.

Amfortas sank down onto his couch. The splendor faded from the wounded king, leaving only a man in bloody robes, tears of bereavement and exhaustion pouring down his face. He stared at the alcove in which Titurel lay in his living tomb. What if the Prodigal Son had returned home and, at the height of the feast, had turned upon his father and struck him dead?

That were blasphemy unthinkable; yet he had thought it. *This is the last time I serve the Grail, Father,* he thought at the hideous old man. *Never again. We are both better off dead.* He clenched his teeth as his squires bore him out. None too gently: this lot, all of a faction, held no love for him.

The doors closed, leaving only the memory of sanctity— and Gurnemanz, glaring at the motionless fool who had so disappointed him.

The old knight stalked up to the boy and shook him by the arm. The rapture of the Grail drained from him now, he was as brusque as he had been fatherly before. "Still standing there, are you? Do you know what you saw?"

The boy shook his head and pressed his heart convulsively. His hair shone in the daylight restored to the hall.

"So," Gurnemanz muttered. "You were truly nothing but a fool. And I was a bigger fool for hoping."

He pulled the boy by the arm he still held and drew him, muttering as he went, toward a small side door. "Off with you, then, to wherever you're going. But listen to old

Gurnemanz one more time. From now on, leave our swans in peace. Go looking—you gander, you—for geese!"

He pushed the boy out the door and banged it angrily behind him. Walking stiff-legged as if his back and legs hurt from wounds or the dampness within even these stone walls, he followed the knights' path out of the hall.

(Abruptly, prophecy erupted in her consciousness, and she knew that all time past and all time present demanded that she rise from her slumber and hasten to the fool so unceremoniously shoved out of Montsalvasche. But sleep overcame her. She groaned and struggled. What was the matter with her? She had yearned for it, begged for unconsciousness just as Amfortas begged for relief from his burdens. This was not rest, though; this was capture, her mind wailed in the second before it was swept away by a powerful undertow and engulfed.)

Sunlight shone in the domed sanctuary of Montsalvasche. The echoes of rejoicing soared up to heaven.

27

AN undertow dragged Kundry out into the black waters of nightmare. As she tried to thrash her way back to consciousness, memories clamored in her head for *more life, more life!*

Even a thousand years was not enough.

A fragment of memory brushed past her thoughts, and she clung to it as to a spar of driftwood. Once, she had accompanied a patron to the Sea of Galilee. Watching the fishermen head for shore under a sky sullen with lightning, she had seen a child escape its mother. Laughing, it dashed out into the water and was swept off its feet—to death, had a sailor not heard her scream for help, seen the child too, and leapt into the dark waters to rescue it.

Her patron had summoned the man, charmed the tale from him, then tossed him silver as if silver could repay the man for courage and story both. "It is the risk of the tide and storm that adds to the joy of swimming," he had told her later. Rome, strongly pragmatic, was as little a nation of the sea as her own: his words, even pompously spoken, amazed her. Kundry herself had sent her maid with gold for the mother and known the gift for a paltry thing.

She knew now that her patron's words were not true. Kundry would have longed now for such a fool of a sailor to rescue her from this current. The ones who had the power and the courage were dead: she could not believe but that all of them were dead.

She herself—she had tasted power before. Had she the power now to crest the wave? She fought. Kicking and gasping as if struggling to snatch breath as her head surfaced above a whitecap, she fought for breath and life. Too long submerged and there might be nothing left of her worth living.

Then a shadow fell. As if she were in truth a fish and a net had been dropped upon her from a boat, she lay immobile, waiting to be hauled in. Her mind went blank.

The water of her restless sleep drained away. She woke and found herself tangled in blue smokes, under blue lights. The air quivered with power. A brass wheel spun, the sound of its passage bat-shrill in the heavy air.

A voice rose in the last rage of an incantation. "Arise! Come to me! Your master calls you, nameless one, chief among she-devils. Rose of Hades, Herodias, you were—and what else? Gundryggia then; Kundry here? Come here, come here now, Kundry! Your master calls: rise!"

Kundry knew that voice: neither male nor female, arrogant in its rage for power. She lifted her head. The mists of gums and spices faded slightly; and Kundry saw pillars, the black and the white. These were not the twin pillars. These were broken at their core, shells of the integrity and strength that the true pillars held. Between them hung the sign of the Tree Reversed. Sullen lights pulsed and erupted along the paths of that Tree.

Placed before it, like a throne set before a tapestry, was a great chair. The long sleeves of his robe draped over his plump arms like a Harpy's wings. In it, white hands caressing the Spear, sat Klingsor. In the years that he had possessed it, he had gained some power over it, if he could touch it and not risk burns. But it had not assuaged the hunger in his eyes.

Kundry threw her chapped hands before her eyes and screamed.

Once, mad with guilt and grief, she had cast herself at the foot of a cross and been hurled instead far away in time and place. But the power she had drawn on to flee Golgotha had been long extinguished. The seasons in Broceliande had restored it somewhat, and the battle in the woods with Klingsor had shown her she could fight and resist. But still, what power she had was suppressed now, stifled by the pressure of the wards that Klingsor had spun over his domain and reinforced by possession of the Spear.

"Awake now, are you? Ha! Once more, when I need you, you fall to my spell."

Trapped again! The sight of Klingsor, so soon after she had seen the Grail through her lover's eyes, shocked a wail from her. If she could put her head down again, curl back in on herself like a babe harbored in the inner sea of its mother's womb, perhaps he would go away.

But the false mage clapped his hands and forbade.

"Tell me, where have you been wandering this time?" he sniffed at her. "Roving with that rabble of knights? What a fool you are to serve them, when they treat you like a beast. I can smell them on you!"

He drew closer. He even offered a hand scented with civet to ease her steps down from the platform to which he had conjured her. She hated the way she was faltering, and she held out her own before she thought: callused, browned, and scratched now from her sojourn in the thickets from which Klingsor had drawn her.

Kundry knew the place: Klingsor's tower. She was a prisoner again.

"Don't you fare much better when you obey me?" he asked in the sweet, reasonable voice she had even more reason to detest. "Didn't I keep you always young and beautiful?"

Kundry shook her head and kept her eyes down. Let him think she preferred this guise. At least, looking as she did now, she would not have to whore her way.

"I don't understand you, Kundry. After you conquered their leader for me"—he laughed, that voice with no maleness in it rising in derisive music—"the Grail's thrice-holy defender, what could tempt you to seek them out again? They would kill you if they knew."

They had had this talk before, Kundry recalled. Twenty years ago, and more than a thousand. That time, she had laughed at him, had reviled him, and been cast back to the moment of her curse. This time, though . . . she flung out her hands. The first thing, she remembered, that the child saved from drowning did was spew up water. In just the same way, the struggle with nightmares had made her dizzy and sick.

"Deepest night," she whispered. "Madness and sorrow . . . sleep, deepest sleep . . . death!"

"What woke you, then? Someone else?" Klingsor snapped. "Answer me!"

"Yes." Assent slipped from her like the ebb tide on which souls flow out to their deaths. "My curse . . . how I yearn . . ."

Again, that damnable laughter. "You're yearning for the knights?" A whole man's voice would have broken on that high note of irony, but not Klingsor's.

"I served them." The knights and squires had laughed at her. They had jeered at her. They had even threatened her. But she had served them well, returning good for ill, Gurnemanz said.

"Yes, yes, to atone for the evil you had caused?" It was uncanny how Klingsor could follow her thoughts. His sarcasm lashed her. "Or because you think you love the man you destroyed? But they cannot help you; I have their price. Even the strongest will fall, sinking into your arms—fall by the Spear I seized myself."

Kundry remembered. Klingsor had caught and summoned her . . . She moaned, fear drowning her rage at him. Never mind that Klingsor had forced her to entice Amfortas to her bed, then laughed when she regretted the Grail king's maiming. Never mind that he had cast her back to her birthplace and birth time when she had turned on him. She had more power now: if she turned on him now, perhaps she would not lose. It would be hard to try again. Every time she had fought Klingsor, she had lost.

"I have a task for you, Kundry." Klingsor spoke as if coaxing a lazy child. "You'll like it, too. Today, you must meet and win the most dangerous knight of all. It is his folly that shields him."

Klingsor cocked his head, as if listening for some sign. He ran to look out over the tower wall. The peacock brocades brought from Persia rustled and shifted in the blue light.

"There he comes, laughing like a child! See the pretty castle, child? Come to play at war? Look at your next sweetheart, Kundry!"

She shook her head and looked down at the stone floor,

past Klingsor, anyplace but at the idols and perversions of power that he had collected about him. Oh, why had she not the strength of Samson to stand between the pillars Klingsor had set up beside his chair, to shake them, and bring them down, the black pillar and the white, upon his unhallowed head?

She remembered Amfortas's eyes when he woke to know himself betrayed by her; she would not violate another innocent again.

"I will not," she whispered.

"You will. You must."

Kundry raised her head. "You cannot compel me."

"But I can," Klingsor told her. He lifted the Spear, and she shrank from the sight of it. "I can force you. I, your master. And do you know why?"

Decidedly, they had had this conversation before. Klingsor would try to make her believe he exulted in his immunity, as a eunuch, to the power she had wielded over men like Amfortas. She didn't want to hear it again; she didn't want to match strengths in a game she had always lost. And she was weary, so weary.

What else could she expect? It was her curse to ruin all she touched, to destroy where she loved, and never to find release.

Klingsor laughed. "Kundry, come here." He drew out the words, an obscene parody of seduction. "You went to the knights who abused you to work out your curse. Now, perhaps the one who spurns you can set you free. Would it be so bad to try with the boy who is approaching?"

He had her by the scratched, filthy arm and was dragging her to the wall. He was like the undertow, too fast, too treacherous to resist, hastening to his own destruction and sweeping her with him. His grip on her arm hurt, and she tried to pull back.

The perfect whore, was she? Just look at her! The laughter forced on her by her curse tore from her. What came out was a wail.

"Is that why you waked me? I won't . . ." His strength had grown since he had thrust her back in time; he must have drawn some power from the Spear her crimes had helped him gain.

"Ha, look out, Kundry girl!" Klingsor urged with a bawd's glee. "See what a handsome boy I found for you!"

She had both hands up over her eyes. He plucked them away and held her by the shoulders. "Look!"

It was the fool who had forsaken his mother and slain the swan.

Klingsor, one arm still about her, snatched up a horn and leaned out over the wall. He blew fierce alarums until his cheeks, beneath his black beard, puffed out red. Then he drew a deep breath and began to bellow.

"Watchmen, ho! Warriors, heroes, wake up! Your foes are near." Again, he clapped the horn to his lips and blew fiercely. The echoes rang in the tower. They made Kundry dizzy, sick, but she tried to muster her own forces. Then his hand was on her, and her strength drained away. Merlin's power was that of vision and patience; it would not help her in this fight.

Klingsor was laughing. "Watch them! My poor fools of warriors, defending the pretty witches they sleep with."

"Courage, courage, my heroes!" he shouted, then laughed. "After all, what do I pay them for, if not to fight and die at my command?"

Amfortas, Kundry thought with supreme irrelevance, would have joined his men, armored, yes, wounded as he was, leading the defense, had this accursed place been his to protect. It was all folly. The fool was young and beautiful, too full of life to be turned into butcher's meat. She did not want to watch. How could one boy prevail against Klingsor's warding spells? She tried to shrink away from the wizard.

Klingsor forced her to the ramparts. There was the fool she remembered, armored only in the crudely stitched leathers she recalled, laying about him with a stick. Wait! Even as she watched, he snatched a sword from a man she remembered as Ferris, chief of Klingsor's mamluks. So Klingsor had healed him after all. A rush of old anger surprised her. Ferris had seized her, fondled her, then threatened her. When Ferris fell, she shuddered with satisfaction.

Gurnemanz had been right to think the fool might make a goodly knight. Though the boy held the sword awkwardly, almost like a club, as he swung it, one knight reeled back, his hands clapped to the red wound that had been his forehead. Another staggered, then fell, his shoulder almost severed even through his mail. A third collapsed, hands cupped at his center. Even this far above the plain, Kundry could hear their screams.

It was butchery indeed that Kundry watched, not battle. The ground became a kind of red muck. Shouting battle cries that turned to moans, the knights slipped in it, struggled up, and turned to flee all the while Klingsor called them girls and cowards and laughed at their deaths. She could not bear to look. So many battles she had seen in her time; and each man whose blood poured down his face and body wore the same look that Joshua had worn after the Romans scourged him—of a human maimed and crying to know why. Involuntarily, her hands went out to Klingsor's mamluks. Even they deserved better than a master who sent them out to die.

Al-Marrekh, he of the spear, whom her Roman masters had called Mars, bestrode the field of battle and laughed at the blood that stained his feet and ankles.

Klingsor's hands worked back and forth on the stonework, as if he kneaded a woman's breasts. His eyes were bright with hunger. He licked his lips, and then he laughed. She could not bear that laughter and bloodshed commingled. She squeezed her eyes shut and clenched her fists, but her own laughter welled up and possessed her utterly as it had not done since she gazed up on a cross and known that all faith was dead, all hope was dead, and she was forever trapped. Like a mailed fist, her laughter struck her down. She cowered against the rock, her breath spent, too weak to do aught but moan.

She shuddered with revulsion, then with something else. As the dying knights' blood washed down their faces and their sides, she felt the fever and the pulse of it in her own flesh. Before her eyes, the aged, callused skin sloughed off. Slack muscles went taut . . .

Stop it! she shouted within herself. Reading her face and thoughts, Klingsor laughed again, a far more evil sound than any laughter of hers. She made a shield of her will and what little strength she possessed. For an instant, the sense of shedding her skin for something fresh and new ceased. Her body turned traitor on her, clamoring for more youth, more life, more blood.

Another knight fell, screaming out of what had once been a mouth. His blood washed over her. Its warmth was welcome, like a hot bath on a winter day. Kundry raised her hands to her mouth. Their nails were rosy, unbroken; the knuckles small; the skin smooth. Now she could feel the muscles of breast and belly grow sleek once more.

Too weak to fight, a voice taunted within her skull. *Just you try.*

"Look at them bleed, look at them fall," Klingsor gloated. "If all the knights in the world fought below and slaughtered each other, I would watch and laugh. And the fool! Look how he stands there, laughing like a boy, proud of his conquest."

"Lean out any farther and you'll fall," Kundry told him. "Or have you finally learned to fly?"

Swift pain lanced through her. Greenish fires, like the lights on the model of the Tree, began to glow in Klingsor's eyes. He would repay her for the gibe later, at his leisure.

"No, child," Klingsor mocked the fool, "there is no one left to fight. You've frightened them away. Come to *me* now, and I will fight you. You there, so childish and free, and so dull—you'll fall right into my hands once you've lost the purity that wards you. Then I will rule you!"

Now Klingsor had her by the arm, was hauling her upward.

"Now, to my work. Even if he cannot break my words, he can overleap them. And when he does, I must be prepared. You must change back to what you were," he said. "I want you looking young, enticing; not like the stinking hag we both know you really are. Pfui! How long since you bathed? I have fine baths here, oils and powders and paints for that skin of yours. And gowns of fine silk, not sackcloth and snakeskins. You'd like that, wouldn't you, hey, Kundry? To be a rose of Sharon once again, fit to snatch a Grail knight's soul?"

He watched to see if she would flinch. The pleasure she took in denying him that triumph twisted in her heart.

Amfortas had called her Rose of Sharon before sleeping in her arms.

"I knew you would come to serve me once again."

Kundry stiffened. "No."

"You must." Eyes bored into hers, a greenish light waking in the blackness. As well quarrel with an image of the Assyrian gods with their monstrous wings, their pitiless eyes, and their talons.

"I won't." She took a deep breath and summoned what strength she had. She dared not think of what would happen if she lost but was not destroyed.

Light wreathed him and spread out to her. She thought that if it touched her, she might die, but she lacked the craft to stop it. Her matted hair and the flesh of her arms seemed to prickle; light shone off her, too. Klingsor's hands fell back. For a long while, they stood opposed, sorcerer and thrall. Even the screams of battle and rout were muted by the circles of light in which they stood as their powers—one tried, one untested—grappled and crackled in the blue-tinged air.

The light lapped at the walls, and a smell of burning rose.

"Well protected, are you?" Klingsor muttered. "But you do not attack. Cannot, I think." He drew his hands together, steepling them before his face. Striding to stand between the pillars, he flung out his arms between those shells of dark and white in salute to the dark tree etched upon the tower's wall. The powers of the dark began to wake and kindle. Kundry flung them frantically aside, but the wards caught them, redoubled them, and cast them back at her.

"I cannot bend you, but I can break you. Keep your petty defenses, girl, and may they serve you well—back in Judaea once again."

Kundry gasped. The light about her flared as her fear

grew. This time, she could not conceal her horror. She recoiled from Klingsor, and he laughed, even that terrible hunger of his assuaged for the moment. In that Assyrian face of his, his teeth shone like knives.

"Yes, I can send you back again. I can, and I will. Think of it, Kundry. So absurd you looked, dwindling and falling down through the pit of centuries. You are not the only one who laughs, you know. I laughed at you as you fell. I laughed at your pathetic fight to turn aside the fate I had set for you. As I laugh now.

"Fight me, and you will live your curse for the third time. Think of it, the nails driven into hands and feet, the crack of hammer through bone and flesh into the wood, and the blood, dripping from the spear that now I wield!"

He might be bluffing. She could not be sure. But she could not bear that sight, that fate, that thousand years' accursedness again. Her hands pressed against her ears until they rang, but she could not shut out Klingsor's threat, Joshua's last words—or the laughter that had damned her twice now. If Klingsor fulfilled his words, then nothing she could do would save her and she would have to hear them again, then relive, again, a thousand years of torment.

And, once she had suffered through that time again, what would stop him from sending her back yet a *fourth* time?

She thought of hurling herself at Klingsor's feet, begging him to do his worst—anything but that! Then she saw the triumph in his eyes. Why feed it by showing just how abject she was before that, too, was demanded of her?

The aureole about her faded, sparks lingering at her fingertips, then dying out. She stood, head down. Beaten.

"Why do you always fight me?" Klingsor purred, sweetly reasonable in victory. His hands grasped her shoulders as they had done at Golgotha. "Come and see yourself."

He led her to his mirror. Her eyes rolled in an attempt not to see. Wild, matted hair; coarse, torn garments as before . . . but worn like a crude mask over youth and beauty. "The change has already happened, while you watched the battle. You *consented* as Sir Ferris died. You laughed." Klingsor shrugged. "My traitor. After all these years, to think he served me best by dying."

Kundry moaned, low in her throat. He had won; and this time, she had no recourse. A laugh began, deep in her throat, which now shed the wrinkles and slackness that it had had. It tore at her as it had the day Joshua died. But she had to laugh. It was all worthless, all her struggles; it had always been—and she had tried so hard.

"Look at you, Kundry. Young and beautiful once again. Fit to win a king, as once you did. Just think how you can inflame a boy—his first woman! I can hardly wait to watch." He ran his hands over her body, like a slave buyer in a market, and she gagged. It was Amnon who was touching her, then a series of men who flung her silver when they were through. She tried to twist free and hurl herself from the walls, but Klingsor's pudgy hands held astounding strength.

"Remember. You could be sent back. The choice is yours."

Now she was young and beautiful again, like a snake who had shed her skin. Was that all that was left her—to *be* a snake, torpid and gleaming in the sunlight? To betray all, including herself?

"Let us complete your transformation, then get you dressed," Klingsor said. "Then you can oversee my second line of defense. After all, you have had so much practice at surrender, haven't you? Perhaps, once I have won, I may reward you. Remind me, Kundry."

He gestured, and Kundry was plunged into blackness, pierced only by the lights of the Tree Inverted, the Tree of Death that was the basis of Klingsor's deepest workings. She shuddered as she heard him call on Samael and Azazel. Wings hovered, driving foul winds before them.

Her very flesh shifted and re-formed without her consent. Was this what witches felt when mobs caught them, and tied them, and the fire touched their flesh? Outside Klingsor's wards, the sky shone blue. She was grateful that the wards stood between the purity of that light and her polluted self.

The maids who served Klingsor and his knights attended Kundry. They bathed her, oiled and scented her; and even as they wept for their lovers, they whispered about this youth who could wound or slay mamluks of such proven skill. They did not weep for long. Kundry dismissed them as quickly as she dared.

Now, her hair arrayed in long curls down a thin robe of white shot with gold thread, Kundry lay on cushions of Persian brocade: crimson, bronze, and indigo. She trailed her hand, its fingertips patterned with henna, along the grass beside the tiny fountain. Overhead, as if trapped in amber, the sun shone with the heat of late summer when gardens and loose women flaunt themselves, overripe. Regardless of the weather of the world, it was always summer here.

Kundry stretched in the sunlight like a serpent who had shed its skin. She had indeed shed one guise for another: hag and knights' drudge for houri. And now she waited until her prey came in sight. She coiled, slow and sinuous on the sleek cushions, not as much for the delight of fine fabrics on supple flesh, as to display herself to Klingsor. Doubtless, he was watching; doubtless, he would say he had a right to approve the changes he had ordered.

She too must watch. She rolled over onto her stomach, rested her arms on a bronze cushion and her head on her arms, and stared at her reflection: dark eyes splendid in a vivid face; red lips; white teeth. Amfortas had compared her lips to a thread of scarlet before he kissed them to a deeper red. Tears rose, threatening the painstaking kohl lines that drew out the corners of her eyes. There was no point in thinking of Amfortas any longer: after a thousand years of trying, Klingsor had finally found a way of controlling her. At least, she thought, until she could get away.

Did she despise the maids who served her for their shaky loyalty? Hers was less secure, for she would flee Klingsor the second she could. For as long as she could. For all the good it had ever done her.

A tear fell into the fountain, mingled with the gentle swirling of the water, and blurred her reflection. She blinked once, and it was gone. It had been centuries since she could truly weep; that single tear surprised her.

Now Kundry could peer into Klingsor's garden. Centuries of care and blooms and herbs from all over the known world had gone into it. Leaves rustled slowly. Fat, lazy bees flew buzzing from one gaudy bloom to the next, even gaudier flower. In a pool that glinted with sunlight, a serene blue lotus floated amid papyrus reeds and rushes. Beyond were orange trees from Jaffa, their fruit shining fit to rival the golden apples of the Hesperides. Palms waved nearby; Kundry would not think of the last time she had held palm fronds in her hand. Not far beyond, she glimpsed plants that were little more than floral cups of sweet-smelling liquid—harmless unless you glimpsed the stripped bones within their chalices: though the plants never moved, they were hunters, nonetheless. Just such a place was Klingsor's garden.

Kundry did not have to walk in that garden to savor the kingdoms of fragrances she would find there or the brilliant, exotic treasures hidden in the shadows of rock and tower and trees. It was all contained in a courtyard as unlike the rough gray stone of Klingsor's fortress as Kundry now was unlike the hag who had scuttled about at the Grail knights' beck and call. Tiles wrought in the shape of stars shone on the walls circling the garden. Arabesques and letters of blue and gold shimmered on each tile. More elaborate designs adorned the high arches and graceful pillars that separated an arcade from the garden itself. Beyond lay only the mountainside and the valley, fading in the distance into the blue shadows of a high pass.

Kundry looked up from the tempting shadows of that arcade. The youth stood upon the ramparts, staring down into the garden. Almost, he wore the look of gleeful triumph that he had worn the day he slew the swan. He was happy to have survived the battle, to have conquered so many men who looked like the knights that he had thought, while still a boy and even more foolish then than he now was, to be angels. So many against one boy; yet he had conquered. He laughed and wiped the sweat of battle from his face, leaving only one smudge of dust and blood on his cheek.

Much to Kundry's horror, she found herself wanting to wipe it away for him and stroke his flushed forehead.

Kundry's eyes fixed on the youth's, reflected in the scrying pool. Once again, she marveled at the blue of his eyes: opaque, brilliant. But not unthinking. Not this time. The heat of battle and exhilaration had already faded, to be replaced first by confusion, now by excitement.

A haze, whether of heat or desire, was rising over the garden; somnolent fat bees hummed, urging languor. Practiced in the game as she was, Kundry knew when the youth first sniffed the fragrances and sighed deeply. His cheeks flushed and now his eyes sparkled with delight.

The haze over the garden grew deeper, brighter. Light seemed to conceal the youth's face from her. Kundry blinked, as if to clear her eyes of film.

Then, as if a kind child plucked a butterfly from a sleeve and set it down in safety, her consciousness was separated from that of the youth; and he strode down toward the bower where Kundry lay, hidden.

Kundry raised her head. It swam. Before she could gasp with the shock, the prophetic fit was on her. She laid her head down on the too-soft cushions and blinked at the motes of light dancing on the water of her scrying pool.

For an instant, she trembled. Prophetic powers enough only for what she needed to make this death-in-life of hers possible. It left her breathless. One word, and its meaning, glowed violet in her thoughts like the afterglow of a lightning bolt.

It was not letters of flame engraved by the hand of an archangel on a palace wall, but it served her well enough for vision. The moment of revelation passed, and the light faded, permitting her to spy again on the lad who strode onward toward his doom.

She knew his name now. He was more than the son of Gahmuret and Herzeloyde, whom she had spied upon from the moment he had left his mother. Gurnemanz had been wrong; if this lad did not fall, becoming less than Amfortas, he was the one foretold.

And she was the one ordained to ruin him as she had ruined his kinsman. Ruin him or be sent back to relive her damnation an incomprehensible *third* time. That was not a choice.

Best get it over with.

To her horror, she found herself eager to see him, to let him see her—a beautiful, living woman. He fascinated her: young and new, unmarked by life, yet so solidly alive. Already, she could imagine the smell and strength of him in her arms. He would hold her close, shaking with the excitement of his first woman, and his passion would keep her young. She wanted to see herself, reflected and glorified in those blue eyes, to know herself cherished, if only for a moment and by a fool.

Klingsor would jeer at her as he had with Amfortas. No doubt, he was watching now.

Then let him, she told herself. She would give him a show well worth watching, just as he had taught her a thousand years ago. And with each kiss and caress, she would let Klingsor ache for the manhood he had sacrificed. That would be revenge, of a very small sort.

From what she said now, there would be no return, forever. But she could not regret it for anything less than peace and redemption; and both were impossible for her now.

Drawing a deep breath, she called the name she now knew to be her quarry's.

"Parsifal!"

28

KUNDRY called again. "Parsifal! Come to me."

In her clear, rich voice, the name seemed to rise up and reverberate from the wards that shut the air of Klingsor's palace away from the honest sky. The boy strode forward.

"I remember!" he exclaimed in wonder. "But how could you know my name? Now I recall. My mother . . . one day she dreamt, and thus she named me."

"Come to me now, and claim your prize!" Kundry invited the youth. "This place holds only joy and welcome for you."

"This garden . . ." Parsifal's voice was dreamy as if he smoked hashish. "Is it all a dream?"

He neared the arch through which Kundry had passed earlier. His hand parted the hedges on either side. The tender branches and leaves brushed his hands, as if unwilling to let him pass without exacting a caress as their toll. Kundry knew what he must see: herself, lying upon a couch rich with flowers and cushions, looking like every man's dream: Lilith, Helen, Guinevere. The gold-shot silk of her thin robe glinted over her every curve, and the boy's gaze followed it with astonished delight.

"Was it you who called me?" he asked. "Me, the man without a name? You have given me one!" Recovering from his earlier wonder, he hastened to her side and knelt. This knightly grace was a far cry from the wild, ungainly movements of the youth who had tried to strangle her by Lake Brumbane. Yet the energy, the quick shifts of mood—those were the same.

Kundry counted over her wiles, then discarded them all.

None of a courtesan's calculations would work with such an innocent.

In his current guise of knight and victor he had called himself the nameless one. In the guise of boy and fool, he had launched himself upon her for raising any question at all about his past. "The nameless one." Tired and keyed up after battle, aroused by heat, and blood, and death, he would need to rest, to trust, to find safe harbor in her compassion and her arms.

In those needs were her key.

"I named you," she told him, her voice warm and reassuring. " 'Fal parsi'—so pure and foolish. Your father Gahmuret cried your name, Parsifal, as he died, far off in Arabia. Even as he perished, he gave a name to his unborn son. Why do you think I'm here? I lingered here to tell you. Why have you come here, if not to learn from me?"

Parsifal's lips trembled. "I have never seen nor dreamed what I see now. Lady, you fill my heart with dread."

Kundry laughed deep in her throat and held out a hand in such a wise that Parsifal had no recourse but to take and kiss it.

"No, Parsifal, you foolish, pure one! I lingered here, so far from my homeland, just to tell you how much I've seen. I heard you laugh in Herzeloyde's arms. Though her heart was broken, she drew comfort from your joy and strength from the light in your eyes. Do you not remember?

"She cradled you on tender mosses and lulled you to sleep, guarding you all night and waking you each dawn with tears that glistened in the light of the rising sun. Mourning your father, she vowed to save you from a fate like his. Small wonder you never saw a knight!

"Can you not remember how she would cry out when you roamed the forest, or how she laughed in relief when you returned, and how she caught you up in her arms—a lad—but in that instant, still her child? And you—you were heedless of all her care."

Careful, Kundry warned herself. This Parsifal was strong; it was not around her neck that she wished to find his hands. She must touch the next subjects with as much caution as she had ever used.

"You left her." She widened her eyes, which drops had made to seem huge, dark, and liquid. "You did not even look back as she cried out in despair and died."

Parsifal sank from his knightly posture onto both knees. His shoulders slumped and he rested his hands, clasped in entreaty, on the silken couch. The flush of wonder left his face; under its tan, his skin was pale.

"What sorrow!" He shook his head, wondering at himself. "What a blind, blundering fool I was! My own mother!"

He glanced around the blossoming garden as if wondering how the sun could shine on such beauty anywhere in the world while he grieved. He rested his forehead upon the couch, blotting out the sight. The time had not yet come to touch him, Kundry judged. She made her voice soft, infinitely comforting, yet mournful.

"If you never grieved, you could never be consoled. Here, let me . . ."

The blond head twisted back and forth upon the silk. Parsifal's hands gripped the couch, and his shoulders shook. "My mother, my mother! How could I forget her?

"I am nothing but a fool," he said heavily.

Kundry leaned over him. Gently, she touched his forehead, smoothed back his tumbled hair, and laid her arms confidingly about his neck. She was as caught up in her spell as he. Still, one last pang of compunction touched her. Must she do this? The youth's hair smelled of sunlight; despite his battle, he was cleanly, fresh.

He must learn love sometime, she tried to tell herself, and with whom better than herself, who was so practiced at it?

Liar, she thought. *You Judas.* She hated herself, yet she kept her brow smooth, her hands gentle.

"Confess your fault, and it's ended. Knowledge will cure your folly. You have seen the sorrow of your mother and father; would you not wish to learn the joy that once they knew?" She brushed hennaed fingertips delicately over his eyelids. The boy suffered the caress and even turned his face up to her.

"Love, that gave you life, will conquer death and folly both. Like this!"

Finally, her moment came, and she was athirst for it.

She lowered her lips to cover his mouth and tightened her clasp upon his neck to pull him fully to her. He overbalanced and fell back against the couch as her mouth sought to warm his, to open his lips and tease him into passion. For an instant, he went pliant in her embrace, and his hands brushed her shoulders. She felt the heat and strength in them, and shivered in anticipation.

His mind, responding to the touch of her emotions, kindled and began to admit her: such riches of spirit and love in this youth! In a minute, his arms would tighten about her, and she could lean on his strength, escape into his passion for the first time in . . . He was himself, not Amfortas, but perhaps she could pretend . . .

His fingers tightened against her. Then he flung her away from him so she lay gasping against her cushions.

He pressed both hands against his heart as if he had taken his death wound. Fear glazed and hollowed his blue eyes.

"Amfortas!" he cried. "The spear wound! Here, burning in my heart."

It was not his heart in which he burned, Kundry thought. She reached for him with practiced arms. A little longer, she knew, and the pain that grasped him could melt into rapture: nothing easier to subdue than lust. But Parsifal recoiled. He glanced about wildly, not seeing the garden, but the inside of a pavilion that Kundry too remembered too well.

"I heard Amfortas screaming. I saw the wound bleed! It bleeds now in me, too. Not the spear wound, no, but the flame in my heart, the fear that captures my senses and chains them . . . this sinful, guilty burning!"

He could not know. He had been a babe when Amfortas fell. And when he had seen the king, he had been mute, sullen. He could not have known. Yet he knew; and knowing, judged, and condemned her once again.

Parsifal struggled onto his knees. Once again, his hands were clasped upon the couch; but this time, as if he prayed.

"Now I *see* it again! The holy cup where the sacred blood glows, bringing peace and healing to all who worship. But not here; not in *this* heart. I hear him scream, I hear him!"

He clapped hands over his ears and swayed from side to side. "I hear the Savior cry out on the cross, mourning the Temple overthrown. 'Redeem me, rescue me from defiled hands!' Does he mean the Grail, or he who wields it? It is itself . . . and I, the fool who fled! How can I redeem myself?"

He trembled and sweated as if prophecy had gripped him, shattered him, and molded him anew. The air shimmered as if it sought to rise up through Klingsor's wards and reunite with the bright sky.

Klingsor had to be watching, Kundry realized. Watching her fail. She rose on her knees and inched along the silk of the couch toward the anguished youth. All might not be irretrievably lost yet. She flicked her eyes down the length of his body. Surely *it*, if not his mind and conscience, desired her still.

"Noble knight," she began, shocked to find her voice hesitant. "Don't fear me. Look up! There is redemption for you"—her voice went throaty—"and for me."

Carefully, she let herself down onto the couch until she lay full length, her head next to Parsifal's where he still knelt on the fragrant grass. Her hands went around his neck again, and she tried to stroke him, to cajole him to rest. She tried to insinuate her thoughts into his own but felt herself barred from such intimacy.

He shut his eyes and drew breath hissingly into his body. Then, gradually, as if in a trance, he muttered, "Yes! This is how it was. It had to be. I know it now—her looks, her laughter, her lips. Just so, she bent her head over his, and the dark, dark hair poured down over his face. She touched his face so tenderly, drew on her own heart's pain, and kissed away his soul's salvation! Oh God, that kiss!"

Parsifal rose and pushed Kundry away from him. She went sprawling, giddy from the way he had thrust her from his mind and body. She raised one hand to her lips, where she could still feel the heat of Parsifal's young mouth.

"Keep away from me!" he snarled.

She *had* failed. Memories of plunging once again down the dusty centuries back in time to Judaea turned her sick. He was pure, this Parsifal, so pure in his recoil from her as if her hands—these courtesan's hands of hers that had touched him only with the greatest gentleness and skill—dripped blood.

There had been other hands, tanned and callused from wood work, writing in the dust of the floor of a shrine. *He who is without sin among you, let him cast the first stone.* So young, this boy, so self-righteous; and was she to relive damnation for his sake? Thoughts of tears and other plots crowded into her thoughts, to be drowned out by that quiet voice: *Go and sin no more.*

That old command of forgiveness whited out her memories. She had tried; she had failed; she was barred from the Mercy forever. What sort of Mercy was it, to exclude her, who had tried so hard?

"You cruel boy. I have longed for you for endless ages. To love and to atone . . . oh God, if you only knew the curse that holds me through sleep and waking, through death and life, pain and laughter, racks me each day to new depths of torment."

He was watching, at least, his blue eyes dark with thought. Before she knew, those eyes had the truth from her.

"I saw Him . . . Him!" She flung the word at him until Parsifal's eyes flashed with revelation. He had not recoiled again. Her heart leapt, because he had not yet rejected her.

"Nailed to the cross—and I laughed! His look fell upon me, and now I seek Him from world to world. To see Him again, to see that look of pain! And when I do, when I think He is near, then once more that damnable laughter fills me, and someone dies. I laugh then, laugh because I cannot weep; and then sink again into a night of shame.

"Now you know. Oh God, if just once, just once, I could put my head on the shoulder of someone who knew me, and pitied me, then let God and the world cast me out! I would be reborn!"

Parsifal's eyes filled with tears. He reached out as if to touch Kundry's fevered cheek, then withdrew his hand.

"For that brief hour," he said with surprising gentleness, "we would both be condemned. I am sorry. For us both.

"My brothers need me." He spoke the words with growing wonder. "I have to go back. I have to heal . . . all of them."

Parsifal pushed himself away and stood reflected in the pool that Kundry had used for a spying glass. Sunlight filtered through the wards and shattered on the still water, then leapt upward to encompass him. He looked like nothing of this earth at all: some creature, perhaps, from beyond the circles of this world, perhaps from beyond the ninth sphere itself come to look upon this world and reveal it—and her—as evil, wholly evil. The light crept up about Parsifal's face, veiling it like the countenance of the high priest during the holiest moment of the Day of Atonement—or like that of Joshua when the power flowed out of him and the dead returned to life.

And all that glory was her doing! Cast out by God she might be, but nevertheless, it had been Kundry the unforgiven, Kundry the whore, who had raised this godling to awareness of his own powers! Let him shield her against Klingsor, and she would never have to fear him again.

"So, my kiss made you see this? Just my kiss? Then, just think! If you loved me, loved me entirely with the full passion of your body, you would surely be a god. Redeem the world, if that's your task. But for this one moment, love me and know what it is to feel like a god."

Her heart leapt up. *Let* him touch her. He must, oh, he must. After that one embrace, she would not be here to wander, to know herself accursed. She would be like Semele, consumed in divine embrace. It would be a better ending than she deserved.

Parsifal shook his head and drew back.

He knew. He knew it all. She had humbled herself to beg, and now he despised her. Anguish made her cower amid her cushions. The blood of her humiliation pounded in her temples until she thought that the drumbeat of her pulse would echo against the garden walls. The air in the bower grew thick. She gasped for breath and drew in pure fury.

"You'll never find them!" she screamed. "The king has fallen, so let him perish, and let me laugh at him, too. The unhallowed, the fool, who fell by his own Spear!"

"Who dared to wound him with the holy Spear?" Parsifal asked.

"It is he who gives me strength. I'll summon the Spear against you myself if you dare plead for that sinner."

Kundry's hands plucked at her long, dark hair. Red lights flickered behind her eyes, worse even than the worst throes of prophecy.

She rose. Her legs threatened to buckle and cast her down into the dirt at his feet. "Would it be so terrible to be mine, for just one hour? Love me. Then I will gladly lead the way to Amfortas!"

She flung herself at him. To hold him, even to touch him: the scope of all her desires over all her centuries had contracted to that tiny hope. Even the poorest shepherdess could hope to embrace and be embraced by her betrothed; but even that innocent hope had been denied to Kundry. Wasn't that the way of her entire, too-long life? Deny her love, a home, even death itself; cast her out; and then, when she fought to protect herself, revile her? All that she had ever wanted, she was forbidden; and now she must see it all lavished upon this fool!

"Begone, you cursed thing." He thrust her away, the revulsion he had conquered for so long finally revealing itself.

She shrieked in wordless rage at first, then for the help that never, never came when she screamed. "Guards! Oh help me! Seize the intruder. Don't let him leave; bar every pathway!"

Her hands curled into talons, and her belly chilled as she saw the smooth flesh wither and develop the spots and ridged veins of age once more before its youthful beauty flickered back. "Though you should escape and search along every road in the world, you'll never, never discover the path you seek, away from my presence. I curse them all to you. Wander! Wander as I must till the world ends!"

A shifting in the air and a rumble of thunder made Kundry look up. Klingsor stood on the rampart. He wore a travesty of priestly robes—black linen and a breastplate flickering with the dark gems of the Tree Reversed. Rage gleamed in his eyes. In his hand, poised to throw, was the holy Spear.

Kundry remembered her first sight of the Spear. It was a Roman *pilum*, scrupulously tended and polished by its first owner, who might have been blind but was anything but slack. Now, however, the Spear was dark, not just with the centuries of its age, not with being buried in sand, but with the use it had endured for the past twenty years. The metal of the Spear's point was dark; darker yet the blood that encrusted it and defiled the wood itself.

Klingsor brandished the Spear, and her eye was caught and held. Overhead, the wards shimmered and darkened, and Kundry knew that Klingsor had used the Spear to reinforce them.

"Stand right there! This weapon will bring you down." He laughed. "And thus the holy fool falls by his master's Spear!"

He hurled the Spear straight at Parsifal's heart. The air shrieked with the speed of its passage. Once again, the castle's wards quivered. Kundry bit her lips against a scream of warning.

Like a hawk returning to its master, the Spear hastened toward Parsifal. Then it paused and hovered over Parsifal's head. Light shimmered about it. Even as Kundry watched, it shed the abuse from years of sorcery. The wood glowed as if newly rubbed with lemon and beeswax; the Spearhead shone bright, except where blood, even brighter than the metal, dripped from it for an instant, then vanished.

Parsifal reached up a hand to pluck the Spear from the air.

About him, the air thickened as Klingsor's wards tightened. Kundry fell gasping to the ground, too weak to do aught but watch as Parsifal held out the Spear and made the sign of the cross.

Some power touched her body, forehead, breast, and shoulders; a voice beyond the bonds of blood or humanity intoned a blessing she had not thought of for a thousand years.

Atoh Malkus Ve-Gedulah Ve-Gevurah Le-Olahm Amen.

The ancient words vibrated through her. Instinctively,

her mind translated them. "For Thou Art the Kingdom, the Glory, and the Power, forever." The invocation might be words drawn from the faith that had sprung up about the man Kundry had mocked; but they were even older than that, part of the faith she had lost in the hills outside Jericho. Faith and faith were the same; for all the bloodshed, all the fighting with which faith sought to conquer faith, they were the same and had always been the same. Forever.

The very simplicity of the idea stunned her. She had been a fool; she had always been a fool. She had not even the comfort of being a *pure* fool, such as he who now wielded the sacred Spear.

She wanted to scream with rage; she wanted once again to sing hosannas. Lacking strength or will to do either, she crouched on the shuddering ground and prayed for death.

Klingsor reeled back, his hands gesturing wildly as thunder rumbled and his castle shook underfoot. A crack appeared in the garden wall, and the blue tiles with their graceful designs fell and shattered.

Parsifal held the Spear. Light flashed from the sky to the Spearpoint, too bright now to look at.

Then Klingsor's wards, so long and so wrongfully reinforced with the power of the Holy Spear, burst asunder; the land and air of the castle, too long separated from the rest of creation, rejoined it. And the archangels, too long banned from this stretch of earth, swept in. Kundry could catch only a glimpse of them. They were too high, too splendid, and too swift for mortal eyes to encompass; she saw only a splendor of wings, colors, and eyes.

From the East rushed Raphael, shimmering in his crimson and pale golds. From the South, with a blast of heat as if blown from some supernal bellows, rushed Michael. One titanic hand brandished a steel sword from which blue flames danced; the other held aloft a spear like unto the Holy Spear, but far larger. Flames followed him across the garden, withering it with their breath. From the West came Gabriel, his robes of blue, tinged with orange, blotting out the sky like the last seconds of sunset. And from the North descended Auriel, the citrines, olives, and russets of his manifestation almost homelike after the arcane brilliance of his brothers, before his wings swept over the castle, shutting out the light.

A terrific clap of thunder made the towers of Klingsor's castle shake, totter, then fall.

"They fly, they fly!" Klingsor screamed. He reeled on the highest battlement, his entire body poised with the desire to call back the bright presences who had wasted his stronghold. They paused. For an instant, the whirlwinds stirred up by their wings subsided. The light they shed upon the world glinted even upon the gems of Klingsor's breastplate. The gems winked into flame, then ash; and still the archangels waited.

Could even Klingsor be caught up in the Mercy?

Auriel descended, hovering near Klingsor. Light glimmered and filled the archangel's hands with bread and wine. Silently, he offered them to Klingsor.

Come and eat.

The magus backed away from the food.

It will satisfy that hunger. The hands raised. The fragrances of grapes and fresh-baked bread sent Kundry's head whirling.

Klingsor took a tentative step closer, then another. Kundry held her breath: to sate that hunger of his . . . to ease the *I want* that had made his too-long life a misery and drawn her in. *Let it be*, she prayed.

In the instant that she truly believed he would take the grace that Auriel afforded, Klingsor's joined fists dashed bread and wine to the paving stones.

"I take no charity!" he screamed, his face contorted.

Was it only Kundry who saw the look of heartbreak on the archangel's face? He stepped backward and, as it seemed, apart. With an effortless flick of his wings, he rose to join his fellows.

"Why should *they* be given wings? Give them to me," Klingsor moaned. His voice whined up into a keen. "My wings. Mine!"

Again, the light blazed up, and the rush of the archangels' passage caused the earth to shake.

"Give me your wings!"

Klingsor hurled himself from the battlements after them.

He fell, tumbled down, and his body was covered by the crumbling walls of what had been a fortress and was now but a ruin. A wail went up for a moment, then was still. Flowers from Auriel's wings lay scattered on the withered ground.

Kundry cowered against the earth, but Parsifal stood over her. Not even a clod of earth touched her as the castle fell. When the earth stopped shuddering, Parsifal, holding the Spear, strode toward what had been a wall. As he left Klingsor's shattered domain, he turned and looked back at Kundry, almost with pity.

He paused as the archangels had for Klingsor. He held out his hand.

Light gleamed about his face. Kundry was afraid to look at him. She wailed, and backed away, on all fours.

"You know where you can find me again," he told her.

Kundry moaned like an old woman who has seen her only grandson tossed on the spear of a bandit. Shaking back matted hair, she raised herself and stared after him—a bright, tiny figure who trudged down the slope into a valley of blue water and green fields. A brief flare of sunlight burned on the point of the holy Spear.

29

WITH a beast's patience, Kundry wandered. It did not surprise her that once again, she tramped the forests like an exile; nothing surprised her now.

Day by day, her body and her world withered around her. Her long hair matted. When she tried to claw the worst tangles from it, long strands came away gray.

Days and nights slipped by. Days let her see the safest path down a road half overgrown or blocked by a fallen bridge or wagon. Others, madder than she and not as helpless, wandered during the day. Nights brought her no rest. It was as much a time to stand on guard as to sleep, to creep up upon deserted cottages and steal as to hide herself.

Time was when Arthur's name as much as Arthur's knights had meant a maiden bearing gold could travel alone and in safety. These days, the maidens hid, and all the gold was long buried.

The flimsy gown she had put on in Klingsor's castle to beguile a knight soon frayed to tatters, exposing her to more dangers than the cold. The few jewels on her when the castle fell had long since been traded for food and a rough cloak. When she saw a tunic hanging outside a cottage and made off with it, a dog scored her leg with his teeth. She lay up for a day, too afraid to retreat into sleep, too weak to defend herself should the cottager come in pursuit of the thief. Her leg ached, and she had forgotten which herbs might help such a wound to heal. Fortunately, the bite bled clean. Madness was a hard way to die—and a harder way to live, especially if you were cursed, it seemed, to live forever. She limped for some time thereafter and counted herself lucky to have fared no worse.

At some point, she stole a loaf of moldy rye. Her memories of that time grew dim—terrible nightmares, flights from a well-trod path into the wilderness, exhaustion that made each fiber in her body scream for rest while a relentless will, seemingly imposed from without her body, drove her onward. She drank from muddied pools and recoiled at the reflection she saw through the mats of her hair floating on the turbid water.

And so, at last, she came to Broceliande. Once she had been an adept in its passageways. Now, the bole of oak, ash, and thorn withstood her like the palisade of a fort; when she tried to force passage within, each leaf and vine and thorn took arms against her. The paths among the worlds were barred to her, at least for now.

Sobbing tearlessly, she wandered still further. Day and night melted into one; if she crossed a river or climbed a hill, she never noticed, except for when she fell. All places were alike: they were not home. All people were alike; their hands were raised against her. It was very cold for spring.

Finally, she came to a field where battle lines had been drawn up. Sunlight smoldered on the armor, and men glared at each other across the trampled green stalks that would never be a harvest now. Helms and armor made them all seem kin. Some, she realized, *were* kin—she saw the hooked nose of an old man on one side handed down to the young man on the other. Fathers and sons had turned on each other; each brother became Cain. Leading their armies, a father and a son opposed each other while standing close together. Kundry crept close to listen as the old man and the young carved up their nation for a kind of shabby peace. Both wore gemmed circlets. The sunlight glinting off the gold looked tawdry.

Then, so quickly that no one could move aside or explain, a man cried out in pain and revulsion. Drawing his sword, he hacked at the serpent that bit his heel. It was the oldest hatred in the world, and it still proved deadly.

"Oath-broke!" screamed his enemies and drew steel. Archers poised, and horsemen spurred their mounts. The old man and the young withdrew to lead their men to death.

The younger man looked smug, the older man anguished in a way Kundry had seen before on a king's face.

Once again, Kundry gazed on Golgotha. This time, the power to cast herself away was as far removed from her as the circles of the moon. Hiding, Kundry drew in upon herself, an ancient child in a monstrous womb, until evening. Most of the shouting had died by then. Rustlings in the bushes warned her of a different danger. Reivers had come out to despoil the slain.

Near her lay a man with his throat cut, the looter bereft of his loot. Only his dagger, flung into the underbrush, remained. Dimly recalling that knives meant safety as well as death, Kundry retrieved it. Moonlight glinted on its golden hilt; blood had darkened on its blade.

And the battle was not wholly over. Resistance yet remained on either side. She cowered in a thicket as she watched a young man and an old man shout defiance at each other and attack. As the young man fell, a spear in his entrails, the older one staggered. Half his helm was shorn away; the other half still bore its crown.

The stream from which she had hoped to drink turned red. What else she saw in it made her shrink back: she had lost the unnatural beauty of Klingsor's spells. Her matted hair was falling out; her face looked only slightly more alive than that of the bled-out man who sprawled propped against a tree across the stream from her. With Klingsor gone, only the ancient curse protected her: wander she must, but as a crone.

She screamed and swooned. When she awoke, the moon was setting. Still, she had light enough to see a boat launched out upon the water. Three women swathed in black sat in it, handling the oars and nursing the old, crowned man whose head lay in the lap of the eldest. This was not flight, Kundry sensed, but withdrawal from the world. She used to travel Broceliande that way; she feared those roads were barred now.

Those crones and the king they bore had found their way; she must find hers.

Numb, she stumbled on a road. Roman-built, it had outlasted the kingdom that had replaced its builders and their conquerors.

Others like herself traveled on it, escaping the wreckage of their homes and towns. They were all wretched, mumbling a little and holding out grimy hands to beg whatever meager food others could spare; they dodged kicks and casually thrown rocks, and hid from those who were avid to steal even the little they had saved. Like chips in a stream, they were borne onward by the road.

The day came when she stood blinking before a town whose walls bore the marks of old attacks. Its gate stood open like a mouth full of rotten teeth. She listened, fearing the too-great silence that meant plague. Then she heard dogs barking. No plague: the town had simply been deserted in the war. Perhaps she might find blankets or even shoes. She summoned her courage and wandered in.

No one saw her as she moved from street to street. From shut-up houses, once or twice, she heard a low, hopeless moaning that she could not bear to hear. Quickly, she moved on. A cape, dropped as someone fled, lay in her way, too torn up to wear; but she bound its rags about her feet and no longer left a track of bleeding prints upon the cobblestones.

At length and at last, she stood in a vast, echoing hall. It reminded her of—there had been a hall she had not entered, except once in a dream. There, too, an altar had stood. Beside it, she was almost sure, had lain a bier or a litter—she forgot. Around it were arrayed tables as if for a feast, but bare of food.

This hall was dark, swept bare even of the rushes and fragrant herbs that must have strewn its floor. At its center stood, not an altar, but a table, shaped like the sun's disk. Sword cuts on its legs made it tilt, unsteady of balance; the chairs that should have ringed it were shattered or overturned.

Curious, she set one upright and saw the blazon of a lord cut and colored on its back: a red dragon, much battered and half effaced. It was not right to leave those chairs fallen, she thought. Laboriously, she set them straight, in attendance around the great table. Still, it remained in the deserted hall as a body might lie, its eyes glaring open, in a house from which the other folk have fled. It troubled her to see it almost as much as it troubled her to stand so alone in a place that should have teemed with noble folk.

She crept from the hall, down the streets, and out the vacant gates. Jerusalem had fallen, the Temple she had entered with such awe lay reduced to rubble in the hands of its enemies. Rome, which had ordered that devastation, lasted a few more centuries, and now its buildings were carted away stone by stone to patch houses or to burn for lime. She had had such hopes of this realm, but the Round Table was hacked and splintered: there was no stability anywhere, and no rest.

Again, she cast herself upon the road, which bore her to another walled-in place. Its bells and the austere robes of those who dwelled there were familiar. They were ladies, not knights, and their coarse robes bore no bright heraldry of a dove, edged in gules. Holiness prickled at Kundry's senses. She shut them stubbornly; the incense and beeswax smells of sanctity and refuge, this place where women worked and prayed in safety, were not for her. She had learned that in Jerusalem, if nothing else.

Her feet had long since passed beyond aching to open sores. A woman, whose robe was as stark but more finely made than all the rest, sat her down and knelt before her. Soaking away the crusted bandages, she unwrapped them and did not flinch or look away. The women about her gasped and offered to take her place as healer. It was not fitting, they protested.

The lady shook her head. She had laid such toys of privilege aside, and now filled her hands with tasks like this. Nothing was more fitting, she told them. If Our Lord washed his disciples' feet, how much more should an uncrowned queen, and one in need of grace, take upon herself? Smiling to take the sting from her rebuke, she commanded herbs, warmed water, and soft cloth for bandages.

The others obeyed so rapidly that Kundry would have fled, but with a gesture of a long, fine-boned hand, the lady forbade. Easing Kundry's fear, she washed and bound her bleeding, swollen feet, then saw her fed and garbed in a gray coarse robe. Then she led her along a low arcade to where women stood by long rows of tables before wooden plates of bread. Light poured in from a narrow window and etched an aureole upon the veil of Kundry's benefactress: thus, briefly, she wore a crown again.

Had Kundry seen her before in another guise? Dimly, she thought about it as she fought not to gobble her food, but to eat with spoon and napkin in seemly wise. Night fell, and the women led her into another hall. Kundry stopped in her tracks. At the end of the room hung a cross and, nailed to it, the wooden figure of a man. A torch flared, and the shadow of the man on the cross flew at her like a spear. She whimpered and shrank back.

Even now, she could not kneel. Even now, she could not look at it. She fled, afraid of the laughter that must surely grip her, accursed as she was.

Behind her women made signs against ill will. But the lady who had washed her feet knelt and wept.

Kundry left the place that very night. Another fugitive might have found the place a safe harbor in a troubled world. But the price of such peace was one Kundry could not bear to pay. And it were far better that one like herself flee than be cast out once they knew her for what she was.

The year waned, and the world's health waned with it. She wandered all that autumn, into winter. People teemed upon the land, once so settled and so peaceful. Refugees wandered the roads, and hid from bandits; bandits hid from armies. And sometimes, no one could even distinguish between them.

Shrines dotted the countryside, tended by aging men whose scars and bearing showed them to be other than simple priests or holy men. Spurs were hung as offerings before rough-hewn crosses. Thin hermits knelt all night long before the relics in their swords. And when Kundry offered to clean the men's poor huts, she saw mold and spiderwebs deface the quarterings of shields stowed out of plain sight. Not all refugees from Camelot were poor, or old, or frightened: some mourned.

A gold brooch given her by one such hermit found her a place on a boat. It brought her to Lesser Britain. Standing

stones replaced the shrines, a dead forest that cast a pall
upon the land. The roads grew chill, then icy; they cast her
at the outskirts of Broceliande. The leaves and thorns that
had cut her hands to the bone were withered now. The
ground was hard. And the trees had enough to do keeping
the sap running through their trunks, without striving to
bar her way.

Like a spy, Kundry slipped into the forest that had been
her refuge and her bane. She had forgotten how to speed
her way upon its paths. The streams that had nourished her
were filmed over with ice. Beasts she had once greeted in
their own chirps and growls fled from her and watched the
intruder, large-eyed, from their lairs. She was not welcome
even here.

She would have wept if she could. Her tears had fled with
her wits. When she turned to go, the flakes of falling snow
covered ice that had formed upon the stone.

It was a harsh mercy indeed; but she found a cave from
which the bears had fled. A spring ran nearby, free even
beneath the shackles of the ice. Even before the sun turned
into a distant ember, glowering at the horizon, she had cut
a double armload of pine branches with the dagger she had
reived from the reiver. Snow fell in icy kernels. She slept,
waking at times as a beast wakes to seek food and water
until the winter passed.

One day, the ice over the spring broke, like a silver knife
striking crystal, and the water ran free, rejoicing. Kundry
woke to what consciousness remained to her. Already, daf-
fodils lanced through the snow beneath the pines; the buds
upon the maples were sticky. Drawing her cloak about her
meager shoulders, she set off once more. Her joints ached,
as if she had lain not upon stone and boughs, but on the
rack.

She reached a crumbling road, no work of Romans, this,
but a track natural to Broceliande. Power tingled through
the rags that bound her feet. She paused, wondering if the
tides of Broceliande would sweep her away or strike her
down. Instead, the power subsided, and Kundry ventured
to trudge along the road.

Beyond the undergrowth that encroached upon the

track, the trees rustled. A white hart leapt across, and Kundry turned to watch it. Where had she seen such a beast before? She cowered back into the brush, awaiting the hunters that must surely come to strike it down: but no hunters came.

Kundry shook her head, clearing webs from the remnants of her thoughts. Memory came, of a grave, aged man warning a youth that the very birds and beasts that roamed this wood were sacred. Names came to her once more: Gurnemanz, the old knight, and Parsifal, the young one who had refused her, but offered her redemption she had not the courage to accept.

She would not see them again, she thought. She was doomed to wander for all time.

Light thrust down through the clouds and glinted off something that lay in the underbrush. Drawn as a beast might be drawn to something new, Kundry shuffled over, knelt by the road, and scrabbled in the earth until her chapped fingers seized the shining thing.

She raised it, brought it to her lips, and blew on it so she could rub the frozen dirt from it on her robe. When the grime was removed, she saw she held a ring—one that she remembered.

She reclined on silken cushions with a dark-haired man, who leaned over her and told her that he had been taught always to gain a lady's kiss and a lady's ring: she had given both.

She had betrayed with a kiss; knowing her false, the man she had betrayed had cast her ring like trash at the side of the road.

Curling her fingers around it until the warming metal bit into her hand, Kundry raised her fist to her lips. Animal moans tore from her throat, and she stumbled off the road into the underbrush.

She would walk no further this day. And when she moved on, she would take pains to journey in a different direction lest she see . . . Sleep clapped manacles on her thoughts. She feared to remember what she feared to see. It was the black sleep that Klingsor had cast upon her time after time, but Klingsor was dead. He had refused the

Mercy offered him, and so had she. Yet even he was safely dead now, while she . . .

Whimpering a little at that unfairness, she wandered until she stumbled and fell into the underbrush. The thorns made havoc of her cloak. Then the pliant branches parted to contain and cushion her. It was so kind of them, she thought. She would have laughed at her idiocy, but her mind was clouding over. She thrust the ring she had found onto her finger and raised it to her lips.

"I am so sorry," she whispered after so many years, and then she slept.

And Broceliande whispered and shifted about her at last, carrying thicket and sleeping outcast inward toward its core.

30

KUNDRY could hear herself moaning. She whimpered again. It was not fair that she be forced back to life again, not after all this time. Some relentless force was lifting her. As if reluctant to release her, the thick undergrowth in which she lay tugged her cloak from off her shoulders. She felt herself borne up, cradled in strong, bony arms. The one who carried her groaned about his aching knees as he knelt, lowering her onto a patch of grass, fragrant and warmed by the sun.

She wanted to twist away from him, to sleep, only to sleep. How long had it been? Why must she wake now? But relentless hands rubbed her hands and temples, and a voice she remembered called her name.

"I knew I recognized that voice. Up, Kundry lass, wake up! The winter is past, the rain is come and gone, and the flowers are blooming. Don't you hear the birdsong? Wake to spring, girl, I tell you, wake!"

It was Gurnemanz, who had found her the last time her fate and erring footsteps had brought her this far into Broceliande.

The chafing hands halted for a moment in their work. "Cold and stiff," Gurnemanz muttered. "This time, I fear she's dead for certain. And yet I know I heard her groan. You can't die today, Kundry, not on a Good Friday morning as fair as this. Look up, lass, look up!"

Kundry opened her eyes and shrieked with loss and grief. She lay on a mound of grass strewn with patches of heartsease and marguerites—homely flowers, not the flaunting blooms of Klingsor's locked garden. Beyond them, meadows stretched out, blossoming sweetly where Kundry would have expected only waste. Beside her a spring bubbled into a pool that drained away into a brook that led toward water glinting in the distance.

Opposite the spring, built up against a mass of gray rock, was a hermit's hut. Beside her knelt the hermit. It was the knight Gurnemanz.

She looked up at the old man. The past seasons had used him as harshly as they had used her. She remembered a man who strode about, bearing the full mail he wore beneath the flowing surcoat of his order as if it weighed no more than a silken tunic. Even then, he had been old, but he had always looked as if he lacked only sword and horse to enter the lists at any moment.

The man who knelt, chafing her hands and feet like a nurse or like the lady who had bathed them, was thin and aged. His hair and beard were gray, fading fast to white. His face was lined, and he had lost so much flesh that his cheeks sagged in dewlaps down to his beard. He no longer wore armor; instead, he wore the Grail knights' surcoat, with its blazon of a dove, outlined in red, as a hermit's tunic. It was scrupulously clean, but almost as shabby as her own robes. Even the dove embroidered on it was frayed. Its heavy folds, shiny from wear, hung on his gaunt body.

He winced as he worked, grumbling at the pain in his joints this close to the spring that fed into Lake Brumbane. Holy water should not, he muttered to himself, make an old man ache thus. When his complaints wrung a tiny smile from her, he looked absurdly pleased. Kundry remembered the knight-hermits who had sheltered her along her way. Like Gurnemanz, they had the look of men whose hearts were broken, but who had learned to live until the pain had healed into scars and the scars had set into a form of rough peace.

Why had she been brought here? Was her fate not tired of toying with her yet?

And it was not fair that Gurnemanz suffer still more on Kundry's behalf. She raised herself on her elbows and suppressed another groan at the stiffness that still ruled all her limbs.

There must be something she could do for Gurnemanz:

hew wood, or carry water as she had done before; clean his cottage; take messages, if they required no great skill or discretion. He would feed her, shelter her, guard her even from the malice of his own brethren. She would have blessed him if she could—and if he could have valued her blessing.

For a long time, she gazed at the old man. Even now, he preserved his old, military ways and cleanliness. He deserved better than a servant who looked like a woodwose cast out from its tribe. His very serenity made her want to attempt a calmness of her own. She raised shaking hands in what she knew must be a futile attempt to tidy her hair and her penitent's robe.

Restlessness had driven her from every refuge she had sought; she had no idea that fate would shepherd her to this place and this kind old man. *Frown, cuff me, drive me away,* she implored, but did not know to whom she pleaded. *But do not be kind to me. I can bear anything but that.*

"No word for me?" Gurnemanz's familiar growl was astonishingly pleasant on her ears. "Not one? Is this the thanks I get for rousing you—again!—from a sleep that could have been the death of you?"

I would have thanked you for leaving me alone, her eyes told him.

His frown grew deeper as he glared down at her. "Why should I be surprised at anything you do?" he demanded. The relief in his eyes, so much at odds with his reproof, made her groan and throw her arms about him.

He smoothed back her hair, ruining her efforts of a moment ago to straighten it. "You crazy woman," he grumbled tenderly. "What have you to say for yourself?"

"Just let me serve," she whispered. Her voice was hoarse, broken.

Gurnemanz rose, pulling her up with him like a poppet. He shook his head ruefully at her.

"You will find little enough to do," he told her. "We need no more messages delivered now. We don't seem to be an order of knights anymore, but a band of hermits. Each of us lives on his own, foraging for roots and herbs. We learned it from our brothers, the beasts in the forest."

Kundry nodded, giving a little bow of her head. Gurnemanz's hut didn't look as if it were ready to fall down
. . . not with the next storm, perhaps; but the one after it
might well bring it down upon his head. In the meantime,
no reason why holiness need live thirsty. She went into the
hut and sought out a pitcher. She could draw water from
the spring.

When she emerged, Gurnemanz was muttering to himself. "How different from what she was before! Do you
think it's the fact that today is Good Friday, old man? She
speaks not at all, and time was, when all her speech was
curses and laughs that chilled the soul. If she were any
Christian, I'd have pledged that she had taken a vow of
silence. With Kundry . . . bah, who can ever tell with
Kundry? You're an old man, Gurnemanz, old and foolish.
But—please God—what a day of mercy this could be for
her!"

Gurnemanz looked into the sun as it climbed. "God, did
You lead me to her so You could save her at long last? Give
an old man his wish and let the poor girl have some peace."

A beam of light slanted down through the immense
branches of the ancient trees that ringed the clearing. It
caressed his face, and he smiled.

He crossed himself and whispered, "Thank you, Lord."
A tear streaked down his wrinkled face.

Do you weep for me? Kundry was too moved to ask. *I am
not worth your tears.*

Gurnemanz began to pace, and a snort of laughter burst
from him. "Your young men will dream dreams, and your
old ones will see visions? Well, I'm old enough—that's
certain—for the vision part of it."

Light sparked in Kundry's eyes, and she whirled. That
shimmer could only be sunlight flashing off metal. She
stood, one hand shading her eyes. Light flashed again, bobbing like a torch as it moved toward her. Someone was
coming, and by that token of light on metal, a warrior.

Anticipation and fear, such as one hears at the far-off cry
of trumpets, prickled along her spine. She opened her
mouth to warn Gurnemanz. Air sighed from her throat, but

no words. Now that all else had failed her, had she lost her speech as well?

Odd that it did not trouble her. The past year had taught her to dread men who walked clad in armor and to flee them. Now, however, she had no wish to flee. The peace of the morning, the beauty of the flowers clustering about the old man's ruined hermitage, soothed her. She had outlived her fear.

She had outlived even the need for speech. Not to serve Gurnemanz for what time might remain; not even to warn him. Calmly, she went to Gurnemanz, tugged at his arm, and pointed. Then she stood, waiting for him to decide. The fragile warmth from the sunlight that built up on her skin was very pleasant. The birds sang, undisturbed by the newcomer.

"What's that you say? Didn't say a word, did you? That's right. What's that you *see*, then?" Gurnemanz demanded. He drew a deep breath to summon the old bellow that had commanded troops and subdued generations of younger men. To her surprise, his words were formal, but far more subdued.

"Who comes toward the sacred spring wearing armor? He is not one of our band, lass, is he?"

She would have stood with Gurnemanz, but he gestured her away. From the door of the old knight's hut, she watched as the moving light drew closer and resolved itself into the figure of a man clad in black armor. He bore a spear and his helm was closed; he bore no sword. Such armor was a heavy burden for a man on foot: he walked slowly, almost as if he had taken a blow to the head and now wandered Broceliande, as mazed as she had been.

He entered the clearing. Drawn by the bubbling of the stream that led to Lake Brumbane, he came at last to the grassy mound on which Kundry had lain. Carefully, as if sparing limbs that were wounded and that now slowly healed, he seated himself.

It might be well, Kundry thought now, to have a weapon. She looked about. Gurnemanz was a knight; he must have a sword. Yes, there it was—but it was propping up a sapling. She fumbled in her breast for the knife she had stolen from a murdered thief and found it gone, replaced by a golden phial. She remembered a phial she had once clawed out of the earth for Amfortas: would he have need of this, or might another?

But the old man showed no fear. "God's greeting to you, guest!" he hailed the knight in black armor. "Are you astray? May I direct you?"

The man shook his head, as if in the grip of a very gentle dream.

"What, *another* wanderer with no tongue?" Gurnemanz muttered to himself. Then he turned back to the stranger. "What is it? Some pledge may have vowed your lips to silence, but I am pledged to tell you plainly what is right. This place you've come to is holy ground. Here, a man should bear no weapons—helmet, shield, or spear—and least of all today! It is a holy day, or don't you know?"

Again, the knight shook his head. Gurnemanz drew in a gusty sigh as if he inspected a squire and discovered him with shabby harness or an unbrushed horse.

"You don't know?" he asked with a hint of his old impatience. "What heathens have you been living among that you don't know today is Good Friday?"

The knight shook his head again, then lowered it as if abashed.

"Lay down your weapons, sir! Do not affront our Lord. This very day, He shed His holy blood to redeem the sinful world. He lacked arms; shall you dare carry them?"

Deliberately, the knight rose. Taking his spear, he thrust it into the ground. Beneath it as if in offering, he laid shield and sword. Raising the visor of his helm, he removed it and laid it on his shield.

Then he knelt before the spear, his hands clasped in prayer.

Gurnemanz gestured Kundry over. In silence, she came, walking softly so as not to disturb the praying knight who raised his eyes to the spear's head. Tears of devotion filled them, and his face, illumined by the morning sunlight, seemed to glow. He was very young. A lark flew overhead, exulting in the sun on its wings. Briefly, he turned his face to follow it, then returned to contemplate the shining spear.

"Do you know him now?" Gurnemanz whispered to her. "The one who slew the swan?"

Kundry nodded slightly. She felt as if her heart had been bound in iron bands, and those bands were now splitting asunder, piercing flesh even as they freed her. And then she recognized the pain as hope.

"The fool I drove away," Gurnemanz breathed. "He was the one, after all. God, what a fool *I* was!"

Kundry studied Parsifal's face. The robust fool who had been silent before the Grail, the beautiful youth she had tried to seduce—she could see the shadows of both in this face. It was the face of a grown man and a knight now, tempered by experience, by lack of food, of sleep, by loneliness, and by pity. He had been a fool in truth; but she thought that Gurnemanz and even she had played tiny parts in bringing him to wisdom.

"Where do you think he came from? By what roads?" Tenderly, Kundry looked at the old man, who had lived in Montsalvasche, at the heart of the world, for so long that he had forgotten how hard it was for others to come there.

Then Gurnemanz stiffened. A breath of sheer wonder came from him. "The Spear—that is the Holy Spear; I know it."

Solemnly, he crossed himself. This time, Kundry did not flinch. "Oh, what a holy day this is."

Knight and Spearhead were too bright for her to look upon. She too might hope; but this was not her revelation. Kundry turned her face away, but only slightly. She could not bear to look, but she could not bear to look away, either.

Parsifal finished his prayer, lowered his hands, and slowly rose.

"Praise God, I have found you again," he said to Gurnemanz, and held out his hand.

Ancient knight and young clasped arms.

"So you still remember me, old and grief-struck as I am? How did you come here, and from where?"

"From error and from suffering, I came here," Parsifal replied, his voice somber. "Now, I think perhaps I can escape them both, now that I hear the wind in the trees and greet you again, you good old man." Seasoned he might be; he still had the same joyous smile. "Or am I wrong again? Everything seems so changed."

Gurnemanz shook his head, his eyes bright with tears and sunlight. Kundry wanted to hold her hands out to them both: the old knight who had mounted guard over a wasted realm, the young knight whose every word—even his doubts—showed how he had grown in wisdom and in power.

Hope washed twenty years from Gurnemanz's brow, but he could barely force the question out. "Tell me who you are seeking."

Parsifal's face twisted with sorrow and guilt. "Once, I heard a man reveal his deepest anguish. And like the green fool I was, I stood stock-still, unable even to mumble a word of pity.

"I can heal him now," he declared. For a moment, the certainty of his words blotted out his sorrow. "I can. I bring him healing and salvation, as foretold." He raised a gauntleted hand to his brow, his fair hair tumbling over the black metal.

"Ah, you cannot know. Never finding the way of healing, I wandered, led astray by a terrible curse. Even when I thought I had found the way, there were always dangers, battles, duels to force me from it. And each time, I was afraid. I could not profane the Spear by using it as a weapon. I fought to defend it, not myself, and took my share of wounds along the way. But I bore it at my side, and I now return it home . . . the Grail's Spear, unstained."

Tears ran down Gurnemanz's face. "Oh wonder," he whispered. "Thank God, I have lived to see this day." He buried his face in his hands and his shoulders shook.

In simple pity, Kundry would have laid her hand on him, but refrained. Knowing her, how could he welcome her touch, even in compassion?

Gurnemanz composed himself and drew himself up as if he stood before his king. Tears ran down his face, but he ignored them.

"Lord," he addressed Parsifal, "if it were a curse that drove you from your chosen, rightful path, you may be assured the curse is ended. This *is* Montsalvasche, the Grail's domain. Our brothers await you. If you *are* the one foretold, God knows, we have need of the healing you bring. Since the morning you first came here, the sorrow you witnessed grew to madness. Amfortas . . ." Gurnemanz's voice broke on the long-loved name.

Parsifal's strong young hands shot out to sustain the old man, who shook his head and would not be comforted.

Would not be comforted *yet*, Kundry thought. Despite his pain, her heart rejoiced for him. Amfortas would not be the only one who was healed today.

Once again, Gurnemanz got himself under rigid control. "Amfortas," he began again, "suffered so in soul and body that he longed for death. Finally, he defied our Order. No pleas, no sorrows of his brothers could move him to fulfill his office. The shrine has lain closed, the Grail shrouded. He thought that since he could not die as long as he saw the Grail, if he cut himself off from the sight of it, he might escape from mortal anguish into death.

"He cast us from its presence, too, and all our power weakened. No Christian king begs defenders from us now. We have drawn in upon ourselves, lost, without a lord. I came here to live in the woods like a hermit until death comes to take me, as it took my old lord. Denied the sight of the Grail, my dear king Titurel died—mortal and mindless, like any other weak old man."

Parsifal struck his breast and cried out in horror. "Then it was I who brought this woe upon you. I have done what I should not have done. I have not asked what I should have asked. I have not been where I should have been and have lost all hope of salvation! God of mercy, why do you load this weight of guilt and sin upon a fool?"

His knees buckled, and Gurnemanz caught him before he fell, easing him to sit upon the grass.

Kundry ran into the hut, poured out a basin full of water, and held it out to Gurnemanz. Once she had heard a man pray that a cup be lifted from him. Soon that cup would be passed to another bearer, and it was no lighter for all the years gone by.

Gurnemanz shook his head at the basin, then said

gravely, as if considering it, "I feel this pilgrim of ours has some holy work to do today, perhaps some sacred rite. Put the basin away. We will use the holy spring itself to wash him clean, whatever his sins have been."

Gently, they moved him to the edge of the spring and began to unarm him. Parsifal turned his head fitfully upon the grass as if upon the newly smoothed pillow of a sickbed.

"This day, shall I truly be guided to Amfortas?"

Gurnemanz nodded, busy with the fastenings of his breastplate. "Most surely. Today is the funeral of my dear lord Titurel. Amfortas swore he would reveal the Grail one last time to bless his noble father."

Parsifal smiled with a child's trust.

Kundry had pulled off Parsifal's greaves. She drew up water in her palms and poured it over his feet. If she dared look up at him, she knew she would see light obscuring his face, as it had another face so long ago.

A gentle hand laid on her head made her look up, startled, into a sweet smile. "So humbly you have washed my feet. Now, dear friend, bathe my brow, too."

Changed as she was, could he possibly know her?

Kundry cast a desperate look at Gurnemanz. He shook his head at her, holding her in her place at Parsifal's feet. Then the old man scooped water in his hand and sprinkled Parsifal's head. The drops of water glittered in his fair hair like a diadem.

"Be purified, you pure one, by this water. Thus, it washes every guilt and pain from you."

Kundry slid her hand into her robe for the golden phial that had replaced her dagger. In such a phial, she had brought useless balm to Amfortas. And ages ago in Jerusalem . . . she had applied a similar ointment to a man's feet. She was drained of love and guilt and hope now: this phial was all she had. Well enough: this new redeemer should have it too. Then her sacrifice would be complete.

If that were true, she might even be permitted to rest. Though she had longed for rest, raged for it, begged for it, done everything but pray for it, the possibility of rest, of making an end, no longer possessed the urgency that it had for all of her prolonged life. She broke the seal upon the phial and poured oil on Parsifal's feet. Hastily, she unbound her hair; tresses of gray and black and white swept over them.

His fingers enclosing her hand for one warm moment, Parsifal took the phial from her and handed it to Gurnemanz.

"You anointed my feet," he told Kundry. "Kings' friend, anoint my head now, for I tell you, today you shall become friend to yet another king!"

His strength restored, his voice rang out with joy.

Gurnemanz knelt and received the phial. He poured the oil over Parsifal's head and brow, where it caught the sun in a golden haze. Then gnarled, strong hands grasped that head in blessing. "A father's blessing on you, and a servant's. As king I hail you now. Oh, you pure one—you sufferer who pities suffering. You have redeemed Amfortas already."

Gurnemanz's hands lifted, steepled in entreaty. "Now lift the burden from his head forever."

"That burden and another," Parsifal assured him.

Water splashed down Kundry's hair, over her forehead, and into her eyes. She looked up, sadly shaking her head. She was not worthy of forgiveness; and, in any case, this was not her rite.

But yes, Parsifal's eyes told her. *But yes. Look up.*

Mirth too deep for laughter glinted in those eyes: it would have been absurd and prideful to refuse this anointing because it belonged to no rite she knew, not even the ones she had betrayed.

And not even she was that great a fool.

At least Kundry remembered something. She had been away from her faith for far too long. Desert-sprung, it had always cherished water. Jews washed before meals, bathed before the Sabbath or after childbirth, purifying body and soul alike—and had done so long before Joshua had stood in the Jordan and overruled Johanan's objections to sprinkling the living water on his brow.

And at the ritual baths, every woman stood naked and alone with God.

She was no bride, less still the Sabbath bride; and she had

never been a mother—except to this second birth of her
own freed soul.

Kundry sighed deeply, astonished to recognize her own
relief. Could one turn apostate from apostasy? She had
been so tired, so thirsty. *No more need to endure*, those eyes
told her. *I have you safe now. Rest in me.*

"You shall be my first care," said Parsifal. "Have faith!"

A moment longer he held her eyes. The intensity of that
gaze kindled between them. Blessedly, the racking, damned
laughter that had always accompanied such moments for
her seemed to have fled forever. Kundry was silent, even
calm. Within Parsifal's eyes, she saw herself transformed, a
woman of great beauty and greater age, her madness washed
away, the sands of her life dissolving into the water he had
poured upon her.

As if it had healed some wound within her, tears poured
from her eyes. She sank weeping on the earth as if on her
mother's breast.

The earth lulled her from weeping into drowsiness. She
rested her aching head upon the grass and gazed out at the
tiny clearing and the great wood of Broceliande beyond it.
They glowed in the morning sun, and the flowers of early
spring shone like tiny stars.

Parsifal sighed with the utter satisfaction of a child or a
creator. "Today, the world all seems so fair! Look at the
flowers. I have seen many a magic flower that went wild,
trying to twine about me and trap me, but I cannot remember when I really looked at meadow flowers blooming since
I was a child and my mother taught me their names."

"Good Friday's magic, Lord," Gurnemanz burst out joy-
ously, though he inclined his head as if he spoke to Amfortas or the old king, who would be buried today.

"That day of agony—and here we are, rejoicing in the
land when all that blooms and breathes should only
mourn," Parsifal said, frowning as the thought struck him.

Gurnemanz shook his head. "You have only to look at
her. How can you say that? It is not so."

He gestured down at Kundry, and smiled at her as she
recoiled. "She has been a great sinner. Yet now, her tears of
penitence fall on the grass and make it shine so brightly that

all creatures rejoice and praise God. They no longer see the pain of the man racked upon the cross. No: they see Man redeemed, set free from sin and fear, and made pure. Today, even the tenderest bud knows that the foot of Man will not harm it. All creation that blooms and dies has ceased to weep today, lord; it sings its thanks to God, and its song is all of love. The world has won her innocence again."

For a moment, all three were silent, as if they heard music: the morning stars singing together, perhaps, or the archangels shouting in joy.

Kundry looked up at the two men: the younger, ardent, still harsh in judgment, especially of himself; the elder, wise and weary. Gurnemanz laid a hand upon her head, then removed it, as if he could not perform what she needed. She turned her gaze to Parsifal, remembering the words she had heard once from a centurion. *Lord, I am not worthy* . . . He had prayed and been answered. For the first time in centuries, Kundry prayed and thought that she, too, might receive the answer that she sought.

"I saw the flowers wither even as they mocked me," he murmured. "Can they too yearn for redemption? Is there hope for them? There must be! But you, dear heart, still weeping? How can you weep, when—just look you!—how the meadows smile at you!"

He kissed her gently on the forehead. Even as she trembled, the bells of Montsalvasche groaned out Titurel's death knell.

Ceremoniously, Gurnemanz rose and bowed. "It is noon," he said, "and the hour has come. Permit me, lord, to serve as your squire and conduct you hence."

Parsifal nodded, and Gurnemanz sighed. Kundry could see him draw his old nobility upon him like a robe of state to perform the role. Both men rose. With the stride of a much younger man, Gurnemanz hastened to his hut and fetched the mantle of the Order of the Grail.

Such service should have been my *task*, Kundry told herself. She might have risen; instead, she wished only to lie still and let her soul flow through her flesh into the earth. She caught a glimpse of herself in the holy spring: so old already! All her years were passing, like the last grains of sand through a fragile glass.

Gurnemanz laid the mantle, less shabby by far than his old tunic, over Parsifal's shoulders; Kundry adjusted the folds at his feet. Vested with the mantle of the Grail, Parsifal pulled the Holy Spear from the earth. Tiny blooms of white and red sprang up where it had lain, infusing the air with new sweetness.

Kundry sighed deeply. Just a little longer, and she could rest forever now. The bells were tolling, but the men stayed. For what? Surely, they did not wait for her; she had all she needed and more than she had dreamed. Parsifal had cleansed her, and God had granted her forgiveness.

Still, they waited, the new lord and the old knight who now served him. They would be late! She wanted to wave her hands at them, hasten them along the path to Montsalvasche; but her hands lacked strength. Gurnemanz scowled at her: did he truly think that *she* would presume to enter the citadel of the Grail when she had spent the very Seder of its consecration wandering Jerusalem alone?

I am not worthy, she thought. Thinking so, in Jerusalem, she had fled the feast, the night of Passover. She had been wrong then in her thoughts and her flight.

She would not be wrong again.

And one thing more remained to do. Kundry might have received God's forgiveness and Parsifal's blessing, but one more ordeal remained: to stand before the man she had betrayed, look her former lover in the eye, and confess her sins. She must let him see her as she was now, immeasurably aged, and penitent—admit her love, and beg his forgiveness.

Just that one task, and she could rest.

Again, the bells rang out. Then Parsifal smiled at her: *Why do you tarry?* he seemed to ask.

Surely I come quickly. Surely I come now. But she must save her strength for deeds now, not for words. She tore the wrappings from her feet, then rose to follow the Grail King and his squire toward Montsalvasche.

31

GURNEMANZ led the way and Parsifal followed, as if he walked behind a herald: the old order and the new. Oldest of all, Kundry followed them along the way she had never dared to come, though she had seen it once, in her dreams.

The walls rose before them and admitted them—much more slowly than her vision of Montsalvasche had shown her and to a realm much changed. Was this reluctance, perhaps, to admit her? She felt no wrongness, save for a sense of malaise, a weakness that made the stones of Montsalvasche insubstantial. Compared with the warmth and light of the forest outside, a chill lay on this place. Kundry's nostrils twitched; a holy place, and yet she smelled not incense, but mold.

The tapestries that covered the towering walls were frayed or missing. The banners were all gone. In several places, metal torch holders seemed to have been hacked from the stone; the pale, rough scars of their removal glistened like leprosy on stone that was smoke-darkened everywhere else. As the bells rang, at times discordant with pain and disuse, the rocks themselves seemed to tremble. A fine dust sifted down from the very arches of the vaults.

Slowly, as if groaning at a funeral, the great doors gaped to reveal the Grail's hall. It looked more like a crypt than a shrine now. The windows at its dome were all darkened. The feasting tables had been removed. Outside in Broceliande, the sun reached zenith; inside the hall, it was dusk.

With a muffled wail of horns, side doors swung back. Two files of knights entered. One group bore the coffin of Titurel. The second escorted both the bearer of the Grail's tabernacle, shrouded and dark, and Amfortas's litter.

All of the knights were old or aging. As sullen faces and
graying hair showed, it was long past the time when the
squires should have gained their spurs. They had made
some effort to appear, for this last ceremony, as a brotherhood, not a rabble of hermits, but some lacked surcoats.
Others, like Gurnemanz, wore surcoats, but no mail. Many
others more wore armor with rings missing from the sleeves
or shoulders, or robes that showed the marks of time and
moths.

The knights who bore Titurel were muffled in rusty black
cloaks. A few padded barefoot. Several even bore arms.
The Order was crumbling along with its citadel. Abruptly,
Kundry feared that the passage of king and Order both
from the world might not be peaceful.

The knights knew their roles and their burdens. They
knew each other, too, past boredom to the point of violence. Lacking the solace either of action or the Grail, the
factions Kundry had suspected long ago had festered.
Ceremoniously, the knights bowed; ceremoniously, they
trimmed their ranks and addressed each other as if the
boredom of their rites without the refreshment of the Grail
had not driven them past snarling into rebellion. Only their
eyes did not share in the discipline. Hungry, angry, unsatis-
fied, they glittered as enemy regarded enemy, and the looks
they shot at Amfortas were filled with hate.

"Who goes there?" asked a senior knight, stationed at the
door. "And what is your duty?"

"We bear the Grail, concealed in this gloomy shrine, to
the altar," recited the leader of the men who conducted
Amfortas within. It had all the sincerity of rote learning.

"You there, dressed in mourning, whom do you bear?"
asked the guard.

"Within this shrine, we bear a hero whom God Himself
once chose as His guard: Titurel the King."

"He who kept God's self within the Grail? How was he
slain?" a knight asked. His glare at the living, suffering king
told Kundry he asked the question as a way of punishing
Amfortas.

Knights glared at knights. Gurnemanz scowled. Then he
looked back at the man he escorted and his face lightened.

Amfortas rested his brow upon his hand, as if unwilling to see his knights' anger and contempt. He seemed a prisoner even among his own men, whose dirge for Titurel's death sounded like a reproach—and a threat. The group of knights bearing Amfortas and the Grail set down their burdens.

My lord, my own dear lord, Kundry thought. It was hard to see in this aged, weakened man the warrior who had won her love and brought his doom upon himself; still, she saw him, and still she loved him. She edged back further behind Gurnemanz and Parsifal. The time when she must show her courage would come; for the moment, they indulged her.

"Once the pure light of the Grail was denied him, the hand of conquering age struck him down," the spokesman for the mourners declared. He was one of the knights who bore arms. Amfortas did not look at him, and the knight did not look at the feeble king.

"Who withheld the light?"

"He whom you escort—the Grail's sinful guard." The answer came swiftly, with more than an edge of resentment. Amfortas visibly shrank in on himself. Was his courage waning with his life? Kundry could not believe that.

The leader of his party stepped forward to confer with the other knight. "We escort him today because he has pledged to fulfill his office for the last time."

Laments rose from the knights as they raised Amfortas none too carefully to the couch behind the Grail altar and set his father's coffin before it.

"For the last time, the last time . . ." wailed out echoes from the dank arched walls. Even the echoes sounded hungry as the knights waited, expectantly, for a sight of the Grail.

The knights knelt and were joined by others, late come to the hall and even shabbier than the others. Gurnemanz frowned again and would have wrung his hands. Parsifal rested a hand briefly on his shoulder, and the old man forebore.

"Let us mourn!" cried the armed knight. "Guardian of the Grail, for the final time, perform your office!"

Amfortas leaned forward on his couch as if he would

have risen but lacked the strength. He drew a shuddering breath, as if he drew in strength with the musty air of the hall. "Yes, mourn. Mourn for me, too. Gladly, I weep with you. Even more glad would I be if you would deal me death—small penance for a sin like mine."

The knight's boots and spurs rang on the bare stone floor as he rose from his knees and opened Titurel's coffin. At the sight of the pale, incredibly withered body within, the knights cried out in woe. Their grief drowned out the solemn clangor of the bells. Kundry shivered. Parsifal straightened: it was this he had come to heal.

Amfortas forced himself up on one arm. He leaned forward over the altar and looked into his father's face. Age and death had smoothed the pain from Titurel's face, but a living anguish burned that of his son. The king raised his hands in prayer.

"My father! My God, what have I done? In my attempt to die, I dealt you death, you whom angels visited and trusted with the treasure of the Grail. Father, now that you dwell on high in glory and behold the face of God, beg that His holiest blood may bring me solace too . . . in death, the only mercy left me now. Hear my prayer, Father! The wound and the poison within—make God destroy their torment. They gnaw at my heart, so let that heart be stilled. Father, hear my plea and beg God: 'Grant my son release!' "

Kundry heard mutterings: this was no proper requiem. Several of the knights, impatient of the Grail King's grief, rose from their knees and pressed forward. Several twitched their hands near the hilts of their swords. Their eyes flicked hungrily at the shrouded Grail.

"Reveal the Grail now!" burst out a barefoot squire.

His mourning interrupted, Amfortas flinched.

"You promised; perform your office!"

"Your father's soul demands it."

"You must . . . you must!"

They formed a ring around the altar and began to close in hungrily on the maimed king. They were a mob in that moment, not a brotherhood of knights, and they dared to command their king.

How could he bear it? If he disobeyed, would they kick him as once they had threatened to batter her?

Amfortas began numbly to obey. Then, as if a chance movement jolted his wound, he cried out in agony. His pain woke anger, and he flung himself down from the altar into the midst of the knights, who recoiled from him as if he were unclean.

"No!" he shouted. "No more! I was so close to death I could hear the pulse of its wings. And you would force me back to life? You madmen, why do you force me to live when you could grant me instant death?"

He opened his mouth again as if to curse them.

"Here I am! Draw your weapons!" Amfortas cried. He ripped robe and bandages asunder. Dark blood began a sluggish welling from the ancient, poisoned wound that Klingsor had dealt. Parsifal drew in a hissing breath.

"Look at this wound. Here is the poison; here is the blood. Unsheath your swords and plunge them—here! Within my heart. Come on," he jeered, "you heroes, afraid now? Just slay this one sinner and end his pain. Then you can have the Grail, and it will shine for you!"

The knights shrank back. Even in the darkness, Kundry could see the pain on her old lover's face. He shook, anguish and despair driving him into ecstasy. She held out her hands to him. The men who were her shields had vanished; and she knelt before the Grail King, face to face.

Near her, Parsifal raised the Spear he bore as if in salute.

Unexpected light threw up huge shadows around the sanctuary of the Grail. Softly, a new knight moved into the center of the throng. Amfortas sensed the motion—*and will one of these men finally strike me down?*—and gazed wildly on him. For a moment, his tortured features eased, then twisted in disappointment. Then he cried out again and rushed at the knights, trying to frighten them into drawing steel.

And in that moment, Parsifal approached. Light poured from no apparent source. It gleamed from his hair and the tip of the Spear he bore. Just as Amfortas, in his frenzy, whirled to confront him, he reached out with the Spear. As

a mother might feel a child's brow for fever, he touched the
gleaming point to Amfortas's wound.

"Only one weapon will serve," Parsifal said quietly into
a sudden stillness. "The weapon that dealt the wound must
heal it. It is finished."

Amfortas halted in his rush to hurl himself on his men's
weapons. He gazed down at unmarked flesh. Convulsively,
he covered himself with the torn white linen of his robe. He
staggered back. Gurnemanz lunged forward, catching him
just before he fell. For an instant only, Amfortas rested his
face against the old man's shoulder and sobbed. Awkwardly, Gurnemanz patted his king's hair. Then Amfortas
pulled free and turned toward Parsifal.

"Be healed and forgiven; you have atoned," Parsifal told
him. "Now I shall undertake your task."

Amfortas's mouth worked, and he raised a hand as if to
protest.

Parsifal shook his head. "No, that's not the way. Even
your suffering is blessed. With all my heart, I thank you. It
was pity for your pain that transformed a fool into a king—
and your healer."

Amfortas sank to his knees as Parsifal strode forward, to
stand before the altar and Titurel's opened coffin. Around
him, the knights, purged of their rage, knelt as one man.
Their faces showed shame, then smoothed into rapture.
Already they looked younger and more hale.

"I bring you the sacred Spear once again!" Parsifal proclaimed and held it aloft.

A globe of light formed a sun on its silvery blade. As it
struck Kundry, she gasped and tumbled to her knees beside
Amfortas. Their eyes met. Amfortas's lips went even whiter
as they formed the syllables of her name.

Changed as I am, you know me? Kundry gasped inside her
mind.

In the hallows, she heard his thought: *Then, now, and
always.*

She began to look away, then paused: her sin was past,
her penance done; and now she had a right to meet his eyes.
She had been changed, and soon, her king would be, too.
She saw herself glorified in his eyes: the sere, bone-white

beauty of experience, age, and the calm that transmutes them all into wisdom.

"Thank God for the miracle!" Parsifal cried. "This holy weapon has healed you. Even now, fresh blood glows upon its point and yearns to flow back to its source. You saw the miracles in this shrine, as through a glass, darkly. Now you shall see face to face."

Kundry gasped as strength flew out of her. Just let her depart now, and she would bless each of the too-long years that she had lived.

Amfortas's eyes kindled like the light now rising in the shrine. He glanced down at her hand, raised to uphold him, should he need it. Recognizing the ring she wore, gleaming in the light of the Holy Spear, he raised her hand to his lips.

"My dear lady," he whispered. "Then have you too been a penitent all these long years?"

It was time to admit how she had wronged him. Kundry parted her lips on the words, but no sound came out. Tears poured down her face, and she knew her tears shone too. She was dissolving before the Light, into the Light, and there was no pain.

Secure in the arms of his oldest friend, Amfortas reached out to touch Kundry, but she sagged down, away from him. So, it was not necessary to confess, after all. She had but to meet his eyes and know: she was forgiven. She had always been forgiven. She had been a fool to doubt or fear—and today, she was not the only fool to bless her folly.

Amfortas leaned forward, alarmed that she had fallen. There was no cause for alarm, she knew. Time and this new grace were simply dissolving what bound her spirit to her flesh.

"We will get the king to restore you, lady," he whispered. "Look up. Be brave for me again."

Wearily, Kundry shook her head. No need, now. He raised the hand he held to his heart as if willing her the strength he had regained.

Head up, his eyes fixed upon a vision he alone saw but would now share, Parsifal began to climb the stairs to the altar. Before him, the squires leapt to their duty and swung open the gates that held the Grail within the shrine.

Parsifal sank to his knees. With shaking hands, he folded back the cloths that hid the Grail. Light shone through them, and burst into radiant day as he revealed the Chalice. It glowed crimson. The fine bones of the hands that held it glowed through their ruddy skin. Light erupted from the highest point of the dome and from the windows that ringed it, revealing the face of the Fool made wise by pity and the faces of the other fools, upturned to watch him. Light poured out onto Titurel's corpse, gilding the pale face and surmounting it with a crown.

"Highest of holy wonders," sang the choir stationed in the dome. "The redeemer, revealed!"

The sweet voices rose impossibly high and pure, past human ears' power to hear them; yet Kundry heard. A dove flew from the dome and out the open clerestory into the noonday sun. She watched its flight and smiled as it vanished into the light.

The last of Kundry's strength fled, and she fell upon the cold stones of the floor. Amfortas rested his head upon her hand. His tears fell on it. This was no time for tears, but for joy, she wanted to say; but then there was no time at all.

Dimming and glazing at this last moment of her life, her eyes beheld the Fool. Parsifal stood transfigured in a pillar of light, holding aloft the Grail. It glowed crimson. Its light began to transform the chill, dark sanctuary, warming it and healing. Pain flowed out of the knights' faces. Satisfied, Kundry let her breath flow from her in a long sigh.

And then, without a warning, the world fell away. The stone walls of the sanctuary vanished. In their place stretched olive-green fields and a warm, muddy stream beside which lambs played and sheep cropped grass. Once again, Judaea's hot sun beat down upon Kundry's head, but its light now held no dangers for her. She stripped off the striped wool shawl she was wearing over her head, and the sunlight poured down like oil over her shoulders.

Something was holding her hand, drawing her back. She freed herself and stepped away from that last barrier to her freedom. Before her stretched her lands, her sheep, her flock—and no harm would come to them or her again. She rejoiced; the elders had promised her that they would spend Passover in Jerusalem, and she would be wed.

From far off came a cry of voices and rams' horns, summoning her to go up to the long-awaited festival. Light pooled in the East. Soon enough, her betrothed would join her. The ring of their pledge gleamed on her hand so brightly that she could not look at it. She could wait for him. With happy certainty, she could look forward to all the time beyond all the circles of the world.

Leaving her body and the old, dark memories behind, Kundry ran to heed the call of horns. Purified and young again, she ran across the water toward the source of light . . .

. . . laughing.

AUTHOR'S NOTE

OF all the different strains of Arthurian romance, perhaps the strangest and most exalted is the story of the Holy Grail.

The skeins of that story are more complex and far longer than we usually think. Probably the greatest corpus of Grail material can be found in the Old French romances, beginning roughly with the First Continuation of Chrétien de Troyes's unfinished Grail romance, the *Perceval*. Here the writer states that the Grail was the vessel that Joseph of Arimathea caused to be made and that he set at the foot of the Cross to catch the blood dripping from Christ's wound—itself a story derived not from the Gospels, but from the apocryphal, fourth-century *Gospel of Nicodemus*.

Some time between 1202 and 1212, the Burgundian Robert de Boron, in a work now called *Joseph d'Arimathie*, claimed that the Grail was not just the cup used at the Crucifixion but also the chalice used at the Last Supper. Conceptions of the Grail varied, proliferated, and grew more complex among the many French writers of the first half of the thirteenth century. The prose *Perlesvaus* calls the Grail the cup used at the Crucifixion. The prose *Lancelot* (around 1215–1230) calls it the "Sankgreal" (and there is a pun on "sang real" or royal blood and "san Greal" or holy Grail). The *Quest Del Saint Graal*, the prose sequel to the *Lancelot*, elevates the Grail to a form of vision that floats into Arthur's hall and inspires his knights—a tradition adopted by Malory from his "French book" and eloquently used by Tennyson.

In these romances, we see developing the idea of a priestly house that serves the Grail and is in direct descent from the great houses of the Bible. Here, too, we see the great distinction (later given eloquent treatment by Charles Williams in *Taliessin Through Logres* and *The Region of the Summer Stars* and, most recently, John M. Ford in "Winter Solstice: Camelot Station") between Camelot, the kingdom of Arthur and of Earth, and Carbonek, the city of the Grail, which Galahad is to wield as king and priest.

These texts form part of the French tradition, which—along with the Celtic strains of Arthurian story—dominates the Matter of Britain as we have come to know it. But there is also a very old and powerful German tradition, influenced by the French and spun off from those texts in and around the twelfth and thirteenth centuries.

The sources I have used for *The Grail of Hearts* begin with Wolfram von Eschenbach's *Parzival*, probably written during the first part of the thirteenth century. Derived in part from the verse romances of the twelfth-century French poet Chrétien de Troyes, Wolfram's *Parzival* owes a good deal to the work of the German minnesingers, those knightly poets such as Hartman von Aue and Walther von der Vogelweide who were the German equivalent of the troubadours.

For a more complete description of the relationship of Wolfram von Eschenbach to the minnesingers as well as their relationship to the Arthurian romances of Chrétien, the reader is referred to *Parzival: A Romance of the Middle Ages*, translated and introduced by Helen M. Mustard and Charles E. Passage (New York: Vintage, 1961).

Flanking *Parzival* in time and theme were two other great works of German poetry—Gottfried von Strassburg's *Tristan* and a compendium of much older Germanic verse about Siegfried and Kriemhild that a now-anonymous Austrian poet wove into the verse narrative *The Song of the Nibelungs*.

The stories of Tristan, the Nibelungs, and Parzival all profoundly influenced Richard Wagner, one of the most monumental and certainly the most myth-obsessed composers to write opera. Probably no opera has been more revered—and more misunderstood—than *Parsifal* (Wagner changed the spelling of the protagonist's name). The combination of music and this particular libretto is highly explosive, considering the ideological uses made of Wagner.

To a great extent, the paradoxes and controversies that are Wagner have brought this odium upon himself and his work. A notorious anti-Semite, Wagner nevertheless recruited Hermann Levi, the son of a rabbi, to conduct *Parsifal* because of his outstanding musicianship. There is no denying that the composer thought of *Parsifal* as more than grand opera; he called it a "Buhnenweihfestspiel" or festival work to consecrate a stage. For a sane and moderate explanation of Wagner's material and possible motivations, the reader is referred to the English National Opera Guide to *Parsifal* (volume number 34, under the general editorship of Nicholas John, published by the Riverrun Press of New York, 1986).

Into the story of the fool made wise by pity and the Grail, Wagner wove the tale of the redemption of Kundry. In Wolfram's story, Kundry is a sorceress, a variant of the Loathly Lady who travels between Arthur's court and the castle of the Grail, announcing the fulfillment of prophecies and, in general, behaving like many of the other damsels-errant within the Matter of Britain. In Wagner's opera, Kundry is a variant of the Wandering Jew, as Wagner himself noted in the 1865 prose draft of the story of the opera. In terms of characterization, as musicologist Dieter Borchmeyer says, she is akin to Wagner's Flying Dutchman, whom the poet Heinrich Heine called "the Wandering Jew of the sea," and even to Wotan, whom Wagner described as a kind of Flying Dutchman.

And in her search for forgiveness, Kundry resembles the hero of another of Wagner's operas, *Tannhäuser*, in which Wolfram von Eschenbach himself plays a moving and lyrical role. Wagner's creation of a woman who laughed at the Crucifixion and who is condemned to wander until she too finds grace is probably the most audacious part of his story and his most daring recasting of the traditional stories.

Though I am no Wagnerian expert, I would refer readers interested in becoming listeners as well to the "discography" for *Parsifal* given in the *Guide*. I myself would recommend the *Parsifal* conducted by G. Solti with the Vienna

PO, and with singers Dietrich Fischer-Dieskau as Amfortas and the great Wagnerian soprano Christa Ludwig as Kundry, or the monumental rendering by the late Herbert von Karajan, featuring Peter Hoffmann as Parsifal, J. van Dam as Amfortas, and Dunja Vejzovic as Kundry.

Finally, I am very much in the debt of the Metropolitan Opera of New York City for the production of *Parsifal* in which, during the lengthy third act, I conceived the idea for what became *The Grail of Hearts*. Much of the dialogue, especially during the last half of the book, has been—at the very least—strongly influenced by the libretto of *Parsifal*, sometimes as translated by Andrew Porter in the opera guide or as translated, adapted, and very much modified by me, on the spot—usually with the music going full blast.

Explanations—or at least a guide—are in order any time a writer ventures onto the very perilous grounds of myth and theology. Wagner's etymology of Parsifal as "fal parsi" or "pure and foolish" is as fabulous as the French etymology of "perce à val" or "pierce through the middle." Both explanations represent symbols important to the individual artist rather than any attempt at linguistic accuracy.

Used as we are to printed texts, to a very definite sequence of stories in terms of their creation and publication, and even to the idea that there is one definitive answer to many questions, we feel frustration in trying to track down the "true" version of any Arthurian romance. The Grail story, with its replacement in the later English tradition (with which we are most familiar) of Perceval by Galahad as the primary hero, is one of the most puzzling. The very transmission of texts for the Perceval/Parzival story is uncertain. Chrétien claims that he has worked from a book lent him by Count Philip of Flanders. Wolfram worked from Chrétien's text. We would like to think that these represent continental versions of an older, Celtic story; but the earliest form of the "Peredur" in the *Mabinogion* is dated about 1225—later than Wolfram's book and long after Chrétien's—while the total manuscript is dated about 1300.

Regardless: As with all other elements of Arthurian romance, the Grail stories too double back on one another.

Ultimately, though some versions of each Arthurian story contain more authoritative text or display more clearly traceable roots to earlier versions, it's probably best to regard the Matter of Britain as a matrix, in which all versions of a story exist simultaneously in our thoughts, fusing into one composite.

As readers—and writers—we have memories of our favorite tales and elements drawn from a period almost as long as Kundry's wanderings.

All Biblical references are taken from the King James version of the Old and New Testaments, with some help from the Vulgate text and A New Catechism. In addition, I consulted the following works on Gnostic material: The Gnostic Gospels, by Elaine Pagels (New York: Vintage, 1979); The Nag Hammadi Library in English, Richard Smith, managing editor (New York: Harper & Row, 1988); and Hans Jonas's classic The Gnostic Religion (Boston: Beacon Press, 1958). Such texts are my sources for the Gospel according to Mary and much of the "religious" material that is, obviously, not derived from the Gospels. I also used G. Vermes's The Dead Sea Scrolls (New York: Penguin Books, 1962) and Francis Legge's Forerunners and Rivals of Christianity: From 330 B.C. to 330 A.D. (New Hyde Park, New York: University Books, 1964). Quotations from what looks like extra-Gospel material are Gnostic, and taken from "The Thunder: Perfect Mind," "The Gospel of Mary," "The Dialogue of the Savior," and "The Acts of John."

Kundry's defiant responses to Sir Ferris in the first section of the book are modern translations of poems written, probably by women, in Islamic Spain. They appear in Elene Kolb's article, "When Women Finally Got the Word," from the July 9, 1989, New York Times Book Review. The poem about the lioness is Spanish/Arabic and was composed by Aisha bint Ahmad al-Qurtubiyya in the tenth century.

Though, clearly, uncovering Judaea of the first century A.D. would be the work of lifetimes of tenure by an academy of scholars, I found myself guided in particular to Paul Johnson's A History of the Jews (New York: Harper & Row,

1987) and *The Jewish War* of Flavius Josephus, translated by G. A. Williamson (New York: Penguin Books, first edition 1959). My first acquaintance with the finding of the Holy Spear came in Robert Payne's *The Dream and the Tomb: A History of the Crusades* (New York: Stein and Day, 1984), in the section entitled "The Dark Roads to the Holy Land." I also acknowledge my debt to The National Geographic Society for its help in locating pictures of Jerusalem, Israel, and Trans-Jordan, most of which were taken before 1948.

In addition to the "orthodox" Arthurian romances and criticism traditionally covered by most university Arthurians, I drew fairly heavily on more psychologically oriented and occult materials such as *The Grail Legend*, by Emma Jung and Marie-Louise von Franz, translated by Andrea Dykes (Boston: Sigo Press, 1986), Nancy Qualls-Corbett's *The Sacred Prostitute: Eternal Aspect of the Feminine* (Toronto, Canada: Inner City Books, 1988), Trevor Ravenscroft's *The Cup of Destiny* and *The Spear of Destiny* (both published by Samuel Weiser, Inc.), and *The Middle Pillar*, by Israel Regardie (also published by Samuel Weiser, Inc.).

In addition, this book would have been impossible if the "revisionist" Arthurian romances of the late twentieth century, such as Marion Zimmer Bradley's *The Mists of Avalon* and Diana Paxson's *The White Raven*, had not shown me the possibilities inherent in departing from the Christian and medieval mind-set of usual Arthurian fictions and recasting them to include additional material. Probably no aspect of the stories of Arthur and his knights that comprise the Matter of Britain is as thought-provoking—or as provoking in general—as the accounts of the Grail and the interpretation of what it represents. In the Middle Ages, the Grail stories could be read as part of consensus belief; though this is no longer true, we still are faced with the fact that the Grail and its stories cannot be interpreted only in secular terms.

The Grail of Hearts is my personal attempt to explain—for my own contentment, if no one else's—a long-standing fascination with this material and the work of Richard Wagner. In it, I have followed, primarily, the German texts, though I have borrowed the idea of Merlin imprisoned in the wild from British and Latin sources and the idea of a quasi-sentient Broceliande from Charles Williams. I will apologize in advance for any inconsistencies, real or apparent, but such confusions are the logical consequence of working within a tradition that is more than a thousand years old.

As always with Arthurian story, no one story can take all possibilities into account. The Grail may have begun as the Cauldron of Ceridwen, or as a magic platter owned by the sixth-century Welsh king Rhydderch of Strathclyde, as a kiddush cup used one Passover, or even, as Wolfram says, the gemstone "lapis exillis," from which the phoenix kindles its death flame; or it may even have been the Antioch cup now in the collection of the Metropolitan Museum of Fine Art in New York. What kind of artifact the Grail actually was—or whether there actually was a Grail—does not matter as much as the fact that it has been transformed into undying symbol. One thing is certain: authors agree that it provided those seated around it with their hearts' desires in food and drink.

A similar gift may be ascribed to all of the stories of Arthur. Probably the truest statement ever made by Geoffrey of Monmouth in his *Historia Regum Britanniae* is that Arthur's name would be food and drink to tale-tellers.

> Susan Shwartz
> December 31,
> 1991

CONTEMPORARY FANTASY FROM TOR

Watch for the next book
in the Tor Fairy Tale series...

THE

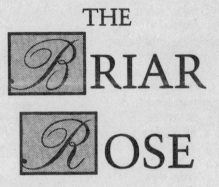

BRIAR
ROSE

❧ by ❧

Jane Yolen

*coming in September
from*

Tor Books